STEALING *for* KEEPS

REBECCA JENSHAK

Bloom *books*

Published by Bloom Books, an imprint of Sourcebooks
P.O. Box 4410, Naperville, Illinois 60567-4410
(630) 961-3900
sourcebooks.com

Cataloging-in-Publication data is on file with the Library of Congress.

Printed and bound in the United States of America.
VP 10 9 8 7 6 5 4 3 2 1

For all the dreamers.

FROST LAKE
HIGH SCHOOL
KELLER
7
GO
KNIGHTS
GO
KNIGHTS
Knights
SOCCER IS LIFE

CHAPTER ONE

DON'T BE AFRAID TO SPARKLE.

My best friend, Lacey, holds up the poster board with that phrase written in big, blue bubble letters—all except the last word, which is covered in glitter—and waits for my reaction.

"It's…sparkly," I say from my spot on the grass outside the high school where we've set up for this activity, leaning back and soaking up the last of the summer sun.

"I know, right? It's perfect." She lets out a little squeal of excitement and places the poster on the ground with a dozen more, all with similar sayings.

We start back next week, and if Lacey has her way, the entire school will be wallpapered with uplifting signs. *Best year ever. Be stronger than your excuses. Dreams don't work unless you do.*

I love her optimism. One of us needs it.

"Are you going to help or just lie there?" she asks in a tone that sounds less like a question and more like a judgment.

"You keep telling me mine are boring."

Her mouth pulls into a wide smile, and her brown eyes light up with amusement. "Well, they're not very colorful."

"I used blue and white." The school colors of Frost Lake High School and ninety percent of Lacey's wardrobe. It doesn't matter that it's still officially summer; she's always decked out in school spirit. Mine is buried somewhere underneath layers of contempt and disappointment.

My gaze drops from her Knights Cheer T-shirt to the posters scattered around us. I went with a more classic and straightforward approach to balance out Lacey's cheery mantras. *Welcome back, Knights. Now entering Knights territory. Knights pride.*

I can't be the only one who doesn't want to walk into school on the first day and be assaulted with pep and optimism at every turn. Or maybe I am. My crankiness about summer ending is making it hard to see reason.

"You should at least add some sparkle," she says, arching one dark brow.

"Not every sign has to be covered in glitter."

"I disagree. Glitter makes everything better."

"Agree to disagree."

She sticks out her bottom lip, gives me big puppy dog eyes, and leans forward, letting her long hair fall over her shoulders. No one can refuse Lacey's pleading expression. Especially me. Not even at my grumpiest.

I feel myself relenting even before she says, "Please? I'm finally captain. I've waited years for this, and I want it to be perfect."

Nothing like setting your expectations at an unreasonable level. But I know how much it means to her. We've been best friends since middle school, and being cheer captain is everything she's dreamed of.

"Fine. Fine. Hand over the glitter." I sit up and hold out my hand. The girls' soccer team is practicing behind us, and the faint shouts and whistles are background noise, along with the music playing from my phone.

"Actually, we're out. Can you run in and grab the extra glitter bottles? They're in my locker."

"I don't know about running, but sure, I can go get them."

Her happy expression falls, grazing over my right foot for only a second. "I'm sorry. I completely forgot. I'll go."

"It's fine. I was only teasing. I'm perfectly capable of walking." Not well, but I am mobile.

"Right. I know." She gives me a sad smile that makes my throat tighten.

I've gotten pretty good at getting up and down with the boot on my right foot. It is a very unstylish black plastic with Velcro, but it's better than the hard cast and crutches I had earlier in the summer.

I'm standing when she speaks again, this time without pity in her tone. "Uh-oh. Here comes your ex."

Without fully preparing myself, I turn in the direction she's staring. The first sight of him makes my breath catch.

Vaughn Collins. Junior soccer star, most popular guy at Frost Lake High School, and my ex-boyfriend.

His blond hair is striking in the sunlight. He's tall and broad, bigger than most of his teammates filing out behind him. They shoulder duffel bags and carry soccer balls. At FLH, soccer rules. They've won state the past two years, in large part thanks to Vaughn.

"Need me to run interference?" Lacey asks, voice tight

and clipped. She's the bubbliest person I know, but if you hurt someone she loves, watch out.

"No. It's fine. I was bound to run into him eventually." It's been nearly two months since I talked to him. I have had a lot of time to wonder what this moment would be like. I imagined playing it cool or walking right by him and not even seeing him. Instead, anger rises up inside of me. Anger that I want to unleash on him.

"Stay strong," my best friend says, voice so stern that it makes me laugh a little.

"I'm not getting back together with him." No way.

"Good. You deserve better. He's…" Her words trail off as I walk away.

I can only focus on one thing right now, and that's the boy across the field who has just spotted me as well.

I cross toward him slowly, but his long legs eat the space faster, and I'm standing in front of him before I've figured out what to say. The anger I was clutching so tightly slips through my fingers, letting in some of the hurt and confusion I tried my best to bury.

Vaughn and I were together for two years. He moved to Frost Lake in the fifth grade, and we became instant friends. We had so many things in common. My parents had just divorced, and his had split up when he was younger. I was passionate about skating, and he never went anywhere without a soccer ball in hand. While our classmates were trying a variety of sports and activities, we already had a single focus.

Our parents both expected a lot of us too, and we struggled with wanting that pressure and despising it at the same time. We understood each other. Even before we were a couple, we shared a bond I never had with anyone else. I guess that's why his decision to dump me right after I had already lost skating turned my world upside down.

"Hey," he says casually. He takes me in with those dark blue eyes, stare trailing down slowly over my small black shorts and bare legs before flicking up. "What are you doing here?"

Why couldn't he have gotten a regrettable haircut or suddenly become unattractive? It would make it easier to ignore the fluttering in my stomach.

I look away from him and back at Lacey, tipping my head and motioning toward our sign-decorating station. She's glaring hard, but she still looks sweet and harmless. "I'm helping Lacey make signs to decorate the school for next week."

"Right. I can't believe summer is already over. We have our first team meeting today and a light practice."

His dad, Coach Collins, appears outside with a coffee cup in one hand and a clipboard in the other. I want to chuckle at the thought of Coach C and light practice in the same sentence, but I hold it in.

Mostly I'm mad, but there's this small part of me that wants to show Vaughn I'm fine and pretend that him breaking up with me while I was dealing with everything else didn't hurt. And then there's the fear that I might do something really embarrassing like start crying.

"So only three hours instead of five?" I ask, keeping my tone neutral.

One side of Vaughn's mouth pulls up a fraction higher. "You know my dad. It doesn't count as a workout until at least one person threatens to quit."

The reminder that I know his dad so well because I spent so much time hanging out at their house is the final straw. I don't want to do this with him, pretend like everything is cool and nothing has changed.

"Right. Well, I should—"

"It's good to see you," he says, cutting me off and stopping me before I go. "I've been meaning to text. . . ." His voice trails off, and he looks a tiny bit guilty. "You look good."

Two months without so much as a hello and he wants me to believe he had any thoughts about texting me? He must read my disbelief.

He breaks eye contact briefly and looks to the ground. "Things were really busy. I did think about you though. How was your summer?"

The reminder of how "busy" he was further annoys me, and that anger I walked over here with resurfaces. His busy schedule is the whole reason he broke up with me. He was going to be gone all summer with his dad, attending and working at soccer camps around the country. Vaughn didn't think it made sense to be in a relationship when we weren't going to see each other. I think his exact words were, *"I can't commit to you and soccer."*

I was blindsided. We'd always supported each other, and as soon as I was no longer able to chase my dreams, he seemingly decided I was no longer capable of understanding his need to chase his.

"It was great." I'm overselling it. The first three weeks, I sulked until Lacey forced me out of the house and reminded me we only had two more summer vacations together before graduation. But there's no way I'm admitting to him that I wasted any of my vacation being sad about our breakup when he obviously didn't shed any tears over me.

"Hi, Claire." Coach Collins approaches with a smile that crinkles his eyes. He's a hard-ass to his players, especially his son, but he's always had a soft spot for me. And he has this posh British accent that makes everything he says sound a little more exciting.

"Hey, Coach C." My tone is far happier as I greet him than it had been with his son. Just because Vaughn is a jerk doesn't mean I have to hate his father.

"How's the ankle?" He glances at the boot.

My smile dims slightly. He's only being polite by asking, whereas everyone else has been tiptoeing around it, but an ache still forms in my chest at the reminder I'm still not fully healed and never will be. I'll be able to resume normal activities, but my competitive figure skating days are gone forever. "It's better. Thanks."

"Good. I'm glad to hear it." His gaze shifts to Vaughn. "Get the balls and cones out, and see if you can find the water coolers. If they aren't in the storage shed, check the locker room."

"Yes, sir."

After another tip of his head and a smile aimed at me, Coach C leaves us alone.

Vaughn shifts in front of me. "I guess I should get to it before he gives me another lecture about stepping up this year now that I'm captain."

"Yeah, me too. Lacey has, like, a hundred more posters to decorate."

His lips curve in what could almost be considered a smile, but Vaughn is far too serious for it to feel anything but polite. "Are you going to Doyle's camp tonight?"

Doyle's camping cabin is where all the soccer guys hang out. It's far enough out of the city limits that cops don't drive by without reason, and most of the cabins are rentals for tourists or used only on weekends.

"I'm not sure." Lacey mentioned it earlier, but it felt weird purposely going somewhere I knew I'd run into Vaughn. I guess now that we've got that out of the way, it doesn't matter.

The rest of the soccer team is starting to take the field as the girls' team finishes. Vaughn reaches forward with one hand, and his fingers brush mine. "You should go. We can catch up, and I want to talk to you about something."

For a moment, I forget about the last two months, how much he hurt me, how he abandoned me when I needed him the most, and just enjoy the feel of his calloused fingers against mine. It would be so easy to get back with him, and no one would even bat an eye. Everyone else was as caught off guard by the breakup as I was. We were a couple that made sense to people. Claire and Vaughn. Vaughn and Claire.

I pull my hand away and clasp it in my other hand behind my back. "Oh yeah? What do you want to talk to me about?"

Vaughn isn't usually cryptic or hard to read—another thing I've always liked about him. But I can't think of a single thing we need to discuss.

His dad yells his name across the field and points at his watch.

Vaughn curses under his breath and starts moving away. "I gotta go, but I hope I'll see you tonight."

I head into the empty school, still reeling from the short interaction. It's good we got it out of the way. We have a lot of the same friends, and school next week would have been that much more awkward with everyone watching our first conversation.

The air inside the school is humid, and it's so quiet that

the only sound is the echo of my uneven footsteps. I take my time, passing by the trophy case and inhaling the smell of fresh paint and bleach. Everything is clean and ready for students to arrive next week.

Lacey's locker is easy to find. Among all the other plain blue ones, hers is the lone locker decorated. Her name is written on a cut-out megaphone. It's covered in sparkles of course.

Inside, I spot the glitter bottles on the top shelf. I grab them while admiring the photos pinned up on the inside of her locker.

There are lots of the two of us from as far back as sixth grade. I wrinkle my nose at one particularly awful picture of me when I dyed my hair a red color that turned out more orange. I keep looking, smiling at all the memories she's captured. There's even one of me and Vaughn from last year's soccer championship game. He's holding the trophy in one hand, his other arm around me, and he's smiling bigger than I've ever seen him smile. That was a good day and a fun night. Vaughn was on top of the world, and I always had a hard time resisting the carefree and fun version of him. I'm surprised she put this one up or didn't at least mark an x over his face.

I'm about to close the locker when another photo at the very bottom catches my eye. My heart stops as I lean down and stare at myself. I'm skating in the middle of the ice, hands lifted to my sides, staring off into the distance, completely lost in the moment. Emotion clogs my throat. What I would give to be able to skate and lose myself like that again.

A door slams somewhere nearby. I swipe at the tears in my eyes and kick the locker shut with my injured foot.

As I do, one of the glitter tubes drops from my grasp onto the floor, rolling into the middle of the hallway. I move to retrieve it at the same time as a blur of a boy comes around the corner and flashes in my peripheral. My heart races with adrenaline, matching the pace of his steps.

Light green eyes snap to mine. I should move or say something, but I'm frozen.

At the last second, I squint, bracing for impact, but somehow, he manages to stop inches from me. His arm wraps around my waist to steady himself. We spin around, him keeping me upright and me clutching the glitter to my chest.

"Shit. I didn't see you." Breathless and deep, his voice makes the hair rise on the back of my neck.

I blink away the weird, dazed reaction his presence seems to have on me, and the twinge of pain in my foot brings me back.

"Yeah, no kidding. You almost ran me over." I remove myself from his hold, but my skin buzzes from his touch.

He's tall, and his skin is a light bronze that makes his dark, windblown hair seem even starker. I thought I knew every student at Frost Lake, but I've never seen him before.

"Is that the way to the soccer field?" He nods his head behind me toward the back doors of the school.

Handsome, but rude.

"So much for an apology," I mutter.

"I'm sorry. I'm lost, and if I don't find the soccer field soon, I'm going to be late for my first practice with Jude Collins."

It takes me a second to register his words. When I do, I allow myself to study him more closely. I was so focused on his face and not becoming roadkill that I didn't notice the signs. Shorts, a faded T-shirt, sneakers, and a duffel bag over one shoulder. Right. A soccer player. Makes sense.

"Relax. You found it. The field is straight out back." I refocus on my task of retrieving the glitter. I groan when I see the top of the tube popped off and glitter has spilled out onto the floor. A pretty good amount. I send a silent apology to the school custodians.

The guy in front of me is having some sort of moral dilemma. He stares down at me and then the back door before finally squatting down to help.

"Here, let me," he says, trying to take the half-empty container.

"No, it's fine," I say a little gruffly. "I got it. You're going to be late."

"It's the least I can do."

"Seriously. I've got it." I pull it back too hard, and a rainbow of colors bursts up into his face. It goes *everywhere.* His hair, his eyelashes, the bridge of his straight nose, and his shirt.

I start to laugh, and then think better of it when his mouth falls open and he glances down.

"You've gotta be kidding me," he says more to himself than me, but then he hurriedly gets to his feet and rushes off, leaving a cloud of glitter as he goes.

The laughter I was holding in finally escapes, echoing in the empty halls.

He's already pushing out the double doors that lead out to the field when I yell after him, "Don't be afraid to sparkle!"

CHAPTER TWO

My hero is scowling at me.

I drop my bag and stand at the back of the group. The guy next to me offers a reassuring chin jut. He's the only one. Everyone else looks as annoyed with me as my new coach.

Coach Collins continues, removing his gaze from me, "We're starting with skill stations in the groups I called off. Rotate around the field clockwise on the whistle. It's day one. Don't hold back. I want to see what you're made of."

He dismisses us with a nod. I groan. I can't believe I missed the entire meeting.

Everyone starts to walk off, but then Coach Collins looks directly at me as he says, "One last thing."

My skin prickles with unease. I've only met Jude Collins once before when my family visited Frost Lake earlier this spring. He let me forego the traditional tryouts for the team based on my stats and performance at my old school. He was friendly, all smiles that day.

Today he looks like he's seriously regretting that

decision. The look he gives me is the same one he used to give reporters after games when they'd ask combative questions to try to get a rise out of him. He never took the bait with words, but that look screams total and complete annoyance. Always cool and collected under pressure. So unlike me right now.

"Practices start at three o'clock sharp. The easiest way to ensure you get cut from this team is to show up late."

No one moves, but I can feel their stares.

"That's all. Let's get to work."

My new teammates break off into groups while I stand there, unsure of what to do. I'm definitely not asking.

"You're Austin Keller, right?"

I turn to see the same guy who offered a friendly smile earlier. His light brown hair is held back with a black headband and brushes the collar of his shirt in the back.

"Yeah. Otherwise known as the guy most likely to be cut first," I joke.

"I was leaning toward Disco as a nickname." He has an easygoing way about him from the slant of his shoulders to the smile he continues to aim at me.

"Disco?"

"Yeah." His smile widens, and he makes a circle in front of his face. "Because of all the glitter. What's going on there?"

I wipe a hand down my face. "It's a long story."

"I'll bet. You kind of look like the *Twilight* dude when he steps into the sunlight." He looks like he's holding back laughter. I guess I can't blame him. "I'm Rowan. You're with us." He motions with his head for me to join him and two other guys standing nearby.

"Thanks. I mixed up the location and went to the gym first."

"Ah, yeah. No, we only start there on Fridays for weight training. Mondays and Wednesdays, we do weights after practice. And sometimes, when the girls' team has a home game, we'll end there so they can prep the field."

Frost Lake High is three times as big as my last school. Back there, everything was in one general area. Here, the gym and the field are on opposite sides of the huge property. My head is spinning, and Rowan must realize it because he laughs.

"You'll figure it out. Until next week, just come here. Before practice starts preferably."

"Thanks. So what are we supposed to be doing?" A few of the groups are already on the field. I'm anxious to get to work. I desperately want to change Coach Collins's opinion of me, and the easiest way for me to do that is with my game.

"Passing drills on the far side." As he points, Rowan leads our group toward the orange cones set up for us.

In the distance, two girls are sitting in the grass. I recognize the girl I ran into in the hallway. She's staring this way but too far away for me to read her expression. I hold up a hand in a friendly wave. She doesn't acknowledge me, which isn't surprising. I'm not usually a jerk, but I was late and frazzled. I didn't see the boot on her foot until after I nearly trampled her. She is beautiful though. Hopefully there are lots of beautiful girls walking around the halls next week when school starts.

We break off into groups of two for passing drills. The other guys introduce themselves as Hunter and Blake before pairing off, leaving Rowan with me.

"What year are you?" he asks as we work out.

"Junior. You?"

"Same."

We fall quiet as the assistant coach walks by and watches each of us in action.

When he's gone, Rowan asks, "What school are you coming from?"

"Valley High."

"Is that near Detroit?"

I give my head a shake as I send the ball back to him. "Nah, Arizona."

"Damn. That's a long way. What brought you to Michigan?"

"Coach Collins. Frost Lake High."

"No shit?" He stops the ball and looks up at me. His brows lift, and one side of his mouth quirks up.

"He's the best, and the program he's built here is everything I've dreamed of." Jude Collins: former English professional footballer, arguably the greatest midfielder of his generation, and my idol since I was seven. I would have walked over broken glass to learn from him. Since he's taken over as head coach, Frost Lake has produced some of the most promising young soccer stars. Many have gone on to receive college scholarships to play soccer and two have even been drafted to professional teams.

"Was your old team any good?"

"We did all right." I shrug. We weren't terrible, but in the two years I played, we never made it past the quarterfinals. Frost Lake's record is unmatched. The best talent in the country in a public-school setting—something that was very important to my parents. I'd be happy if soccer was my only priority, but they feel differently.

I'm excited to see how I match up with these guys—if I don't get cut before I get a chance to show my new coach what I can do.

The whistle blows, indicating we need to switch to the next drill. For the next hour, I do nothing but focus on playing my heart out. I get to know Rowan as well. He's a midfielder with the best spatial awareness of anyone I've played with.

We're taking a water break, and the other guys are chatting with one another. There's one group still going, and Coach Collins stands on the sideline watching.

After splashing some water over my head, I approach him.

Without looking at me, he says, "What can I do for you, Keller?"

"I wanted to apologize for being late. I got confused about the schedule and went to the gym first."

He glances over at me. His dark shades keep his eyes hidden, but I can feel his scrutiny. "Were the instructions I sent out not clear?"

"No," I blurt out quickly. "I mean, yes, they were clear. It was my mistake." Water drips down my temples, and I swipe it away with the back of my hand. "Anyway, I'm sorry, and it won't happen again."

He nods and returns his gaze to the field. "Good."

I start to walk off, and he says, "Keller?"

"Yeah?"

"Do you usually wear glitter to practice?"

I want to sink into the ground. I glance down at my shirt. Even my hands are covered in it from wiping my face. "No, sir. I had a run-in with a girl holding what I think was an entire glitter aisle as I was rushing out to the field."

The tiniest smile pulls at the corners of his lips. "Let that be a lesson. Nothing good happens when you show up late to my practices."

—

After another grueling two hours, I've survived my first practice. I walk almost numbly with the rest of the guys to the sidelines where our bags are stashed.

"Yo, Disco."

I'm pulling off my sweaty T-shirt when Rowan walks over. He tips his chin at me.

"I'm stuck with that nickname, aren't I?" I wipe my face with my shirt and grimace when I somehow find more glitter on it.

"It's catchy." He laughs. "Congrats. You made it past day one."

"Was there any doubt?" I smirk. Aside from showing up late, practice was good. I worked hard, and I kept up with the biggest, fastest guys on the team.

"A bunch of us are going out tonight. Matt Doyle's family has a camp out on Highway 2. You know the area?"

"Not really," I admit.

"No problem. Hand me your phone."

I do, and he puts in his number and hands it back.

"Shoot me your address, and I'll swing by and pick you up on the way. If you want."

"Uhh…" I hesitate. "Are you sure it's cool? We have practice tomorrow."

He waves me off. "It'll be chill. Mostly just the guys here and a few other people. It'd be good for you to meet some more of the team. Even our captain will be there. Right, Vaughn?" He opens his stance as the star forward of Frost Lake's soccer team approaches. "Did you meet Disco here? He did his makeup for us, hoping to make a flashy first impression."

I wipe my face again, but I'm sure it's futile.

"Of course I'm coming. Someone has to make sure everyone stays out of trouble," Vaughn says coolly. He tosses Rowan a practice jersey.

We spent all day in the same groups, which meant I didn't get to put names with faces, but I recognize Vaughn. He's the best high school forward in the state. Maybe the country. He's broken every school record in the state and led Frost Lake to two championships. He's magic on the pitch. Everything you would expect of Jude Collins's son.

His blue eyes meet mine and scan me in question.

"I had an unfortunate glitter incident," I say in case he thinks Rowan is serious.

He cracks a small smile. "You're Austin Keller, right?"

"That's right."

"Your stats last year were pretty good. Especially considering your season ended so soon."

I stare at him, slack-jawed. Vaughn Collins knows *my* stats?

Rowan chuckles. "You're gonna give the new guy a big head. Our dear captain makes it his job to know everything about everyone."

Vaughn hands me a jersey. "I said pretty good. Your footwork under pressure could be better."

Damn. He's right. "I've been working on it this summer. It'll get there."

Whatever flaws he sees in my game, I want him to know I won't rest until I fix them. Lucky for both of us, there aren't many flaws in my game.

"What kind of drills have you been doing?" Vaughn asks.

Before I can answer, Rowan groans. "Oh no. There's two of you now."

"He means that as a compliment," Vaughn says to me.

Rowan shoulders his bag. "Excuse me for caring about more than soccer. Practice is over, and I'm exhausted. We can chat drills and stats tomorrow."

With a laugh, Vaughn walks backward. "I gotta hand the rest of these out, but I'll see you both tonight. Keller, let's chat. I have some ideas that might help."

"Yeah, that'd be awesome." More than awesome. It's perfect.

I met my hero, and the captain of my new team knows my stats and wants to help me improve my game. What a freaking day. Not even a look at my sparkly face in the rearview mirror when I get in my Jeep to drive home can ruin my mood.

CHAPTER THREE

ROWAN SHOWS UP EXACTLY AT EIGHT. I HURRY OUT TO THE driveway and climb into his old Ford truck. It suits him. It has a well-loved, rough-around-the-edges kind of vibe to it.

He takes one look at me and says, "Aww, man. No glitter tonight?"

"Ha, ha." I shut the door and prop an elbow on the open windowsill.

He stares past me toward the house we moved into just last week. "You have siblings?"

"Yeah. A sister and a brother," I say as I glance up at Torrance's window. The light is on. It's the only indication, other than her closed door, that she's home. She's not my biggest fan right now.

Wyatt is eight and thinks everything is new and exciting, but Torrance hasn't spoken to me since we left Arizona. She's only a grade younger than me, so I know how hard it was to leave her friends. I miss mine too, but I wish she could be just a little excited for me. Playing soccer at Frost Lake could open so many doors.

Rowan drives through town and then onto a gravel road that winds through a dense forest area. I can't get over the trees. They're massive, and everything here is so green.

The night air blows through the truck. I lose track of the time as he drives down a narrow country road. Small cabins pop up in clearings as we talk, mostly about soccer. He tells me about Frost Lake and asks me about my previous teams. When we finally fall into easy silence, I note how quiet it is out here. The only sounds are the trees swaying in the wind and the tires crunching on gravel.

I'm about to ask him how much farther when a larger cabin comes into view. It's the only one for miles that's had the lights on—and a line of cars out front.

Rowan pulls a U-turn and parks along the side of the road. We're greeted with music as soon as we exit the truck. Voices drift out as we walk up the steps of the front porch.

Rowan walks in without knocking. The reaction is immediate. Every head turns, and a group of guys sitting around a table with cards in front of them yells, "Rowan!"

I've known him for less than a day, and it's easy to see he's well-liked by everyone.

"What's up?" he asks no one in particular.

"We saved you a seat for poker," Barrett calls. He's a senior and the starting goalie for the team.

"Absolutely not," Rowan says. "I don't have any money, and if I did, I wouldn't gamble it with your cheating shenanigans."

"I don't cheat," Barrett says, grinning wide. He gives me a polite head nod. "What about you, New Guy? Do you like poker?"

"Yeah, it's okay."

He kicks out an empty chair for me. "Since it's your first night, we'll even take it easy on you."

Rowan snorts in a way that tells me he thinks Barrett is lying.

"Another time."

"Good choice," Rowan says. "Come on. Everyone else will be out back." He goes straight past the table and through a small kitchen to a back door. He steps out onto the porch and holds it open for me. "Word of advice: never gamble with Barrett. He's a shark. His parents are loaded too, so he doesn't think anything of dropping a few hundred dollars on a bet."

"Noted," I say, scanning the backyard. The porch is small, but it steps down into a yard that stretches toward the forest behind it. In the center, a fire is going, and people sit around it. A lot of the guys I recognize from the team, but there are others that I don't know. And girls. I should have expected it, but there are more girls here than guys.

I look for the girl from today but can't find her as Rowan leads me out to the party. A couple of people are on four-wheelers, and they head out into the tree line.

Rowan stops next to a group of guys that includes Hunter and Blake. "You already met these two, and these are the Whitlock twins, Eli and Eddie."

They nod their heads in unison. They are identical but their hair is different. One has longer, curly black hair, and the other's head is shaved.

"This is Disco," Rowan says. "Junior forward all the way from Arizona."

"Hey." I nod. "My name is actually Austin."

Rowan keeps walking, pausing at each group and introducing me. Always as Disco. At some point, I stop correcting him.

When we've gone around the entire party, we take a seat next to the twins.

"Is Vaughn here?" I ask. I was hoping to see him so I could follow up on our conversation from earlier. I have so many questions.

"Nah. He probably stayed late to practice more or get in an extra workout," the twin with the short hair—Eddie, I think—says.

Rowan grabs a beer and a soda from a cooler and offers them to me. I take the soda, and he grins like he knew I would, then pops the top on the beer. I don't mind drinking, but I'm not about to do anything that might make tomorrow's practice go poorly. I will be on time and well rested and definitely not hungover.

"He usually shows up later," Rowan says. "Parties aren't really his thing, but he comes to keep an eye on us and make sure things don't get too rowdy."

My disappointment must show on my face, because the next question out of Rowan's mouth is, "Did you seriously move all the way from Arizona to Michigan just to play soccer for Coach Collins?"

"Yeah." I feel like maybe I should be embarrassed about that, but I'm not. This opportunity is everything.

"Well, shit, we got another diehard on our hands, boys." He claps me on the shoulder. "I respect it, but tell me, Disco, how do you feel about putting all thoughts of soccer on hold for a few hours and just enjoying the night?" He leans back and tips his head up toward the sky. "The stars are shining, the music is pumping, and there has to be at least one pretty girl here who wants to dance with the new guy."

"I don't dance."

"Well, we won't tell them that."

"I think I'll hang here," I say as Rowan stands and looks at me expectantly.

"All right. You're sure? Girls at Frost Lake are in a league all their own."

"We do have some hot chicks," the twins say at the same time.

Chuckling, I nod. A vision of the blond girl I ran into earlier comes to mind. "I'm sure."

"Okay. Have fun." With a wink, Rowan leaves.

Eddie and Eli get pulled into conversations with other people, so I walk over to the side of the yard where Hunter and Blake have started playing cornhole. Barrett has abandoned his card game and sits on the bottom step, watching them.

"Can I get in the next game?" I ask.

"Yeah," Hunter says, flicking his head and sending the light brown strands out of his eyes. "But there's another one if you don't want to wait."

"New Guy!" Barrett calls from where he sits. He points at me as he stands. "Me and you."

I follow him to the other cornhole setup.

"Care to make it interesting?" he asks as we pick up our bags.

I chuckle, thinking about Rowan's warning that Barrett likes to bet. Unfortunately for him, he's not getting anything from me. "I don't have any money."

He waves it off. "We'll play for a dare."

"A dare?"

"Yeah. You win, and I take a dare from you. I win, and you take one from me."

"Can't we just play for bragging rights? I don't need you to do anything but shake my hand when I win."

He throws his head back and laughs loudly toward the sky. "I like you, New Guy. This is going to be fun."

"What's the dare?" I ask. I feel a small beat of hesitation, but I never back down from a competition.

He tosses one bag up and catches it, smiling. One of his front teeth is chipped, and he has a sparse black mustache that blends in against his dark skin. "If I win, you have to kiss that girl over there before the end of the night."

I follow his gaze to the porch where two girls have just stepped out the back door. My heart trips when I see her. She's wearing jeans and a tank top tonight instead of the shorts and T-shirt she had on earlier, and her hair is down, falling over her shoulders and teasing her bare arms. It takes a beat before I even fully see her friend. The same brunette she was with today. She's cute too, but there's something about the blond that draws me to her. I hope she left the glitter at home.

"Which one?" I ask, tearing my gaze away.

"The one with the boot."

Otherwise known as the blond goddess I nearly trampled.

"That's it? I just have to kiss her?"

"Yeah. That's it. Easy, right? You're the mysterious and unknown new guy. The girls will be fighting over you before the end of the night."

I highly doubt that girl has ever had to fight for a guy. They probably just fall at her feet. It doesn't stop me from imagining what it'd be like to make out with her. It's been a while, with the move and everything. Not that I've ever had a lot of time for dating. Soccer takes up so much time that I've only done the girlfriend thing once.

"I'm not even that good," he says. "You'll probably beat me."

Kissing her wouldn't be the worst way to end tonight. I shrug. "Let's do it."

Twenty minutes later, he's not only beaten me, but he's beaten me so badly that I can't figure out how it happened. I'm usually good at cornhole.

We've attracted a crowd, including Rowan, who shakes his head at me and gives me a look that says, "I told you so."

"Pay up, New Guy."

"What'd you bet him?" Rowan asks, stepping up to pat me reassuringly on the shoulder.

"Uh-uh." Barrett interrupts. "This is between me and the new guy."

Rowan's brows lift. I think he mutters, "This can't be good."

"I have all night, right?" I ask. She's gorgeous, and I didn't exactly make the best impression earlier. I'm going to have to play the long game.

"Yeah, but I wouldn't wait. Once Vaughn gets here..." He trails off, tilting his head to the side and wincing.

"Is there a rule against hooking up during the season or something?" I look from Barrett to Rowan. The last thing I need is to do something stupid and get cut. I'm already on thin ice after showing up late today.

"No, no. You're all good. He just gets bent out of shape with my dares sometimes."

Rowan's brows lift. "You nearly sent Chad to the emergency room after you bet him two hundred dollars that he couldn't surf the hood of your truck."

"That was unfortunate," Barrett says. "I didn't account for his terrible balance, and that massive pothole came out of nowhere."

I have an uneasy feeling in my stomach.

"But he was totally fine. And the new guy here just has to get a girl to kiss him or embarrass himself trying."

Not just any girl. The hottest one at the party and the one I almost ran over trying to rush to practice. But I do love a challenge.

My new teammates are watching, and I have a feeling they aren't going to stop until I've completed my dare. Might as well make my move.

She's sitting on the back of a parked four-wheeler with the brunette.

As I approach, her friend notices me first and elbows her in the side.

Her mouth pulls up into a half smile that's playful but mocking. "Well, look who it is. I must say, the glitter was a good look on you. You sparkled all the way across the field."

Glitter jabs. I'm getting used to those. And if she's joking around, then maybe she's already forgiven me.

"Hey. I'm Austin. I didn't catch your name earlier today."

"Oh, you mean when you were running me over?"

Or not. "I'm so sorry. I was late, and I should have been looking where I was going. And if it's any consolation, the guys are never going to let me live it down. They're calling me Disco and asking for makeup tips."

She lets out a small laugh. "That does make me feel a teensy bit better."

There's another beat where she seems to consider if she's going to tell me her name or not. Finally, she says, "Claire." She tips her head to the side. "This is Lacey."

I glance over at her friend, who's smiling *big* as she watches my interaction with her friend.

"That was quite a beating you took," Lacey says. "Didn't anyone warn you about Barrett?"

"Yeah." I rub the back of my neck. "I swear he cheated, but I don't know how."

Claire's laughter tinkles in the air. "He definitely cheated. He always does."

"Would you believe me if I said I was taking it easy on him?"

"No," she says adamantly. "Just like I wouldn't believe you came over here just to apologize. What'd he dare you to do?"

My jaw drops.

"Oh, please. It's obvious. He doesn't do anything without betting on it. Plus, everyone is staring at us." She glances behind me.

I turn, and she's right. My teammates' expressions range from excited to impressed. Except Rowan, who looks almost nervous. I offer a reassuring smile.

"So what is it? Do you have to get my number? Maybe ask me out on a date? We might as well get this over with." Her bored tone borders on annoyed. If I had to guess, she's the object of many dares.

"I have to kiss you."

"Kiss me?" Her brows lift in surprise, then she laughs. That doesn't bode well for me. "And if you don't?"

I don't plan to find out.

"I'm a good kisser," I assure her.

"Wow." Her laughter doesn't deter me. I work hard at the things I like, and I like kissing. "That's not happening. I don't even know you."

"Like I said, I'm Austin." I hold out my hand, but she doesn't take it.

"I'll make out with you, Austin." Lacey smiles. Her dark hair falls over her shoulders. "You're cute."

I wink at Lacey and then glance back at Claire with a cocky grin plastered on my face. "I could just kiss you on the cheek or forehead or something?" He didn't specify where I had to kiss her, and I'm about to take any loophole I can to get out of this with my pride intact. "Would be a waste though. You're hot, I'm hot..."

She hops down from the back of the four-wheeler and steps closer while crossing her arms over her chest. She's shorter than I remember, but she holds her head up high and pushes her shoulders back. She's got this fiery attitude and sass that I didn't pick up on this morning. I like it a lot.

"You really know how to sweep a girl off her feet," she says dryly.

"Well, I kind of did if you think about it."

She smiles with a soft laugh. "You're a real charmer."

"What can I say? It comes naturally around you."

She shakes her head like she thinks I'm making it up, but for her, I'm ready to pull out my A game.

"Tell me, *Austin*, what do I get out of this?" Her tone sounds almost bored. Almost. There's just a hint of amusement and maybe intrigue.

"What do you want?"

She studies me closely. "I'm not sure yet."

"You can have anything you want."

"Anything, huh?" Claire steps closer until I can feel the warmth of her skin next to mine. I think I hear Lacey squeal with excitement behind her, but I can't look away. Claire's eyes are different colors. One is blue and the other is hazel. Both are framed with long, black lashes. And her lips, which keep catching my eye, are coated in a glossy pink. She might be the prettiest girl I've ever seen up close.

"Anything." If she wants to get out of here and go somewhere more private, I'd be down for that too.

Her eyes dart to my lips, and she moves another inch forward, laughing quietly. "You owe me so big."

My heart is beating so fast. It must be because it's been so long since I've kissed someone. I don't remember ever having this reaction before.

"You're sure?" I ask, then slam my mouth shut. What the hell? Am I really trying to talk her out of it? Forget the dare. I just want to taste her.

"No, but I'm rarely certain of anything anymore." Another small laugh escapes, but then she tips her head up in invitation.

I close the distance, leaning down and brushing my lips over hers softly.

Instinctively, one hand finds her hip, and the other goes up to the column of her neck where I can feel her pulse racing in time with mine. She smells like cotton candy, and the way her mouth molds to mine, I already know I'll never get enough.

Somewhere in the back of my mind, I remember we have an audience and reluctantly pull back. We can continue this later. There's no way I'm not kissing this girl again.

We stare at each other, still inches apart. *Thank you, Barrett.*

Someone taps me on the shoulder, and I turn, almost floating. Not kissing anyone for a month can really fuck with a guy.

I smile and shake the fog from my brain when I realize its Vaughn behind me.

"Hey. You made it. I was looking for you earlier." It's only after I speak that I realize he's glowering at me.

"Hey, Vaughn," Claire says, tone icier than it was with me.

I open my stance and look between them as I try to piece together the situation.

He doesn't even acknowledge her, just keeps staring hard at me. I don't know what's happening, but he's pissed. Then he levels me with seven words. "What are you doing kissing my girlfriend?"

CHAPTER FOUR

"What the hell, Claire?" Vaughn steps in front of Austin.

Bringing a hand to my lips, I move back. I'm in a daze, so it takes a moment of my ex-boyfriend staring at me with anger and disbelief etched onto his face before I remember he has no right to be mad. He broke up with me.

"Hi to you too." I return to the back of Doyle's four-wheeler where I'd been sitting when the new guy walked over and asked to kiss me. I'm ignoring Vaughn's question. And why did he call me his girlfriend?

It's obvious from the panicked look in Austin's eyes that he had no idea why Barrett dared him to kiss me out of all the girls here tonight.

Vaughn follows me, but when I glance back around, Austin is nowhere to be seen. Figures. He's smart to put some distance between him and his team captain. Right or not, it was a predictable outcome for Vaughn to react the way he did. If I had known he was here, I would have acted differently.

In fact, I'm not sure why I kissed Austin at all. I could have easily told him to get lost. I should have. Cocky jerk. Then I wouldn't have to deal with Vaughn pretending like he still has any claim over me.

"If you're trying to make me jealous, it's working." He leans closer and speaks quietly. We have an audience, and everyone within a five-foot radius has an ear turned in our direction to catch the latest Frost Lake High drama.

School hasn't even started, but the rumor mill is always alive and well.

"Jealous?" I can't help the huff of air that leaves my lungs as I watch Vaughn's brows furrow.

"I'm sorry, did I miss the memo?" Lacey gets to her feet and puts herself between me and my ex-boyfriend. "Are you two back together?"

I don't have to see Lacey's expression to know she's pinning Vaughn with a murderous stare. She is tiny but terrifying when she wants to be. She was never a huge fan of Vaughn, because he's so serious and stoic—basically the opposite of her—but ever since he broke up with me, she despises him.

"Lace, this is between me and Claire," he says softly. A muscle in his jaw gives away his irritation, but he understands that making my best friend angry isn't going to get him anywhere.

I don't need her to protect me, but she always does anyway.

She crosses her arms over her chest. "Yes, but she doesn't want to talk to you."

I probably should talk to him. I know him well enough to know that he isn't going to let this go. Once he's got something on his mind, he won't rest until it's resolved. It's a trait I admired when it was focused on something other than me.

He doesn't get to race in here all jealous when he sees me with another guy. He broke up with me.

When Lacey doesn't budge and I don't speak up, Vaughn finally relents. He takes a small step back and flicks his gaze up from Lacey to me. "I'm sorry about the way I ended things. I messed up, but we belong together, Claire. *We're* not over."

He turns on his heel and walks away. Air slowly returns to my lungs, and I inhale deeply, then let it out in a whoosh.

"Are you okay?" Lacey asks in a much gentler tone than she'd used with Vaughn.

"Yeah, I'm fine," I say automatically. I'm aware people are whispering and still watching, like they hope we'll shout at each other across the party and don't want to miss it.

"Hey, who wants to play flip cup!" Rowan appears out of nowhere with a six-pack of beer in one hand and a stack of Solo cups in the other.

There's a beat of silence, and then people are calling out and moving toward the makeshift table laid out on top of a large tree stump.

I breathe a little easier as soon as the focus is off me. Rowan glances at me, and I know he's doing it for my benefit—or at least partially. He doesn't usually need a reason to party, but he's the kind of guy who knows when to step in and change the mood.

"Thank you," I mouth to him.

He winks in response.

"Well, that was interesting," Lacey says with amusement in her tone. "Tell me, are you planning on kissing any more boys tonight? Because it might be fun to watch Vaughn's head explode."

I hadn't planned on kissing Austin. My lips tingle at the memory. I also hadn't planned on liking it. The last thing I need is another guy like Vaughn.

"The night is still young," I joke.

"I think I'm going to like single Claire this year." She bumps her shoulder against mine.

For the rest of the night, Lacey sticks to my side. She doesn't say it, but I know she's acting as a shield from Vaughn. He rarely comes to these parties, and if he does, he usually doesn't stay this late.

As he finally heads toward the gate to leave, he glances back at me. Our gazes lock, and I feel a thousand different emotions pass through me. My anger and frustration at the way he ended things and how he thinks we can just pick up where we left off has fizzled out, and I'm left with a twinge of sadness and remorse.

I wouldn't have kissed Austin if I knew Vaughn was here. I probably shouldn't have kissed him at all. But it reminded me that there are a lot of guys out there. I don't have to settle for someone who only wants me when it's convenient for them or someone who is just doing it for a stupid dare.

I look away first.

Lacey and I are saying our goodbyes to everyone when I finally spot Austin. He's in a circle of soccer players, talking and laughing. As if he can feel my eyes on him, he looks up. I quickly avert my gaze, and my cheeks heat at being caught staring. The last thing I want is to feed his ego.

I drop a hand to Lacey's forearm to get her attention. "I'm going to use the bathroom before we leave."

"Okay." She nods. "I'll meet you inside in five."

I cross the yard and head into the house. It's empty. The dining room table where the guys had been playing cards earlier is abandoned, decks of cards and empty bottles and cans littering the top.

When I finish in the bathroom, I come back out to find Austin standing in the dining room. His gaze is on his phone, but as soon as he hears me approaching, he looks up.

My steps slow as he pockets his phone and stands tall.

"Hey," he says with no uncertainty or trepidation in his tone. I expected him to avoid me, maybe give me some weak apology. He had no idea why Barrett dared him to kiss me, that much I know, but I guess I expected him to look…guilty or regretful. He looks neither of those things. Instead, he seems happy to see me. Which doesn't explain why he kept his distance all night.

I decide to pretend like nothing happened. So we kissed a little. He was doing it because he was dared, and I was doing it…well, I'm still not sure why I did it. But it didn't mean anything. It was a nice kiss. Okay, better than nice. He's a great kisser. He didn't lie about that. But maybe I just forgot what it was like. It's been almost two months since I've so much as held hands with anyone.

"Hi." My lips pull up into an amused smile. "I'm surprised you're still here and that you're talking to me." I place a hand on my chest and lean in to whisper, "Does Vaughn know?"

His light green eyes are laser focused on me as he cocks his head to one side. "I don't need his permission to talk to you."

That is not the response I was expecting. It pulls a laugh from me, and Austin steps closer.

"I'm sorry," he says.

"Sorry that you kissed me or sorry that you got on the bad side of your team captain?"

"Nah, he'll get over it."

He's so cocky. So confident.

"But I am sorry that I put you in that position. I'm still finding my place with my new teammates, but I should have just told him to screw off. That was a crappy way to have our first kiss."

"Our only kiss. I don't date soccer players."

"You dated Vaughn."

"A mistake I don't intend to repeat with one of his minions."

"Minion?" One of his dark brows lifts. "I'm no one's minion."

"No? Because I think you set a world record with how fast you ran off when you found out I was his ex-girlfriend."

"He didn't say ex. He said girlfriend. Current."

"We broke up," I say, feeling a little of that earlier irritation rising.

"Well, either way, it didn't seem like a conversation I should be a part of." He shrugs one shoulder.

"It's not a conversation that needs to happen at all. Vaughn and I aren't together, but you'd be smart to stay on his good side. The guys respect him, even if they like to mess with him from time to time."

"Like daring me to kiss his ex?"

I nod. "Exactly."

"I'll be all right." He gives me another shrug. "What year are you?"

I'm surprised by his determination. Most guys would have given up by now. After a moment of silence, I say, "Junior."

"Me too."

I shift my weight. My foot is bugging me a little from being on it more today than I have previously.

His gaze drops to the boot. "What'd you do to your foot?"

"I broke my fibula and tore the ligaments in my ankle." I move to go around him. I'd rather talk about Vaughn than my injury.

Lacey is coming inside as I head toward the door. She smiles at me, then her expression morphs to confusion when she sees Austin behind me.

"Sorry," she says, a smile slowly forming on her lips. "I can wait outside for you."

"No, it's fine. I'm ready to go."

"Wait," Austin calls as both Lacey and I turn to go through the house to the front door. "Can I get your number?"

"Why?" I ask, genuinely surprised that he thinks that's a good idea. Did he not hear me? Vaughn is the captain this year. And the best player on the team. Making him mad would be stupid.

"So I can text you. Maybe you could show me around next week."

Lacey giggles, and when I glance over at her, she is fighting to keep it together. I can't help but smile back at her. The new guy is incorrigible.

"Student council has volunteers to help acclimate new students," I tell him.

"Or you could just volunteer."

"I don't think so."

Austin is following us toward the door, but he stops when we reach it. Lacey pats him on the chest as she goes by him. “I admire your determination in the face of certain social ruin.”

She opens the door and steps outside. I hesitate in front of Austin. I don’t know what to say to this guy. I can’t believe he’s for real.

“You don’t even know me,” I say.

“That’s the point. I want to get to know you.”

I don’t want to be flattered that he’s so determined in his pursuit of me, but a spark of excitement flickers inside me anyway.

I can’t think of a single thing to say as I move out the front door.

“See you around,” he says to my back.

And it feels like a promise.

CHAPTER FIVE

THE GIRLS' SOCCER TEAM IS STILL ON THE FIELD WHEN I arrive to practice the next day. A few of the other guys are stretching. I look around for Vaughn, but he isn't here yet. I need to make sure there's no hard feelings about what happened last night.

I explained the situation at Doyle's before he left, but all he would say is "It's okay. You didn't know."

And I hadn't. But even knowing what I do now, I can't say I don't want to do it again.

I drop my bag and take my ball over to where the team has huddled, waiting to take the field.

Barrett spots me first, his grin pulling up one side of his mouth. "New Guy, you showed. Good for you. Kiss any more of Collins's ex-girlfriends last night?"

The entire group snickers. I decide not to let them get to me. I know guys like Barrett back in Arizona. He wants to get a reaction out of me, but I'm not letting any of them see me sweat. I can be a valuable player on this team. No way petty drama is going to get in my way.

"Not that I know of," I say, matching his grin.

Their laughter grows louder. Moving my gaze to the girls on the field and hopefully dissuading my team from razzing me further, I raise the ball over my head and stretch.

When the girls finish practice and we take over, I still haven't spotted Vaughn. He doesn't show up until the very last second, falling into the back of the group as Coach blows the whistle and gives us warm-up instructions.

We jog circles around the field in a pack. Vaughn is at the back, and I'm in the front. I assumed he'd naturally make his way forward since he's one of the fastest on the team, but after two laps, he hasn't. I fall back until I'm beside him.

Sweat trickles down my forehead, but my legs are beginning to feel warm and loose.

"Hey," I say, nodding my head.

His gaze stays locked forward. Coach blows the whistle, and we finish the lap and grab water. I stick next to Vaughn. Rowan side-eyes me from a few feet away.

"Last night was wild, right? I should have expected that the guys were going to pull something. Are we good?"

"It's fine, Keller." Vaughn doesn't look me in the eye, but I take him at his word.

He seems like a straightforward guy, and I'm looking forward to playing soccer with him. Everything I know about him points to us having a similar love and determination for the sport.

"How long were you two together?" I'm not exactly prying, but I do find myself hoping he'll share a little more about his ex. When he doesn't, I add, "I wouldn't have kissed her if I'd known, but she seems cool."

Rowan clears his throat nearby. I glance quickly at him,

and he's shaking his head in warning, but I'm not sure why until I notice the stony expression on Vaughn's face.

I try to backpedal, but I'm not even sure why he's so mad. All I said was that she seemed cool. "I just mean I can see why you were into her. She's superhot and—"

The daggers shooting out of his eyes only intensify, but luckily Coach blows the whistle again before I can put my foot in my mouth any further. I mean, does he really think no one else has noticed Claire is a knockout?

"Break into groups of three for defending drills," Coach bellows from the middle of the field.

I glance around to see trios forming all around me.

"You want to be in our group, Keller?" Vaughn asks. He has Doyle with him, the senior defender whose family owns the cabin Rowan took me to last night.

"Yeah," I say quickly, not able to hide the surprise in my voice. I noticed yesterday that Vaughn always positions himself to go up against the best guys in practice. Maybe I misread him, and he's not pissed about Claire. I'm happy to put it all behind us.

Coach has laid out cones down the field for each of the groups. One person is on offense, another on defense, and one person is out. The idea is simple: offense passes the ball to defense, defense passes it back and then rushes the offense, who tries to get past the defender.

I'm first up on defense. Vaughn passes me the ball, and I pass it back, then run toward him. He's a great ball handler, maybe the best I've ever played with, but I dig deep. He goes right, and I match him. Vaughn is patient though. He moves from side to side, waiting for an opportunity. It comes when he fakes right, then left, and gets me on my heels. He's past me on the right before I regain my footing.

"Nice job," I say and offer him my hand.

He turns without acknowledging me and kicks the ball to Doyle, who is now on offense.

It's a quick drill but high intensity. Offense becomes defense, then gets a short break. But with how fast everything moves, it isn't much of a breather.

Doyle and I are tired after only a few rotations. He's wheezing, audibly dragging in air to his lungs at every pause in action. Vaughn doesn't seem to be struggling at all. If he weren't sweating, I'd call him a machine.

On my fourth try, I wipe my forehead and concentrate. Vaughn is talented, but he prefers faking left and going right. He's done it two out of the three times we've done this drill. We pass the ball back and forth, and then I attack, leaving enough room between us that I can react and keep him from blowing by me.

Just like he's done before, he takes his time. He moves quickly, but in control. Right, left, baiting me and trying to get me out of position. But I stick with him.

"Nice, Keller!" Coach Collins calls.

It's the first time he's given me any kind of positive feedback, and it distracts me just enough that my reaction time slows, and Vaughn wastes no time in punishing me.

"Shit," I mutter under my breath. I jog to take my place behind Doyle while I wait for my next turn on offense, but Coach moves toward our group.

"Let's switch things up," he says. "Keller, you're fast but sloppy, and you're too easily distracted. Focus."

I take in the critique, silently berating myself for stupid mistakes and ready to do better.

"Let's reverse the order now and get fresh groups," Coach instructs.

This means that I'm now on offense against Vaughn. It's my chance for redemption. I take a deep breath as I pass the ball to him. Almost lazily, he passes it back, but then he's sprinting toward me. I know he's expecting me to take my time, but instead I go for a straight line past him. I almost make it, but he steals the ball from me at the last second, and I let out another curse.

"Again," Coach says to me. "Did you have any defenders in Arizona?"

Vaughn kicks the ball back to me. I take my time, but he crowds me and gets a swipe at the ball before I can make my move.

My frustration grows. Coach continues watching with his arms crossed over his chest. He tips his head as if to say, "Keep going until you get it."

Vaughn looks almost gleeful at my irritation. It fuels me, but I'm dog-tired. I do my best to make him play at my pace just like he did and like I'd done with Doyle, but Vaughn is bigger and faster than the guys I played against in Arizona. He doesn't fall for shoulder fakes or any other half-assed attempt to trick him. He makes me work. I'm quick to the left and then back right. I keep the ball away from him, kicking it behind me and switching frequently.

"You've got to move toward the goal to score, Keller." Coach sounds exasperated.

Fuck. I know he's right. It doesn't do me a lot of good to keep the ball away from him if I never get a clear shot. I'm not going to get an opening, so I decide to make one. I fake hard to the left and then move right. I get the jump on him, but he lowers his shoulder, and the impact of his body colliding into mine sends me to the ground.

I hear some of the guys laughing. Coach blows the whistle. "Take five for water."

I stay sitting on the ground with my elbows resting on my knees. My jaw hurts from where his big shoulder rammed into me. It could have been an accident, but I doubt it. He knew I had him beat, and he took a cheap shot.

Vaughn kicks the ball up and catches it. "Better luck next time."

Practice goes downhill after that. Vaughn ices me out, and by the time we're finished for the day, the rest of the team has noticed and are giving me a wide berth. Only Rowan dares to talk to me.

"Well, that was painful to watch," he says, falling into step next to me. "You really pissed him off."

"I don't understand. This is all over some girl?"

"Not *some* girl. Claire Crawford."

"What is the big deal? She said he broke up with her."

"It's...complicated," Rowan says as we walk over to the sideline.

"How so?"

"Listen, forget about Claire. It's not worth going to war with Vaughn."

"All because I kissed her?" It seems like an extreme reaction, even if she is the most beautiful girl I've ever seen. There's just something about her. Those eyes. And that hair. And those legs.

Rowan's voice pulls me from my Claire-obsessed thoughts. "And you all but implied you were into her."

Did I? That wasn't my intention, but I am intrigued by her. She was so...something.

"You called her hot," he says, as if clarifying.

"Well, I'm not blind." I squirt water into my mouth and then over my head.

Rowan chuckles softly and squeezes me on the shoulder. "When it comes to Claire, my advice is to pretend that you are."

—

When I get home from practice, Mom is in her office on a call, and Wyatt is in front of the TV in the living room.

Most of the house is unpacked, but a few boxes of miscellaneous shit that we haven't found a home for yet sit in front of the couch acting as a coffee table.

I sit next to Wyatt and prop my feet up on one of the boxes.

"Did you get the master sword yet?" I ask him. He's playing *Legend of Zelda*.

"Not yet," he says, then his nose wrinkles. "You smell. Mom is going to yell at you for stinking up the new furniture."

He is a wise kid for only eight years old.

"I'll just blame you," I tell him, swiping the controller out of his hands.

He lunges for it, but I hold it up high where he can't reach. Undeterred, he climbs up on me to get to it.

"You've been playing all day. It's my turn."

"You have to do your chores first," he says in a matter-of-fact voice that I'm sure Mom used on him earlier.

"She's on a call."

"Yeah, but it's not fair." He's in a phase where everything has to be fair. Last night at dinner, he made sure we all had the exact same number of fries.

Torrance comes from the kitchen and stops in the

entryway. She leans against the wall, and her features tighten. "Didn't you know, Wyatt? The world revolves around Austin. Get used to things not being fair."

Her words shouldn't get to me—she's been mad ever since we moved to Michigan—but it's been a long day already. I hand the controller back to my little brother and stand.

I don't bother engaging her as I walk into the kitchen. I open the fridge and pull out a container of leftover macaroni and cheese. Grabbing a fork, I dig in without heating it up.

She follows me, disgust etched into her features as she watches me shovel in the cold noodles.

"Want some?" I offer as I hold up a forkful in her face.

"Gross. No." She pushes my hand away from her.

The fact that she's in the same room as me is progress though. Last week, every time she saw me, she burst into tears.

"Can you drop me off at the mall?"

Ah, well, now it makes sense why she's tolerating my presence.

"What for?" I ask.

"I want to go clothes shopping for school next week," she says like the need to justify the free ride annoys her.

"I thought Mom was going to take you," I say as I shove another bite into my mouth.

"She was supposed to this morning, but she's been in back-to-back meetings."

I nod, feeling something like guilt. Mom used to only work part-time, but she's had to take on more hours since we moved. The house in Arizona still hasn't sold, and the van needed a new fuel pump last week.

I know that our moving here has put a strain on

everyone. I appreciate what they've given up for me, but I don't want to be held responsible for every bad thing that happens from now until eternity. Frost Lake is my opportunity, but it isn't like it's a bad place. The summers here are way better, I know that much already. I do not miss practicing outside in one-hundred-and-fifteen-degree heat. And maybe we'll finally have a white Christmas.

"Yeah. I'll take you," I say as I drop the empty bowl in the sink.

"Thank you." Her tone is begrudging gratitude.

We used to be close. She's only a grade younger than me, and back in Arizona, we even had a lot of the same friends. "Actually, can I come with you? I need to get a few things too."

"We can't leave Wyatt here by himself."

"He can come too. We'll hit up the arcade while you shop."

A hint of a smile appears, but she masks it quickly. "Sure. Whatever."

CHAPTER SIX

The first day of school arrives before I'm ready. When I get downstairs, Mom is dressed for work, drinking coffee as she stands in the kitchen. Ruby is eating breakfast at the island.

"Excited for fifth grade?" I ask my little sister.

She shrugs one shoulder but then grins. "Layla and I got the same teacher again this year."

I smile. I miss the days when having my best friend in my homeroom was all it took to make me excited for a new year.

Everything about this year feels different. No boyfriend to hold hands with between passing periods, no rushing to skate practice right after school and then cramming homework and studying in before bed. At least I still have Lacey. Maybe a great best friend is all I need.

"I bookmarked some colleges for you to consider." Mom tips her head toward her laptop on the counter. "And we need to talk about your schedule this year. You're going to need much better grades if you're going to get into a top college. Is it too late to add a couple of AP classes?"

It's her new dream for me: attend a good college, get a fabulous job, and forget that I spent the past ten years putting all my effort into figure skating.

"I have to go. Lacey is waiting," I say, ignoring all her questions, and swipe a granola bar from the pantry.

Lacey grins from behind the wheel of her new Bronco Sport. It was a guilt gift from her dad after he forgot her seventeenth birthday. It's decorated in blue-and-white window paint with things like *Juniors*, *FLHS*, and, of course, *Cheer Captain*.

My stomach is in knots as she pulls into a parking spot, and it only intensifies as we walk into the chaos. This year feels exciting and terrifying. I knew who I was as a sophomore, or at least I thought I did, and now all that has changed.

The halls are already packed with students. People stand in front of their lockers, talking and catching up after the summer break. Glittery signs hang on every wall, catching the light and temporarily making me smile. The smell of new perfume and unrealistic expectations hangs in the air.

At our lockers, I stand with my back against the cool metal, watching the excited faces of my peers and trying to summon some of it for myself.

"I can't believe we don't have a single class together this semester." Lacey frowns at my schedule.

I swipe my phone back. "That's what happens when you're an academic overachiever."

She grins. Lacey is supersmart and in all AP classes. My mother would be so proud of her schedule.

"Well, here's hoping I don't regret that by the end of the week. I heard the new AP Calculus teacher is really hard."

"How could anyone possibly know that yet?"

She shrugs. "I guess someone heard from a student at his last school."

"You'll be fine," I reassure her.

The first bell rings.

"I better go." Lacey clutches her laptop and notebook to her chest with a nervous, excited grin. She is perhaps the most hopeful of anyone today, and I don't want to take that from her, so I smile back.

"See you at lunch," I promise.

The morning goes by in a blur of welcome speeches from teachers and seating arrangements. My class schedule isn't that strenuous since, until a couple of months ago, school was not the biggest priority in my life. I don't see the point in changing that now. I'm not a brainiac like Lacey, and I'm not even sure I want to go to college yet. It was never my plan, but now I don't know what I'll do after high school ends.

I manage to dodge Vaughn until lunch. He's texted a few times since Doyle's party, but I'm not interested in whatever he has to say. It's too late for apologies, and there's no way I'm getting back together with him. I'm sure with the start of the school year, he'll move on quickly. He's not exactly hard up for attention.

He's sitting at the same table as last year. Several of his teammates are with him, and the tables nearby are occupied by girls all trying to catch the eyes of the team. Vaughn looks directly at me the moment Lacey and I enter the cafeteria. There are two seats next to him, the only open spots at the crowded table, like he was saving them for us.

"New year, new table?" Lacey suggests.

I breathe a sigh of relief. "Definitely."

Breaking his gaze, I follow Lacey through the lunchroom to the other side.

The cafeteria is broken down in your typical high school cliques, which each have their own table. Frost Lake High has all the usual groups: the jocks; the trendy girls who spend their allowances on designer labels and come to school every day looking like they're ready for a glamour photo shoot; the supersmart kids; the kids who despise high school and ditch more often than they show up (I have no idea what they do instead); and our little group.

Me, Lacey, Andie, and Brandon have been friends since middle school. Andie and Lacey are both on the cheerleading squad, and Andie also does theater. She routinely has the lead in the school plays. Brandon is on the hockey team, but he didn't start playing until high school, so he isn't as tight with those guys. Plus, he's always had a huge crush on Andie. There were more of us who hung out before high school, but several have found new clubs and friend groups.

The four of us each fit into other cliques, but we've stuck together. Not always. Last year, I sat with the soccer team more than them. Lacey disappeared for a month when she dated a guy on the basketball team, and Brandon was gone for a few weeks when he was trying to fit in with his new varsity hockey buddies. But we seem to always make our way back to each other.

They're the friend equivalent of a pair of really comfortable sweatpants. We've all known one another a long time, and it's just easy being together.

Or it was easy being together before Andie and Brandon became a couple nine months ago. Sometimes, I forget, they're a couple and then they do something sweet like share food or kiss. I still remember in seventh grade when Brandon told Andie she was flat-chested, and she cried for two days straight. He hadn't meant to hurt her feelings—he thought he was just stating facts and probably wanted to acknowledge that he'd noticed her, not that she didn't yet need a bra. Anyway, he seems to be just fine with her cup size now.

"Hey." Lacey sets her tray down in front of them.

They pull their heads apart and look forward.

"Hi," Andie chirps happily. "Love the new bling." She motions toward the new C patch on Lacey's cheerleading top, denoting her as captain. All the cheerleaders wore their uniforms for the first day.

Lacey pushes her dark hair back and smiles down at it proudly. "It looks great, right?"

"You were made for the job," Andie assures her, then rests her elbows on the table. "I'm thinking of getting a nose ring. Thoughts?"

"Since when?" I ask.

"Since today when I realized I look exactly the same as I did last year." She lifts a hand to the left side of her nose. "A tiny little gold hoop."

"You were hot then, and you're hot now," Brandon states casually. He let his hair grow out over the summer, and it hangs down to his chin. Plus, he got glasses. He looks like a cross between Jungkook and Clark Kent.

Andie blushes at the compliment, and I'm certain they're going to start making out right in front of us, but instead her stare slides over to me. "How are you, Claire?"

It's clear from the vague question and sympathy in her tone that what she's really asking is how I'm doing with my foot still in a boot and my skating dreams blown to smithereens. But even I realize it's too early in the year and the day for that kind of pessimism.

"I'm great." I open my chocolate milk carton and avoid looking directly at her or Brandon. My foot is hurting today. It doesn't bother me much anymore, but I've done a lot more walking this morning without elevating it. However, the last thing I want to do is talk about my foot.

Luckily, nobody presses, and my three friends fall into easy conversation about the new school year and all the classes they're taking. Talking about school then turns to talking about the parties to celebrate the start of the new year. Every year, someone throws a big party during the first week. It almost always gets busted by parents, but this year it's at Bobby Boone's house, and his parents are these big-time lawyers who are always traveling. People are excited.

"We're going," Andie says, motioning her head to Brandon.

"Really?" I ask. It's not really either of their scenes. They usually go to the parties after dances or homecoming, but neither of them has ever attended a back-to-school party. Lacey drags me every year. It's not that it isn't my scene, but I rarely had time for them. I skated every night until seven or eight, and I was so exhausted after. Also, my mom was really strict about staying out late any time I had morning practices. I can hear her canned reply: "An athlete needs a good night's sleep."

"We're juniors now!" Andie's face lights up with excitement and pulls me from my thoughts.

"Yeah, I suppose so." I attempt a smile back at her. My face muscles are starting to hurt from all my forced smiles today.

"You're going too?" Lacey asks, surprised. I guess she wasn't planning on dragging me this year.

"Maybe." I shrug. "Aren't you?"

She shakes her head. "I can't. Dad just finished a big work project, and he wants to take me to dinner, and then we're going to watch a movie. I'm making him watch *Bring It On*." She grins, and I have a hard time imagining her buttoned-up dad watching a cheer comedy.

"Sounds S-U-P-E-R!" I mock, bumping my shoulder against hers.

"R-U-D-E." She bumps me back harder.

I take a bite of my ham and cheese sandwich. Andie and Brandon go back to talking between themselves, and the table falls into a comfortable silence. I'm happy to just be for a bit. No talking. No expectations. No having my life figured out.

Until Lacey breaks that silence. She can't help it. She's an only child, and her mom died when she was a baby. But that must be where she got all her extrovert genes, because her dad is this super introverted researcher who gets lost in his work for days at a time. "I was thinking now that you don't have figure skating every day after school, we can hang out in the afternoons when I'm done with cheer practice."

My reply gets stuck in my throat.

Her eyes widen, and then her black lashes drop, making her look like a hurt puppy. "I'm so sorry. God, Claire. I'm an idiot. That was a crummy thing to say. I just meant—"

"No, you're right. I'm wide open, and I'd love to hang out in the afternoons. It'll keep me from dying of boredom." I haven't figured out what to do with all the extra time I have without skating. The moping and feeling sorry for myself that I did all summer filled that void, but now...now it's time to do something. I'm just not sure what.

She squeezes my arm and drops her voice low. "I'm sorry. Truly. I should have thought before I spoke. I think I used my brain too much already today."

"It's okay," I tell her. "Really."

Her gaze lifts, and a slow smile spreads across her face. "If it's any consolation, the new guy looks like he wants to take full advantage of your empty schedule."

I glance up to see Austin walking toward us behind Rowan. The latter tips his head toward us.

"Hey, Rowan." Lacey laces her fingers together and rests them on the table. "Hey, New Guy."

Rowan stops, holding his tray in one hand. "Have you met Disco?"

"Briefly." I feel his gaze turn to me, but something else has stolen my attention.

Vaughn. He's several feet behind his teammates like he was on his way over. His stare volleys between me and Austin, jaw clenched. My stomach drops. I can feel the hurt and anger radiating off him even from ten feet away. I know that I shouldn't feel bad for him, but I can't help it. For all the ways he let me down, I still never want to be the reason he's hurting.

The whole interaction lasts only seconds, but it feels like an eternity before he gives me his back and stalks in the direction he came.

"Right, Claire?" Lacey elbows me.

"Sorry, what?" I refocus on the two guys who are both looking at me expectantly.

"They should sit with us." Lacey waves her hand to the empty spot next to me.

Andie is already moving over to make more room.

I can't think of a single good reason to say no, so I nod.

"How's the first day?" Rowan asks to the table.

Lacey jumps in for all of us. "Amazing. I just love the first week of a new semester. Everyone looks great, and the drama is relatively low."

"That's because no one is weighed down yet with homework and the constant social pressures that turn us into anxious, hormonal assholes," Brandon points out.

"True." Andie nods her head in agreement.

"What about you, New Guy?" Lacey asks Austin.

"What about me?" he asks in a slow drawl that oozes confidence. He's wearing a white T-shirt and jeans. The white is a stark contrast to his dark hair. It's a touch shorter on the sides than when I saw him last.

My cheeks grow warm at the memory. I have worked really hard to forget about that kiss. Cocky soccer players are not on my new year to-do list.

"Where are you from?" Lacey asks. I'm thankful that she's mid-interrogation, and no one is paying attention to the shade of pink I'm sure my face is turning.

"Arizona," he says.

"What position do you play?"

His brows lift as if he's surprised by the question. He'll learn quickly that he should never be surprised by what comes out of Lacey's mouth.

"I'm a forward."

"Oh, like Vaughn." I recognize the glint in her eye. She's dying to know every last detail about him, and she won't stop until she does.

"You play?" he asks her.

"No."

"You did once when we were kids," Rowan says.

"One season when I was six hardly counts."

"Play is the wrong word. You mostly just stood in the middle of the field and cheered on your teammates," I say. I wasn't there, but she has told the story enough times that I feel like I was.

One side of Rowan's mouth pulls up into a grin. He was there. "She really did."

"It should have been obvious to my dad right then and there that I was destined for cheerleading." Her face lights up as we share a smile, and then she turns back to Austin. "What do you think of Frost Lake so far? Aren't the signs and decorations great?"

"The decorations?" He looks from her to me and then around the cafeteria.

I cover my mouth with a hand to stop a laugh. He couldn't possibly know that she's responsible for, like, ninety-nine percent of it, and he's acting like he hadn't even noticed them.

"The cheerleaders are the ones who made the signs on our lockers," Rowan explains.

"Oh, right." His attention moves to me. "I should have known. They're very sparkly."

"Thank you." Her smile grows impossibly bigger.

I'm not sure he meant it as a compliment, but he doesn't know about Lacey's obsession with glitter.

"So, do you have a girlfriend back in Arizona?" She continues her interrogation, and Rowan and I share an amused look.

"Nope."

"Interesting," Lacey says and shoots another sly glance at me. I'm going to kill her.

A group of sophomore girls on the soccer team call out to Rowan from across the room, then stand to make their way over. Rowan is probably the most liked guy at Frost

Lake. He's friends with everyone, and no one has a bad thing to say about him. He'd be the most popular guy at Frost Lake if he put any effort into it at all. But even as it is, he's always nominated for stuff.

Amanda and Sophie stop next to our table. They give all of us cordial smiles before pinning their gazes on the new guy.

"You must be Austin Keller," Sophie says. "I'm Sophie. This is Amanda. We're on the girls' soccer team."

"His reputation precedes him," Rowan jokes. "He goes by Disco."

Austin hums low in his throat as he shoots Rowan a playful glare and then tips his head slightly at the girls. "Nice to meet you both."

Sophie sits in the tiny space between him and Andie. My friend shoots me an amused look as she scooches closer to Brandon.

"Are you going to Boone's party tonight?" Sophie asks him. She's facing the other way, but I can just make out the question above the noise in the cafeteria.

"I'm not sure," he says.

"You should totally come. Everyone will be there. A bunch of the girls from the team are going, and, Rowan, you'll be there, right?"

"Wouldn't miss it," he says.

I truly don't know how he goes out so much and still maintains his grades and soccer.

"And I'll be there," Sophie says. "Give me your hand."

Austin does, looking slightly confused.

She pulls out a pen and proceeds to write her number on his hand in blue ink. When she's done, she stands. "Now you can text me, and we can meet up."

He nods a few times, saying nothing. I can't read him. Sophie is pretty. She dated Blake from the team last year. I wonder if she's Austin's type and then scold myself for the thought. I do not care. I just think it's ridiculous how girls are already falling all over themselves to talk to him. He's cute, but what do they even know about him?

Sophie beams. "Okay, we gotta go. See you later!"

As soon as they're gone, Lacey erupts into laughter. "Wow, New Guy. That was impressive. You said less than ten words and somehow managed to get a date. Bravo."

"If only it were always that easy." His stare lands on me, and I find myself unable to look away. The bell rings and jolts me back to the present.

I stand abruptly.

"Where is the fire, Crawford?" Lacey asks with a grin.

"I gotta go." My gaze briefly flicks to Austin, who is watching me with those light green eyes. I hate that he makes me feel so off-balance. Looking back at Lacey, I say, "My next class is in the east building."

"I won't see you the rest of the day." My best friend sticks her bottom lip out in a pout. "Hang tomorrow afternoon?"

"Definitely," I say. I smile at the rest of the table, carefully avoiding meeting Austin's gaze, and then book it out of there as fast as my boot will allow.

—

By the time I hoof it all the way to the east building, my foot is throbbing. The doctor warned me to ease back into things, but I didn't think that walking would be so tiring.

Mrs. Randolph is standing outside the classroom, greeting students as they walk into her room. A smile curves my lips when she calls out to me.

“Claire Crawford.” Her gaze briefly drops to my foot, but she doesn’t let it linger there. “I was so glad to see you signed up for my class again this year.”

“Thanks,” I say, feeling a little embarrassed at the attention. It never made me uncomfortable when I was being praised for skating. I think it’s because I worked so hard at it. Hours and hours of practice nearly every day. While art is just something I’ve always liked to do. It’s fun, but it feels weird to be complimented when I’ve spent so little effort trying to be good at it.

None of my friends take art. I recognize a few faces from art class last year, but I don’t know any of them well enough to do more than wave and say hello.

I take a seat at an empty table by the back closest that houses the supplies. The moment I take the weight off my foot, I breathe a sigh of relief.

Mrs. Randolph comes into the class seconds before the tardy bell rings.

“Good afternoon, everyone.” She takes her place in front of the giant chalkboard. Most of the classrooms have whiteboards now, but the east building is part of the original school, and someone decided to preserve as much as possible. Including windows that are drafty in the winter and offer no resistance to the heat in the summer. They finally added some air-conditioning last year, but Mrs. Randolph has it turned off and the windows are open.

“For those of you who are new,” she starts, but a figure fills the doorway.

Austin Keller.

He steps inside and offers our teacher a polite smile. “Sorry for interrupting. Is this Visual Arts?”

“It is. Take a seat anywhere you like.”

There must be a giant neon sign flashing over my head, because Austin looks past all the tables in front and directly at me. I swear a hint of a smirk ghosts his lips as he heads my way.

While Mrs. Randolph continues introducing herself to the class, Austin drops into the empty chair beside me.

"Are you following me?" I whisper the question. I know it's dumb. He couldn't possibly have known I was taking Visual Arts, but I cannot sit next to this guy all semester. He's so cocky and frustrating. I do not have any room in my very free schedule for soccer players. Except Rowan, but we're just friends.

"No. Well, I would have liked to, seeing as how I also needed to find the east building, but you booked it out of the cafeteria so fast I didn't stand a chance."

A smidge of guilt works its way in, but it isn't like I knew he was taking art.

Another student enters the classroom. This one is holding a piece of paper, which she hands to Mrs. Randolph, who reads it and then sighs. "It's the first day and already somehow filled with interruptions. Give me two minutes, class."

She steps out into the hallway, and quiet chatter starts around the room.

I squirm in my seat and try to ignore the pain in my foot.

Austin stands, and I watch in confusion as he goes to another table and takes one of the empty chairs. Is he moving seats? I kind of hope so, but then I'll also feel like an asshole. Instead of sitting, he moves the chair over in front of our table.

I stare at him blankly.

"For your foot," he says finally. I don't make any move to prop up my leg, and he adds, "I can tell it's bothering you. I had a broken foot once, and by the end of the day, it hurt like a bitch if I didn't elevate."

"Thank you," I say, heat flaring in my chest. "How is your first day?"

"Good. Better now that I know I'm going to see you every day." He flashes a charming smile that I'll bet works every time. Except this one.

A laugh tumbles out of me. "Have you been using that same line all day?"

"Nope." His grin inches higher. "Just came to me." He comes back around and takes his seat next to me again. "So are you going to Boone's party tonight?" he asks.

"I'm not sure," I say.

"Why not? Something else to do? Not your scene? Hate fun?" He grins. "I can't make you out yet."

"Why do you care? You already have a date." I stare at Sophie's number scribbled on his hand.

He glances at it and looks back at me. "Jealous?"

"Hardly." I scoff. "By all means, date the entire school. I couldn't care less."

His hard stare makes me want to squirm in my seat for an entirely different reason. This guy is just…too much. I know his type, and I'm not going there again.

Austin leans closer, bringing a sweet, smoky scent with him. I hold my breath.

"Yeah, well, at least kissing her won't get me black-balled by my entire team," he says with a smirk that seems to contradict the seriousness of his words and then moves away, finally tearing his gaze from me.

CHAPTER SEVEN

Austin

I'M IN THE KITCHEN LATER THAT NIGHT, LOOKING FOR something to eat. I settle for sour cream and onion Pringles and I'm peeling off the lid when the back door off the kitchen slowly opens.

It's dark in the house. Everyone else is asleep. Or so I thought. When Torrance quietly shuts the door behind her and turns, I say, "Welcome home, dear sister."

She yelps and jumps, then presses a hand to her chest. "Dammit, Austin, you scared the shit out of me."

I look over her outfit—short skirt and tight shirt. "Where the hell have you been?"

"Bobby Boone's party," she says as she leans down to take off her sandals. She tosses them onto the pile of shoes by the back door. "Are you going to tell Mom?"

"No." I pull out a stack of chips from the container. "But she's not an idiot. She probably already knows."

"Are you kidding? Since we moved here, she's too busy to notice anything." She takes the Pringles can from me, then moves to the counter and pulls herself up to sit. "You were a hot topic at school today."

My brows lift. "I was?"

"Rumor has it you broke up Vaughn Collins and Claire Crawford. Impressive work for your first day, bro."

"That's the dumbest thing I've ever heard."

"So you didn't make out with her at Doyle's bonfire party last week?"

I start to deny it, but, well, I kind of did. "How do you know so much already?"

Frost Lake is so much bigger than our last school, I feel like I learned a hundred names today and retained only a few.

"I have ears."

"They didn't break up because of me."

"Well, that's not what people are saying."

"You need to get a life. Find some new friends, and stop listening to stupid gossip."

"Why? So you can sleep with them?" She cocks her head to the side in challenge.

Annoyed, I give her the middle finger. I dated her best friend back in Arizona, but it's not like I make a habit of hooking up with her friends.

"Kaylie asked *me* out and I learned my lesson. Your friends are drama. Like you."

"Whatever." She draws the word out and rolls her eyes.

"People say lots of shit that isn't true. Just like back in Arizona." Different school, same exaggerated gossip.

"Yeah, well, Vaughn was there tonight for a while, and he did look pretty upset. Also, he's hot. I have no idea why she'd break up with him for you." She wrinkles her nose up in disgust.

Flipping her off again, I ask, "Was Claire there?"

My sister's smile turns mischievous. "I'm surprised you don't already know."

I roll my eyes. "I did not break them up. They broke up months ago."

"But you did hook up with her?"

"We kissed. Once." One kiss that I still can't stop thinking about. "It was a stupid dare. That's all." I snap my mouth shut. My sister is as likely to spread that around as anyone right now, with as pissed as she's been about moving.

"A girl in my algebra class is friends with Hunter Lester's sister, and she said that they've been a couple for years. That it's only a matter of time until they get back together. He's still hung up on her."

That last part I'd already figured out on my own, but the fact that they dated for so long is news to me. I don't like the idea of them getting back together. I try not to think too hard on why that is. I have enough problems without getting myself further involved in high school drama.

"Seriously, how do you know all this already?" I ask, swiping the Pringles can back from Torrance.

"How do you not? They're your friends. Or, well, not Vaughn." A devilish grin spreads across her face. "Is it true that he punched you at practice?"

"For the love of..." I mutter and then sigh. "Of course it isn't true."

She laughs like she thought as much but is loving the image of me getting decked.

In truth, practices have been rough. Vaughn is still pissed, and the rest of the guys are watching him for their cues. Last Friday, someone swiped my clothes and all the towels while I was in the shower. I had to walk out bare-ass naked into the coaches' office to find something to cover myself with.

And today, my practice jersey went missing, and I had

to show up to the field without it. Coach made me run five laps and then chastised me for losing his property and not coming prepared.

Maybe they'd be messing with me regardless of Vaughn. I'm coming in as the new guy, and not everyone is stoked about sharing the field with an outsider, but I have a feeling if he was embracing me as a teammate, they would too. Which means I'm going to have to figure out how to make amends.

—

The week passes in a blur of school and soccer. During the day, I see Claire at lunch and in art class. She doesn't say much to me in either scenario, but I've gotten to know her friends, and they all seem cool. Rowan's cool too. He's the only guy on the team who says more than two words to me at a time.

In the middle of the second week, Mrs. Randolph gives us a free day to work on anything we want. She's a pretty laid-back teacher, and the class has become my favorite. The room is stuffy and smells of paint and clay, but I have an entire hour that feels like a break. School has never really been my thing. My grades are okay, but I've always preferred an extra hour of soccer practice to doing homework.

I pull out my sketch pad and pencils from my backpack. Claire watches me but doesn't say anything.

"I like to draw," I offer, flipping to a blank page.

She nods, stare still on the book. "Can I see?"

"Sure." I stop flipping and push it over to her.

Her lips curve up as she stares down at a drawing I did of Zelda for Wyatt. She keeps going, stopping at each page for so long that I start to get a little nervous. I'm not embarrassed about my sketches, but it feels different sharing them with her.

"There's a lot of soccer balls," she notes, one side of her mouth pulling higher.

"It's my go-to when I'm bored and trying to look like I'm taking notes in class," I say.

She hands it back to me. "I used to do that with my figure skating routines. I would sketch them out. I'd draw little figure skaters in varying positions all over the paper." A small smile lifts the corners of her mouth. "Your drawings are much better than mine."

"A figure skater, huh?" I can see it. She has that grace about her. Always poised and a little hard to read. I bet she lights up when she's on the ice.

"I *was* a figure skater. I don't do it anymore."

Every little nugget of information she gives me just makes me want to find out more.

"How come?"

She moves her right foot with the boot out from under the table and glances down at it.

"I assume the boot is going to come off eventually."

"Yes," she says with a little sass in her tone. Then it takes on a slight edge that's mixed with something else. Sadness, maybe. "It comes off in a few weeks, but I'm done skating."

I want to ask why, but she drops her gaze to her paper, dismissing me. We fall quiet as we both go back to working, me sketching and her painting with watercolors. It's nice. I enjoy being with her, even when we aren't talking.

At the end of the class, I fold up my drawing and hand it to her. She eyes me with some trepidation before taking it.

"What's this?" she asks.

We walk out of the classroom together. She's still clutching the folded paper in one hand.

"I was inspired."

She looks even more nervous at that, but slowly she unfolds it. Her feet stop moving as she stares down at it.

"It's rough. I don't know a whole lot of figure skating poses. The form is probably all wrong and—"

"It's great," she says, voice shaky. She doesn't meet my gaze as she folds it back up. "You are really talented, Austin."

That sadness I detected in her earlier resurfaces, making it hard to accept the compliment. Whatever her reasoning for not skating anymore, it's obvious I hit a sore spot.

"I'm sorry. I didn't mean to upset you."

"You didn't. It's..." She trails off. "It's beautiful. I love it."

CHAPTER EIGHT

He drew me skating.

The backs of my eyes sting as I open my locker and grab my chemistry book for sixth period. The familiar chatter of my peers around me is all background noise, like I'm trapped inside a bubble and they're all on the outside.

Someone bumps into me, knocking me out of my spiraling thoughts.

"Shit. Sorry, Claire," Matt Doyle catches himself as I turn around, clutching my books to my chest. He points at Eddie with a smirk. "No shoving in the halls."

Then he shoves him back playfully. It's the usual chaos between passing periods, but today I feel like an outsider. I catch Vaughn's gaze. His rowdy teammates are between us, but he only watches me. The slight furrowing of his brow feels invasive, like he sees more than I want him to.

Spinning around, I head for chemistry. I'm still carrying Austin's drawing and I duck into a corner and pull it out so I can stare at it again.

I wasn't lying when I told him it's beautiful. He's so talented.

I wonder if he has any idea just how badly I wish I were still this person. No, of course not. How could he? I hadn't even meant to bring it up.

I have been able to mostly avoid talking about skating since my injury. Everyone who knows me well has given me space to deal with it without asking a lot of questions. And I have appreciated that, but I think it gave me a false sense of how well I'm dealing with it. Like if I didn't say it out loud, I would be able to move on and heal my heart along with my foot.

But this drawing has tears welling in my eyes. I can almost feel myself in the very position he drew me. One leg raised behind me like I've just landed a jump. I miss that feeling of flying through the air and the sense of accomplishment after weeks or months of practicing and finally nailing a new skill.

"Claire." Vaughn appears in front of me. The furrow of his brow is more pronounced.

I blink rapidly, and tears trek down my cheeks. Swiping them quickly away, I stand taller and shuffle the drawing into my chem book.

"Are you all right?" he asks.

"Fine." He's the last person I want to talk to right now.

"You're not fine." He steps closer. "I haven't seen you cry since you lost the junior grand prix freshman year."

Those were tears of frustration. Is it twisted to think I'd be willing to lose a million times over if it meant I could compete again?

"It's nothing. I was just having a moment." I clear my throat and then inhale through my nose.

"I'd say that's allowed. You're going through a lot."

I don't like the way he continues to stare at me or the attention we're starting to garner from others spotting us. I can almost see the spark of excitement in their gazes, like they think they're seeing us reconcile.

"I need to get to class."

"Don't run away, Claire." His fingers circle around my wrist gently. "Let me be here for you. Tell me what you need."

"*Now* you want to be here for me?"

Vaughn's expression shifts from sympathetic to guilty. "I'm sorry about this summer."

"Not as sorry as I am." I slip out of his grasp and push past him.

—

By the time I get home, I'm exhausted from holding in my emotions. I fling myself down on my bed and curl up on my side, hugging my pillow to my chest. Austin's drawing is tucked away in my backpack, but I can see it vividly if I concentrate hard enough.

Maybe I should have let Vaughn be there for me, but I'm still so mad that his affection seems conditional. When it's convenient for him, he wants to be there for me. But what about all the rest of the time? When I needed him most, he wasn't there. I don't know if I'll ever be able to move on from that.

I'm in slightly better spirits when Lacey comes over after cheer practice.

"What is happening in here?" she asks, looking around at the mess I've made. All my clothes are out of the closet and lying on the bed.

"Cleaning and organizing." I pull out a pair of tennis shoes that are several years old; one shoe is missing the laces. Mom has been on me to do it for months, but I've finally reached peak boredom. "I got inspired by some closet organization videos."

"Okay." She drops her bag on the floor with a small laugh, then makes a spot for herself on the edge of my bed. "How was your day? I hate our schedules this year. Besides lunch, I barely see you."

"Fine," I say. The word is basically my default response at this point, but then I remember that this is Lacey. The one person I don't have to pretend for. "Actually, it sucked."

"What happened?" The fierce protectiveness in her eyes is the balm I need.

I stop my work in the closet and face her. "I was talking to Austin, and I mentioned that I used to skate. It's the first time I've really talked about it in months. I thought I was..."

"Over it?" she asks, quirking one brow in disbelief.

"No," I say quickly. "I'm not sure I'll ever be over it, but I thought I had accepted it at least."

"Claire..." Her voice trails off, and she smiles sadly. "I'm sorry."

I can feel the sincerity of her words so strongly.

"Anyway, I was upset, and then I ran into Vaughn."

The change in her expression is so swift, it pulls a laugh from me.

"He wanted to be there for me." I scowl at the idea the same way I had earlier.

She snorts. "Too little too late, Collins."

"Exactly. I don't get what game he's playing. He broke up with me because he didn't have time for a relationship, and now he's acting like he wants to pick up where we left off, like nothing has changed."

"Maybe he just realized what a big mistake he made. You're a catch, babe. I told you months ago that he would rue the day."

"Don't tell me that you think I should consider taking him back?" Is that even what he wants? Really? Or is it just guilt?

"Of course not, but if you do, then I'll still be here." She sounds mildly disgusted, but I appreciate her saying it anyway. "And there's no shame in being upset and letting people be there for you."

"I'm not getting back together with him."

"I don't just mean Vaughn. You have a tendency to keep things inside and pretend you're okay. Everyone knows that this is hard on you. You don't have to be so tough all the time."

"I'm sharing with you."

"What about Austin? Are you sharing with him?" She grins all too knowingly.

I toss a shoe at her, then get back to work, digging through the many sneakers and sandals buried at the back of my closet.

While I organize, I think about Austin. I'm not sure how I feel about him. On one hand, he seems like a good guy. It's buried under layers of arrogance, but it's there. On the other, am I really ready to date again? Especially someone so much like my ex?

"Hey, do you want to help me pick out fish next Monday after school?" Lacey asks from her spot on my bed. She's started to sift through my clothes and put them in piles based on type.

"For what?"

"The Meet the Knights carnival. They're for the fish bowl toss game. I have to pick up the fish from the store and take them to the field."

"I have no idea where you find the time to do all these things."

"Me either, which is why I'm begging you. Please go with me?"

"Fine." I have plenty of time in my schedule.

She squeals with delight. "You're the best."

When there's only one item left in my closet, I sit down on the floor and bring my old skate bag into my lap. The familiar weight makes goose bumps climb up my arms. I tossed it in here the day after my surgery, where I wouldn't have to see it and be reminded that I wouldn't be picking it up and heading to the rink any time soon. As if it being out of sight was truly going to keep it off my mind.

Unzipping the bag, I peek inside, only catching a glimpse of one white skate before I decide I'm not ready to deal with them yet. I put the bag back where it was.

One step at a time.

CHAPTER NINE

As I walk into my English literature class, Vaughn, Eddie, and Doyle go quiet. It's been the same since the start of the school year. I considered switching my schedule around, but I know the only thing that could make the situation worse would be letting them run me off.

I take my seat next to Jenn. She's a junior too. Her family moved to Frost Lake last year when her mom took a new job in the area. Her friendly smile is a nice contrast to the icy welcome from my teammates, and she knows what it's like to move in the middle of high school.

"Hey," she says, glancing over her shoulder quickly, then back at me. "Still on Collins's shit list, huh?"

One side of my mouth quirks up.

"I'm at the top of the list though, so that should count for something," I joke.

She shoots me an apologetic smile.

Our lit teacher, Mr. Kepfler, takes attendance and then instructs us to break into groups and discuss the first six chapters of *Pride and Prejudice*. He is big on having open discussion and talking among ourselves to further our own understanding of the material we read. Mostly that ends up with people talking about anything but the book.

While Jenn and I move our desks closer, I can hear Vaughn and the rest of the guys talking about tonight's scrimmage game.

Meet the Knights, from what I've been told, is a celebration of the upcoming season. We're broken into two teams, blue and white, and we'll play a full eighty minutes.

Rowan says it's a big, showy night with carnival games and food trucks. The student council group and the parent booster club put it together every year. People come, watch the game, see the new team in action, and then eat burnt hot dogs and cotton candy, all for donations to the athletics department at Frost Lake.

I'm just happy the season is almost here.

"Has your dad said how he's breaking us up into teams?" Eddie asks loudly behind me.

"No." Vaughn's voice is quieter. "He decides right before the game so we can't strategize."

Adrenaline starts to pump through me. Practices have been intense, and I've never had to work harder, but I'm earning my spot, whether they like it or not.

"Hey, do you know Claire?" I ask Jenn when the guys turn their conversation away from soccer and the team.

"You mean Collins's ex?" she asks, looking up from the book. Soft laughter escapes from her lips. "Yes, everyone knows Claire. They were *the* couple."

I really hate the visual of them together.

"Why? Considering doing something dumb like kissing her again?"

A sheepish grin pulls at the corners of my mouth. "You heard about that, huh?"

"Everyone did. I imagine that's why you're sitting here with me and not back there with them."

"Partly," I admit, then point toward her backpack. She has a figure skating patch stitched onto the side. "Did you skate with her?"

"No. I don't skate competitively, just for fun. I'm on the hockey cheer squad. I don't really know her that well, just things I've heard. Are you two together?"

"Hockey cheer squad?" My brows rise as I try to imagine that.

"Yeah." She smiles. "We cheer at the hockey games."

"I had no idea that was a thing." I shake my head. Only in Michigan.

"So are you?" she asks.

"Am I what?"

"Are you and Claire together?"

"No. We aren't together." Though she has been occupying a lot of my thoughts.

"You might want to let Collins know that, because rumors around school are saying differently."

Fucking rumors.

By the time I make it to art class, I'm so keyed up for tonight, that it's all I can focus on.

Well, almost.

Claire smiles at me as I take my seat. Something has shifted between us over the past week. She talks a little more freely. I haven't asked about skating again, sensing that's a tough spot for her, but otherwise, I think I'm finally starting to win her over. I'm not sure exactly what my plan is. Asking her out would likely make things worse with Vaughn, but I'm starting to wonder if it matters. And if it doesn't, I might as well get the girl.

"Are you coming to the game tonight?" I ask, thoughts still on soccer but also her.

Nodding without looking at me, she says, "Pretty much the whole school shows up for Meet the Knights."

"Including you?"

She meets my gaze. Her multicolored eyes really get me. Unique. Like her.

"Yes," she says finally. "Including me."

—

When I get to the locker room before the game, the entire team is already there and dressed. Coach Collins eyes me, one brow cocked. "Good you could join us, Keller." Lazily, he rotates his wrist to check the time on his watch. "Did I not say to be here tonight at five o'clock on the dot?"

"I thought it was changed to five thirty..." I trail off when I notice several of the guys fighting off laughter.

Fuck me. I did think it was odd Coach—who has never sent an email out before—sent out a last-minute time change an hour before we were supposed to arrive at the field for Meet the Knights. But clearly not odd enough to question it like I should have.

His stare moves around the locker room, and everyone's faces go to stone. A few guys look down, so he can't read their expressions.

"My mistake. Sorry, Coach." I move past him and take a seat on the bench between Rowan and Blake.

"Starters on the board," he says. "I want to see everything

you have out there. You know your opponent tonight better than you will all season. I'll be making a lot of switches and moving you around. Work together, and take your time."

With a nod and a small upturn to the corners of his mouth, he gives us a smile and turns on his heel to leave.

When I glance at the board, my name has been crossed out and Eddie's added next to it. I don't have to guess why I'm not starting.

"Did somebody tell you the wrong time?" Rowan asks, keeping his voice low.

"Yeah." I tamp back my irritation. That's what they want, and I refuse to let them see it.

"I should have warned you they might try something tonight."

"Not on you," I say, meaning it. He's the only guy in this room that I know for sure didn't send it.

"Don't let them get to you. They'll get bored of it and move on." He tosses me a blue jersey. "Welcome to the blue team."

"Thanks." I pull it on over my head.

The guys are lining up to go out. Vaughn is wearing a white jersey. I can't decide if that's good or bad news for me.

"Use all that frustration you're feeling right now on beating the white team. I have never been on the winning side for Meet the Knights, but this feels like the year."

I nod and think about doing just that. I sit on the bench in front of the locker and pull on my socks and shin guards. "Is your family here?"

He pauses, then shakes his head and smiles. "Nah. They're busy, and it's just a scrimmage. Yours?"

"Everyone but my dad. His flight was delayed."

"Bummer," Rowan says.

It's the first time he won't be at one of my games. Sure, it's just a scrimmage, but it still feels wrong.

By the time I'm finished getting dressed, I can hear the music and noise on the field. Adrenaline starts to pump inside me. I shift from foot to foot, eager to get out there.

When we walk out, all the guys in front of me hit the top of the doorframe. Rowan says from behind me, "It's tradition."

I lift up on my toes and hit the worn spot. At my old school, we had something similar. Every team I've been a part of has had their own superstitions and traditions. I've always enjoyed the group aspect of soccer. The friendships, the sense of community, and working toward a common goal. I hope eventually this team will feel that way for me. I can't help but think if I can show them how much I can contribute, that'll happen sooner rather than later.

I can just make out one side of the field as we walk up toward it. There are bleachers on the near side, but on the far side, people have set up lawn chairs and blankets.

A group of cheerleaders waits for us at the edge of the field. They unroll a large white banner, and over the sound system, I hear a man with a deep, heavily upper Michigan accent say, "And now, let's meet your Frost Lake High Knights!"

The music changes to something with a heavier beat, and I can't help but laugh. All this for a scrimmage? At my old school, football was king. People came out for soccer games if there wasn't anything else going on that night or when we had a big game, but this? This is like nothing I've seen.

I glance back at Rowan to find him grinning at me like

he can read my thoughts, and then the line starts to move, and the first guy runs through the paper. As I step out onto the field, a wave of excitement rushes through me. This is what I've been working for. Playing in front of a big crowd with a team that is better than any other I've been a part of.

We make a lap around the entire field and then split into our teams, each taking one side.

The music continues as we warm up. I scan the bleachers until I find my family. Mom waves, as does Wyatt. Torrance looks like she'd rather be anywhere else. My chest squeezes at the empty spot next to them. Dad should be here.

One of my favorite parts of playing soccer is after the games, talking about it with him. I guess in a way, that's the only real tradition I've had for myself.

I force a grin at Wyatt. He's bouncing in his seat and pointing, like Mom and Torrance can't see me for themselves. His excitement is a nice contrast to Torrance. I thought we'd come to some sort of nonverbal peace treaty last week when she snuck in past curfew, but since then, she's been as cold to me as before.

I scan the bleachers between taking practice shots. There are still a lot of people I don't know at Frost Lake, but I'm starting to recognize faces. One in particular stands out.

Claire is sitting a few rows up on the bleachers with Brandon and some other guys I recognize as hockey players. A bunch of them are in my world history class.

Several of the girls from the soccer team are sitting in the row directly in front of Claire and her friends. When I lift my hand to wave at her, she looks away. Maybe it's a coincidence, but I think she might enjoy giving me the cold shoulder. Sophie waves back instead. She, on the other hand, is giving me two very warm shoulders. She's asked me out almost every day this week. She's nice and cute. I'm not feeling it with her, but maybe I've just been too preoccupied.

I've got a fascination with the sassy blond playing hard to get that's making it difficult to notice anyone else.

Before the game starts, the announcer calls out the coaches and then the players. I spot Lacey and Andie with the other cheerleaders, standing on the field and yelling as each of us runs out to applause from the crowd.

Lacey does some sort of backflip combo as they call my name. She ends with a grin, raising her hands over her head.

I tip my head to her and make a face that I hope shows how impressed I am.

She grins back as she brings her hands to her hips. "Go get 'em, New Guy."

The game starts out friendly. We've been going up against one another every day in practice, so this feels like that with a few more people watching. But when the white team scores the first goal and the scoreboard lights up with it, things get more competitive.

Coach rotates everyone at regular intervals so that we all get the same amount of time on the field. It's fair and keeps us from getting tired, but I don't want breaks. I want to be out there.

Rowan and I are rarely on the field at the same time, and the rest of the team is still unsure what to make of me. More than once, I'm wide open, and someone hesitates before passing it to another teammate.

I'm frustrated when Coach subs me out for another breather. The first half is winding down, and I've barely touched the ball.

Even with the light atmosphere, I can tell he's making notes on who will earn starting spots for our first real game next week. I want one of those spots, and I know I deserve it. Now I just have to show him.

CHAPTER TEN

"He is so hot," Sophie cries as Austin takes the field, clapping her hands and then holding them up to her mouth to yell. "Go, Austin!"

I glance over at Lacey and roll my eyes. "Someone needs to get her a thesaurus. That seems to be the only adjective she knows."

For the past hour, I've had to listen to Sophie, Amanda, and the rest of the soccer girls talk about Austin and what they'd like to do with him or have him to do them in more detail than I needed. At one point, he lifted the hem of his shirt to wipe his face, and the screams they let out have my eardrums still ringing.

"Cut the girl some slack," Lacey says with a smile, stare leaving the field only long enough to grin at me. "Her vocabulary may be limited, but you have to admit she's right. The new guy is easily top three of the junior class, maybe of the whole school. Plus, he has that new guy mystique."

"I don't have to admit anything," I grumble, feeling a teensy bit jealous at all the attention he's getting.

Lacey's laugh gets lost in the noise as the blue team scores. My gaze manages to go directly to the guy in question. He and Rowan high-five as they jog up the field.

"Who scored?" I ask.

"That was Rowan," Lacey yells over the crowd.

The buzzer sounds, ending the first half. People around us get up to grab concessions or move around.

My best friend straightens the big bow on top of her head. "So what's going on with you two anyway?"

"Who?" I ask, glancing at Andie and Brandon next to me.

"You." Lacey elbows me with a giggle. "And New Guy. He's obviously into you."

"What do you mean obviously? We barely talk."

"Yeah, but he's always watching you."

"It's true. Brandon and I were talking about that yesterday," Andie pipes up. She has a matching bow in her hair and a shiny new gold hoop in her nose. She pulls it off well.

My face heats, and an uncomfortable feeling stretches across my skin. "He's just a flirt. Nothing is going on."

"If you say so," Lacey singsongs. "We gotta go. Yell loud for us, okay?"

"You know it." I tip my chin at her. "I'm only here for the cheerleaders."

Her grin widens as they head down the bleachers. The squad doesn't usually cheer during soccer games, but tonight they're doing their routines on the field during halftime, then they have to go to the carnival, where they're running a cotton candy stand.

Brandon and his friend Miles scoot down the bench closer to me. Someone walks by with a plate of nachos, and the smell of cheese wafts around us.

"Ooh, that smells good." Miles sits taller, leaning toward the food as it goes by. He stands and rubs his stomach. "Be right back."

"Get me some too," Brandon calls after him.

The two of them have been eating nonstop. Hot dogs, candy, chips. I have no idea how either of them could still be hungry.

"You're a bottomless pit," I tell him with a smile.

"Coach says I need to add some weight."

Brandon plays hockey. He grew a few inches over the summer, and he's tall and lanky. Probably not ideal when you're being slammed against the boards.

With the row in front of us empty, I prop up my boot on the bleacher. Brandon glances down. "How much longer do you have to wear that thing?"

"Two weeks."

"That's not long." His face brightens. "Can you go right back to skating, or do you have to rehab and stuff?"

My stomach swirls with sorrow and disappointment. I consider giving him a vague reply, but then I remember what Lacey said about sharing my feelings with people. "The doctor said I could get back to regular exercise, but he warned me that if I continued pushing myself like before, I'd risk doing permanent damage."

"Oh." His dark brows slant. "Shit. Claire, I'm sorry. I didn't know. Wow. You've been skating competitively since…forever."

"Since I was six," I say, then try to smile through it. "The break has been kind of nice."

No, that's total bullshit. Aside from sleeping in and having a laxer schedule, which admittedly has been nice, I've been bored out of my mind.

I loved skating with all my heart. It was all I ever wanted to do. And sure, it ate up all my time, but there was nowhere I loved more than being on the ice. Now it's gone.

I still wake up every morning thinking about my routines and what I need to work on, and then seconds later, it all comes crashing back. Technically I will be able to skate again when the boot comes off, but not like before. The doctor warned me that going back to that level of intensity would just cause more injuries that would eventually compromise my everyday activities like walking.

Brandon nods slowly, his lips pulling into a half smile. "Yeah, I can see how that might be kind of cool. And hey, now you've got time to do lots of other fun stuff."

The cheerleaders start yelling from the center of the field, Lacey's voice clear through the others. I turn my attention to them. "Yeah. Exactly."

Yes, lots of other fun stuff. I just haven't figured out what that should be yet.

—

By the time the second half starts, my foot is tired from sitting in one position. I get up and walk over onto the grassy area next to the bleachers where the self-professed Knights fan club stands and cheers and, during normal games, razzes the other team.

A group of senior girls are giggling and talking about one of the guys on the field, only I don't realize it's Austin until he runs by us.

"I heard he dated a college girl back in Arizona."

"A girl in my physics class said he was on the cover of some soccer magazine."

"Sexiest Soccer Player Alive?"

They all giggle.

The desire to roll my eyes is so large, but then the people around us erupt into cheers and drown the girls out. On the field, Vaughn holds one hand up as his teammates rush to congratulate him on the goal. My attention goes to Austin. The look of annoyance on his face as he glances up at the scoreboard makes me feel for him. Vaughn is hard to beat.

In the final minute of the game, the white team is up by one goal. Even the people in the bleachers are on their feet. Nervous energy has me tapping my thumb against my thigh. It's been so long since I competed, but I can feel that last-minute surge that I'd get just before I'd step on the ice. For a moment, I'm lost in memories of skating. The lights, the music, the feeling as I let go of everything and just lived for those few minutes where nothing mattered except the routine.

I swallow around the lump of emotions as I push away the likely truth that I'll never get to do that again.

Someone grabs my arm, and I glance over as Lacey comes to stand beside me.

"Hey, I was looking for you." She holds out a cone of cotton candy toward me. "Want some? I made it myself."

Her happy grin loosens the sadness, like it always does. I don't know what I'd do without her.

I take a handful, and we turn back to the game. She yells, "Go, New Guy!"

I hear someone else around us say, "Pass it to Disco!"

People seem to know and like him despite him having only been in Frost Lake for five seconds.

On the blue team, Eddie has the ball stolen as he tries to go around Vaughn to the goal. The crowd lets out an "Oooo."

"Looks like that's it," Lacey says.

The words have barely left her lips when Austin comes out of nowhere and steals the pass Vaughn sends to one of his teammates. Everyone in the crowd goes wild. Austin dribbles, fakes around a defender, then another. It's impossible to look away from him as he weaves through opposing players. He's far enough back, and there's just enough time left on the clock that they could probably set up another play, but Austin is headed toward the goal, and he doesn't look like he's going to pass off to anyone.

Vaughn catches up to him, and it's like no one else on the field exists. I hold my breath with the rest of the crowd as they battle. I'm pretty sure Austin takes an elbow to the jaw, but he doesn't back down. He fights back, pushing around Vaughn until he finally gets a clear shot and kicks it toward the goal.

I want to close my eyes, but I can't. There's no way that's going in. I haven't seen anyone pull something like that off except maybe Vaughn. My ex-boyfriend might currently be on my shit list, but his talent on the soccer field is unmatched.

Barrett jumps to the left inside the goal, but the ball flies just beyond his fingertips.

"Gooooooaaaaaaaaal!" The announcer's voice booms over the loudspeaker.

"Oh my gosh!" Lacey jumps, latching on to my arm and forcing me to bounce with her.

Cheers for New Guy and Disco, a few for Keller, ring out all around us. No matter what they call him, all eyes are on Austin. His face is pure joy as Rowan bear-hugs him, and then the rest of the team piles on.

CHAPTER ELEVEN

"THAT WAS UNBELIEVABLE!" BLAKE SHAKES HIS HEAD IN DISBElief, a big grin on his face as he holds out a hand for me to slap. "We're going to be unstoppable this year."

The mood is light and happy. We tied, which isn't the way I hoped it'd go down, but it feels like that last shot helped me turn a corner with my teammates, so I'm taking that as a win.

A cautious win. I'm not holding my breath that they won't go back to hating me tomorrow.

The only person that doesn't seem all that happy is Vaughn.

Coach Collins comes into the locker room, and we quiet down to hear what he has to say.

"Nice job tonight. I saw some good things. I also saw some things that weren't so good." One side of his mouth tips up in an almost smile. "Practice tomorrow after school. Come ready to work."

With a nod, he leaves us. The atmosphere isn't quite as jubilant with the reality of practices and hard work to come tomorrow, but then Rowan turns on some music from his phone, and everyone slips back into party mode.

"Are you heading to the carnival?" Rowan asks as he pulls a clean shirt over his head.

"Yeah. I promised my little brother I'd take him."

"Nice." My buddy's face lights up. "Great job out there. I told you they'd come around." He cuffs me on the shoulder and then says, "I'll see you there."

He shuts his locker and heads off. I dress slowly, hoping I'll get an opportunity to talk to Vaughn without a bunch of other people around, but before that chance arrives, one of the assistant coaches calls for him, and I decide not to creepily wait in an empty locker room for him.

The carnival is set up in a grassy area beyond the parking lot. All the usual carny games are represented—ring toss, hammer strength, goldfish bowl toss—plus food vendors and more. Mom is making new friends with the other parents, so I take Wyatt with me. Torrance disappeared before I got out of the locker room.

"What do you want to play first?" I ask my little brother as we walk down the row of games.

I spot Claire with Lacey and Andie next to a cotton candy cart.

"That one!" Wyatt takes off at a run toward where other kids are tossing Ping-Pong balls at small plastic bowls with goldfish swimming around.

By the time I reach him, a woman behind the table has already given him three balls, and Wyatt has launched the first one. It goes beyond the tanks by about two feet.

"Easy there, killer. Not so hard." I ruffle his hair. "Which one are you going for?"

"The one on the right corner," he says, pointing. He's the biggest.

"He's also in the hardest spot to get. If you aim for one in the middle, the ball might bounce or roll into another."

"I don't care. I want that one." His tone leaves no other option, so I buckle in to watch him toss all his balls into the gravel.

"A kid that knows what he wants." Lacey steps up beside me, smiling at my little brother. A rush of adrenaline spikes through me when I see her.

"Lacey, Claire," I say, finding my voice, "this is my much cooler brother, Wyatt."

"The much cooler was obvious from the haircut." Lacey runs her hand over the top of his Mohawk.

Wyatt grins, but he is far less impressed by the hot girls standing with us than me. He tosses another ball toward the fish he's decided he can't live without and misses again.

"Nice goal tonight," Lacey says. "Consider me impressed."

"Thanks, Lacey." My gaze moves to Claire. She hasn't said anything. "Did you also enjoy the game?"

"The cheerleaders were great," she says with just a hint of a smile. I could talk with her all night long and never get enough of her feistiness.

Lacey laughs and then covers it up by clearing her throat. "Speaking of, I better get back to the cotton candy stand. You're good to keep Claire company for a while, right, New Guy?" She backs away and wriggles her fingers at us.

Claire takes a small step closer once her friend departs. "I don't need you to keep me company. I know lots of other people here."

"Of course," I say. Wyatt is out of balls, and I hand

over two more tickets for three more chances. "Maybe you can keep me company though. He has his heart set on a fish."

She nods, and a small smile tips up the corners of her lips. "I had a goldfish once."

"Really?" Wyatt finally gives her his full attention.

I lean closer to her. "If this tale ends in a tragic death, maybe not the audience."

She huffs a laugh and ignores me. "He stays at my dad's house, so I guess I still do, but I don't see him as often. Wanna see a picture?"

Of course Wyatt does, and Claire humors him by opening up the photos app on her phone and finding a picture of a big goldfish in an aquarium with pink rocks and a fairy-tale castle.

"That's so cool," he says. "What's his name?"

"*Her* name is Princess Goldiefin."

My brother scrunches up his nose, but his excitement over winning a fish is reignited, and he focuses hard on aiming.

"Your parents split?" I ask, guessing by the tidbit she offered up about her living situation.

"Yeah, a while ago."

I think it's the first personal piece of information she's given me since she told me she used to skate. It makes me greedy for more.

"I'm sorry."

"It's okay." She shrugs one shoulder.

We stand side by side, her arm brushing mine, as Wyatt tosses another ball that hits the rim of the tank and bounces away. His face falls with clear disappointment.

"That's all right." I place my hands on his shoulders and squeeze lightly. "Try again."

"I only have one more, then I'm out of tickets, and Mom already said she wasn't buying me any more if I blew them all on one game."

I hold back a chuckle.

"Which one are you aiming for?" Claire asks.

He points, and I add, "The big guy in the far right."

"You know." Claire squats down at eye level with Wyatt. "I bet if you get the ball in any of the fish tanks, you could ask the nice lady if you could swap the fish for the one you want."

He considers her carefully. "What if she says no?"

"Well, then, I guess you'd still have a really cool fish anyway. Wanna know a secret?"

He nods his head quickly.

She leans in. "I helped picked out all these fish."

"No way! That's a lot of fish."

"Yep. It was really fun. And I promise." She holds one hand over her heart. "I only selected the coolest fish. You're safe with any of them."

His grin widens, and he turns back to the game, ready to take another turn.

"Thanks," I say to her quietly.

"He's cute."

"Well, he takes after his big brother."

She looks like she wants to debate that but then smiles. Wyatt misses again and turns with slumped shoulders.

"Actually, you know, I have all these tickets left, and I have to go soon. Maybe you could use them?" Claire holds up at least twenty tickets. I'm going to be at this one spot all night.

Wyatt hesitates until I nod my permission.

"Thank you," I say again. "So…you picked out the fish?" I raise one brow in question.

"Lacey is head cheerleader and vice president of student council, so I got roped into helping."

I chuckle, because I'm easily able to picture Lacey handing out orders to anyone and everyone to pull the carnival together.

On his next try, Wyatt sinks the ball into one of the bowls. His excitement is contagious. Claire and I are all smiles as he bounces with joy in front of us. The woman gets the fish and brings it to us. He can barely hold it.

"Easy. Don't shake him too much." I help him steady the fish.

"I won't," he says like he wasn't doing just that a second ago.

There are two balls left, but he has already forgotten about them. He's staring at his new fish and talking to him through the bag. I pick up one of the remaining balls and look over at Claire. "Have a favorite?"

One brow lift, and she surveys the fish. "Second row from the back, fourth over."

With my right hand, I aim while holding her gaze. "Are you sure?"

She lifts one brow in challenge. "Third over."

I move my hand over an inch to the left and wait for her to decide if she's going to keep fucking with me. I hope so. I like it.

"Fourth," she says defiantly.

I slide my hand back over.

"There's no way," she says.

The ball leaves my fingertips, and I hold Claire's gaze a beat longer. I know I've made the no-look shot by the shock on her face a second later. The rush is almost as good as making that last goal tonight. Almost.

She covers her surprise quickly. "Nice trick."

"No trick. All skill." I wink.

The woman brings her fish over to me.

"Now you've got a fish at each house," I tell her.

Her hard-ass expression morphs slowly, then she laughs, and a real smile plays over her face as I hand over the plastic bag with a squirming goldfish swimming in it.

"Thank you." She looks touched by the gesture, which makes me want to do a whole bunch of nice things for her.

"Want to hit up another game with us?" I ask. "I could win you a big stuffed animal to go with it."

"I should probably go if I'm going to set up my new fish tank and still finish my chemistry homework."

I nod, kind of wishing now that I hadn't given her a reason to leave. "See you tomorrow?"

"Yeah." She looks at Wyatt. "Have any ideas for fish names?"

He thinks hard. "I was trying to decide between Dash and Flash. I think I'm gonna go with Flash."

"Good name."

"You can have Dash if you want."

"Hmm." She nods and looks at her fish. "How about Captain Dash?"

Wyatt giggles. "That's even better."

She smiles at him, then me, and holds up a hand as she backs away. I watch her go, and then Wyatt and I continue perusing the games.

When Mom catches up with us, she shoots me a weary look as Wyatt shows off his new fish.

"Isn't it great, Mom? I named him Flash!"

"Yeah…great."

He hands the fish over to her, and she holds out the bag hesitantly.

Wyatt takes off for the next game, leaving Mom to carry Flash.

"Have you seen your sister?" Mom asks as we follow him.

"No," I say at the same time as I hear someone yell my last name.

I swivel around until I see Vaughn standing behind me. He's the last person I expected to track me down tonight.

He closes the distance between us, then glances between my mom and me. "Can we talk?"

My surprise makes me slow to respond.

"Yeah," I say finally, then to Mom, "I'll be right back."

"Not too long. I have an early meeting tomorrow. I want to be in bed in the next hour," she says and gives the fish another dismayed look.

With a nod and a promise that I won't take long, I head off with Vaughn. He says nothing as we walk slowly through the carnival. Did I imagine it, or did he ask if we could talk? This is painful. Maybe he's leading me toward some other prank. Are they going to tar and feather me next?

I shove my hands in my jeans pockets and stop walking. "What's up?"

His jaw ticks as he stares back at me. "I didn't send the email."

I didn't really think he had, but I'm sure he knew about it. I can't think of a single thing to say in response, so I stay quiet. If he wants to talk, fine. I don't have to talk back.

"It was a good goal," he says, almost like it pains him to do so.

I start to smile. Jesus, is it that hard for him to give someone a compliment?

"The right thing would have been to set up another play. What you did was risky, but tonight, it paid off."

A backhanded compliment. Okay, that's more of what I'd expect.

"It was the only way I was going to get a shot," I say, arching a brow. He knows as well as I do that I wasn't getting passes from my teammates, apart from Rowan. Sure, I could have stalled and given us time to set something up, but I wouldn't have been the one to shoot the goal, and I knew I had it.

He doesn't outright admit it, but he nods. "I saw you talking to Claire earlier."

"Yeah." I don't bother denying it. Then I think about what Torrance said, how everyone is saying I broke them up and how Jenn basically confirmed that the rumor around school was that I was into his ex. "Just talking."

"So there's nothing going on with you two?" His gaze narrows while he waits for me to answer.

"There's nothing going on," I confirm. It's true, there isn't anything going on right now, but that doesn't mean I haven't thought about it.

The relief on his face is immediate. "Things with Claire and I are complicated. We're not together right now, but..." The implication is obvious. He thinks they'll be together again. "I know you didn't realize the situation when you got here, but I guess between the kiss and everything else, I got in my head that you were interested in her."

He doesn't phrase it as a question, but I can tell he wants me to confirm.

"It's just you two have been sitting at lunch together, and I heard you have art class together, then tonight..."

"We're just friends." The word doesn't quite sum up how I feel about her, but it's technically true. She's not exactly jumping at my offers to hang out. Even tonight, she ran off at the first opportunity she had.

He considers me for a moment. "All right. I appreciate you being honest with me."

A feeling an awful lot like guilt wraps around me, making my skin feel tight. But I don't owe him anything. He's made my life hell.

"You're a good soccer player, and we have a real shot at state again this year." His words take a moment to land, and by the time they do, he's holding out a hand to me. "Truce?"

I hesitate before I take it, then Vaughn bumps his shoulder against mine with a wide smile.

CHAPTER TWELVE

THE FOLLOWING DAY, I DON'T SEE AUSTIN UNTIL ART CLASS. HE wasn't with Rowan at lunch, and I haven't caught so much as a glimpse of him in the hallway. I wondered if he was even at school today, but then I overheard a group of freshman girls talking about how good he looked in the purple shirt.

I'm embarrassed to admit I knew without a lot of thought that he hadn't worn purple all week. I wasn't aware that I was tracking his outfits like some sort of fan girl, but maybe I do have a teeny-tiny fleck of interest when it comes to the new guy.

He's kind of hard not to notice, considering the entire school is obsessed with him. My interest isn't about that though. It's not because he's easily one of the hottest guys at school, though he is. It's not because he's talented and cocky, but again—he is. It's little things. How he spent last night at the carnival with his little brother instead of his teammates. And the way he always seems to know what I need—a chair to prop up my foot or a goldfish because mine is being held hostage at my dad's house.

I didn't even realize I missed the fish until I was holding Captain Dash in my hands. I like how low-maintenance fish are, just chilling in their bowl, waiting for food.

I set up my fish last night and then promptly took a photo to send Dad to let him know we were now twins. He sent back a selfie of him giving a thumbs-up with Princess Goldiefin in the background. I'm surprised the thing is still alive.

I never really wanted to leave her, but it didn't seem right to take my fish when every other living thing in the house was leaving. And Dad had liked the fish more than Mom did anyway.

Maybe they're small, but Austin seems to notice things that other people don't. I like that about him.

And the second he appears in the classroom, wearing a light purple shirt that sparks the green in his eyes, I have to admit that one: the freshmen girls were right, and two: I more than like him. I have a full-blown crush.

The bell rings as soon as Austin slides into his seat.

"Hey," I say in the exact same way I have all week. Except today the excitement thrumming through my veins is notched up a level. I like him. What's the use in fighting it? Maybe this could be something. If nothing else, some flirting and fun getting to know each other better.

Except Austin doesn't look nearly as happy to see me as I am him. He barely looks at me as he gives me an errant chin dip.

"Hey." Even his tone is off.

My stomach drops, and my face warms with unexplained embarrassment like I've done something wrong, only I don't know what I did. Austin continues to stare toward the front of the class. Taking a deep breath, I try to shake it off. Maybe it's not me and he's just having a bad day.

Mrs. Randolph takes her place in front of the blackboard and begins explaining our first big assignment of the quarter. I'm listening but watching Austin out of the corner of my eye.

His body language is casual and disinterested in everything happening around him. He's got a black pen in his right hand, and he absently scribbles on the front cover of his sketch pad.

I take out my notebook under the guise of taking notes on the assignment but instead write out *Everything okay?* and slide my notebook in front of him.

His gaze slowly flicks from his notebook to mine, and then he nods. A half smile pulls up one side of his mouth, easing my worry and confusion.

"Yeah, all good," he says quietly.

I write off the whole encounter, but when Mrs. Randolph tells us we'll be working with partners for the assignment, Austin won't meet my eye.

Heat creeps up my neck, and I try to play it off like I didn't assume we'd work together.

He glances around like he's hoping to work with someone else, but neither of us have really talked to anyone else since the start of the class, so it's unsurprising when they all pair up and we're the last two left.

"Everyone got their partner?" Mrs. Randolph asks.

Austin finally turns and looks at me. My cheeks are hot, and I'm certain my face is painted bright red.

"Austin? Claire? All set?" Mrs. Randolph asks.

Everyone looks toward us.

I'd honestly rather work on it by myself than with

someone who clearly doesn't want to be my partner, but when Austin says, "All set," I don't see how I can get out of it without seeming like he's hurt my feelings. Either I have seriously misread his signals, or something is up.

"Great. You can use the rest of class to get started." Before Mrs. Randolph has finished speaking, people are already moving around, dragging chairs closer and talking to their partners. "You'll have some class time to work on it each week, but you're probably going to need to find times to get together outside class. This is a big project and a significant portion of your grade. Have fun with it!"

Her smile is meant to be reassuring, but I am filled with dread as she takes a seat behind her desk, leaving us to begin. An awkward silence hangs between me and Austin while everyone else starts talking about the project and how they're going to break it down.

In any other circumstance, I'd be excited. It's essentially an art show. Eight pieces, four each, with a cohesive theme and feel. We also have to put together a marketing plan: flyers, social media campaign, etc. In terms of homework and school assignments, it's not as terrible as writing papers or studying for a test. But the weird shift in Austin's attitude today makes me wish for a fifteen-page research paper instead.

"So…" I say, trying to sound like I am completely unaffected by whatever his deal is. "Any ideas?"

Surprisingly, he does have some. We spend the class coming up with a concept we both like and deciding on our eight show pieces. His love of sketching and my love of painting are harder to combine in a way that feels like one collection, but when we have it all outlined, the weird tension has shifted.

It's only when we're smiling at each other, both excited about the project, that he slips back into the Austin who suddenly doesn't seem to want to be near me. Like he's controlled by a switch, his smile falls and his gaze drops. "I think we got it." His voice takes on that distant, bored monotone again. "I'll get started on my pieces tonight."

I have no idea what to think about his sudden personality changes, but I decide that I'm not going to let it get to me. He's just another immature boy, and my crush… definitely crushed. I must have imagined his sweet and charming traits, because this guy is far too much like all the others in this school: hot one minute, cold the next, and always wanting what they don't have. I am not playing that game again.

"We should probably work on them together. At least in the beginning to make sure it works the way we think it will," I say. I'm not letting his crummy attitude earn me a bad grade. My mom is already on me about not having the GPA or course schedule to impress colleges.

His green gaze pierces into me, making my nerves jump around. He nods slowly. "Okay."

"What about after school today?" I suggest.

"I have practice."

"After that?"

His stare is blank, but eventually he nods again. "Sure."

"Do you want to come over to my place? My sister has dance rehearsals, so we'll have the place to ourselves." As soon as the words are out of my mouth, I realize how they might sound and want to groan. I keep smiling like it is no big deal. It's not. We're just working on a project together.

"Yeah." He clears his throat. "Okay. Text me the address."

The bell rings, and he stands up so fast, his chair almost falls to the ground.

By the time I make it to my locker, the halls are filled with people. Austin is leaning against his locker, looking far happier than he had all class. Sophie stands in front of him, Rowan and Vaughn off to the side. They all laugh, then Sophie leans forward and touches Austin's arm. A flicker of annoyance passes through me. I stop at my locker to get my notebook for my next class, but I watch them out of the corner of my eye. Sophie eventually walks off, and as does Rowan. It's just Vaughn and Austin. My ex and my… art class partner.

Austin is taller and his dark hair is longer. Vaughn is broader and his features harder. They're each handsome in their own way, but seeing them together, it's hard to imagine a time that I thought no one could ever compete with Vaughn.

I slam my locker closed. Nope. Not handsome and not interested.

I repeat that lie to myself the rest of the day.

—

"The guy couldn't get away from me fast enough," I say to Lacey as I walk around my bedroom. She just finished cheer practice, and I'm video chatting with her while I nervously pace and wait for Austin to arrive.

"Maybe he was just having an off day."

"No." I shake my head. "Something is different. He would barely look at me."

"Maybe Vaughn?"

I still and consider that. "No. Austin all but told me he didn't care what Vaughn thought."

"Yeah but…"

"But what?" I ask when she doesn't immediately finish her statement.

"I didn't want to say anything, but rumor around school is that the entire soccer team was hazing Austin pretty hard until the Meet the Knights scrimmage."

"Why?"

"Why do boys do anything? Vaughn was clearly mad that Austin was moving in on his girl."

"I am not his girl," I say immediately.

I walk over to my bed and sit on the end. I knew Vaughn was pissed the night of Doyle's party, but that was weeks ago. "I'm not sure that's it. I saw them today at school. They seemed fine. Better than fine. They were friendly."

"Doesn't that seem suspicious? The day he starts acting chummy with Vaughn, he also starts avoiding you?"

I pause and reconsider the past few weeks. Austin and Rowan sitting with us at lunch instead of the rest of the team. Austin hanging out with his brother at the carnival. A text notification comes in on my phone.

Austin: Outside.

"I gotta go," I tell Lacey. "He's early."

"Call me later," she blurts out before I can hang up the phone.

I hustle downstairs and to the front door, but before pulling it open, I take a deep breath.

When I do open the door, Austin is standing on the other side. His head is down, looking at his phone, and his smile is carefree. As soon as he glances up at me, it disappears.

The embarrassment and irritation I feel at him treating me so coolly are almost enough for me to turn him away, but I need answers.

"Hey. Come in," I say.

He steps in, gaze tipping up to look around. "What do your parents do?"

"My dad is a financial advisor, and my mom is a real estate agent." The house is big. Way bigger than the one I grew up in as a kid. It was a foreclosure, and Mom got a good deal from the bank. I used to joke with Lacey that it was haunted by the ghost of other people's crushed dreams. Now they're just my dreams that haunt it.

"I thought we could work in my room." I take off without waiting for his agreement. Every step, I get a little bit angrier. Who does Vaughn think he is? And why the hell would Austin listen to him?

I sit down on my bed and don't bother to watch as he comes in and sets his backpack on the ground. I don't care if he's comfortable. We're going to get through this and then hopefully not need to work together anymore. He can do his pieces, I'll do mine, and we'll divide up the rest.

"Wow. That's a lot of trophies."

When I glance up, he's standing in front of my dresser, where all my skating trophies are displayed, with his back to me.

I ignore his comment and dive right into the project. "Do you think we should do a social media campaign or keep it grassroots?"

"The latter, for sure." He turns to me. "Much artsier. Maybe we could have a secret password to get in too."

I start to smile at the idea but I catch myself. "That isn't a terrible idea."

Austin walks over to the bed but then hesitates before he sits as far away from me as possible. He's so close to the edge that it's almost laughable. But it confirms what Lacey suggested. I don't know why I didn't want to believe it. Maybe I hoped Austin wouldn't be so eager to stay away from me just because of Vaughn.

He was so convincing that night we kissed, pretending like he didn't care what Vaughn or anyone else thought. I think his exact words were "He'll get over it." Clearly not.

The whole thing makes me want to scream. At myself and at him. Instead, I scoot closer. I need to know for sure what's happening here.

"You're really good at this," I say, forcing my voice to be much sweeter than I feel. I reach out and place a hand on his forearm. He visibly flinches at the contact but remains still. His skin is warm under my touch, and my fingertips tingle.

"Thanks." He stands again and goes over to his backpack to retrieve his notebook and a pen. When he comes back, he doesn't sit. Instead, he goes over to the desk and grabs the chair, pulls it a foot from the bed and then sits.

The frustration that's been sitting on my chest all day loosens. This is ridiculous.

"It's kind of hot in here, isn't it?" I ask as I get to my feet and go over to my window. It isn't. The air-conditioning is blasting so cold I put on a sweatshirt over my tank top when I got home. I open the window anyway and then turn to face Austin as I pull the sweatshirt over my head. My tank top rides up with it all the way to the band of my bra. Not planned, but it helps my plan, and Austin's gaze gets stuck on the bare skin above my belly button. His throat works with a swallow, and his eyes widen. It would be funny if I weren't vibrating with anger.

"Oops." I pull the fabric down too far, and it dips at my cleavage. I almost feel sorry for him. Almost. I sit back on the bed and lean forward, giving him what I am sure is an eyeful. "So…"

He says nothing for too long, and the atmosphere in the room is heavy with tension.

"Austin?"

"Hmm." His gaze slowly moves up to my face, then he scowls and looks down at his notebook.

Okay, so he's still into me. Or embarrassed for me because I'm all but flashing him. I want to face-palm. This is so dumb and equally infuriating. What am I trying to prove? He's a straight teenage guy. Of course he's going to look if I take off my clothes. That doesn't mean he likes me.

And who cares if Vaughn told him to stay away from me or he decided on his own that he wasn't interested in me anymore? Either way, I just want to crawl under the covers and wallow in my stupidity for thinking he was different.

"Any suggestions for the secret password?" he asks as he doodles absently, clearly avoiding looking at me.

"Boys suck," I mutter softly.

"What's that?" His light green eyes find mine in question.

"Nothing. I will think on it."

For the next five minutes, we manage to talk about our project. We come up with some ideas and split the work between us. My mood has gone from annoyed to disappointed.

"I guess that's it," I say when we both fall silent. I get up from the bed and take my stuff over to my desk. The backs of my eyes prick with tears, and I want to cry or yell. This year is starting off all wrong. Junior year was supposed to be a new start. No skating, no boyfriend, just me and whatever I wanted it to be. The problem is I don't know who I am without those things.

Austin is slow to get up and even slower as he grabs his backpack and walks to the door. "Well…I guess I'll see you tomorrow."

"Sure," I say without looking at him.

He doesn't move, and I don't glance his way. Instead, I walk over to my new fish and toss a few flakes of food into his bowl. He rushes to the surface, and a smile spreads across my face.

"Is that the fish from last night?" he asks.

"Yep. Captain Dash."

"You really named him that?" Some of that easygoing friendliness I'd grown used to is back in his tone.

"Of course." I finally glance over my shoulder.

Austin stands in the doorway, backpack over one shoulder, looking conflicted. "Wyatt will be thrilled. He asked me about a million times this morning if I knew how your fish was doing."

"You can tell him he's doing great."

"Or you could tell him."

My brows tug together. "What do you mean?"

"We could hang together at my place tomorrow." He shifts uncomfortably from one foot to the other. "I know we have it all basically outlined, but it might be nice to work on the pieces together."

"I don't get you." The words are out of my mouth before I can stop them, but it feels good, so I keep going. "One day, you're flirting with me, inviting me out, and winning me a fish, and the next, you can barely look at me. Now you want me to come over to your house?"

"I'm sorry." Both hands wrap around one strap of his backpack, and he steps forward. "It's just..." He struggles to continue, finally saying, "Soccer is everything to me. My family gave up a lot to move here for me. I can't risk it."

"And I'm a risk?"

"Vaughn—"

The second his name is out in the air, I decide I don't need to know.

I hold up a hand. "You don't have to explain. I got it."

"Claire..."

"It's cool. Really. I understand." The thing is I do. It's exactly what Vaughn did, always choosing soccer and the team over me when he had to make a choice. I'm not even sure it was the wrong decision, but it still hurts.

"I'm really sorry. I'd like it if we could be friends?" He removes one hand from his backpack and holds it out to me with a sheepish smile on his face.

I fight the disappointment that settles like a pit in my stomach, then slip my hand into his, ignoring the zap of electricity that shoots up my arm as his fingers close over mine. "Friends."

CHAPTER THIRTEEN

The second Claire walks into our chaotic house, I'm second-guessing myself. Her house was quiet and tidy, two things ours never is.

Mom is making dinner in the kitchen. The smell of garlic bread hangs in the air, and she has music playing loudly to drown out the noise of the TV in the living room.

When she sees Claire, she smiles and hurries over to her phone to turn it down. "Hi. You must be Claire."

"Hi, Mrs. Keller." Claire lifts a hand to wave.

Mom looks like she's five seconds away from embarrassing me. She's got that happy smile on her face, obviously pleased with Claire's politeness. Her gaze darts between us like she wants to ask me if this is my new girlfriend. *Groan.*

"We're going to work upstairs," I tell her.

"Okay," she says. "Dinner will be ready in about thirty minutes. Will you join us?" Mom asks her.

"Oh, I..." Claire glances at me for help.

I shrug. Mom was always trying to feed my friends back in Arizona.

"Thanks. That'd be nice."

"Come on." I take off toward the staircase.

"Leave the door open!" Mom calls after me.

"Moooom," I yell back. I shake my head when I get to the top of the stairs.

Claire's easy smiles makes it a little less awkward.

"I'm in here." I motion toward the first room on the left and then walk in and flip on the light.

When her gaze scans the small room, I rub at the back of my neck and feel a creep of embarrassment. Since we got here, I've done very little to make this place my own, aside from the furniture—a bed, a nightstand, a bookcase my dad built, and a desk. The only other signs of life are the laundry basket of clothes Mom has been nagging me to put away and my sketch pads scattered across my desk.

I move toward them and stack them in a tidy pile. "You can work here if you want."

"Is that where you usually draw?"

I nod. "Yeah, but it's no big deal."

She drops her bag onto the carpet and then sits, crossing her legs as she starts to pull out her art supplies. "It's okay. I usually sit on the floor while I paint."

I stare at her, looking all cozy in the small space between my bed and the wall. Claire has this way of always seeming like she fits in wherever she goes.

"Don't worry. I have a small tarp I can put down so I don't get anything on the carpet."

The carpet was the least of my worries, but my mom will be thankful.

We've barely gotten started when Wyatt comes storming into my room. I left the door half-open per Mom's request, but now I'm wondering how we'll ever get anything done.

This house isn't exactly quiet, and someone is always invading my space unless I have the door closed and locked.

"What are you guys doing?" Wyatt asks, running in and jumping on my bed. He peers down at Claire like she's the most fascinating thing. I can't say that I really blame him there.

"Working on an art project," she answers, not seeming at all bothered by him. He has that effect on people, for a few minutes anyway.

"What's that?" he asks, pointing to her paper.

"Well, this is going to be a painting of the supply closet in the PE room at the high school."

His little face scrunches up as he stares down at the mostly blank paper. "It doesn't look like a closet."

She laughs lightly. "No, it doesn't. Not yet, but it will."

He grins at her and then moves to sit next to her on the floor. "Can I try? I bet I could paint something better than that."

"Wyatt." I shake my head at him. "Don't be rude."

"Sorry." He dips his head.

"It's fine." She grabs a blank page and hands it over to him.

"Really? Austin never lets me touch his art supplies."

I roll my eyes. "That's because you use my pencils to make slingshots."

He looks the tiniest bit guilty.

"Well, you can't hurt anything here."

I notice she hands him the widest brush instead of one of the small, precision ones. I tip my head to her in thanks.

It takes my little brother less than five minutes to finish his masterpiece.

"It's very good," she tells him. "That looks just like the

swings at the elementary school. Glad to know it hasn't changed."

"Thanks." He beams.

"You should take it to show your class," she suggests.

"I don't think so." His tiny head shakes rapidly.

"Why not?" I ask. Back in Arizona, he was always taking shit in for show-and-tell. One time, he took in a scorpion he captured in a jar without any of us knowing. Mom got called to the office. It was a whole thing.

"They'll think it's dumb."

"Who will?" I press.

"The other kids. They think everything I do is stupid. Nobody wants to be my friend."

White-hot rage floods my veins. "You're not stupid."

He shrugs.

"Hey." I rest a hand on his shoulder and squeeze lightly until he turns his blue eyes up to me. "You're the coolest third grader I know."

He giggles, looking less sad than before, but the tightness in my chest is still there. I had no idea he was struggling to make friends.

"I didn't know you were in third grade." Claire smiles at him. "Who is your teacher?"

"Mr. Wave."

"My sister had him two years ago."

"You have a sister?"

"Mm-hmm. Ruby."

"Is she pretty like you?" Wyatt's eyes widen with the possibility.

I fight a laugh, which Claire notices, and then she blushes.

"We look a lot alike," Claire says. "Except her hair is

a reddish blond, and she's a little bit shorter. I'll tell her to look for the supercool third grader at recess."

He gives her a toothy grin that falls before he says, "Are you just saying that to make me feel better?"

"Not at all. If you have any trouble with kids being mean, you ask around until you find Ruby."

"Or you just text me," I say.

Claire arches a brow. Maybe threatening eight-year-olds isn't the answer, but right now, I'd do anything to make the look of hurt disappear from my brother's face.

"I'm gonna go show Mom my painting." He bounds off like the conversation never happened.

"His mood swings give me whiplash sometimes," I tell Claire with a small half smile. That uneasy feeling of him being picked on at school isn't gone, but I'll have to figure out how to deal with it later.

"He's a cool kid. I'll tell Ruby to keep an eye on him."

"That's really nice of you, but I'll talk to my mom. Maybe she can ask the teacher what's going on or something."

"Spoken like someone who was never picked on." Her light laughter gives me pause.

"You were picked on?" I shake my head with disbelief. Why would anyone mess with a girl like Claire? She's beautiful and nice, and from what little I've come to know about the Frost Lake High social hierarchy, she's pretty high up there.

"I was shy, and my mom made me wear these frilly dresses every day. Kids thought I was weird or stuck up. And then Jimmy Hannah told the entire second grade that I liked to eat hair."

I laugh, unable to hold it in, but thankful when she joins in.

"I'm sorry. Eat hair?" I say the last two words slowly to make sure I heard her right.

Her face takes on an adorable shade of pink. "I would sometimes put the end of my braid in my mouth."

She looks up at me like she's back in second grade, waiting for me to mock her. I would never, but...

"Why?" I hold a fist over my mouth as I continue to stifle my laughter.

"I don't know. I guess I did it when I was nervous or bored or something. I didn't eat it!" She throws her arms up, paintbrush still in one hand.

"Just licked it."

The pink on her cheeks is redder now.

"I never should have told you," she says, but her smile says the opposite.

"I'll never say a word." I get up and go sit on the floor in front of her with my sketch pad and pencil. "You still do it, you know."

"I do not eat my hair."

"No." My gaze moves from her eyes to the end of her ponytail draped over one shoulder. "When you get nervous or you're concentrating really hard, sometimes you'll play with your hair." I reach over and tug the end gently.

"Oh." She reaches up to touch it self-consciously, and our hands brush and hold.

My gut twists, and my pulse kicks up a notch.

Somewhere in the very back of my brain, I hear Vaughn's voice asking if I'm interested in her. I'm not. I can't be. I realized yesterday that I'd been given an opportunity to finally have the guys accept me. I got to school, thinking it didn't matter and that I didn't owe Vaughn anything, but then suddenly my teammates were all happy to see me and wanted to talk soccer and invite me to hang.

And practices have been incredible. I'm no longer fighting for every possession, every shot. I forgot what that feeling is like. Being a part of a team, especially a good one, is magic.

Which is why I can't risk things going back to the way they were. Not even for her.

"Austin, dinner's ready!" Torrance yells as she walks by my open door.

I drop my hand and jump back.

I clear my throat as I stand. Claire does as well, neither of us saying anything.

Wyatt and Torrance are already seated when we get downstairs.

Mom is at the stove. She glances over her shoulder. "Everything is on the table. Austin, get Claire something to drink."

I walk over to the fridge and hold up a can of Diet Dr Pepper in one hand and Brisk iced tea in the other.

"Dr Pepper," she says.

"Good choice."

I get two, and we sit at the table. Wyatt fires out question after question until Mom has to tell him to stop so Claire can take a bite of her food. Dad calls in the middle of dinner, and Mom takes her phone into the office to talk. Torrance leaves without saying a word to anyone, and Wyatt stuffs the rest of his food in his mouth and hurries off to play video games before Mom tells him to start getting ready for bed.

Claire and I eat in silence and then take our plates to the sink. I load up the dishwasher while she watches me.

"Your family is nice."

"Nice?" I ask, popping in a tab of soap and closing the dishwasher to start it.

"Yeah. I mean, I don't think your sister likes me very much, but you all have a nice dynamic together."

"I'm sorry about Torrance. It's not you. She still hates me for uprooting the family and ruining her life. Wyatt likes you, though. In fact, I think he has a crush on you. He must have asked you fifty questions tonight."

"I don't mind," she says, and I believe her.

"Do you want to work on our projects a little more?"

"I should probably get home."

I really don't want her to go, but that seems like something someone who was interested in her would think or say, so I just nod.

We go back up to my room where she packs up all her painting supplies, and I tidy up my desk. Once her backpack is zipped and she lifts it to one shoulder, she looks at me.

"Can I ask you something?"

"Sure." My heartbeat accelerates.

"What did Vaughn say to you about me?"

I open my mouth to answer but stop myself.

"It's okay if you don't want to answer. I suppose it doesn't matter anyway." She looks a little sad, which has guilt washing over me.

"He's my teammate, and he cares about you."

"You don't owe me an explanation. We're just friends, right?"

"Right."

She hesitates, and then her lips curve up into a smile that seems fake as hell. "I gotta go. See you tomorrow."

"Yeah," I say as I watch her go. "See you tomorrow."

CHAPTER FOURTEEN

"I wish I didn't still have this stupid boot." I stare at myself in the floor-length mirror.

"No one is going to be looking at your foot." Lacey's brows rise as she gives me a once-over in my lilac dress. "You look amazing. That color is great on you."

"Thanks." I turn side to side, admiring the flowy skirt. The bodice is fitted, and the straps hang off my shoulders.

Tonight is the first school dance of the year. The seniors throw it every September as sort of a final hurrah to the beginning of the year. It's fun and well attended and a good excuse to dress up.

"Boone is having another party after the dance." Lacey smooths a hand down her silver dress. It's short and sparkly and looks like it was made for her.

"I heard, but I don't think I can go. Ruby has a dance competition tomorrow."

"So?" My best friend faces me. "Why do you have to sit through hours of torture on a Saturday morning? It's not like you're the one competing."

I know her words aren't meant to hurt, but they still do. I don't know if it will ever stop hurting.

"I don't know. I think I'm providing moral support and an extra pair of hands in case someone needs a headpiece sewn in at the last minute or something."

"You have attended enough of Ruby's competitions since you hurt your ankle. Your moral support should be covered for a good twenty years. And you're shit at sewing."

A rough laugh escapes from my lips. She isn't wrong. I went to rehearsals and competitions all summer for Ruby. Mostly I just sat through the hours and hours of other dancers to get to Ruby's two minutes of stage time. I don't mind being there for her. She sat through plenty of my skate practices and competitions too.

"Go ask your mom." Lacey puts her hands together in front of her chest. "Please?"

"Okay. I'll ask, but don't get your hopes up."

My mom is in her bedroom at the end of the hall. The TV is on and plays quietly as she sits on the bed with a needle and thread, sewing sequins on a red top.

"Mom," I say, knocking lightly on her open door.

She glances up, blinks several times, and then smiles. "You look pretty." Before the compliment can even land, she adds, "You should wear your hair down though."

My hand flies up to the side Dutch braid Lacey did for me. "It'll just get all messed up at the dance."

The gym is always warm and sweaty at the big dances with everyone crammed into the small space.

She makes a hum of disapproval and goes back to her work. "We're leaving at five tomorrow morning, so don't stay out too late."

"Actually, I was wondering if I could skip the competition tomorrow."

She looks up again, that stamp of disapproval still staring back at me. "Why?"

"We'll be gone all day, and Ruby is only doing one dance. Plus, I have this big art project I need to work on."

"Is this because you want to stay out late tonight at some high school party?"

"No," I say quickly, then nod. "Partly. There is a party after the dance."

She sighs.

"But I do have a lot of school stuff to do this weekend, and it would help to be home tomorrow."

"Okay." The heaviness in her tone speaks of her displeasure. "Focusing on your classes is a good idea. You'll never get into college with no extracurriculars and a B-plus average. Did you decide on which colleges you'd like to visit? I need to make plans around Ruby's dance schedule."

"Not yet. I'll make a list this weekend."

"Okay."

Okay. It takes a second for her words to sink in. I haven't gone to an after-dance party...ever.

"Thanks, Mom."

She nods and goes back to her sewing as I leave.

When I walk back to my room, Lacey is standing there with a huge grin like she was eavesdropping. Who am I kidding? Of course she was listening in.

She squeals. "Tonight is going to be so much fun!"

—

The school gym is decorated with balloons and streamers.

One side of the bleachers is pulled out for seating, and the DJ is set up on the stage.

Lacey twirls in front of me, already dancing as we make our way through the crowd. When we get to the middle of the basketball court, she stops and looks around with a huge grin.

"Next year, we're going to do it up even bigger than this," she promises.

I smile at her and the way she's always thinking ahead. I haven't even thought about next week, let alone next year at this time. Right now, everything feels so up in the air. It's like I can do anything now, but anything feels so wide open that it's overwhelming. All I ever wanted was to skate at the world championships. I was so close. Everyone said that it was my time. And then it all just fell apart.

"New Guy is here," Lacey says, interrupting my thoughts.

I swivel around to look in the same direction as her, and there he is, looking as good as he always does in jeans, a long-sleeve white Henley, a matching white baseball cap, and tennis shoes. My heart rate speeds up, and I run a hand over my braid.

"Is he coming directly from soccer practice?" Lacey asks, commenting on his casual appearance. Most everyone dresses up for the dances. Even the guys will at least throw on a button-down shirt or dress pants.

"I don't know," I say, unable to look away from him.

"Aren't you two BFFs now with all the *studying* you're doing lately." She smirks and puts air quotes around the word *studying*.

I push at her shoulder lightly. "That project is worth fifty percent of our grade."

She snorts. "Uh-huh. I'm sure that's the only reason you're hanging out every night."

My face heats. It's been two weeks since we were assigned together in art class, and we've fallen into a rhythm, working on our pieces every night after school. We mostly go to his house instead of mine. I like being around his family. Even without his dad present, they have this warm, welcoming house. Ours wasn't really like that even before my parents separated.

And Austin and I have fallen into a friendly if not sometimes flirty routine. He hasn't hit on me again, and I've stopped trying to get a reaction from him. After spending some time with him, I decided it doesn't matter if his feelings changed because of Vaughn or not. They did, and I don't want a guy who folds so easily.

Even one who is as hot as Austin.

He weaves through the crowd, looking around. When he spots us, Austin smiles in greeting. Lacey waves, and he heads toward us.

"I think I missed the memo on the dress code," he says, looking from me to Lacey and then back. "I'm surprised they let me in."

"It's not mandatory or anything, so I guess you're safe to stay," Lacey teases. "But that's a good idea. Next year, we're instituting a dress code, so you've been warned."

He laughs lightly. "Thanks. I'll pencil that information into my calendar."

His sarcasm isn't lost on Lacey, but she nods her approval as the song changes to something slower. "Good."

The noise in the gym has quieted along with the music.

"So," Austin starts, looking at me, but then there's a shrill scream from our right.

"Austin! Austin!"

The three of us watch as Sophie and her friends hurry our way.

"Looks like your fan club has spotted you," Lacey tells him.

"Oh no." He looks around. "People dress up at these things, *and* they dance?" He groans. "I'm going to kill Rowan. He could have at least given me a heads-up."

"You don't dance?" I ask, smothering a laugh.

"Not if I can help it." He looks like he's sweating bullets at the prospect, which is hilarious. I didn't think Austin was shakable. He always seems so confident in every situation.

"Well, I do," Lacey says. "And this is my favorite song."

She waves as she backs away from us. I listen until I recognize the music. I know for a fact Lacey doesn't even like this song. I glance in the direction she went. She's standing in a group with some fellow cheerleaders off the dance floor.

"Austin!" Sophie calls again.

He tips his head down and looks up at me from under the bill of his cap. "Think she'll keep going if I don't look up?"

She stops directly beside him, a huge smile on her face.

I shake my head. "Sorry."

"Austin, hey!" the eager sophomore says.

He hesitates a beat and then raises his head and smiles back at her. "Oh, hey."

Sophie is wearing a black dress with pink high-top Converse. She has a whole sporty, dressed-up thing going on. Her hair is curled, and the cut of her dress is low, but it's like she didn't want to fully commit to dressing up. She looks nice though, and I know Austin notices. He can't not notice. But for some reason, he still looks a little pained at the idea of dancing.

"I'm so glad you came," she says. Her gaze drops over his casual attire. She doesn't comment, but she seems just as thrown by it as Lacey had. Without giving him time to reply, she adds, "Do you want to dance?"

"Actually," I cut in, giving her an apologetic smile and stepping closer to Austin. "He just asked me to dance."

"I did?" His brows disappear under his hat, but then he nods. "Right." He sort of smiles at Sophie, but it almost looks like a grimace. "Sorry. Maybe later?"

"Yeah, of course. I'll come find you on the next one. Oh, and you're going to Boone's party later, right?"

"I think so," he replies.

"Yay!" She claps her hands and lifts her shoulders.

When she turns to leave, Austin lets out a long breath. "Thank you."

"Don't thank me yet. Now we have to dance, or she'll just follow you around all night."

He chuckles softly, looking as uncomfortable as if I suggested we walk over hot coals barefoot, but takes a hesitant step closer to me.

"You cannot be that bad of a dancer," I say, slipping my arms up to his shoulders. The height difference means our bodies are close.

His hands go to my waist, and I suck in a breath at the contact. Suddenly I'm wondering if I should have just backed away and let him dance with Sophie.

"Oh yes, I can be." His body is stiff, but his touch is soft. He smells like laundry detergent and a whiff of cologne.

"Relax," I say. "And don't step on my bad foot."

He chuckles and looks pained again as he glances

down, like he's ensuring he knows where it is so he doesn't stomp on it. It's adorable really, how out of his element he is right now.

"How is your foot?" he asks. "Do you need to sit?"

"Oh no, you're not getting out of this that easily."

One side of his mouth pulls up in a sheepish grin.

"My foot is good. The boot comes off next week if everything looks good."

"That's great."

We fall into a rhythm, swaying to the beat, and he seems to let go of some of the tension he was carrying.

"Oh, I meant to tell you, Wyatt is in love. Your sister came up to him today at recess and introduced herself."

"Oh really?" I smile. I mentioned him to Ruby last week, and she promised she'd keep an eye and ear out for him, but we've barely seen each other since. She's busy with dance rehearsals every night, and I've been spending evenings at the Keller household.

"Yeah, he asked me tonight if I could put in a good word for him." His grin widens. "So consider this the good word."

I laugh and picture Wyatt. "Wow. I'm impressed he has the guts to go after a girl two years older than him. Confident kid, like his big brother."

"If she looks like you, then I understand his obsession." He smiles. "You look really great tonight. Always, but I like the dress. And the braid. And the glittery stuff around your eyes."

I laugh at that, and he winces.

"Fuck, I'm going to shut up now."

My laughter trails off, and my face heats with the compliments.

"So how did you manage to avoid slow dancing this long? Did your last school not have dances or something?"

"They weren't like this, I'll tell you that." He looks up and around at the decorations. "They were held in this small, old gym, and the PE teacher also DJed on the side, so they'd get him to set up and play. It was awful. He'd play exclusively eighties music, and everyone would end up sitting around and talking or leaving early and hitting a party or something else. Do people stay the whole time at these things?"

He really is too cute when he lets his insecurities show. I'm used to cocky and confident Austin. "Most people will leave by ten."

"But not you?"

"Lacey is a diehard. I'll have to drag her off the dance floor."

"She's a trip. How'd you two become friends?"

"She came up to me on the first day of sixth grade and said she liked my dress and declared we were going to be friends." I shrug.

He lets his head fall back and laughs. His light green eyes sparkle, and a little of his dark hair is visible around his ears.

"I'd be lost without her. Especially this year."

"She's a good friend to you," he states. "I bet she'd say the same about you."

"I don't know about that. Although I do get roped into helping her with her many extracurricular duties, like making all those signs for the start of the school year."

"Oh, I remember," he says. "That was the day you dumped glitter over my head and I showed up late to practice looking like I had spent the night at a rave. Even people around school who don't know the story are calling me Disco."

"You ran into me," I point out, fighting a laugh. "It's not my fault that Rowan's nickname for you has spread like wildfire."

One corner of his mouth kicks up. "Worth it. I met you, and here we are dancing."

"And dodging your fan club," I add. I feel the need to remind him we're only doing this because he needed an out. "You should just put them out of their misery and date one of them already."

"Nah." He shakes his head.

"Not interested in having a girlfriend?"

He bobs his head side to side. "The right girl…maybe. But I'm not interested in any of them."

The song is winding down to the final notes, and immediately after, a more upbeat song starts. I remove my hands and step back. His fingers graze along my stomach as I pull away.

"Thanks for the dance. You're not so bad."

"I think that was all thanks to you, but I appreciate it anyway." He lifts his hat from his head and runs his fingers through his dark hair. "Do you want to maybe go get some air? I'm underdressed and not skilled enough to be in here."

I open my mouth to taunt him, but I had planned to agree. I want to keep talking to him. Being near him is fun and exciting. But I see Vaughn out of the corner of my eye. He looks like he just got here. He's scanning the gym and nods when he sees Rowan and some other teammates.

"We probably shouldn't," I say.

Austin turns and follows my gaze.

"If he sees us together, he might get the wrong idea."

"Right." He nods, but there's a hint of disappointment in his tone.

"You look good." I reach up and take off his hat, then muss his flattened hair. He lets me, watching on amused. "Better."

I hand him his hat, and then we stand there, neither seeming to want to move.

"Well, I guess I'll see you later?" I ask.

"Yeah," he says as I back away slowly. "Thanks for the dance."

CHAPTER FIFTEEN

Austin

The schools are bigger and nicer in Frost Lake than my old ones back in Arizona, the dances more elaborate, the funding for sports much more substantial. The houses are larger, vehicles nicer, and the girls hotter, but I'm glad that one thing seems to be universal: teenage parties mean booze and loud music, and the promise of hooking up.

Rowan rode over with me, but he's already found the center of the party and is thriving in it. I walk through the living room to the dining room and kitchen area. There's a game of flip cup happening on a long, wooden table with a big-ass chandelier hanging over it. Others are gathered around the island with drinks in hand, talking and laughing.

I spot Sophie and her friends and take a sharp turn into another room. She's a cool girl, but she seems to think we're going to be something more than friends, and I just don't see that happening when there is a cute blond I can't get out of my head.

A cute blond who's standing in the corner with Lacey and another girl I recognize as a cheerleader.

I catch Claire's eye as I enter the room. She smiles and cocks one brow in a teasing, flirty way. Something shifted between us the past week. We've become friends…at least when we're alone. I made a truce with Vaughn, and I don't plan to break it, but remembering why is getting more difficult the more time I spend with her.

Instead of going over to her like my feet want, I wink at her and keep walking. I circle back through the party, and I find that my teammates are gathered in the living room, Rowan included.

"There you are," he says, tipping his chin up at me. "I thought you left already."

"Got lost," I joke.

"His grandparents own the paper mill in the town over," Blake says. "You should see the pool in the backyard."

It's cool out tonight, rained on and off all day, but by unspoken agreement, we head outside anyway.

"Do all these people go to our school?" I mutter, more or less to myself, though the guys chuckle.

The pool, as promised, is impressive. It's lit up with multicolored lights along the edge, and the water sparkles under the moonlight. Everyone in Arizona had a pool in their backyard, but this is a spectacle. It has two lanes roped off for lap swimming, a diving board, and a swim-up bar.

No one is braving the pool tonight, but a few girls are sitting on the edge, letting their toes dangle under the surface. In warmer weather, I can see how this pool gets a lot of action. Not that Frost Lake gets a lot of warm weather, a month or two tops. Seems like a waste of money, but something tells me these people aren't worried about saving a few hundred grand.

All around the giant pool, people stand in groups,

drinking and talking. Off to the side of the pool is a grassy area with a firepit and chairs gathered around. It looks like they're playing some sort of game, because shots are being knocked back by several as the others laugh and cheer.

But the main attraction in the backyard filled with my classmates (and then some) is the hot tub. It's built next to the pool, and steam rises from it. Girls are stripped down to their bras and panties, and guys are in their boxers. I can practically see the pheromones in the air.

"I love high school," Rowan says, clapping me on the shoulder and heading that direction.

"That hot tub for sure has bodily fluid in it of some kind." Blake grimaces.

"Definitely," Vaughn says.

I recognize more people than I don't after a quick appraisal. I don't know if I'll ever get used to the size of Frost Lake. And still, everyone seems to know everyone.

"Yo, Keller."

I turn at the sound of my name, and some guy from my English class tosses me a beer. I catch the lob pass and tip my head to him in thanks.

Blake is next to me with an already open beer and another in his free hand. "You want this?" I ask him.

"You don't?"

"Nah, man. I'm driving."

"Stack me up." He holds out the hand with the closed beer, and I put the other on top. "Fuck it. You know what?" he asks no one in particular. "What's a little bodily fluid gonna hurt? The hot water probably kills anything too gnarly."

"Don't get pregnant!" Vaughn calls after him. He shakes

his head, then glances back at me and Hunter. "You guys want to kick the ball around?"

"Where?" I ask.

One side of his mouth lifts. "You'll see."

—

In a side yard that's nearly as big as the backyard is a small soccer field. Goals with nets and all.

"Why does he have this?" I walk onto the field in amazement. There are even lights around the perimeter, like the designer considered after-dark games.

"He was on the soccer team freshman year," Hunter answers. "We used to come over here on the weekends and play until all hours of the night."

"I'd never leave if I had something like this." I'm still amazed. My parents put up with me kicking the ball and using laundry baskets or whatever else I can find as a makeshift goal and only complain when I'm too noisy (kicking the ball against the side of the house) or break something (a window or two or three).

Vaughn and Hunter peel off their button-down shirts, and the three of us kick the ball around, warming up, taking shots at the goal to get used to it. It's obvious that they've played here as much as they said, because they move around the smaller space with an ease that takes me a few minutes to achieve.

Before long, we've attracted three others, and we've got a game of three-on-three and a crowd forming to watch.

It feels good to play, even like this, with guys who love the game as much as I do. We're competitive, and there's no taking it easy on one another, but we laugh and chirp, and it's just fun.

Well, mostly fun. Neither Vaughn nor I can resist a challenge. It's me and him, back and forth. I've learned his game. I'm ready for him to push his forearm against my chest and extend his body away from me. I've gotten quicker, and I love seeing the lines of frustration on his face.

When I glance over at the sideline, Claire has joined the crowd. She and Lacey stand off to the side. I'm not the only one who's seen her. Vaughn stands taller and peels off his undershirt. I thought the guy was unflappable, but it's clear he has at least one weakness: Claire.

Smiling to myself, I take off my shirt as well. We toss them to the sidelines.

"You want me to stop taking it easy on you now?" I ask.

"Bring it on."

"I don't want to embarrass you."

"You fucking wish, Keller."

The fire that is lit under him from my words and Claire's presence is almost enough to make me wish I'd kept my mouth shut. But it's so damn fun to go up against him like this. Scrapping and pushing and cheap shots. No holding back.

He tackles me off a pass, and our feet get tangled up, both of us going down. I elbow him, and he makes sure he pads his fall with my body. I glance over at Claire. Her gaze goes from me to Vaughn, which is how I realize he's also staring at her.

"Do you need some water?" Sophie appears at my side as I stand.

I take the cup from her, drink half of it, and toss the rest over my head. Claire and I lock eyes again. Her gaze lowers like she's tracking the drops from my face to my stomach. Her eyes on me feel like being struck by a lightning bolt.

I toss her a wink when she finally lifts her gaze, but not before I notice the blush creeping into her face.

Her response is to turn and leave. The disappointment I feel is swift. I like it when she watches me. I like it when she's around, period. Maybe I shouldn't flirt with her, but I just can't help it. I want her. There, I've admitted it. Now what the fuck do I do about it, knowing Vaughn will have the team turned against me in a flash if he finds out?

The game continues. People slowly lose interest, and eventually, the noise from the party starts to die down.

"Shit. It's almost one. I gotta get home." Hunter grabs his abandoned shirt and then walks over to me and outstretches a hand. "Nice game."

"You too." We slap hands.

"I should go too," Vaughn says. He leans over to get his T-shirt, then wipes his forehead with it. He puts his nicer shirt on, leaving it open and his bare chest and stomach visible. Some of the girls who are still sitting around and watching giggle and ogle him, but he's oblivious again now that Claire is gone. "Are you free tomorrow after practice?" he asks. "I thought we could work on some speed drills. If you still want."

Even though things have been cool between us since the truce, he hasn't offered to help me again. The pranks have stopped, and the guys don't seem to have it out for me anymore, but I'm well aware that one nod from Vaughn, and I might be right back to looking over my shoulder.

"Yeah. That'd be cool."

"I'll text you." He scans the side yard, giving the girls no more than a second of his attention before heading out the gate to the front.

I head back to the main yard. The party stragglers are

gathered around the firepit, and a few couples are in the hot tub, but they're making out, and people seem to be giving them a wide berth. I don't blame them there.

I spot Rowan in a chair in front of the fire, so I start toward him. He has a familiar blond sitting next to him. Claire.

They're sharing a chair. She's perched on the very end, a cup of something that I'm guessing isn't water in one hand. Her smile is wide, and her body language is loose. When they all start laughing, I can pick hers out even though she's not the loudest.

She must feel my eyes on her, because she turns, and we stare at each other from across the yard. Her lips curve higher, and she has this sort of sassy, flirty shift in her that lets me know instantly that she's not sober.

My thoughts are confirmed when I get closer, and she stands and stumbles toward me.

"Did you win?"

"Should have stuck around to find out," I say.

She rolls her eyes. "Please. You have a big enough fan club without me."

"Is that right?" I enjoy her fiery attitude more than I should.

"Yep. I just have to keep an ear to the ground at all times to know your location, outfit, and actions. The girls in this school are obsessed with you."

"Not all of them," I point out. Not the one I want to be, even though I know it wouldn't matter.

"You're talking to me in public," she says too loudly. "Does Vaughn know? Would he approve?"

Her tone is mocking but playful, and luckily no one except Rowan is paying us any attention.

"Probably not." I grab both of her arms to keep her steady. "You good?"

"Great."

I start to remove my hands, and she wobbles again.

"How much have you had to drink?"

"This is only my second," she says, looking down at her mostly empty cup.

"I know you're good at art, but maybe math isn't your strong suit." There's no way she's this drunk after two drinks.

Rowan steps closer.

"She's a lightweight," he says in a loud whisper, like he's trying to be funny.

"As opposed to a lush like you," she snaps back at him.

"Fair point, Crawford."

Claire suddenly looks tired, like the alcohol has flipped a switch from tipsy and fun to drunk and needing to pass out.

"I think it might be time for you to go home."

"I think it might be time for you to go home," she mocks back.

"Wow," I mouth to Rowan and twist the bill of my cap from front to back.

She thrusts her cup at him. "Here. I don't want any more."

He downs it in one gulp.

Lacey joins us. She doesn't seem quite as bad off as her friend, but judging by the giggly way she approaches us, I'd say she's drunk as well.

"Do you want to go in the hot tub?" she asks her friend.

"I think I want to go home."

"No!" Her friend grabs on to her arm. "You have the whole night for once. We're going to stay up until dawn and then get French fries and milkshakes, remember?"

Claire winces and puts a hand to her stomach, then her face pales.

"Are you…" Lacey doesn't finish the question before Claire's eyes widen in panic.

"I don't feel so well."

"Did she drive?" I ask Lacey.

"No, I brought her. We were going to catch an Uber after the party."

"Can you catch a ride with someone else?" I step closer to Claire and wrap an arm around her waist. She leans into me like she's thankful not to be holding herself upright. "I'm heading out now, so I can take her home."

"I'll Uber with you," Rowan tells Lacey.

Lacey nods at me. "Maybe I should go with her."

"I'm okay," Claire tells her. "I just need to sleep."

Her friend comes forward and hugs her. "Love you, Claire Bear. Text me when you get home." She then looks at me. "If something happens to her, I will shove a glitter bomb up your—"

"Oooo-kay." Rowan takes Lacey by the shoulders and pulls her close to him, then drapes one arm around her. "We're good here."

With a nod of appreciation to Rowan and a weary smile at Lacey, I take more of Claire's weight and start toward the side gate to the street.

She's quiet as I help her into the passenger side of my Jeep. I go around the front and slide behind the wheel. The music is blasting from my drive earlier, and I turn it down and glance over at Claire. She hasn't budged, so I lean across her to buckle her seat belt. The movement puts us close—too close. She smells like cotton candy and rum. Her eyes lock with mine, and when she glances down at my mouth,

I realize if I leaned forward even an inch, our lips would touch.

I've thought about kissing her again every day since the first time. I wonder if she's ever thought about kissing me again.

"How are you feeling now?" I ask, not recognizing my own voice. It's deep and sounds like I chewed on gravel. I pull away and start the vehicle, only daring to look at her again when I pull out onto the road.

"Better. I think. My stomach doesn't hurt anymore." She offers a weak smile. "I probably won't puke in your car."

"Reassuring," I say dryly, focusing on the road. It's dark out, and there are only a few streetlights. I still don't know my way around yet, and the last thing I want is to get lost so Claire can have time to start feeling bad again and vomit on the floorboard. I do not do well with the smell of vomit. Just thinking about it makes me queasy.

She laughs a little. "You'd deserve it."

"For what?" I ask, looking over at her. Her eyes are brighter now, more alive, sparking with their usual heat and playfulness.

"You know what."

I clamp my jaw shut.

"What did Vaughn say exactly anyway?" she asks.

I guess it was too much to hope she'd forgotten about that, but she hasn't brought it up in weeks. I don't want to talk about Vaughn.

"It must have been pretty bad, because you went from not caring what he thought to avoiding me like the plague only a few hours later."

"I'm not avoiding you now," I point out, then add,

"It wasn't bad. Vaughn has never said anything bad about you."

She doesn't look convinced. She turns in her seat, angling her legs toward me. "It's okay. I can handle it. What did he say?" Silence follows, then she says, "I bet I can guess. Did he say I was a distraction that you didn't need? That you were better off not getting involved with me? Or maybe that since my injury, I just don't understand what it takes to be an elite athlete in the same way."

He didn't say any of those things to me, but now I'm wondering if he said them to her. What a fucking idiot. Does he really think those things, or is Claire just trying to con me into talking? I don't know, but I can tell she isn't going to drop this. I make a wrong turn and curse myself. Could I make this drive any longer or more painful?

"Austin," she says my name softly. I think it's the first time I've heard her say it without mocking me, and I want her to do it again.

I let out a long breath. I don't see how I could make things any worse at this point. "He said things were complicated between you two, and he implied that you'd end up back together."

Actually, now that I've said it out loud, I wonder if it's true. Does she want that? Maybe I've misread her signals. Am I a decoy in her plot to get back with Vaughn? The idea makes *me* feel nauseous.

Claire is quiet, and I wish I hadn't said anything. Although if she's going to end up with him anyway, maybe it's better she knows. They can work shit out, and I can go back to not being distracted and focusing on soccer.

Laughter spills out of her while I'm still muddling

through my thoughts and assuring myself I won't be jealous or care at all if she and Vaughn get back together.

I roll to a stop at a light. Inside the city limits, the lighting is better, and I can see the warm pink of her lips and the way the purple strap of her dress slides down off her shoulder.

"That's the most ridiculous thing you've ever said." She's taken with another fit of laughter. "Complicated? Ha!"

"So you're not getting back together?" I ask, then hold my breath while I wait for her answer.

She stifles her laughter and hits me with those multicolored eyes. "Why? You're not interested in me, so does it matter?"

I start to tell her that I never said that, but I can't tell her what I really want to, so what's the point of clearing up that I'm very interested in her? I have just enough self-preservation to know when to hold my tongue.

I manage to find her house without taking any more wrong turns.

"Don't pull into the driveway," she says, so I pull up to the curb.

"Is anyone home?" I ask, wondering if it's okay to leave her alone. She seems less likely to be sick, but she's still very drunk.

"My mom and sister, but they have to get up really early for a dance competition, so I don't want to wake them." She fumbles for the door handle and goes to step out, but the seat belt stops her.

She laughs as she realizes her error.

"Do you need any help?"

"I got it." She pauses on the sidewalk next to my car and takes off one sandal. She lets it dangle from her fingertips. "Thanks for the ride."

"Thanks for not puking in my car."

We stare at each other for a beat. She doesn't shut the car door, and I don't put it in drive.

"Okay. I should go now." She still doesn't budge for another few seconds, then steps away. She attempts to shut the door but doesn't quite get it.

I lean over to shut it myself, watching her walk up to the front door. She's stumbling and laughing. There is zero chance she's not waking up the whole house.

I keep watching as she fumbles around in her purse.

"Don't do it, Keller." I grip the steering wheel. I tell myself she'll be fine. So her mom wakes up and sees she's drunk. It'll be fine, right? Ugh. Dammit.

I kill the engine and get out of my car. I jog up quietly, joining her at the porch.

"Hey," she says too loudly. "I can't find my key."

"I'll help you," I whisper. Taking her purse, I rummage around until I find a key ring. There are several on it, with color-coded rubber rings. "Which one?"

"Yellow." She sighs. "Yellow for Mom's house, green for Dad's. I'm saving the pink one for my house someday. I want to live in a pink house."

One side of my mouth lifts as I slide the key with a yellow rubber ring into the lock. "A pink house?"

When I push the door open, she stumbles ahead of me without answering. The house is dark. There's some dim lighting along the bottom of the cabinets in the kitchen and a lamp at the bottom of the stairs that glows in the corner.

She heads for the stairs before I get the door shut. Her footsteps are heavy, and she's humming. My palms start to sweat as I ease the door closed and hurry after her. I catch her about halfway up.

"Why are you following me?" she asks loudly.

"Shh." I whisper, placing a hand at her back when she leans back too far. If we don't fall down and break something, I'll be shocked. "I'm just making sure you get in your room."

"I'm fine." She wobbles again, and I catch her around the waist.

"Yep. I can see that."

I hold on to her as we walk up the remaining steps. She's still humming and generally just totally unaware of how loud she's being. Does she always walk this loud? I mean, I know the boot is noisy, but it's like she's hammering into the hardwood floor with every step.

Thankfully, this house doesn't creak as we walk. I guess it's too new and fancy for that. I note the closed doors as we navigate to her room.

"And I made it." She throws up her hands and spins in a circle, somehow not falling down. I bet that's a move she did a million times in figure skating.

"Even with a boot, you're graceful."

She laughs again, still not quietly.

"You're gonna wake up your mom."

"Unlikely. She's probably got her white noise machine going."

I don't know how to tell her she's way louder than any white noise.

"Well, I'm here. Safe and sound. Thank you for bringing me home." She tosses her purse onto the end of her bed and then reaches around behind her back.

"You're welcome." I breathe a sigh of relief. "I'll see you later."

"Wait. Can you help?" She turns around and lets her arms fall to her sides. "I can't get the zipper."

"Yeah." I take two steps to her. The small zipper runs along her back. My fingers brush against her bare skin as I grab ahold of it. I'm suddenly very aware of how good she smells, how alone we are, and how fast my heart's beating.

She's quieter than she's been since we entered the house, and it's more unnerving than her stomping around. I step back when the material falls apart and clear my throat.

"Okay."

She turns to face me, holding her dress to her chest so it doesn't slip off her. "Thank you."

"Yep. Get some sleep. I'll, uh, talk to you later."

I turn to go, but she moves forward and grabs my arm. "Wait."

My body vibrates with how much I want her. When I turn, she releases her hold on me, and we stand inches apart, staring at each other.

Reaching forward with one hand, I let my fingertips brush against her thigh.

My brain is yelling, *Not the time, asshole*, but weeks of being near her, thinking about her, dreaming about touching her, have all led to this moment, and I can't stop.

We're both silent as my fingers glide over her smooth skin. Her eyes are locked on mine, and time seems to stand still. I think about kissing her, not for the first or even the hundredth time tonight. She's so beautiful.

My hand lifts to the side of her face. My knuckles brush against her skin, and I drop my thumb over the bow of her lips. They part, and I slide my thumb to the corner. Her head tips back in clear invitation.

To hell with all the reasons I shouldn't; the reasons I *should* feel far more important right now.

"Austin," she whispers my name. I don't know if it's a

warning or a reminder that I'm me and she's her and that we're about to cross a very big line.

I'm seconds from leaping over it, really. I don't just want to kiss her. I want to kiss her until the sun comes up.

I swallow thickly as my heart continues to hammer in my chest. She lets her dress drop to the floor. "I dare you to kiss me."

My heart jumps in my throat, and all the blood rushes south.

I feel her inhale a breath as my fingers drop lower to the swell of her breasts.

A door creaks open somewhere in the house, but the noise is slow to register. I'm focused on Claire's perfect pink lips, the way her heart beats in sync with mine, and the smell of cotton candy.

Suddenly, footsteps in the hallway cut through the moment. We both freeze, eyes wide with panic. Claire lets out a yelp and jumps back from me.

"Oh shit." Her voice is a whisper. She looks around the room, then grabs on to my arm and hauls me backward with her into the closet.

We're chest-to-chest in the small space. My back is against the shelving, and she presses into me. I don't know why she's hiding, but I can't bring myself to question it out loud. Her body molded against mine feels so good.

"You smell nice," she says. "You always smell good. Like sunshine in the middle of the forest."

"I—"

Footsteps continue. I can't tell if they're coming closer or not.

"Is it your mom?" I ask.

"Or a ghost," she says, then starts to giggle.

I place a hand over her mouth and fight my own laughter despite the situation. I can feel her lips moving under my palm. She then wiggles her body to get free and trips on my feet. I catch her a second before her mom calls out, "Claire? Are you home?"

She squeaks, a tiny little noise. I haul her to me. Now her back is to my chest, and she's crushing me into the hangers and shelves. We hold still, listening closely. Our cover is definitely blown.

"What do I do?" she asks, turning her head.

"Tell her you're changing."

"Good idea."

"Yeah, it's me," Claire yells. "I'm just changing."

She starts to giggle again. My heart beats so fast in my chest. The last thing I need is to get caught in this closet with a half-naked Claire by her mother.

My hand drops to her side, and I lean my head back to keep from eating her hair.

Everything is quiet, and then the closet door is wrenched open. Claire's mom stands with her arms crossed and a death glare aimed right at me. *Oh shit.*

"What is this?" her mom asks.

We stumble out, and I'm very aware of how bad this looks.

"I give you a little bit of independence, and you bring some boy back at two o'clock in the morning?"

"It's not like that," Claire says.

"I was just helping her up to her room," I say, running a hand through my hair.

"Helping?" her mom asks, incredulous.

Fuck, fuck, fuck.

She steps closer to Claire and sniffs. "Have you been drinking?"

I'm caught between wanting to sprint out of here and staying to make sure Claire doesn't get in too much trouble. But the looks her mom is giving me make it clear that my presence isn't helping.

"I should go," I say, glancing at Claire. "Are you going to be okay?"

She nods tentatively.

"You shouldn't be here to begin with," her mom says coolly. "Do your parents know you're sneaking into drunk girls' houses late at night to take advantage of them, or should I give them a call tomorrow?"

"Mom!" Claire's voice rises, and her eyes widen with disbelief. "He didn't. He wouldn't."

"No?" Claire's mom waves a hand in front of her daughter's half-naked body. "So you're not drunk, and he wasn't just feeling you up in the closet?"

Claire blushes and pulls a pillow from her bed to hold in front of herself. She looks a lot like her mom, but where Claire's features are soft and inviting, her mom's are hard and harsh.

Her mom narrows her gaze on me and points. "If I catch you anywhere near my daughter again, I will call your parents and the school. And maybe the cops."

Claire shoots me an apologetic look as I head toward her bedroom door.

I think I mutter "sorry," but I don't know which one I'm apologizing to.

CHAPTER SIXTEEN

ON SATURDAY, I MEET UP WITH LACEY AND ANDIE AT THE school. We signed up for dance cleanup duty, which sounded fine before the events of last night. I feel better than I should. I think my mother walking in on me half-naked and Austin about to kiss me flushed the alcohol right out of my system. I had the slightest headache when I woke up, but I'm nursing more of an embarrassment hangover than anything else.

"What did Austin do?" Lacey asks as she pulls a streamer down from the basketball goal.

"What could he do? He ran out of there before my mom woke the entire neighborhood threatening to call the cops. Then she spent the next hour lecturing me on perverted teenage boys."

Andie snorts a laugh. "I got that same talk from my parents when I started dating Brandon."

"But it wasn't like that," I stress to them. "If anything, I was to blame. I was drunk, and he helped me out of my dress, and I just…I wanted to feel something besides sadness and anger."

I wanted to feel it with him, but I don't admit that part.

Lacey looks to Andie. "Two drinks, and she's tearing off her clothes. Who would have thought?"

My face heats. Maybe it was the alcohol, but it isn't like I hadn't thought about it before I drank too much and was all alone with him in my room.

"I am mortified," I say.

"Why? You're hot. You just showed him what he was missing."

"Poor Austin. He must have been so conflicted. Pretend not to notice how hot you are or get pummeled by Vaughn." Andie and Lacey continue to laugh, but my stomach rolls with unease.

"That's not all…"

My friends both stop and stare at me.

"I dared him to kiss me." I want to curl up in a ball and die.

"What?!" Lacey's voice is shrill, and Andie squeals with excitement.

"He didn't," I say. "We didn't."

He was going to though. I felt it. One minute longer and my mom would have walked in on a completely different scene. She probably would have called his parents and the school then.

"Have you heard from him today?" Lacey asks.

"He texted last night to check on me, but I didn't respond."

They both seem surprised by that.

"If I respond, he's going to want to talk about it, and I'd rather pretend it didn't happen."

"Oh, sure. No problem." They laugh.

"Do you think I can switch to home school for the rest of the year?" I ask my friends.

"Your mom would love that. Are you kidding? She'd have you back skating every hour of the day as soon as that boot is off." Lacey's tone gives away her feelings on that. But she's wrong. Now that I can't skate competitively, I'm not sure she'd see the point.

"Would you really want to spend all day with her?" Andie asks. She's spent less time around my mom, but she knows enough to realize how torturous it'd be.

"Right now, it sounds better than facing Austin on Monday."

"It's fine," Lacey insists. "It's not like you slept with him. You didn't sleep with him, did you?"

"Oh my god. No, of course not."

"Good, because once you sleep with them, they lose all interest. That's why this one is still making Brandon wait it out."

"That is not why." Andie shoves Lacey playfully before she bends down to pick up more decoration trash from the gym floor. "We're waiting until our one-year anniversary." She blushes. "I want it to be special."

"It will be," I tell her. "Ignore Lacey. She's still salty about Zach touching her boobs and then getting back together with Maureen the next day."

"It wasn't even the next day. It was one hour later. He was copping a feel in the pool, and then we got out to dry off, and the next thing I know, they're hugging and kissing and back together." It's been a year, and she's still not over it. Zach isn't even her type, but he's the first person she let grope her, and I think the experience scarred her for life.

"Those two have been on and off for years. It had nothing to do with you or your boobs," I remind her for at least the tenth time. One of these days, she's going to believe me.

Andie nods her head in agreement. "Boys don't think like that. Boobs are boobs. They're all the same."

"Is that true?" I ask. "Remember Tasha?" She had DDs in seventh grade, and the guys were obsessed with them.

"She's an outlier," Andie says.

"Maybe I am too." Lacey sticks out her chest for our appraisal. "Are mine so bad you would want to get back with your ex?"

"Only to a blind man. They're perfect." I purse my lips to give her an air kiss.

"She's right." Andie nods. "Yours are way better."

Lacey smiles. "I bet he thinks that every time he touches hers now."

The three of us laugh, and for a brief moment, it makes me forget about last night and Austin. Since I hurt my foot, everything has felt off. Then Vaughn and I broke up, and it's just been one change after another. But these two always make me feel better.

"So...what are you going to do?" Lacey asks after we fall quiet again.

My stomach tightens. "Easy. Avoid him forever. That shouldn't be too hard, should it?"

Lacey fights a laugh. "Sure, babe. No problem. It's not like you go to the same school or anything. Or have the same lunch. Or any classes together."

I stick my tongue out at her. "Not helping."

"You don't need to avoid him."

"Easy for you to say. You should have been there. If Lacey is scarred by Zach touching her boobs and then getting back together with Maureen, then imagine Austin seeing me mostly naked and then being tossed out by my angry mother."

"The girls at Frost Lake will be so sad when he announces his decision to remain celibate for life," Lacey says, laughing.

Andie joins in, nodding. "No kidding. You should have seen them during the soccer game. I watched one girl have a full-on fainting swoon when he lifted his T-shirt up to wipe his face."

That girl might have been me. I don't know what it is about him. He's hot, of course, but it's more than his nice abs.

"He's probably not stressing about it, so you shouldn't either." Lacey gives me a reassuring smile.

"I'm going to turn red and get all weird when I see him again. I just know it. I can still see the shocked expression on his face when I dropped my dress to the floor." I groan and walk ahead of my friends to clean another section of the gym.

"I have an idea," Andie announces. I turn in time to watch her drop the trash she's gathered into the big janitor's bucket and brush her hands off. "Follow me."

I give Lacey a questioning glance. She shrugs, and we fall into step behind our friend as she leads us out of the gym and through the school.

"Where are we going?" I ask as she heads down the hallway.

"You'll see," she chirps over her shoulder with a smug smile that makes me feel uneasy.

It's only when she pushes out the back door and I hear voices and the familiar sound of Coach Collins's voice that I realize what's happening. The soccer team is here. They're practicing on the back field.

"Andie, no!" I stop and shake my head.

"They won't see us," she says. "Come on. See him, let the embarrassment wash over you, and you'll be fine when you talk to him on Monday."

"This is a terrible plan," Lacey says, but I consider it. Maybe it'll help? Or maybe I just want to see him. Whatever the reason, I find myself stepping outside.

It's almost fall, and the cool weather is here to stay. I pull the sleeves of my sweatshirt down over my hands as the three of us veer to the left where the side of the building blocks half the field from view.

I stay in the back for added protection, but just knowing that Austin is out here has my pulse racing.

The girls' team is on the far field, and both teams are in the middle of practice.

"How did you know they were here?" Lacey asks Andie.

"I saw Rowan when I got here. He looked a little rough."

"Looks fine now," Lacey points out. The three of us huddle against the wall, peeking out around it.

I find Austin first. His cheeks are red from the wind and exertion, and his dark hair is messy for the same reason. He's standing next to Vaughn. Both have their hands on their hips while they exchange words. Austin gives a firm nod, and they jog down the field.

Rowan is pointing and calling out something I can't make out. While they wait for the action to begin, he bends over with his hands on his knees. It's the only indication he's tired. Otherwise, he has that same relaxed, nonplussed expression on his face, like he didn't drink more than anyone else at the party last night. And as soon as the ball is kicked into play, he perks right up without missing a beat.

We watch from our hiding spot until Coach Collins

blows the whistle and tells them to get water. The girls' team is also on a break, and the teams mingle as they get water. Sophie approaches Austin. A twinge of jealousy picks at my already wounded pride.

He says something to her as he bends down to get his water bottle. It's a short interaction but long enough for her to touch him and laugh and for Austin to smile back at her. He said he wasn't interested in her being his girlfriend, but that doesn't mean he's not going to hook up with her at some point.

"Well, I guess he's not traumatized," I say glumly and move back away from the wall.

Andie and Lacey follow me.

"Well, you saw him, and you're not blushing. How do you feel?" Andie asks.

"Like he doesn't know I'm standing here, so it's not the same. Monday, I'll have to face him and talk to him."

"Or not," Lacey says. "You could just avoid him forever."

She's kidding, but it sounds like the best plan I've heard all morning.

I spend the rest of the weekend watching TV, doing homework, researching colleges, and avoiding thinking about Austin. Mom and Ruby get back late Saturday night, and they're still sleeping when I get up on Sunday. Mom doesn't bring up Austin, and I don't say anything to her. She didn't punish me for the drinking or the boy being in my room, but I'm convinced it's only because she's been too focused on Ruby to remember me.

By Monday morning, I've worked myself into a full-on frenzy over running into Austin. I go to the art room and ask Mrs. Randolph if I can use her supplies to keep working on my art project. If I can finish my pieces, then there's no reason for Austin and me to get together after school this week.

I do the same thing at lunch, which works great until the bell rings. I know I'm not going to be able to avoid Austin any longer.

I feel the second he enters the room. Breathing is harder, and my skin flushes. I'm at the back, rinsing out the paintbrushes I was using, as he takes a seat at our table. I hide out there until class starts, then slide into my seat with a smile. I turn my head but don't meet his eyes. Instead, I look somewhere over his head.

"Hey," he says in that familiar deep voice. "Where've you been all day?"

"What do you mean?" I ask, feeling my face get warmer.

"I haven't seen you all day."

"Weird," I say, voice tight. "I guess we've just been missing each other."

I'm grateful when Mrs. Randolph asks us all to quiet down. She spends the rest of class going over the next section. We're moving from a drawing project to painting. She shows us some examples from her students last year, including one of mine. "We'll spend today and tomorrow on this assignment. You'll need to use your time wisely to get it all done, so focus on technique, not perfection. By the end of today, your drawing should be complete so you can paint tomorrow."

I get to work more eagerly than I have for any assignment ever. Out of my peripheral, I can see that Austin is flipping to a blank page in his sketchbook, but he's glancing at me.

"So how was the rest of your weekend?" he asks.

"Fine." I stand abruptly. "I need to ask Mrs. Randolph about something."

I flee, then spend the next five minutes asking our teacher questions about the assignment I already know the answers to. Austin seems to take the hint though, because when I take my seat, he doesn't engage again.

I work with the kind of distracted concentration that makes my hand hurt from gripping the pencil tightly. I keep my head bowed over my work, the hair falling around my face keeping me from seeing the guy next to me.

I can hear his quiet sketching, feel every time he shifts in his chair or taps his pencil against the desk in concentration.

As the class winds down, I start to worry about how I'm going to escape. We usually walk back to our lockers together, but it's at least a two-minute walk, and that's far too many seconds where he can bring up seeing me half-naked.

I groan and squeeze my eyes shut. I promised myself I would not even think the word *naked*, let alone reimagine that night. Now I'm doing both.

When the bell rings, I gather my stuff quickly. My pencil drops to the ground. Before I can grab it, Austin leans down and picks it up. He's wearing a confused smirk as I contemplate how badly I want my pencil back.

Slowly, he extends it out to me. I wrap my fingers around the eraser end, but Austin holds on for a few seconds longer before letting it go.

"Thank you," I say as I feel my face heat. "I need to talk to Mrs. Randolph."

"Right," he says in a tone that's not completely believing.

"I'll, uh, see you later."

He nods and finally goes ahead without me. I don't need to talk to Mrs. Randolph, but I do need to unclench my hand before I break this pencil and get a freaking grip on myself.

I take my time, waiting until everyone is gone, and then approach her desk.

"Hi, Claire," she says, brightening as she greets me. "More questions about the assignment?"

"No," I say with a small laugh. God, how ridiculous she and Austin must think I am. I have only a few seconds to come up with something else, so I go with the first thing that comes to mind. "Do you have any suggestions for colleges with good art programs?"

"You're considering art as a major?" she asks, crossing her arms over her chest and smiling.

"Maybe," I admit. "I'm not really sure what I want to do, but I like art." That much is true. It isn't exactly the same feeling as skating, but it's uncomplicated and peaceful.

"That's great, Claire. I can put together a list for you if you'd like."

I nod and give her what is maybe my first real smile of the day. "Thank you."

When I finally leave the class, Austin is still waiting for me. He's leaned back against the wall, one foot over the other. I pause when I see him. Panic washes over me.

"You waited."

"Yeah." He shifts his bag higher on his shoulder.

"Go ahead. I need to go to the restroom."

I start to dart away, but he grabs my wrist. "Are you okay? You're doing a lot of running off in the other direction every time you see me."

"I'm fine," I say brightly. "Just really need to pee."

His brow furrows. "If this is about the other night—"

Warmth creeps up my neck and face.

"I really gotta go," I say, breaking free and not stopping until I'm safely behind the door of the girls' bathroom.

Avoiding him forever is a lot harder than I expected.

CHAPTER SEVENTEEN

"What in the hell did you do to her?" Rowan asks as we're standing at our lockers at the end of the day on Tuesday. It's been another day of Claire avoiding me at all costs. We're talking all costs. She just ignored Rowan too, all because he happened to be next to me.

Lacey offers an apologetic shrug when I shoot her a questioning gaze.

Yesterday, I knew something was up but thought maybe Claire was just having a rough day, but this morning, I pulled into the parking lot at the same time as her, and she proceeded to stay in her car, pretending to be really into fixing her makeup, until I went in without her. She skipped lunch in the cafeteria again, and in art class, she did her best to pretend like I don't exist.

I should be grateful she's leaving me alone. I spent the weekend half-afraid her mom was going to make good on her threats. I don't know what my parents or Vaughn would do if they found out I was with a drunk and mostly naked Claire Friday night, but I'd rather not find out.

We play Stoutland next week, and that should be my only focus. It has to be. I can't bear the thought of screwing everything up after my family literally moved across the country for this opportunity.

"Nothing," I say. I didn't tell anyone what happened when I dropped her off. But maybe she did. "Have you talked to her?"

"No." He squints. "I've not seen her at all. That's weird, right? You definitely did something, and you need to fix it." I start to protest that I didn't do anything, but Rowan holds up both hands. "I don't want to know. Just fix it. If Vaughn gets word that Claire is upset with you, he'll ice you out again, and we need you in the starting lineup next week."

With a pointed stare, he walks away.

I blow out a breath as I lean my back against the lockers. Fix what? I don't even know why she's avoiding me. I need intel.

I get changed for practice quickly and then head to the far field where the cheerleaders are practicing.

Lacey straightens out of a stretch when she sees me approaching.

"Hey," I say, stopping a safe distance away, so I'm not in her squad's way while they warm up. "Can I talk to you?"

"Sure," she says, moving to me in quick, short strides. "What's up, New Guy?"

One side of my mouth quirks up, but then I remember why I'm here. "What's up with Claire?"

"What do you mean?" she asks in a tone that tells me she knows exactly what I'm asking.

"Come on, Lacey. She's avoiding me: ducking into bathrooms, turning and going the other way when she sees me. She even bailed on our group project last night."

"She ducked into a bathroom?" Lacey asks, brows rising.

"Yeah. She really had to go apparently."

A small snort escapes, and she drops her hands to her sides. "Just when I think the girl is too mature for high school dramatics, she goes and gets herself into a situation with her ex-boyfriend's teammate and turns into one of us."

"I don't follow," I say, trying to repeat whatever she just said in my head to make sense of it.

"She's embarrassed, genius," she says dryly. "She got drunk, took off her clothes, and threw herself at you, and then her mom tossed you out."

Hearing it all laid out like that makes me wince. She didn't throw herself at me. I mean, maybe, but I was ready to catch her. Is that really what this is about? She's embarrassed? I don't know why.

"That's it?"

"Claire isn't used to putting herself out there."

"She was drunk."

"Yes, but she's gotten drunk in front of *me* before and never taken her clothes off."

"It was no big deal." Except it's burned into my brain for eternity. But she shouldn't be embarrassed. She had to feel the chemistry between us that night. We were so close to crossing a line, and I was all in.

"I've told her that, but she's freaking out."

"What do I do?"

"I don't know, but you better figure it out, New Guy. Be charming or whatever. I'm really tired of eating lunch in the art room."

—

The next day, I don't even bother looking for Claire during

the day or trying to talk to her in class. I wait until art is over and "accidentally" leave my sketchbook behind.

Like I knew she would, Claire texts later to let me know she grabbed it for me.

> Me: Thank you. Any chance you can bring it by my house tonight? I really need it.
> Claire: Sure. 6 okay?

At six o'clock on the dot, I'm waiting at the front door when she knocks. I pull it open fast, before she has a chance to change her mind.

"Hey." My gaze drops down to my sketchbook in her hand. "Thanks for coming."

I open the door wider.

"I can't stay. I just wanted to make sure you had this."

"Did you look inside?"

"No."

She definitely did. Her cheeks are turning pink. I drew a picture of Claire in her dress from the dance. She looked so good that night, and I just want her to know that's the image I remember most from that night.

"Come on, Claire. You can't avoid me forever."

She says nothing, but she looks like she's two seconds from fleeing.

"Would it help if I took off my clothes?"

"Oh my god." She buries her face in her hands.

"Because I'm happy to even the score." My hands go to the button of my jeans. "You have to promise not to laugh at my Bugs Bunny boxers though. Wyatt bought them for me for my birthday last year."

She's still hiding her face and muttering.

"It's not a big deal." I pry her hands away so I can look her in the eye. "You were drunk and beautiful and...we'll never speak of it again," I quickly add when it's clear talking about it is making things worse.

"Promise?" she asks quietly.

"Sure. If that's what you want."

"I want." Her voice is still wavering just above a whisper.

"All right then. How about those Cardinals?"

The light in her eyes sparks, but her smile is slow to turn up.

"They're a football team in Arizona. Terrible. Always losing."

"Claire!" Wyatt yells from behind me.

Her gaze goes over my shoulder, and I open up my stance as he barrels by me and comes to a screeching halt, inches from ramming into her legs.

"Hey," she says. I try not to be too offended that her tone just shifted from tortured to ecstatic for my little brother.

"Wanna see Flash?" he asks her.

She looks to me hesitantly as if I'm going to tell her no.

"Come on." He rushes off, giving her little chance but to follow.

In his room, he leans against his dresser in front of Flash's tank.

"He looks very happy," she says and rests a finger on the glass. Flash swims by excitedly.

In true Wyatt form, he bounces on to the next thing quickly. He takes a seat on the floor in front of his latest Lego creation.

"Wow. Did you build that?" She looks impressed by him, and I feel a little jealous of my eight-year-old brother.

"I just finished," he says proudly.

"You built all these?" Her gaze scans the room. He has Lego sets on nearly every surface.

"Uh-huh," he says, not looking up. "Watch what it does."

I hang in the doorway as Claire goes to sit in front of him on the floor. She sits patiently and eagerly listens as he shows her all the cool things it does. She's more interested in his Legos than she's been in me all week.

"I am seriously impressed," she says. "I had no idea you were holding out on me. I love Legos. I used to have this three-thousand-piece Harry Potter set. It took me weeks to put it together."

"That's cool. My mom won't buy me any that are more than five hundred pieces, because she says I'm too little." He looks properly put out by that, then busies himself with moving his new Lego set onto an empty space on his bookshelf.

"Very important question," I say as I walk into the room. "Gryffindor or Slytherin?"

She scoffs. "Hufflepuff."

"Oh no. I'm a classic Gryffindor. I knew this friendship was doomed."

The shyness in her smile is back, but she stands and doesn't immediately jolt out the door, so I'd say we've made some progress.

"I should get home."

"Are you sure you can't stay? Mom ordered pizza, and then we can work on our art project." I also just really don't want her to go.

"I need to study for a chem quiz."

"Are you sure you're not just fleeing again? You're pretty fast with that boot. Guinness record level in fact. The way you sprinted away from me all week was impressive."

Her face flushes slightly, and she bites on the corner of her lip. "I'm sorry. I was embarrassed. *Am* embarrassed. I was a mess the other night."

"You were fine." Better than fine. Perfect, though something tells me she wouldn't believe me if I said it.

"My mom yelled at you."

"Not the first time a mom has chased me out of her daughter's bedroom." I chuckle. "Kidding. First and hopefully last." Although I'd be willing to chance it with her.

"Anyway. I'm sorry about all of it."

"You don't need to apologize. Well, except maybe for avoiding me. School is a real bummer without you keeping me company."

"I'm sure you managed." There's a challenge in her tone, and I'm a little bit happy that she sounds jealous thinking I might have been talking to other girls.

"Stay."

She drops her stare to the floor. "I can't."

I lean closer. "Did I mention I'm wearing Bugs Bunny boxers?"

She laughs softly. "I'll see you tomorrow."

"Promise?"

"I promise." She finally looks up at me and smiles in a way that makes my chest tighten. I am in so much trouble with this girl.

CHAPTER EIGHTEEN

ROWAN LOOKS OVER THE SEAT IN FRONT OF ME. "WHAT ARE you drawing?"

"Nothing, really, just messing around." I flip the book shut. We're on the bus home from Stoutland. We won, but it was close. I'm aggravated with how I played and the stupid mistakes we made as a team.

"Do you want to play cards with us?" he asks, motioning with his head for me to move up a row to where he, Hunter, and Blake are sitting, legs angled to the aisle, playing cards.

"Nah, thanks though."

He hesitates a beat as if he thinks I might change my mind. "You good?"

"Yeah," I say easily. Then because it's Rowan, I add, "Frustrated about the game."

No matter how many I've played in—hundreds at this point—the expectations for myself and others get harder to meet. At least for me. My teammate looks like he doesn't have a care in the world.

"We all struggled with their defensive setup. We've seen it, and we'll adjust before we play them again later this season."

It's a calm, mature response that gets a half smile out of me. "How are you so chill all the time?"

"It's just soccer," he says and flashes a grin, turning back around in his seat.

I don't think it's been just soccer for me since I was nine and realized that the better I performed, the more people noticed. Coaches, parents, peers.

I shut my sketchbook and put it away, then glance back to where Vaughn is sitting. He has his headphones on and sits alone. Getting up, I move toward him. His gaze flicks to mine as I take a seat next to him.

"Hey," I say.

He has his laptop open and is doing some sort of multiple-choice math assignment.

"Homework?"

"Practice test." He moves one side of his headphones slightly off his ear. He doesn't look back at me but asks, "What's up?"

"Stoutland was good. Better than I expected." And I expected them to be good. Since coming to Frost Lake, working with Coach Collins, and playing with top-tier high school talents had made me think we were unbeatable. Now I know that's a myth.

"They were ready, and we weren't," he says, still not looking away from the screen. "They're in better shape, work better as a team, and they have five seniors that have been playing together forever."

"And here I thought talking to you was going to make me feel better," I mutter.

He stops what he's doing and sits back in his seat. "Do you know how we've managed to win the past two years?"

"By being the best team in the state?" I ask with a slight smirk.

"Good teams get beaten all the time. We have a lot of talented players, but it doesn't mean much if we can't find a way to work together. They came at us strong tonight, and we didn't have that mesh as a team to deviate from plays and adjust."

Shit, this really is the most depressing after-game pep talk I've ever heard. Vaughn isn't exactly sunshine and rainbows, but I thought with soccer he'd be the most likely to understand this gnawing desire to step off the bus and go immediately to practice.

"I can't fuck this up," I say, more to myself than him. But since I've said it, I turn to him. "My family moved a thousand miles for me to play at Frost Lake. For me to win here."

"I hear you, but if you let one bad game get into your head, we're already screwed."

He's right about that. I used to let things roll off me a little easier, but now every chance feels like a make-or-break moment.

"Yeah." I run a hand through my hair. "Yeah, I know. I really hate being caught off guard."

One side of his mouth pulls up in the slightest smile. "And here I thought I'd been doing a good job of keeping you on your toes in practice. Guess I'll have to step it up."

I'm sure he means it as a threat, but I welcome the competition. Vaughn is the best guy on the team, maybe in the state. If I can play with him, I can play with anyone at our level. Not that I'd ever admit that to him.

His phone pings in his lap. As he reads it, his expression falls back into a scowl.

"Everything okay?"

"Yeah." He sighs. "No. I asked my teacher for an extension, and he just emailed me back to say that he's not going to make an exception."

I glance back at his open laptop. "I wish I could help, but I'm barely keeping up in class myself."

"I'll figure it out." He waves me off. "Or my dad will kill me."

I do not want to imagine how Coach Collins would react to his star player not making grades for the team. The fact that player is also his son…yikes.

"Well, I'll leave you to it." I get up and stand in the aisle.

"Hey," Vaughn calls after me. The stressed expression is gone, and he's smiling. "We'll be ready for them next time."

It's a promise that fills me with relief and anticipation. I nod my agreement.

—

Dad is home when I walk in from the game. He and Mom are in the kitchen. His suitcase is in the middle of the room like he abandoned it mid-step.

"You're here," I say, feeling my grin widen. I step forward, and we embrace. "I didn't think you were coming until next week."

He squeezes me and pats my back. "A couple of meetings got canceled, so I was able to get away early."

We pull back, and I look at him. His hair is grayed at his temples, and he's wearing his glasses that he used to say were just for reading. I know he hasn't changed that much in the weeks since I've seen him, but when was the last time I really looked at him?

"Congrats on the game," he says. "I heard you won."

"We did," I say, considering if I should tell him it felt more like a wake-up call than a victory, but I decide that I don't want to ruin this moment with all that tonight. So instead, I tell him all the things I've been holding on to while he's been away. My teammates, practices, working with Coach Collins. Mom has already gone to bed, and the clock on the oven reads after midnight when I've stopped thinking of more things I want to tell him.

His eyelids are droopy, and he covers a yawn. "I should get some sleep so I can get up in the morning to see your brother and sister when they wake up for school."

We don't have another game this week, but now that he's here, I have a thought. "Will you come to practice tomorrow? Some of the other parents stop by and watch. As long as you don't yell, Coach doesn't care."

"When have I ever yelled?" Dad asks. He's the quiet, introspective type, so it's not usually his style.

"Conference finals, freshman year."

"That was an exception." He waggles a finger. "That kid on the other team was trying to hurt someone. It was blatantly obvious."

It's true. That kid was out for blood and sneaky. The refs had a hard time catching him in the act. Still, the memory makes me smile as I picture my calm and collected dad on his feet with the rest of the parents, yelling and standing up for us.

"Let me see what your mother has planned for me in the morning, but I'll make it if I can."

I smile. "Night, Dad."

When I get up to my room, I change and get ready for bed, then lie back on my mattress with my phone.

Vaughn has already sent some video content from the game for us to analyze. Usually, I'd be all about replaying my performance so I can make adjustments for the next game, but Claire's name catches my attention.

Claire: I have some ideas for our project. Meet tomorrow at my place, six o'clock?

She texted about thirty minutes ago. Nothing else. Not about her avoiding me or the game. Maybe she doesn't know if we won or lost. Maybe she doesn't care. She hasn't wasted any opportunity to let me know how she feels about me and my soccer bros. But she's talking to me again, and that feels like the biggest win of the night.

Me: Sounds good. See you then.

CHAPTER NINETEEN

Claire

"YOU GOT THE BOOT OFF." AUSTIN PAUSES IN MY DOORWAY, stare immediately going to my right foot.

"Yep." I lift it off the floor. It feels light without the weight of the plastic and metal.

"Congrats." He sets his backpack on the floor. "You're all healed now?"

I nod, not trusting my voice. All healed is relative. They've done all they can, but the years of wear and injury will never be able to support the hours and hours of practice needed to continue my skating career. But I'm still glad to be cleared for normal activities.

"Have you checked off all your 'I can't wait to get off this boot ands'?"

"My what?"

"I remember when I broke my arm, I couldn't wait to get off the cast and wash my arm or toss a ball two-handed over my head or sleep with that arm over my face. All the things you don't realize you enjoy so much until you can't do them."

"I thought you hurt your foot?"

"I did that too. But the arm was worse. Fell off the monkey bars." He shoots me a boyish grin.

"I'm excited to wear two shoes," I say, because the other answers are too depressing. The only thing I want to do, I can't. That's less depressing than not having a bunch of other things on the list. My life was all skating, and now what?

"Fair enough." He grins as he looks at my feet again. "So what's this idea you had for art?"

Thankful for something else to focus on, I latch on to the subject change. I pull out all my pieces for the show. I still need to put a few finishing touches on two of them, but they're done enough to get an overall feel. Austin pulls out his portfolio, and I add his completed sketches to the mix.

He is so gifted. Each piece is stunning and interesting on its own, but together you really get a feel for his talent.

"This was my favorite," I say, resting my fingers on the edge of one sketch.

"I redid it, like, three times before Lacey gave her approval." He smiles and gives his head a little shake.

He did a great job capturing her. It's a side angle, in her cheerleading outfit. He really captured the joy and excitement that Lacey brings to all things.

The other drawings are of the cafeteria and hallway. Both drawings focus less on specific people and more on the overall feel of what it's like to be inside Frost Lake High. But in the hallway drawing, there are two girls side by side opening their lockers, and I can't help but notice they look a little like me and Lacey.

He focused on the inside of the school, and I did paintings of places outside. The front of the school, the breezeway between buildings, the cluttered gym closet, and one of our beloved Knights mascot.

"These are really good," he says, looking over my work like it's the first time. He's watched me paint most of them.

"Thanks." With them all laid out in front of us, I admire them but get the same nagging sense that they lack cohesion. "I love all the pieces, but when I lay them out next to one another..."

"They don't quite work together." He nods thoughtfully as he continues to stare. He moves them around on the floor like he's trying to see if the order matters. "Shit. Yeah, I think you're right. Maybe once we have them all matted, that'll help."

"Maybe," I agree. "But what if we did something together? Your sketch work with my painting."

We toss out ideas, some focusing more on the sketches with pops of color, others with a more detailed painting approach. Neither feels quite right. They're all too different from the other pieces.

"Something will come to us," Austin says when we're both frustrated and out of ideas.

"Yeah."

He starts to pack up.

"Plans tonight?"

"My dad is in town. We're going out to dinner."

"Oh, nice."

"What about you?" he asks. "How are you going to celebrate your ability to wear two shoes?"

"Oh..." I laugh lightly. "I don't know. I'll probably order takeout or something. My mom and sister are at rehearsals until late."

His movements slow as he zips up his backpack and lifts it to his shoulder. "Do you want to come with us?"

"No. I'm not crashing your family outing."

"Why not?" He shrugs. "My parents won't care."

"Thank you, but I'm fine."

"How about tomorrow then?"

"Yeah, let's meet up to come up with some more ideas."

"Not that. Let me take you out to celebrate."

I can't explain the weird sensation in my stomach. Butterflies do flips and twirl around, stealing my breath and making me nervous.

"It's really okay. I don't feel much like celebrating." I can tell my answer gives him pause, so I add, "People break their leg and tear all their ankle ligaments all the time. It's no big deal."

"Fine, then let's meet up to talk art ideas tomorrow night over food. It's not celebrating if we're talking about school."

"Fine." Another short laugh escapes.

Austin's mouth curves into a smile. He walks to the doorway and then pauses. "See you tomorrow."

"This is the best milkshake I've ever had," Austin says, eyes closed as he leans back in the booth across from me. His Oreo milkshake is gone, along with the burger and fries he ordered to go with it.

"That's only because you haven't had this one." I point to the strawberry one in front of me. I got brain freeze and had to stop halfway through.

His brows lift in disbelief. "There's no way strawberry is better than Oreo."

I push my glass toward him, and he leans forward, rubbing his stomach like he couldn't possibly eat any more, but then he drinks from my straw, gaze locked on me.

I wait for the verdict.

"That's really fucking good." The way his face lights up fills me with smug satisfaction.

"Told you."

"I didn't say it was *better* than Oreo."

I cock a brow in challenge.

"It's a tie," he says, then takes another long drink.

When he tries to pass it back, I wave him off. "You can have the rest. I'm too full."

"I guess that's a no to dessert then?" he asks, smirking. He pulls out his wallet.

"I got it," I say quickly. I picked this place, so it feels only fair.

"No way. I invited you. I'll pay."

"At least let me pay for mine."

"Nope."

"Why not?"

"Because."

"Because..." I wait for him to fill in the rest of that sentence.

"Because then it wouldn't be a celebration."

"I knew it." Laughter filters out of me. "This was supposed to be a group project hang, not a celebration."

"Titles aren't important." He stands. "Be right back."

He heads off to the front counter to pay, and I shake my head. It isn't the worst thing being treated to a celebratory dinner, even if the only thing I did is heal. To which I didn't really contribute that much. Bones break and heal. The other stuff is trickier.

"Claire?"

I lift my head, shaking the thoughts free and staring straight at two of my old skating friends, Lauren and Zoey. They obviously just came from the rink with their shorts over their leotards and hair pulled back. Seeing them steals the breath from my lungs.

"Oh my gosh." I get to my feet and move toward them. I hug each of them, and then we continue to stare at one another, happy and surprised expressions on all our faces.

"How are you?" Lauren asks and glances to my foot. "I haven't heard from you in so long. Gosh, girl, I miss you at the rink."

She hugs me again, and I feel a pang of guilt and sadness. Both of them were great about texting and checking in when I first got injured. It was me who rarely returned their messages and flaked on meeting up the times they tried. We never hung out that much outside skating before. We never needed to, since we spent so much time there.

I could have made more of an effort. The truth is, I knew seeing them would be hard. They're still doing the thing I so desperately want to and can't.

I feel Austin step up behind me. I open my stance and introduce him. They both gape a little, looking between us and getting the completely wrong idea.

"You and Vaughn are really over then?" Zoey asks. "We heard, but I didn't believe it."

"Yeah." I shift uncomfortably. "But he's doing good."

He's doing good? I have no idea why I say it. I don't even know if that's true. We barely talk, so all my knowledge comes from Lacey, who isn't exactly his biggest fan. Austin would know, but it's weird talking about my ex with him.

"And you?" Lauren asks. "Are you really not coming back?"

I shake my head. "No. The doctor says it would be too risky."

Lauren's expression is pained. "That sucks. I'm so sorry. I know it must be killing you not to skate. You were there more than any of us."

"I'm doing okay," I say, because while I do wish I were there, their pity makes me want more for myself. There has to be another chapter for me after skating.

"You should come by sometime," Lauren says. "Just to say hey. I know everyone would be excited to see you."

"Maybe," I say. Right now, the thought is too painful. I can't even look inside my skate bag without feeling an intense pang of loss.

"We better go." Zoey reaches forward to hug me again. "I'll text you."

"Okay." They move away, and I glance back at Austin. "Sorry about that."

"It's fine. They seem nice."

"Yeah."

It looks like he might push to say more, but instead he asks, "Are you ready?"

Outside, we walk down the sidewalk silently toward his Jeep. It's windy out and overcast. I pull my sleeves down to cover my hands and wish I'd brought a jacket.

"Here." Austin pulls off his sweatshirt. His dark hair sticks up as he holds out the wad of black material to me.

"I'm all right," I say.

"Take it," he says. "That way, I won't feel bad about making one more stop before I take you home."

That stop ends up being Wyatt's soccer practice.

"I promised him I'd stop by and watch him in action," Austin says as we walk across the field to where kids are taking turns kicking balls toward the net.

My smile loosens as his brother spots us. He waves with his whole body, hand shot up high over his head, waving back and forth, stretching him up on his tiptoes.

Austin and I wave back in unison and then take a seat on a metal bleacher. A few parents are set up nearby with lawn chairs, and smaller kids run around the sidelines.

We watch quietly, only commenting on Wyatt and the other kids for a while. They're pretty cute. The skill level is all over the place, as is their ability to focus.

Austin waits until I'm too enthralled by their adorable, chaotic cuteness to say, "I'm sorry."

"For what?" I ask, everything except this moment temporarily forgotten.

"For forcing you out to celebrate. I wasn't thinking. You told me you were done with skating, but I didn't really understand until back there. It was everything for you."

"You mean you didn't understand that I can't do the one thing I want to do more than anything?" I ask softly. "My only 'I can't wait to get off this boot and' is skating."

He's quiet again, and I appreciate that he doesn't try to fill the silence just to make me feel better. Not that it'd work anyway. I hate the saying "it is what it is," but it feels very appropriate in this instance.

I'm the first to speak again.

"It's not just that I can't skate," I say. "That part does suck, of course, but the other thing is, I don't have any other hobbies. I don't have any other 'I can't wait to get off this boot ands.' Aside from skating, my only other interest is hanging out with friends. I didn't realize before now how busy they all are. Lacey and Andie have cheer every day and lots of other hobbies on top of it, and I'm just sitting around waiting for everyone to be free so they can hang out."

"Yeah, I get that. I don't have a whole lot else except soccer."

"Isn't it funny how at such a young age, we're forced to choose between all the things we enjoy for the few things we're good at? Sports teams are competitive, which I get, but what if you really loved soccer and weren't any good at it? Do you have to give it up?"

"Most people probably do," he says.

"Why?"

"I think at some point it stops being fun when you realize the people around you are better at it."

"But you can't get better unless you keep doing it."

He grins. "You're not wrong."

"I get what you mean though," I say. "It's why I haven't joined anything new. I'll be the worst at whatever it is."

"And that bothers you?"

"It'd definitely bother my mother." I dip my head into the neck of his sweatshirt. His scent wraps around me, making me as warm as the material. "What about you? Are there other things you would want to do if you couldn't do soccer?"

He thinks for a moment, and silly as it may be, I'm thankful that he doesn't give me some bullshit answer to appease me. "I hope so, but I'm not sure if there's anything else out there that would feel the same."

"You love it," I say, knowing exactly how he feels.

One side of his mouth inches up, and those green eyes spark. "I'd play soccer all day, every day. By myself, with toddlers, in the snow, even if there wasn't a winner or a future in it."

The last part is hard for me to wrap my head around. My parents, my mom specifically, have always drilled into me that winning is important. Whatever you choose to do, do it all out. Be the best.

"But if I couldn't, then there are other things I'd try."

"Like?"

He blushes a little, and it makes me more curious.

"What? Tell me."

"I think it'd be kind of cool to be a stuntman."

I'm taken aback by his reply. It's so not what I expected. I fight a smile, but when his own goofy grin appears, I let mine loose with a laugh.

"A stuntman? Like in the movies?"

"Yeah. Chase scenes, jumping off buildings, all the stuff the actors don't want to do."

"Because they don't want to risk death."

His grin turns into a lopsided smirk. "I'd be a good stuntman, obviously."

While I'm still laughing at him, I'm also swooning a little as I imagine him coolly walking away from an exploding vehicle.

"What would you want to try?" He sits with his hands braced on either side of him. His pinkie finger brushes against mine. "What interests you?"

"I don't know. Everything. Nothing."

"I see you've narrowed it down," he says dryly.

"If I had it figured out, I wouldn't be sitting here with you."

"Ouch."

"I mean I'd be busy doing whatever amazing thing I'm newly obsessed with."

"What happened?" he asks, then looks to my foot. "How'd you hurt it?"

"Years of pushing through injuries and practicing too many hours a day." I shake my head. "I was warming up before a competition. I went up, and when I came down..." I trail off. It was wrong. Everything was wrong.

"I'm sorry."

I nod, throat clogged with too much emotion to speak.

His gaze locks on me, then drops to my lips. "Let's do it then. Let's find you some new hobbies."

His green eyes spark with hope. He makes it sound so simple, but I've thought a lot about other things I could do, and except for binge-watching TV shows, I haven't done any of them.

Still, I can feel how badly he wants to help, and I guess I get a little swept up in that too.

"How would we do that?" I ask.

My stomach flutters as he grins wide at me.

"Leave it to me."

Practice is coming to an end. The kids are huddled up, and the coach is trying to give them a few final words, but they're inching away, barely listening.

Wyatt barrels toward us, ball tucked under his arm. "Did you see me out there? I scored two goals!"

"You were on fire." Austin holds out a fist for his little brother.

"Did you see it too, Claire?" Wyatt's hair is windblown, and his cheeks are red.

"I did. You're sure to be the next Sam Kerr."

"She's a girl." He scrunches up his cute face.

"And incredibly talented. You would be lucky to kick like Sam Kerr."

He smiles at me but he still seems skeptical.

The three of us eventually head to Austin's Jeep and then they drive me to my house.

"Tomorrow, same time?" Austin asks as I open the passenger door.

"That depends. What are we doing?"

"You'll see. It'll be fun," he says and winks.

CHAPTER TWENTY

"I THINK WE CAN CROSS OFF SOCCER," CLAIRE SAYS, DROPPING to the ground on her butt.

"Can't blame me for trying." I wink and take a seat next to her with the ball in my lap. "You weren't too bad."

She shoots me a knowing glance.

"I could coach you." Again, I have to try. Claire plus soccer is like one of those weird mash-up dreams that combine people and places from different parts of your life and don't make a lot of sense. Fun, but not realistic.

"I don't think I could ever get used to people running at me and kicking at my shins."

"That's what the shin guards are for."

"It still hurts."

It sure does.

"How does your foot feel?" We took it easy since she just got cleared to start exercising.

"Good." She rubs a spot just above her ankle.

"All right then. Up. On to the next activity." I stand and take her hands.

She groans as I pull her to her feet. I don't let go when she's upright and our joined hands hang between us.

"I can't run anymore. I'm out of shape."

"This one doesn't require any running. I promise."

"Is it napping? Or eating? Those both sound like good hobbies."

"You're already good at both of those."

"I feel like I should be offended, but it's true."

The wind blows, and the end of her ponytail whips into her face, getting stuck on her lips.

Laughing, I drop one hand and bring it up to brush it away. We've spent the past hour together in close proximity, but while we were focused on other things, I wasn't thinking about how badly I want to kiss her. Now it's all I can think about.

There's a beat where it seems like neither of us breathes. She's waiting like she knows what I'm thinking and is curious if I'll do it or not. Or maybe I'm misreading it, and she's horrified and temporarily too stunned to move or speak.

I step back, putting some much needed distance between us. "Come on. We don't want to be late."

—

The lights are off in the school library. The windows on the back wall let in a smidge of light through the overcast skies.

"I think we're late," she says as I close us in, quietly shutting the door behind us.

"Nope. Right on time. Mrs. Finch is at a teacher meeting. We have the place all to ourselves."

"I don't even want to guess how you know that."

"I have my ways," I say, grinning. It wasn't actually

that hard. I have a study hour in here, and I overheard her talking with one of the other teachers about going out for drinks after the meeting.

"What are we doing here?" Claire asks, a hint of nervous laughter disrupting the silence. "Besides breaking and entering?"

"We didn't break anything." I wink, then pluck a book off a shelf at random and hand it to her. "And we're here to read."

"We're reading?" She glances at the cover.

"Yeah. Books. Fiction. Nonfiction." I wave around the rows and rows of books. Like everything at Frost Lake High, the library is big and well taken care of. It has that same musty smell that all libraries have though.

"I know how to read," Claire says, putting the book back on the shelf.

"Good. Now when's the last time you did it for fun?"

Her mouth opens, and her head tips side to side while she thinks. "A while. You?"

"Just yesterday. Wyatt and I are making our way through the Bad Guys series."

"Never heard of it." She grins.

"I'll loan you the first book."

Laughing again, she moves ahead of me, staring at the shelves. I follow behind, browsing her more than the titles. She stops and pulls one out, then turns to me. "Is this where you learned all your moves?"

It's a biography about Coach Collins. The picture on the front is of a younger him when he was playing for Arsenal.

I snatch it from her. "No. *Soccer for Dummies*."

"That one I do need to borrow," she says, continuing on.

"Can I ask you a question?"

"I think you just did," she says, glancing over her shoulder and hitting me with one of her sexy grins.

I choose my words carefully, not sure the best way to ask but wanting to know, even if it isn't polite. "Why haven't you gone back to skate? I know you can't compete, but you could still do it for fun, right?"

She selects another book off the shelf and then faces me, clutching the hardcover to her chest. "I don't know. I guess doing it without a goal or purpose feels weird. I liked competing. The nervous energy just before, the rush of adrenaline when the music starts..."

"How long have you been skating?"

"Since I was six. My mom signed me up on a whim, and I loved it. I begged her to let me take more and more classes until I was there every night after school. It's all I ever wanted to do." Her smile was dreamy as she spoke, but now it turns bittersweet. "Which I guess is why we're here. I found a book. Now what?"

We sit on the floor in the very last row, our backs against opposite shelves and our legs sprawled out in front of us, knees touching. She has a fantasy book, and I have the Coach Collins biography.

The only sound is the occasional flip of the page, mostly by her. I'd usually be happy to learn more about my favorite soccer player of all time, but in this case, it comes at the expense of watching Claire.

Her blond ponytail hangs over one shoulder as she hunches over the book reading. Her lips are parted, and her long lashes flutter as her gaze slowly moves from left to right. She looks up, catching me watching her.

"What?"

"Nothing." I turn my stare down to the early years of Jude Collins, but I only read a sentence or two before I find myself glancing back up at her.

Her lips curve in a shy smile when we lock eyes again.

"How's the book?" I ask.

"I don't know. Someone keeps talking to me."

I smash my lips together and hold the book up higher. I hear her laughter as I attempt to get lost in the book. My knee knocks against hers as I shift to get more comfortable. There are beanbag chairs and pillows at the front of the library that would have been more comfortable than the hard floor. But being back here with her feels like we're hiding together in an epic game of hide-and-seek, waiting to be found. The excitement, the nerves, the heightened awareness of every sound and the beat of my heart.

I'm not sure how long we continue to sit there—long enough that my butt is numb when she nudges my knee with hers.

"How are things going with the team?"

"Oh, now you want to talk, huh?"

She gives me a shy smile.

"It's good. Why?"

"Lacey mentioned that maybe the team wasn't so accepting of you because of the kiss and rumors around school about us." Her cheeks pinken, like maybe she's remembering just how good of a kiss it was.

"Eh." I shrug both shoulders. "I don't know how much of it was me being the new guy and how much was about that kiss. Things are good now. They've stopped making my life hell."

She looks appalled. "What did they do to you?"

"You really want to know?"

She nods and leans forward.

"It was mostly normal locker room pranks—taking all the towels and stealing my clothes while I was in the shower, hiding my practice jersey, swapping my cup out for an extra small."

Her mouth drops open, and then a small giggle escapes. Everything feels heightened in the quiet, dark library. Like how much I want to pull her onto my lap and kiss her again.

"What else?"

I'm so focused on her lips that it takes a second for the question to register.

"What do you mean?"

"You said it was *mostly* pranks."

"Let's just say they made it clear they didn't want me on the team."

Her expression shifts immediately, concern tugging her brows together in the middle.

"It's all fine now," I quickly add. "Promise."

We fall quiet again. She glances back at her book, and I do the same, not that there's any hope of me reading anything. I want to keep talking to her, keep staring at her mouth.

"Hey, did you hear that?" she whispers.

I lift my head and listen intently. I start to say no, but then Mrs. Finch's high-pitched voice breaks through the barrier of my current Claire fog. I glance at my watch.

"Shit," I hiss, scrambling to my feet and pulling Claire up to hers.

She starts to giggle a lot like she did the other night.

I can't help but smile as we crowd together, our books smashed between us.

"Well, this seems familiar," I say. "Hopefully this time, I don't get yelled at."

"Let me." She straightens, then laughs heartily like I just said the funniest thing. "I love that book. Have you read the sequel? It's even better."

She takes a step toward the end of the row and then motions with her head for me to follow. I don't know how I feel about this, but she's already blown our cover.

"No, I haven't," I say, not nearly as casual and convincing as she had. "I'll have to pick that one up."

We step out from behind the shelves. The librarian stands behind her desk at the front, looking at us over the top of her cat-eye glasses.

"Oh, Mrs. Finch," Claire says brightly.

"What are you two doing in here?" Mrs. Finch asks, tilting her head to the side. It might be my imagination, but she seems to be eyeing me specifically with a look of skepticism.

"The door was open, and I wanted to see if you had this one." Claire lifts the book.

Mrs. Finch cracks a smile, and the tension leaves her face, smoothing out the lines around her eyes. "That is one of my favorites."

"I saw it on your recommended reading list."

"You did?" The librarian seems surprised.

Recommended reading list? I look between them.

"Oh yeah. I look at your list every month, but this is the first year I've had time to finally read some of them. Is it okay if I check it out? I meant to come by earlier—"

"Of course."

While Claire steps forward, I stare at her, jaw dropped. She lifts her brows at me and practically skips forward.

I'm still staring at her in awe when Mrs. Finch's gaze slides to me. "And, Mr. Keller, would you like to check out that one?"

"Yeah. That'd be great." I move up to stand next to Claire.

"Oh, good choice." Mrs. Finch beams at me.

When we get out into the hallway and are several feet away, I look at Claire. She has a pleased smile on her face as she walks next to me.

"Impressive," I say. "Recommended reading list?"

"It's in the monthly newsletter."

"Must have missed that." I shake my head, then hold up my rented book with my coach's face on the cover. "If any of the guys see me with this book, they're going to give me so much shit."

She pulls her phone out of her back pocket and snaps a picture before I know what's happening.

"Yo, Disco!"

I swivel my head around as I continue to pull my practice jersey over my head. Today, we had a brutal practice followed by a conditioning session that had multiple guys throwing up. It was not pretty.

We had another away game last night, and you'd think from the way Coach punished us that we played badly or lost. We did neither. We finally found a rhythm. We were connecting passes, being patient with the ball, and staying in control.

Rowan walks toward me. His jersey is balled up in his hands. Vaughn is with him.

"You have plans?" Rowan asks. "We were going to grab pizza."

"Oh." My brows scrunch together. "Right now?"

"Yeah. Immediately." Rowan's expression is pained. "I'm starving, and the only cure for one of Coach's hell workouts is greasy pizza with extra cheese and pepperoni."

Vaughn has his keys in hand. "There's a place a few miles from school. I'll drive."

"I can't," I say, checking the time on my phone, then hurriedly grabbing a clean T-shirt. Practice went twenty minutes long, which means I'm already late to meet Claire.

I invited her over for my second favorite hobby: video games. Wyatt is almost as stoked as me that she's coming. She's good with him, and he adores her.

"Got a hot date?" Rowan asks with a smirk.

"Did you finally ask Jenn out?" One side of Vaughn's mouth lifts. He and the rest of my teammates in my English lit class seem to think I have it bad for Jenn. I haven't corrected them. Jenn is great, but my obsession with Claire has made it hard to focus on anyone else.

They're both already grinning and hooting without waiting for my answer.

"We're not together," I say finally. "I didn't ask her out."

They both continue to stare at me like they expect more of an explanation.

I consider telling them the truth: I'm meeting up with Claire because I'm helping her find a new hobby to fill the void of skating. But something stops me.

Maybe it's the thrum of anticipation that's been pulsing under my skin all day when I think of spending more time with Claire. Or maybe it's that I don't want Vaughn to get the wrong idea. I like Claire. I like being with her, watching her try new things. She's tough and determined, and she really hates losing. But that's all it is. As much as I have thought about what it'd be like to kiss her again, I've not acted on it.

And then there's Vaughn. Things are good between us, but I have a feeling that my growing friendship with him balances on a thin wire that would easily be broken if he knew I was into his ex.

"I have family stuff tonight," I lie.

"Ah." Rowan lifts his chin and then lets it fall into a nod slowly.

"Next time," Vaughn says, stepping over to his locker. "And, uh, you better get on it with Jenn. She's not going to wait around for you forever."

I chuckle, gut twisting with guilt. If he knew the only girl I was waiting around for was Claire Crawford, I don't think he'd have the same advice.

CHAPTER TWENTY-ONE

I GO OVER TO AUSTIN'S HOUSE TO WORK ON OUR ART PROJECT and then play video games for our daily activity. He picked *Mario Kart*, which was actually in my favor, because Ruby loves it and it's one of the few Nintendo games I'm good at.

I beat him three times in a row before he lets out a little grunt of frustration.

"Again?" he asks, but he's already cueing up the game for another race.

"No thanks. I think I'll quit while I'm ahead." I set the controller on the couch next to me. "I don't dislike video games, but I get bored with them fast."

"Not Austin," Wyatt says. "He once played *Legend of Zelda* for ten hours straight. He smelled so bad."

"Okay." He tosses a pillow at his little brother. "Enough secret sharing between you two."

Laughing, I stand. "I need to get home anyway."

"You're not staying for dinner?" Austin asks. He always invites me to stay, and I love watching the way his family interacts with one another. His sister doesn't say much, and what little she does say is clipped and moody, but his mom asks about their days, and Wyatt provides comic relief, and when his dad is in town, they all joke and smile more. It's nice.

"I can't tonight. It's my sister's birthday, so we're going out."

"It is?!" Wyatt stands on top of the chair cushion he was just sitting on. "I didn't get her anything."

"It's okay," I tell him.

"But Mom says birthdays are days to tell people how much they mean to you."

It's hard to argue with that and makes me love him just that much more. As much as I enjoy Austin, his little brother is climbing up my favorite people list.

"Why don't you make her a card?" I suggest, unzipping my backpack and pulling out a piece of paper.

"Okay." With no hesitation, he jumps off the chair to me and swipes the paper.

Austin laughs, those light green eyes glinting with humor.

"It's going to be the best birthday card ever," Wyatt announces.

"All right." I sit back down next to Austin, and he hands me the controller again. "But I have to leave in ten minutes."

—

I get to the restaurant five minutes late. My mom and dad are sitting across from each other. Dad looks stiff and uncomfortable, and Mom is smiling in that big, fake way that I know is her way of trying to make us look like a happy, adoring family. Ruby perks up when she spots me.

"Hi," I say as I slide in next to Dad.

"You're late," my mom announces, like I don't already know.

"They haven't even taken our drink order yet," Ruby says with a hint of annoyance in her tone. She is only eleven, but she has teen angst down pat.

"Sorry, but I had to wait a few minutes so I could deliver this." I set the birthday card in front of my sister. Her smile brightens as she takes in the hand-drawn card. "It's from Wyatt."

"Awww. This is so nice." She opens it up and reads it.

"Who is Wyatt?" my dad asks.

"He's my friend Austin's little brother. He's planning on marrying Ruby."

"Oh good." One side of Dad's mouth lifts. "I was worried no one would want her."

"Hey." Ruby's mouth drops in surprise, and Dad and I laugh. For the briefest of seconds, it feels like old times. Well, the good old times. There were plenty of bad old times too.

Mom and Dad spent most of the time fighting before they divorced, and when they weren't, Dad would hide at his office, probably to avoid fighting. But he has always been the softer of the two. He's fun and no schedule, and Mom is all schedule and zero fun.

"Hopefully I won't find this one in my house at two o'clock in the morning." Mom's gaze is pinned on me. She hasn't mentioned that night since it happened, but I should have known she was just waiting for the right moment.

My face heats, and my dad glances over at me. Somehow his disapproval always feels worse than Mom's, because with her, I expect it.

"It isn't what it sounds like," I say quickly before he can assume the worst.

"She was in her bra and panties, drunk, and had a boy in her room." Mom smiles at the server who has now approached our table.

I recognize the girl from school. I think she's a junior, but I only know her name is Cameron because of her name tag. She takes our drink order and then leaves us to our super fun family dinner.

"Claire Bear?" Dad says my name like it's a question, clearly still hung up on whether I'm sneaking boys in and having drunk sex.

"Okay, it's what it sounds like, but nothing happened. I had a few drinks, and it hit me harder than I expected. So I did the responsible thing and got a ride home. We're just *friends*."

"Friends do not hang out almost every night," my mom says.

"We're on a group project together." Although most of our time isn't spent on that anymore. I squirm in my seat, feeling uncomfortable under their scrutiny.

"You might not be thinking about him like that, but I guarantee he is." My mom has all sorts of thoughts on the teenage boy, and none of them are good. I settle in to hear how horrible they are for the nine millionth time. They only want one thing, and when they get it, they're done with you. I shouldn't waste my time, blah blah blah. She didn't even really like Vaughn, and he is every parent's dream.

"I got it, Mom," I say when she's done. "We're not dating. He's on the soccer team, and he's friends with Vaughn."

I don't know why I say it. Maybe as a reminder to myself.

"No boys in your room after ten." Dad leans over and bumps his shoulder against mine. "And no drinking. You're only sixteen."

"You drank in high school."

"Which is how I know it's a bad idea."

A small smile pulls at the corner of my lips, and I nod my agreement, or at least my note of consideration.

"That's it?" my mom asks, sounding incredulous.

Dad sighs. "What do you want me to do, Marie? Ground her for eternity for being a teenager?"

"Nothing. I don't want you to do anything. Let me be the bad guy, as usual."

Ruby and I exchange a look, neither of us wanting to be here.

"Happy birthday," I mouth to her while attempting to smile.

—

After school the next day, Austin stops by my locker.

"Hi," I say, pulling my backpack out and shutting the door. He doesn't usually talk to me outside of lunch and art class. I glance around for any sign of Vaughn. Neither of us has outright admitted we're still avoiding being seen hanging out alone because of my ex, but the knowledge hangs over me.

"Meet me in the breezeway in fifteen minutes," he says.

"Don't you have practice?"

"Yes."

When he doesn't expand, I ask, "How do you plan to be in two places at once?"

"I can teleport, obviously," he deadpans. "I gotta go. See you in fifteen."

"What am I supposed to do until then?" I ask myself, because he's already gone, jogging down the hallway toward the back field for practice. I find Lacey in the locker room where she's getting changed for practice. I'm antsy, excited, and a little nervous.

"What do you think he has planned?" I ask her after explaining Austin's cryptic remark.

"I don't know," my best friend says as she pulls her hair up in a ponytail. "The only reason I've ever met up with anyone there was to exchange homework notes or make out."

Her eyes light up with possibility.

"He didn't ask me to meet him there to make out," I say. Probably. No, definitely.

She looks at me skeptically.

"It's not like that."

She laughs, not even bothering to pretend that she believes me.

"Okay, yes, there have been a few moments." The dance. The closet. The soccer field. The library.

She's no longer laughing, but her lips are slammed closed like she's fighting it.

"But nothing has happened. The night of the dance was an anomaly. We're friends." I really hate that word, but we're not *more* than friends, so it's close enough.

"Whatever you say." She swipes her phone off the bench and starts toward the door, turning and walking backward so we're still face-to-face. "Text me later to tell me about your *friend* hang."

I wait it out another few minutes and then walk slowly

back through the school toward the breezeway. The halls are empty, but a lot of the teachers are still in their rooms grading papers or preparing for tomorrow.

As I get closer, voices filter in from outside. I stop at the doors and stick my head out to see a group of students sitting at the tables. I duck back inside quickly before I'm spotted, then peer back out to check and make sure Austin isn't among them.

"Hey." He comes to a stop behind me, making me jump. He's breathing hard, like he was running to get here.

"Hi." I turn to face him. He's in his practice clothes. A blue jersey with FROST LAKE HIGH SOCCER written across the chest, black athletic shorts, shin guards covered by tall socks, and soccer cleats. I've seen him in his soccer gear before, but I don't know. There's something about seeing him like this and knowing how much it means to him that makes him even more handsome.

"There are people out there," I say, hitching a thumb over my shoulder.

"I know." His grin widens. "Let's go."

Confused but too curious to object, I follow him out the double doors to the breezeway. There are four tables, two on either side of the doors. Students, mostly guys, a couple of girls, sit at two of them. It's only as we walk closer that I notice the chess boards set up in front of them.

Before I can tell Austin that there's absolutely no way I'm joining the chess team, he's holding out a hand to José and greeting him.

"You know Claire?" Austin says.

"Hey, José." I wave awkwardly, then shoot Austin a "what the hell" look that he either doesn't read correctly or ignores.

"José has graciously agreed to let you sit in on one of their practices to see if you're interested."

Someone calls for the chess team captain, and he holds up a finger to us. "One sec."

When he's gone, I step closer to Austin. "No way."

"It might be fun," he insists. "How do you know unless you try?" He opens his mouth like he's about to deliver another cheesy, trite saying.

"On this one rare instance, I think I just know." I might be willing to accept that I'll never be as good at anything else as I was at skating and even that there are things I might love that I wouldn't know unless I tried. But chess?!

"How are you going to be here and at practice?" I motion to him.

"I'm not." He gives me a boyish, hopeful grin steeped in remorse.

Then I remember what he said. José was going to let *me* sit in.

"You cannot leave me here," I hiss.

"José is cool, and the others seem…focused."

"Is there anyone in this school you haven't befriended?" I ask instead of running away, which honestly, I think should count for something. I didn't try chess, but I considered it for all of three minutes. I'd say that deserves two gold stars.

"We have study hall together. He's nice, and he promised to show you how to play as a favor to me, so you can't back out now."

"I know how to play chess. Kind of. I know that the queen is important."

He chuckles. "Good. That'll come in handy."

"I cannot believe you," I say and then give in and laugh with him. This is a terrible idea but also strangely sweet.

"The Frost Lake High chess team has gone to state the last *eight* years, and two of their players are among the top twenty juniors in the nation."

"That's pretty cool," I admit.

"Right?" He continues grinning at me, obviously pleased with himself. "Now, have you ever considered chess as an opportunity to try a new sport and make friends?"

José waves from the table. He is a nice guy. We had English class together last year, and he offered me his notes any time I missed class. Bailing will make me look like a jerk. Maybe it'll be fun.

I hold in a groan and glare at Austin. "I am so getting you back for this."

"For doing something nice?" He holds both hands over his heart. "Can't wait."

CHAPTER TWENTY-TWO

"I can't believe I let you talk me into another activity," Claire says as we step into the theater. The lights are on above the stage, but the rest of the theater is shrouded in darkness. "If you leave me alone in here, I'm never speaking to you again."

"I'm sorry," I say in a whisper, fighting a smile. Yesterday, she practiced with the chess team, and she's still grumpy about it. "Most of the other groups around school meet at the same time as soccer practice, and I didn't want you to miss out just because I couldn't go."

Onstage, the theater group is rehearsing. Two actors hold scripts, facing each other. They speak in tense, passionate voices. We walk over to the side where an open door leads up and around the stage.

"I was so bad, they all stopped what they were doing to help," Claire says in a soft, low voice.

"That sounds nice."

Her beautiful eyes narrow into slits. "Does it?"

Well, now I'm not so sure.

"Apparently I am an exceptionally slow learner when it comes to chess," she adds and gives me the same puppy dog face that Wyatt does when he gets in trouble.

"Aww." I reach out and take her hand, squeezing her fingers, then running my thumb along her knuckles.

"They were really great, but it was mortifying."

"We all start somewhere," I tell her.

"If someone would have shown up to an advanced figure skating class and didn't know how to skate, everyone would have ignored them." She looks like that bothers her the more she considers it.

"José is very passionate about passing on his love of chess."

"It shows. I almost agreed to join."

"Really?" There's something endearing about it. I like that she went along with letting them teach her even if she was embarrassed.

"No, but I did tell José I would help him come up with fundraising ideas, and I promised to ask Lacey and Andie about having cheerleaders at home chess tournaments."

That has me laughing. "José was working it."

"He's very convincing."

The scene onstage comes to an end, and suddenly there's movement from everywhere. People moving set pieces, actors coming and going from the stage, light changing overhead.

"Claire!" Andie bounds toward us with a huge smile on her face.

"Hey," Claire replies. "Thanks for letting us drop in."

"Are you kidding? We can always use extra hands, especially backstage. Let me show you."

Within five minutes, Andie has Claire painting a

backdrop onto a large wooden sign on wheels and me moving heavy props and nailing together a frame for another bulky set piece.

I'm facing her, a dozen or so people between us, but we make eye contact so often I find I'm blushing. I don't know what it is about this girl. She has me building theater sets when I should be doing homework or resting. We have another tough game coming up, and practices have been brutal. Coach Collins never yells, but when he cranks up the intensity, I know he's displeased with how we're performing. And he's been less than thrilled a lot lately.

When I nearly staple my finger, I decide to take a break. Claire has a brush loaded up with blue paint, and she pauses with her hand midair when she spots me.

A knowing smirk tugs at her lips. "Done already?"

"Just taking a break."

"We've been here for, like, thirty minutes."

"You're just painting. Andie has me moving stuff all around and building."

"It was your idea."

"Did you ever do theater?" I ask, opening my stance to watch the action onstage.

"No." She shakes her head. "Well, outside the plays Andie used to make us put on when we were in junior high, but our audience was mostly our stuffed animals, and they let me be in charge of costumes."

"Makes sense."

She continues painting, and I just watch her unabashedly. I don't get to do that a lot at school.

"Better pick up a paintbrush," she says, breaking me from my trance. "Andie's coming."

No sooner than I've picked up a brush, I hear her friend.

"Is the balcony piece done?" Andie asks.

"Almost. Just giving Claire a hand."

Andie smiles like she knows exactly why I'm over here. No use in trying to hide it. I like Claire, and I'll take any opportunity I can to spend more time with her.

As soon as Andie leaves again, I take Claire's free hand. She drops the brush into the paint tray, and I drag her with me off the stage to the side and behind a curtain.

"Where are we going?"

I don't even know. I just want her alone and all to myself. Out of the corner of my eye, I spot a pile of costumes, and an idea forms.

"You were in charge of costumes, huh?" I head for them, still pulling her behind me. I pick up a wool jacket that looks like something my grandpa might have worn in the seventies. "Were they as good as this?"

The smile that breaks out on her face is magnetic.

"I think that's actually from her dad's closet," she says, then reaches for a cowboy hat and sets it on top of my head.

I toss the jacket, then adjust the hat, pulling it low over my eyes and winking.

For her, I grab a gaudy necklace that is heavy and has big, fake jewels. Draping it around her neck, my fingers brush her collarbone.

She turns and lets me clasp it, then she swivels around. "How do I look?"

"Stunning," I say without a second thought. My heart is beating faster than it did running field sprints at practice. We're standing close. Her sweet cotton candy scent wraps around me.

Stepping forward, I lace my fingers through hers. Every

notion I've had about this being a bad idea is pushed away. It can't be. This feels too good.

"Austin." My name is barely a whisper.

"That's a wrap!" The booming voice onstage jolts us apart.

"We should get back," Claire says, turning away from me and taking off the necklace.

I drop the hat back on top of the pile, then we go to the front where we help them clear the stage, putting sets and props in the wings and tools where they belong.

"I guess this didn't end up being much different than art class," I say as I help her rinse out paintbrushes.

Claire lifts one shoulder and shrugs. Smiling, she says, "I still had fun."

"Me too."

We're locked in, grinning at each other, when Andie bounds to Claire's side and wraps an arm around her shoulder.

"Thank you both. It was so fun having you here. Did you see my scene?"

Claire's mouth opens, and then she nods. "Yeah. You were great."

She definitely didn't see it. Neither did I.

"I gotta go home and get ready. Are you two coming to the hockey game?" Andie asks, walking backward away from us.

"Oh, I completely forgot," Claire says.

"I'll be there," I tell Andie. "Wish Brandon good luck for me."

"I will." She smiles at me. "You should come, Claire."

"Yeah, maybe."

"Talk her into it, Austin. I'm counting on you!" With that, she jogs away.

"What do you say, want to check out hockey tonight?"

She laughs. "That's your idea of talking me into it?"

"It's worked so far."

"True. Promise me you won't secretly ask the coach if I can sit on the bench to observe them."

"Of course," I promise. "I wouldn't want you to lose any of your teeth. I like your smile."

She blushes, and it makes my pulse race. We walk together out to the parking lot to our cars. I bump her shoulder with mine, then let it linger. The backs of our fingers brush, and I link my pinkie with hers. "Want me to pick you up?"

"That's okay. I can meet you there."

"Are you sure?" The more time I spend with her like this, the more of it I want.

"It's probably not a good idea. What if Vaughn saw us together?"

Fuck good ideas. That's what I think, but dammit, I know she's right.

"All right. See you there." I will be counting down the minutes.

—

"Do you want to sit with me and my friends?" I ask Torrance when we walk into the arena for the hockey game. I was surprised when she said she was going to the game and even more surprised when she asked if she could have a ride.

She hasn't said a lot to me in the past couple of weeks. I overheard her talking to Mom, begging to fly back to Arizona to go to homecoming with her friends. Mom told her it wasn't a great time and assured her we'd go back for Thanksgiving, but since then, she mostly stays in her room blasting her music.

My sister scoffs. "No way. Please pretend like you don't

know me." Then she veers off like she's afraid someone might see us together.

Well, all right then. I head down the stairs, scanning the bleachers for Claire. I don't see her, but Rowan lifts a hand and moves over to make room for me to sit between him and Vaughn.

"I didn't know you were coming tonight," Rowan says.

"Andie talked me into it."

My buddy grins, then tips his head to where Andie is sitting two rows ahead of us. Or standing. She's up out of her seat, yelling, "Let's go, number forty-seven!" and holding a sign over her head.

"She definitely has team spirit."

"Oh yeah. She's been this hyped since warm-ups." Vaughn is holding a bucket of popcorn and extends it toward Rowan and me.

"No thanks." I shake my head.

Rowan takes it and proceeds to toss big handfuls in his mouth.

"I can't believe Brandon doesn't say something to her about it." Vaughn gives his head a shake. "I think I'd have to break up with a girl if she screamed at me the entire game. I get enough of that from my dad."

"I don't think he minds." Rowan juts his chin to the ice. Brandon skates by and waves at Andie, and even through the cage of his helmet, I can tell he's grinning.

"Ah, she's not hurting anybody. Let her cheer on her boyfriend." Maybe it's not my personal preference to have my girlfriend screaming nonstop from the sideline, but there's no question she's here to support him.

"When did you become such a romantic?" Rowan elbows me.

It's then that I spot Claire and Lacey making their way over to us. Lacey leads the charge. I'm initially too distracted by Claire and her short black skirt, long blond hair—down and curled—and those full, shiny lips to notice anything else. But as the world comes back into focus, I realize Vaughn has gone tense beside me.

Have he and Claire talked? She hasn't mentioned it if so.

"Hello, ladies," Rowan says, smiling at them both.

"You want to sit here?" Lacey points to the row in front of us as she turns to Claire.

I've gone back to staring, so when Claire looks to me, I'm sure I have a goofy grin on my face.

"Sure," she says. Her gaze briefly drifts to Vaughn, but she doesn't smile or say anything to him. He remains stiff next to me.

The girls settle in, not directly in front of us but to the right, where if I turn my head to look at Rowan, I can't miss her. They're taking off their coats and watching the ice.

"Yo, Lacey." Rowan tosses a single piece of popcorn at her. "Are you gonna join the one-woman hockey cheer team with your friend?"

Lacey picks the popcorn off her sleeve and tosses it into her mouth before saying, "I never cheer without my uniform. It's like Superman without his cape." Her lips curve up into a pleased smile. "Besides, they have their own cheerleading squad."

Just then, the hockey cheerleaders skate onto the ice. I spot Jenn among the small group and smile at her. Then I glance down at Claire, wondering what she looked like on the ice. I bet she was incredible.

There are only a handful of cheerleaders, but they yell and get the crowd fired up. They're no competition for Andie though.

Lacey claps as they exit the ice. Then we all fall quiet, watching the game for a few intense moments as the Frost Lake team gets the puck and takes a lot of shots on goal. Their goalie isn't letting anything through, and eventually, the puck heads in the opposite direction.

At some point, I must start staring at Claire again instead of the game, because it catches me by surprise when Rowan nudges me with his knee.

"Yeah," I say, blinking a few times and giving him my attention. "What's up?"

He laughs quietly. "Nothing, Disco. Nothing at all."

CHAPTER TWENTY-THREE

"It's so sweet," Lacey says as Andie recounts how Austin asked her if we could come by theater rehearsal. It's intermission, which is the only reason Andie's talking to us. She's very focused on the game any time Brandon is on the ice.

"It was. He even helped me move some of the bulky set pieces. It usually takes, like, three of us. You think I can recruit him every day?"

I laugh and shake my head. "Probably not."

"He asked me if he could bring you to cheerleading practice, but I told him absolutely not," Lacey says, grinning at me.

"What?" Andie shrieks in surprise. "Why not?"

"Because I still remember when she went to tryouts in seventh grade. She did one cheer and then said absolutely not and left me there alone."

"You were in cheer heaven. You didn't care if I stayed."

"You'd be a great cheerleader. We could teach you all the cheers, and it'd be fun to do it together," Andie says.

"I don't like the idea of being tossed up into the air," I

tell her. Which is true. The other reason I only lasted half of a practice is because I could just hear my mother in my head. She thinks cheerleading is for people who can't cut it as gymnasts or dancers. I don't agree, obviously. Lacey has a special something about her that would be all wrong for dance or gymnastics, even though she's great at both. And Andie loves cheering. It's a natural fit for both of them.

"What about the hockey cheer team?" Andie asks and nods her head to where the small squad is standing just off the ice.

The sight of the girls in their skates makes a whirl of emotions stir inside me. It's been months since I laced up my skates, but I can still remember that feeling, the first glide onto the ice. Nothing beats fresh ice. The smooth surface and the way the skates cut across it.

The cheerleaders skate to the center and do a cheer to get the crowd going. Their skill levels vary from good skaters to great. The latter incorporate some jumps and spins. At least two of them are good enough that I know they had to have taken years of figure skating lessons. I can hear my mom's voice in my head, nitpicking their sloppy landings or the lack of height on their jumps.

"They do have great outfits. We need to work new ones into the budget for next year," Lacey tells Andie.

Then they both look at me, and I realize I've gone silent as I think about skating and my mom. An ache has formed in my chest.

"I don't think I have enough pep for cheering of any kind," I say, which is true.

"Pep can be taught." Lacey bumps her shoulder against mine and gives me a look like she knows where my mind just went.

When the Frost Lake hockey team comes back out onto the ice, Andie goes back to focusing on the game and cheering for Brandon.

Lacey scoots closer to me so I can hear her over our friend's screams. "So have you found anything you liked during all this extracurricular fun with Austin?"

"The only thing I've realized I like is him."

Lacey looks like she wants to burst with excitement. She clasps her hands together, and her shoulders inch up to her ears.

"It can't happen," I remind her.

Her shoulders fall, and she cocks her head to the side. "It's been four months since you and Vaughn broke up."

"I don't want to cause problems for Austin."

Her happy expression returns. "Vaughn can deal with it. I mean, look at him. He seems fine."

I glance over to where the guys are coming back down the stairs to their seats. My ex is smiling, talking. By all appearances, he seems to have completely moved on. Maybe it's me who needs to come to terms with it. It isn't like I've been pining away for him, but there's this part of me that knows Austin is a lot like Vaughn, and that scares me.

"Come on," Lacey says. "You're making too big a thing of this. Let me prove it to you."

Before I can ask what she's up to, Lacey stands and moves up a row to sit next to Rowan.

"Let me get in on those nachos," she says to him.

"You're lucky you're cute," he says in reply, looking a lot like he doesn't want to share.

Vaughn takes a seat next to Lacey, then Austin sits on her other side. I can either move to the far side to sit by Rowan or sit beside Austin. Lacey's eyes widen, and she tips her head slightly to indicate I should sit next to Austin. So I do.

One side of his mouth lifts in a crooked smile. I feel a zing from head to toe. I like him. *Really* like him.

He holds out a bag of Skittles toward me. "Want some?"

I hold my palm out, and he empties a large handful into it, then steals the red ones back.

"What are you doing?" I ask with a small laugh.

"They're my favorite." He winks and tosses the red candies into his mouth.

As the second period is about to begin, more of the soccer team fills the bleacher in front of us: Barrett, the twins, Blake, and a couple of freshmen. They're talkative and loud, but I'm struggling to pay attention to anyone. It's like all my senses are attuned only to Austin. The brush of his shoulder against mine, the smell of his familiar woodsy scent, and the occasional smile he gives me when I chance looking at him.

Vaughn hasn't said anything to me directly, but he does give me a chin lift as the nachos are passed down and we make eye contact. I relax a little. It's chill. We can all hang out, and it's fine.

As the action on the ice starts up, I stop stressing about it completely. I'm still acutely aware of every move Austin makes, but I start to enjoy myself cheering on the team and sharing Skittles. He bought three packs.

He's divvying out another handful for me when Eli turns around in front of us.

"Yo, Disco. There's your girlfriend."

At first, I think he means me, and an icy feeling rushes from my head to my toes. But then all the guys look out onto the ice where the hockey cheerleaders are in a line and doing a school cheer. Carefully, I keep my smile intact and my attention forward.

It's easy to spot which one they mean when Barrett says, "I would not throw Jenn out of bed with me."

"You wish," Eli tosses back.

"She's not my girlfriend," Austin says quickly with a hint of annoyance in his tone.

"You two look pretty cozy in English class." Eli angles his body to grin at Austin.

"We were paired up on a project," he says. "That's it."

"Oh, and the library during free period?"

"Again, working on a project." Austin's voice sounds like he's gritting his teeth.

"Figures you get the hottest girl in class, and I get paired up with this idiot." Eli nudges Eddie next to him.

The twins banter back and forth, and nobody mentions Jenn again, but my mind is reeling.

The whole thing sounds so similar. I bite on the corner of my lower lip as I consider this new information. Is it possible I've misread all the signs with Austin? We've become friends, sure, but is that all I am? Have I been freaking out about my feelings for no reason?

Austin's knee bumps against mine, bringing me out of my thoughts. It could be an accident, but then he keeps it there.

"You gotta admit she's smoking hot, bro," Barrett says without glancing back. His eyes are still glued to Jenn as the cheerleaders take a seat in the front row.

"I've seen hotter."

The guys all hoot and laugh at him.

When I finally chance looking at him, Austin is smiling at me.

—

After the game, people leave quickly. Vaughn left the second the buzzer sounded, as did several of the other guys. Lacey, Rowan, Austin, and I walk out together.

"Where'd your sister go?" Rowan asks Austin.

He stares down at his phone, jaw tight. "Left early, I guess. She texted me a few minutes ago that she didn't need a ride."

Rowan bobs his head. "Are you still good to take me home?"

"Of course," Austin says, sliding his phone into his pocket.

"I can take you," Lacey says. "You're on my way home, and I'm taking Claire anyway."

"I live in the opposite direction of Claire." Rowan smiles at me apologetically.

"I don't mind," I say. "She can take you first, or I can call my mom and see if she can come get me. She'll sigh all annoyed, but she'll do it."

"Claire's on my way," Austin says. "Lacey can take Rowan, and I'll drop you."

No one says anything, so I nod, heart jumping around wildly like he offered more than to let me sit in his car and drive me the few miles home.

His Jeep smells like him: woodsy, like opening a cedar chest, mixed with some kind of laundry detergent or soap. He turns the music down after starting the car. Neither of us speaks until he's pulled out of the parking lot, headed toward my neighborhood.

"Are things with Torrance better?" I ask him.

"I thought so, but she didn't want to be seen with me at the game and then took off before it was over."

"I'm sure she went with one of her friends."

"Yeah, you're probably right." He takes his eyes off the road only long enough to attempt a smile.

"So you and Jenn?" I mean for it to come out teasing, but I'm not quite sure I hit the mark.

"Do you know her?"

"Not well. She moved here last year, and we haven't had any classes together."

"That's what she said." Austin nods his head. "That she moved here last year."

It occurs to me that they probably have a lot to talk about, having both moved to Frost Lake so recently. A feeling that is awfully close to jealousy surges through me.

"What's your project over?" I ask, staring out the window.

"We have to do a book trailer."

"What's the book?" I don't know why I keep asking questions about it. I guess so I don't seem jealous, but it's just making me more jealous.

"*Pride and Prejudice*. The whole class had to read it, and now we're making trailers to convince our friends to read it."

Of course, only the most romantic book on the required reading book list.

"We did this role-playing thing where she's Elizabeth Bennet and I'm Mr. Darcy." There's a hint of laughter in his tone like they had a fabulously fun time.

I feel hot all over and also cold and like I can't breathe. Austin comes to a stop in front of my house, and I fling off my seat belt to flee.

"I could show you the video if you want."

"That's okay. I'm sure it's really good." I need air. I reach for the door handle. "Thanks for the ride."

"Hey." He captures my wrist to stop me from getting out of the car.

I should smile and fake that I'm fine, but I can't manage it. Disappointment swirls in my lower stomach settling like a rock. It's hitting me just how much I like him and how he likes someone else. I should have just gone out with him that first night after he kissed me and then asked for my number.

But I didn't know him then. Austin is sweet and fun. He loves soccer and his family and making people smile. I know because he's made it his mission to make me smile, and I have, more than I can remember doing in a very long time.

"I thought you weren't going to run from me anymore," he says.

"I'm sorry," I say. I can't make any other words come out of my mouth. If I do, I'll tell him everything.

He studies me closely, fingers still circling my wrist. I wonder if he can see the jealousy oozing off me. If he can, he doesn't call me on it.

Instead, he leans over the middle console. His light green gaze darts from my eyes to my lips. My heart pounds in my chest, and my throat is thick with emotion.

I don't know what's happening, but I'm frozen. I want to run away, but I can't. Not when he's touching me. His thumb glides slowly over the inside of my wrist along my pulse point.

It's only when his lips hover over mine that I realize he's going to kiss me. Austin is going to kiss me.

"We shouldn't," I say with absolutely no conviction in my tone. I'm not even sure why I believe that. Because of Vaughn? Because we've become friends? Neither of those feel important with the way he looks at me.

"I disagree," he says. "Strongly."

Then he leans all the way in. My lips part as his press tenderly against mine. My heart flutters, and my pulse races as a giddy sort of surprise and excitement flows through me.

His other hand comes up to my jaw and skates across my skin until he's holding the side of my neck and guiding me through the kiss.

It isn't my first kiss, not even my first kiss with him. It's so much better.

His tongue sweeps into my mouth. He tastes exactly like Skittles, sweet and addicting. He's tentative at first, matching my hesitancy, but when the shock wears off, I urge him on by opening wider. His response is immediate, kissing me in a way that makes my head dizzy.

Austin pulls back, and his green eyes pin me in place. "Best idea ever."

CHAPTER TWENTY-FOUR

WHEN I SEE AUSTIN AT SCHOOL THE NEXT MORNING, MY pulse speeds up, and my heart flutters.

A bunch of us are standing around our lockers, killing time before the first bell. He comes to stand next to me casually, talking with the guys like normal. To everyone else, his choice to stop beside me probably seems accidental. But I know better the second his pinkie finger links with mine.

He doesn't so much as glance at me, and his body is angled so none of the guys can see. When the bell rings, I jump, and our fingers break apart. I gather my things for first period. Austin goes to his locker and gets his stuff, but once our friends have gone off to class, he steps back over to me.

"Hey," he says, his stare holding on my mouth long enough that I know he's thinking about that kiss last night too.

"Hi."

"Can I walk you to class?"

I nod, and we fall into step next to each other. For some reason, I feel almost shy around him.

"Are you free tonight?"

"To work on art?" I ask. He already told me last night after the kiss that he didn't have any other activities planned for us this week, since he has two away soccer games.

"That and I really want to kiss you again."

My pulse picks up speed. I want that too.

"Wait," I say, head spinning. We've reached the door of my class, and we both stop walking.

I was so caught up in everything last night and in him, I didn't ask about one important detail. "What about Vaughn?"

The happy expression on his face falls momentarily, but then that playful, easy smile lifts at one corner. "It'll be okay. I'll talk to him eventually. I don't want to keep it from him, but we have a team get-together tomorrow and then back-to-back games this weekend."

"I understand," I say. I can't help but feel a little disappointment that we have to hide. Then again, if everyone knew, they'd be all up in it, asking a million questions and giving their opinions, so maybe it's better this way. And who knows how Vaughn will react? His texts have stopped and he hasn't tried to talk to me again, but I still feel uneasy about the situation knowing how he treated Austin last time.

"I want to kiss you so badly. Right here. In front of everyone." The way he looks at me, I know he means it. He glances around and then back to me. His pinkie brushes against mine so fast and so soft I almost miss it.

"Me too."

"Soon," he promises, then hands me his sketchbook and takes off for his class.

I wait until I'm at my seat to flip it open. On the last page, he sketched a picture of a boy, presumably him based on the dark hair. In the drawing, the boy's heart is beating out of his chest, protruding against his shirt. I fight a smile and run my fingers along the edge next to the paper.

I don't see him again until lunchtime. I already have my food and am sitting with Lacey and Rowan.

Austin takes the seat next to me and asks how my morning went.

"Good," I tell him and then hand over his sketchbook. With a grin, he slides it into his backpack.

"I need a vacation," Lacey announces.

"Thanksgiving break will be here soon," I say.

Her voice dips into a whine. "I need a vacation sooner than that."

"There, there." I pat her head with a teasing smile and then, because I do love her and know she's been working really hard on school and cheerleading, I rest my head on her shoulder.

"We should go to Whittie Lake," Rowan says, opening his chocolate milk and taking a long gulp.

"What's Whittie Lake?" Austin asks.

Lacey perks right up. "The Whitlock twins have this family cabin on a private lake. It's this amazing property. Lots of room and right on the water. They don't like to throw parties out there because their parents are really strict about things, but occasionally they invite the soccer team. And very good friends of the soccer team."

"Oh, right." Austin nods. "I think I heard Eddie talking about it."

"Do you think he'd be into it?" Lacey asks, hope in her voice and eyes pleading.

"I don't know, but we have a free weekend coming up, so it's the perfect time to do something." Rowan sets his milk down and then shouts across the lunchroom. "Yo, Double E."

One of the teachers gives him a stern look for yelling, but it works. A second later, Eli and Eddie are getting up and heading our way.

While everyone else is focused on the twins, Austin moves his leg over until it's flush against mine, then drops his hand under the table and rests it against my knee. I feel warm all over and wonder if I'm blushing.

Lacey pleads her case with the twins, even promising to make sure everything is clean before we leave. She's very convincing when she wants something, and she must want this very badly.

Before the bell rings, they've agreed.

"So, are you gonna go?" Austin asks me after we're away from the group and heading for art class.

"Yeah, I'm pretty sure my sister has a dance competition in Ohio that weekend, so I'll be on my own."

"What about your dad? You don't go to his house when they're gone?"

"No, not usually. He likes to do his own thing, and it always feels like I'm imposing on him." As I say it out loud, I realize how bad it sounds. "He's just really busy right now at work. I'm going to spend Thanksgiving with him. We go to my aunt's house—his sister—every year."

I'm thankful when he smiles and doesn't press further. "What about you?"

"If you're going, I'll definitely be there."

—

Austin comes over after practice. My mom and sister are already home from rehearsal. Mom gives Austin a disapproving scowl as I rush him up to my room.

"Your mom hates me," he says as I close the door.

He steps into my space. The cold from outside clings to his sweatshirt, and that along with his proximity sends a shiver down my spine.

"She doesn't really like anyone," I say, realizing it's true. She's not even that warm with Lacey, and she's been my best friend forever.

I kiss him this time. All day, we stole glances and secret brushes of hands, and I don't want to wait one more second.

This time, we're more urgent. He backs me up against the door, both hands resting lightly on either side of my neck. I'm holding on to his sweatshirt like I'm afraid he'll try to run away.

I'm lightheaded, and my body tingles everywhere he touches me.

"Claire!" My mom shouts my name and then knocks loudly from the other side of the door.

Austin and I freeze, and then slowly, he steps away. My hand trembles as I reach for the door and open it.

"Hi," I say brightly.

She pushes the door wider with one hand and glances past me to Austin a foot away.

"No boys in your room," she says. "Especially this one."

"*Mom*, we need to work on our art project." Which is true, but I had hoped we could kiss a little more before then.

"You can do it downstairs at the dining room table or in the den." And because she's told me a million times not to paint in either of those places because she doesn't want me to get paint on anything, she adds, "Make sure you put down a sheet or something so you don't make a mess."

I know I'll never win this argument, so I nod. "Okay. Can Austin stay for dinner?"

She sighs like it's the biggest inconvenience ever, and I feel like shit that she's being so mean in front of him when his family is always so great to me.

"It's okay," he says. "I have plans."

Mom finally smiles, a tight-lipped curve with no warmth to the action.

As soon as she's gone, I shut the door again.

"I'm sorry about her."

"It's fine. She thinks I'm bad news, and to be fair, I feel like it right now." He fists the hem of my shirt, but then instead of tugging it, he steps toward me.

I push up on my toes and wrap my arms around his neck, pressing my body flush against him and kissing him again. Everything feels a little bit better when we're together.

—

After we finish working on our art project, I walk him out. He links his pinkie with mine and swings our hands lightly between us.

"Sorry about tonight. She's gone tomorrow night if you want to come back." I really want him to come back.

"What's the deal with your mom? Does she hate all your boyfriends?"

My stomach dips as the last word hangs in the air. "Did you just call yourself my boyfriend?"

"I guess I did." He smirks. "Is that okay?"

"Yeah, I like it."

"Good. Now how do I win over your mother?"

I laugh. It's hard not to. "If I knew, then we'd both be happier. Since I stopped skating, nothing I do pleases her."

"How come? You still have a lot of great things ahead of you. You might be the next great chess grand master."

I narrow my gaze on him, but another laugh escapes. "She's always pushed me to work hard. When I was skating, she made sure I was doing everything I could to be better. As annoying as it was at times, her constant push made me a better skater."

"And now?"

"She wants me to throw myself into school, take extra classes so I can go to a great college and become a doctor or lawyer or something else that sounds important so she can brag about me."

"Come on. She's not really that shallow, is she?"

"I don't know." I shake my head. "I've stopped trying to figure her out. You should too."

"If I don't understand her, how can I win her over?"

"That is highly unlikely. You're a distraction."

He lifts both brows, then kisses me, stealing my breath. I never thought a kiss could feel this good.

"See you tomorrow night?" I ask when we finally break apart.

"I can't. We have a team get-together at Coach's house."

"Right." And then the next two days, he has away games.

He leans in to kiss me again. This time, it's quick, but no less exciting.

"See you tomorrow." He doesn't make any move to leave.

"See you tomorrow," I say back, and then we continue to stand there.

"Claire!" My mom's voice eventually calls from inside.

"I better go." I kiss him one more time. I could easily become very addicted to his kisses.

CHAPTER TWENTY-FIVE

The Collinses' home isn't as extravagant as I expected, though it's still the biggest house I've ever been in.

The living room has a huge sectional where my teammates are camped out in front of the large TV on the wall in front of it. There isn't a lot of other decor: a clock, a large canvas art piece that looks like one of those you can get at a home good store, and a framed jersey.

"Who is Cooper?" I ask Rowan, nodding toward it.

"Not sure." He raises his voice and yells, "Cap, who's Cooper on the wall?"

Vaughn's gaze quickly darts to the jersey and then back to the bag of chips he's opening as he stands in the kitchen. "A friend my dad played with his first year on Arsenal."

I make a mental note to look him up later. He wasn't mentioned in the Jude Collins biography. I finished it in two days and returned it to Mrs. Finch, who proceeded to convince me to check out two more sports biographies: Arnold Schwarzenegger and Michael Jordan.

"Disco! You're on my team." Barrett holds up a

PlayStation controller in invitation. "Let's see your gaming skills."

I'm happy to sit down. I twisted my ankle today in practice during a drill. I'll be fine, but putting my full weight on it is uncomfortable.

For the next hour, we all hang in the Collinses' living room playing video games and eating junk food. When Coach arrives with pizza, we all disperse to the kitchen to fill our plates and then sit around the long dining room table. While we eat, Coach goes over the schedule for the rest of the week. We're missing a day and a half of school, leaving Thursday afternoon after lunch to take the bus to our first game, then staying the night in a hotel before heading to our Friday night game.

My parents aren't able to make it because they didn't want to pull Torrance and Wyatt out of school. I get it, but my dad still hasn't seen me play with my new team. Next weekend, we have another home game, and it can't come soon enough.

When I told Claire that I'd play soccer even if no one was watching, I meant it. But if I could only pick one person to be in the stands, it'd be my dad. It's his love of soccer that got me into it in the first place. He never played, except kicking the ball around with me, but he watched it and talked about it like it was this magical, extraordinary thing. I get it now, but as a kid, it was just a fun thing to do, the two of us.

Coach leaves us and heads upstairs where I assume the bedrooms are. I could easily get lost in this house.

"Where's the bathroom?" I ask Rowan after I toss my trash.

"Down the hall on the left." He nods his head in the direction.

I walk through the house, slowly, taking in the details. There are a lot of blank walls that make me wonder how long they've lived here. We've only been in our new spot for a few months, but Mom has last year's school photos up on the wall and art that the three of us made over the years.

I pause when I get to the first doorway, then suck in a breath. My feet move in without me giving them permission. There's a large oak desk on one side with one of those comfy, leather office chairs behind it. On top of the desk is a MacBook, a few notebooks, and other miscellaneous office supplies that I only give a cursory glance.

Because the rest of the room is filled with trophies and awards, signed soccer balls, jerseys...and so much more. A full-body tingle rolls through me. It's like stepping onto hallowed ground.

I read the name of the award and the date on each one. In many instances, I can picture the photos of him accepting them or the games that led to it. A lifetime of achievement, a career that any player in my shoes could only dream and hope for.

I pick up the ball with his Arsenal teammates' signatures. His final team. They won the FA Cup that year. I can't imagine going out like that.

"Hey."

I jump even though the word is said quietly.

I turn, ball still in hand, to find Vaughn standing in the doorway.

"Sorry." With a sheepish smile, I set the ball back in its spot. "I couldn't help myself. This room..." I turn and take it all in. Every team Coach was a part of is represented, the jerseys he wore, team photos... I could spend days in here. Weeks maybe.

"That ball is his favorite thing in here."

"Who could pick a favorite?"

"Wanna know my favorite thing in this room?"

"Definitely," I say. What can be better than a signed ball from the FA Cup–winning team?

A small grin lifts one side of Vaughn's mouth. He walks over behind the desk and opens one of the drawers, then pulls out a bottle of booze. Unscrewing it, he takes a sip, then holds it out to me.

"What is it?" I ask, stepping forward and taking it.

"Twenty-five-year-old Macallan. It's a three-thousand-dollar bottle of whisky," he says as I'm taking a sip.

The liquor warms my throat as I swallow. I cough at both the burn and the number.

He takes another drink and then drops it back into the drawer and closes it.

"I'll take the ball over the whisky any day," I tell him.

Laughing, he leans against the side of the desk, then scans the room like he's taking stock of something he hasn't seen in years. Too quickly, he looks back to me. "How's your ankle?"

I shift my weight and roll it gently. "Feels pretty good."

"Good. We're going to need everyone tomorrow."

"I'll be ready."

He nods but doesn't move from his spot, and I get the sense there's something he wants to say, so I don't go anywhere either. I could live in this room forever.

"How's everything else?"

It's an odd question, and I'm not sure what he's digging at, but I shrug. "Fine."

Nodding, he doesn't say more, but the fact that he's still sitting here says plenty.

"Something else?" I ask, prompting him. As much as I enjoy sitting in here, his silence is awkward as hell.

"Claire."

Maybe I should have been expecting it, but I wasn't.

"What about her?" I ask, feeling a warmth spread through me. Claire and I have been spending as much time as possible together. Walking to classes, touching when we think no one is looking, kissing while we should be working on homework. I can't get enough of her. And maybe Vaughn's noticed.

"How is she?"

I open my mouth to answer, then close it. "You mean... What do you mean?"

"Skating was her whole world before, and I know how tough it must be now that she's got the boot off but still can't compete. Plus, her mom is intense. She scares me."

A strangled laugh escapes. "Yeah."

"You've met her?"

Oops.

"Briefly. We have that art project and worked on it at her place a couple of times. In the dining room," I add, shifting uncomfortably under the weight of his stare.

"She's incredibly hard on Claire. Ruby, her sister, too. But Claire was her golden ticket. Since she was a kid, Claire's mom had her competing every chance she could, traveling all over. Claire was unbeatable in competitions. She's got the face and the talent, the whole package. You should have seen her on the ice."

"She loved it though, right? The way she talks about it, skating is all she ever wanted to do."

"Yeah." His head nods, but he doesn't look convinced. "Maybe. I don't think her mom gave her a lot of other options. I remember this one time, Claire wanted to do the talent show at school. I think we were in sixth grade. Anyway, no big deal, right?" He shakes his head. "Wrong. Her mom threw a fit. She made Claire feel like shit for wanting to miss one practice to do something else. She loved skating, sure, but her mom pushed her hard. Year-round curfews, diets, practices before and after school, the best coaches and choreographers, you name it. It was a lot. And that's coming from a guy whose dad used to wake him up to run five miles every morning during the summer." He gives me a rueful grin.

My throat tightens. I knew her relationship with her mom wasn't the best, but hearing it from Vaughn's perspective makes it all sound so much worse than I imagined. No wonder she didn't have time for other hobbies or interests. My parents have always supported me, but they never pushed.

"Anyway." Vaughn stands. "I'm glad you two have become friends. You'll keep an eye on her? Let me know if there's anything I can do?"

"You still care about her," I say. I don't mean it as a question, but he nods.

"Always. I love her. I'll always love her. I didn't stop wanting to be with her. I just couldn't be there for her like she wanted. You know what it's like. Soccer has to come first."

A month ago, I would have whole-heartedly agreed with him, but there's something about it that just feels wrong when I put Claire on the other side of things.

My voice is tight as I reply. "Yeah. I get it. My entire family moved so I could do this."

"Then let's fucking do this. You and me." He holds out a hand, and I take it without hesitation.

"Let's fucking do it." I follow him out of the office. "Great teammates are better than good players."

He arches one brow as he looks over his shoulder at me.

"It's from your dad's biography," I admit.

"Oh, right. He was talking about his last team with Arsenal."

"You've read it?" I don't know why, but I'm surprised.

"When I was thirteen, I read everything I could get my hands on, looking for proof he was as big of a prick as I thought he was."

I can't help it; I bark out a laugh. "And?"

"Aside from some seriously bad fashion choices and questionable haircuts, I didn't find much."

"The fur coat, right?" I ask, an image coming to my mind of Coach walking hand in hand with Vaughn's mother at some movie premiere.

"He still has that in his closet."

"No way."

"I'll show you sometime. Just don't touch it. He would definitely kill me."

"Over the ball?"

"He's a complicated man, Keller."

CHAPTER TWENTY-SIX

It's afternoon by the time I wake up on Saturday. We got back super late last night after our road trip games. We won both, and the entire drive back, the team was on a high.

In the kitchen, Torrance looks like she just woke up as well. She sends me a glare over her cereal bowl.

"Where is everyone?" I ask.

"Dad got in late last night. He and Mom are at Wyatt's game."

"Right." I spot the note on the counter.

A + T,

At W's game. Clean your rooms and bring your dirty clothes to the laundry room. And don't make plans tonight. I'm making calzones.

Mom

My stomach grumbles. We haven't had Mom's calzones

in forever. I open the pantry and grab the Lucky Charms, then shake the box. It's nearly empty.

"Sorry," Torrance says, mouth full of my cereal.

I'm annoyed but too tired to fight with her. I grab a banana instead and head out to the backyard. I pull my phone out of my shorts pocket as I take the first bite of fruit. At the far end of the yard, I toe a soccer ball. The cool air nips at my bare chest. I don't know if I'm ready for winter in the north yet. This time of year in Arizona, I'd still be wearing shorts every day and swimming any chance I got.

Claire picks up on the second ring.

"Hey." Her face fills the screen, and my heart lurches in my chest. "Just wake up?"

I get a glimpse of myself and run a hand over my messy hair. "Yeah."

Her laughter puts me at ease. Fuck I missed her. "How are you? What are you doing? What have you been up to?"

She continues to laugh as I toss out more questions. We texted a little while I was gone, but I don't feel like I've really talked to her in days.

"Things are good. I'm at Ruby's dance competition."

"I guess that means you can't hang out today. I was hoping you were free." I kick the ball up and catch it on the top of my foot.

"I wish I could," she says, and I can hear voices and music in the background. "I'll be back tonight. Probably around seven."

"I've got dinner with my family. You could come though."

"Haven't I crashed enough of your family dinners?"

"No."

"What about tomorrow?" she asks.

"Yeah, I'm free."

"Let's hang out tomorrow then. I'm sure your family missed you."

I know she's right, but... "Not as much as I missed you."

She laughs again, eyes sparkling and smile turning a little shy. Then she glances over her shoulder like someone called for her. Looking back at me, she says, "I gotta go. See you tomorrow."

—

Family dinner starts out nice. It's been a while since just the five of us sat down to eat together. Wyatt is tired from his games today and falls asleep within minutes. Mom carries him off to bed, and then Dad gets a phone call.

"No phones at the dinner table," Mom admonishes him.

He mouths, "Sorry" and then hurries out of the room. Mom turns her attention to Torrance, who has her phone out like always.

"Ahem." Mom holds out her hand.

"But, Mom, I'm making plans for homecoming with Kaylie."

"I told you we can't make that work right now." Mom sounds tired, on the verge of exasperated.

"But her mom said it was fine. I can stay with them."

"I'm sorry, the answer is no." Mom beckons with her fingers. "Give it. You know the rules." Then her stare moves to me. "Are you texting under the table as well? If so, give me yours too."

"I left mine upstairs," I say, holding up both hands where she can see them.

Torrance glares at me like I've betrayed her.

"What?" I ask her.

"You never have my back." Torrance sets her phone in Mom's palm with a huff. "I hate this family."

Mom's lips purse and twist. "You don't mean that."

"No. I do." My sister's voice rises, and her green eyes, several shades darker than mine, light up with anger. She stands and pushes her chair back. "I hate this family and this town. I wish you'd just let me go live with Kaylie or someone who really wants me."

She's gone with a huff, storming up the stairs and then slamming her bedroom door so hard the house shakes.

"Should I go talk to her?" I ask. It is my fault we're all here, and while I doubt she's going to want to have a real conversation, maybe she just needs to yell at me for a while to feel better.

"No. She just needs to cool down for a bit."

Angry music starts blaring.

"What'd I miss?" Dad asks as he comes back into the room. He glances to the empty chair next to me and then in the direction of the music. "Where'd Torrance go?"

"Her room." Mom sighs.

Dad doesn't press for more information. He slides back into his seat and reaches for his fork.

"Who was on the phone?" Mom asks him.

"My client finally got the funding approved for the site upgrade."

"Does that mean you have to leave?"

He nods, mouth pulling into a firm line. "Monday morning."

My head snaps up. "Wait. You're leaving Monday? When will you be back?"

He takes too long to answer, and I know. I just fucking know.

"You're not going to make my game on Thursday, are you?"

"I'm sorry, Austin."

I don't trust myself not to say something I might regret, so I get to my feet and take my dishes to the sink.

"Son, if there were any way—"

"No, I get it." I grab my keys from the counter.

"Where are you going?" Mom asks as I head to the door.

"Out."

I left my phone at home in my haste to get away, so when I pull up outside Claire's house, I contemplate whether I should ring the doorbell or try to scale the side of the house to climb in her bedroom window.

The light is on in her room, but the curtains make it so I can't see her. I pace as I figure out a plan. There are flower beds along the house and sidewalk, and they're outlined with small gravel before it turns to grass. I pick up several small rocks.

It takes two attempts before I hit her window. I wince, grateful when it doesn't break. I've never actually tried this, only seen it in movies. I can't even hear it hitting the window from here, so maybe she can't either.

But then, there she is. With one hand, she pushes the curtain to the side and comes to stand in front of it. I lift a hand in a wave. It takes another few moments for her to unlock and push open the window.

"What are you doing?" she asks in a hushed voice, just loud enough for me to hear.

"Still want to hang out?"

Her smile alone makes the sting of my dad leaving again lessen. "Meet me at the door in the back of the house." She motions for me to go around the side.

By the time I get there, she's waiting for me.

"My mom's not here, but my sister is in the living room," she whispers and then holds a finger to her lips. She grabs my hand, and we quietly move up the stairs to her room. When she shuts the door, she laughs and wraps her arms around my neck. "I thought you were busy tonight."

"I couldn't wait to see you." I kiss her.

She giggles into my mouth, and our teeth clink lightly. My hands go to her hips. She's wearing a big, baggy T-shirt, and when I slip my fingers underneath the hem, they brush against her soft shorts that are several inches shorter than the shirt.

Our kisses grow more insistent. She pulls on my neck like she's trying to bring me closer. Leaning down slightly, I pick her up and then walk back to the bed. We fall onto it together, laughing again.

"I like you," I say, brushing a piece of hair that's fallen into her face back behind her ear.

"I like you too."

The words don't feel like enough.

We make out until we're both breathless and my head swims with only thoughts of her. Her smile, her laugh, her taste. I'd give up just about anything right now to stay in this moment.

My hand skims up her ribs to the side of her bra. She stills, then nods slowly. "It's okay."

"Tell me if you want me to stop."

She nods again.

My fingers slowly graze along the soft material until my

palm is covering her breast. My gaze stays locked on hers. I want to see every reaction from her. It's not the first time I've felt up a girl, but my chest tightens like it never has. As I explore her, Claire's lashes flutter closed, and she arches into me slightly. But her lips stay curved into a smile.

I am so far gone for this girl. The realization makes a lump form in my throat. Everything feels different and better and also just…bigger, like there's no going back.

She's sweet but tough. Her heart is big, but she's careful about who she lets in. She is someone who has known incredible joy and great heartbreak, and it's shaped her into this extraordinary person that I can't imagine my life without.

Being with Claire feels like a milestone that can't be undone. I'm sure she'd think I was exaggerating if I said any of that out loud, so instead, I bring my mouth to hers and say, "I *really* like you."

CHAPTER TWENTY-SEVEN

LACEY AND I ARE SITTING ON MY BED, FACING EACH OTHER, laptops and notebooks spread out around us.

I hum along with the music playing on Lacey's phone as I pull out my notes for chemistry. We've reached the point in the semester where the teachers are piling on homework and all the tests seem to fall on the same week. I have no idea how Lacey is managing. My regular classes are kicking my butt, and she's in all AP.

When I glance up to check on her, Lacey is grinning at me. I stop singing and hesitantly smile back. "What?"

"You're smiling…like kind of a lot."

"I'm smiling *back* at you."

"You are smiling as you do homework."

"So are you," I insist, laughing a little. I so do not get her point.

"Yeah, but that's normal for me. You usually scowl more and insist we take snack breaks."

"Ooh, good idea." I get up and walk over to my desk. Opening the first drawer, I grab a small bag of chocolate chip cookies and hold it up. "Want one?"

"Do you have any Oreos left?" She unfolds her legs and walks over to me. "And would all this smiling have anything to do with Austin?"

"Maybe," I admit. I rifle through the drawer, then say, "No Oreos. My studying junk food drawer is nearly empty."

She peers in and frowns, then takes a bag of the chocolate chip cookies. I turn to lean against the desk as I pop one in my mouth.

"Umm, excuse me," Lacey says, giggling and digging into the drawer again. "What is this?" She holds up a condom between her thumb and pointer finger.

My face heats, and I rip it out of her hands, toss it back in the drawer, and slam it shut. "It's a condom. Duh. Did your dad not have the safe sex talk with you?"

With a snort, she shakes her head. "He handed me a book about the female body and told me I could always ask him anything."

"It's better than the 'Boyfriends are a distraction to achieving your goals. They're selfish and they only want one thing,' talk I got from my mom when I started dating Vaughn." To be fair, she had been right about the selfish part.

"Back up. Are you and Austin sleeping together?"

"No." I quickly shake my head. "Andie gave it to me as sort of a joke."

"But you want to sleep with him?" She studies me closely, and my blush increases.

"Yeah. Maybe. I'm not sure."

"That does not sound convincing enough to be hoarding condoms."

"Condom. One singular. And I don't even know that I'll use it."

She takes her cookies back to the bed and sits quietly. Silence hangs between us.

"Wow," she says finally. "I knew you really liked him, but this is big."

"I do. I really, *really* like him," I say, taking a seat back in front of her. "I know it's cliché, but everything feels so perfect." Emotion makes my chest feel tight.

"Babe, nothing is perfect."

"I know that, but it feels perfect. All I want to do is talk to and kiss him for hours." It's only been a few weeks, but I've been falling for him for so much longer.

"And let him put his dick inside you." One of her dark brows rises, and she aims a smirk right at me.

"Oh my god!" I toss a cookie at her.

She finally laughs, and the tight feeling in my chest loosens.

"I don't want to see you get hurt again. I like Austin, but all the sneaking around..."

"It's just for now."

She doesn't look convinced. "In a way, it feels like he's pulling a Vaughn."

My lips part, and I have a sudden rush of defensiveness.

She continues, "You're not telling people because it's what is good for him. What about what's good for you?"

"Do I want to hold his hand walking down the hall? Yes, of course. But it's not forever. He's going to tell Vaughn when the time is right. Besides, it's kind of fun keeping it hidden from everyone. Secret looks, brushes of hands, kisses in dark corners." Heat pools low in my stomach.

"Forbidden love." She sighs dramatically. "Promise me that you'll really think about it before sleeping with him? It should be what you want."

"I promise."

"And one other thing." A hint of insecurity flashes in her eyes, and her voice loses the usual spark as she says, "Promise me we'll still hang out even if you and Austin start banging and spending all your free time together? I can't protect you if I don't know what's happening."

"Are you kidding me? You're never getting rid of me. I will always make time for you. Always," I vow. "But I'm okay. Better than I've been in months."

"Claire!" my mom yells from downstairs. "That boy is here."

"She means Austin," I say, getting to my feet. A smile stretches wide across my face. "He's dropping by to get his sketchbook."

Lacey snorts a laugh. "I see your mom is really starting to warm up to him."

I hear Austin's low voice greeting my mom and then his footsteps as he comes up the stairs.

My door is cracked open, but I fling it wider as he comes into sight. My stomach flips, and my pulse races. His dark hair is still wet from a shower after practice, and I can smell his familiar body wash.

"Hi," I say, voice breathy with excitement.

"Hey." He leans in to kiss me. After his lips swipe over mine, he looks to Lacey. "Hey, Lacey."

"New Guy." She stands and gathers her stuff into her backpack.

"You don't have to go," I tell her.

"I should check on my dad anyway. Make sure he eats dinner." Glancing at Austin, she explains, "He has a tendency to get so wrapped up in his work he loses track of everything else."

If I didn't know it was true, I'd think she was exaggerating.

Austin links our pinkie fingers, and once Lacey has all her stuff, she walks over, stepping into his space. Both of his brows lift, but he doesn't move back or say anything.

"If you hurt her, I will glitter bomb you every day until graduation."

"Always with the glitter," he mutters, then nods. "I won't hurt her."

"Good." Lacey smiles brightly, like she didn't just threaten my boyfriend. "See you guys tomorrow!"

As soon as she's gone, Austin turns to me with an amused grin that looks maybe a hint nervous.

"I'm a little afraid of her."

"I think that's her plan."

He circles an arm around my waist and pulls me to him. His head drops so he can press his mouth to mine. I melt into him, kissing him back and losing myself to his touch and the warmth spreading through me.

When he pulls back, my head is light and fuzzy. He takes my hand and pulls me to the bed.

He leans back, resting on his elbow and foot hanging off the bed. "How was the rest of your day?"

"Good." I get his sketchbook from my desk. His face lights up as I walk toward him with it in hand. As soon as I give it to him, he flips to the last used page.

His head falls back, and he laughs. I glance at the rough drawing. I'm not nearly as talented as him when it comes to sketching, but I managed to draw a decent-looking scene with a boy (him) and girl (me) playing chess, in which I'm winning. I even drew a bubble over my head that says "Checkmate!"

"This is great," he says. "I love it."

I climb onto the bed next to him. He sets the sketchbook aside and lies back, looking over at me.

"How was practice?" I ask.

"Tiring but good." He gets a goofy grin on his face any time he talks about soccer, and he's doing it now. "I am meeting up with Vaughn and Rowan in twenty minutes to watch some game video of the team we play next week."

The mention of Vaughn makes me wonder if Austin has thought any more about telling him. "Should we make a plan on when to tell Vaughn and everyone else about us?"

"If it means I can start kissing you any time I want, then yes." He leans in and brushes his lips over mine.

"This weekend is out," I say. A bunch of us are going to Whittie Lake and if Vaughn did take it badly, it'd put a damper on the whole trip.

He nods, looking deep in thought. "We have games pretty much nonstop until the end of the season."

It turns out there is no good time.

"How about after the season?" I suggest.

"You want to wait that long?" He seems surprised by that.

"I don't want to risk Vaughn trying to make things difficult for you. Plus, it's not that long. Conference championships are in a few weeks."

"Yeah, but then there's still another month after that until state. I really want to still be playing in November." One corner of his mouth lifts.

"You will," I say. "And after you win state, we'll celebrate. Together."

CHAPTER TWENTY-EIGHT

It's a forty-five-minute drive to Whittie Lake from Frost Lake, and the perfect distance for a weekend trip with no parents and no one checking up on us for the next twenty-four hours.

We drive up in a bunch of different vehicles early Saturday morning. I'm in the passenger seat of Lacey's Bronco. Ashley and Rachel are following us. Ashley is dating one of the twins and Rachel has been talking to Hunter.

We have the windows down even though it's overcast and chilly. We're singing along with the radio, sunglasses on, hair blowing, and smiles on our faces.

Austin was riding with Rowan. A text from him lights up my screen, and I wrangle my hair out of my face to read it.

"The guys just got there," I say, raising my voice over the noise, then return my gaze to keep staring at the selfie he sent along with his text that they had arrived. His dark hair is covered by a white hat that makes it hard to see his eyes, but he's got that crooked grin aimed at the camera, and the lake is in the background.

My excitement builds with each mile marker we pass. Within fifteen minutes, we're pulling up behind Rowan's truck.

Austin is waiting in the open garage. Lacey glances over at me with a smirk but doesn't say anything. Austin and I haven't told people we're...kissing. A lot. Like every possible second we can.

Lacey knows, of course, and I suspect Rowan has his suspicions if Austin hasn't outright told him, but otherwise it still feels like this new, secret, and exciting thing. I like him more than I've ever liked anyone. We're having a blast together. Vaughn and I understood each other, and we were compatible in a lot of ways, but it was never this fun.

"I'm gonna go scope out the rooms and make sure I get a good one for the night," Lacey calls, pushing her sunglasses up to the top of her head. "I am not sleeping on the floor."

"Ooh, us too." The other two girls hurry after her.

"Disco, use those muscles for something productive and help Claire with the bags?" Lacey winks at him before disappearing into the house with the girls trailing behind her.

Austin shakes his head, laughing softly as I shut the car door and walk toward him.

"She's something."

"At least she isn't calling you New Guy anymore."

"True." He links his pinkie finger with mine and squeezes. "Hey."

"Hi."

My face warms, and the urge to kiss him is so strong.

"Are there a lot of bags?" he asks.

"What do you think?"

"You know it's only one night."

"You'll be thanking us when you're hungry later."

Together, Austin and I get all the grocery bags and take them inside. The boys are all gathered in the kitchen, and as soon as we set the groceries down, they're digging in and ripping open chip bags.

"Told you," I say to Austin.

—

The day is spent mostly outside. The boys kick a soccer ball around in the grass and alternate trying to push one another into the lake in between. The girls sit on the deck talking, watching them, and occasionally getting involved in the plot to throw people into the lake madness.

As it starts to get dark, more people arrive at the lake house. Some of the football guys couldn't make it until after practice, same for the hockey team. Suddenly the yard and the deck are filled with people. The music is turned up, and coolers are set up everywhere.

"Bet you're glad I grabbed us a bed about now," Lacey says as she quickly pulls her feet in to avoid being trampled by two guys wrestling.

We're sitting on a towel in the yard. Austin is still playing soccer. They're mostly just messing around, I think. They stopped playing for real hours ago, but it's like they just can't help themselves. There's a ball, so they've got to kick it.

"So, Claire..." Rachel leans over from the other side of Lacey. She has a wicked glint in her eye and a smile that tells me she has something juicy to say. "What's the deal with Austin?"

My heart rate picks up. "What do you mean?"

"Does he like anyone?"

"How would I know?" My voice is tight as I try to play it off as coolly as possible.

"You two are friends," Rachel says, leaning farther so I can see the excitement in her eyes as she tries to get the dirt. "Don't hold out on us. Has he mentioned anything to you? Is he talking to anyone?"

"I heard that he's into that girl from the hockey cheer team, Jenn something or other."

The four of us all glance over where Jenn is standing. She and a couple of her friends came with guys from the hockey team. We're still watching as Austin jogs by them with the ball and Jenn glances up and stares at him with a smile on her lips.

"No." Lacey shakes her head. "We were sitting with him at the hockey game when the guys asked him, and he said they're just friends."

"Are we sure he's into girls, because he's friends with her and friends with Claire..." Rachel waves her hand toward me. "They're, like, the hottest girls at Frost Lake."

I feel the blush creeping up my neck.

"Disco!" Lacey yells for him.

He stops jogging and looks over at us. My best friend waves him over.

"What are you doing?" I whisper, feeling a slight panic.

She gives me an "it's no big thing" smile right before Austin comes to a stop in front of us.

"What's up?" he asks. He's turned his hat backward, and he's a little out of breath.

"Sit. Answer some questions for us."

He cocks one brow but does as she says.

"Keller," Vaughn calls from the game and then stands there expectantly.

"I'm out for a while," Austin says. He looks at Lacey. "This is going to take a while, right?"

"Smart guy." My best friend pats the ground.

I'm still uneasy about whatever she's going to ask him, but I can't deny that it feels good to be sitting near him. His gaze drops to my drink.

"Thirsty?" I ask and hold it up to him.

"Thanks." He chugs it, then makes a face. "What was that?"

"Lacey made it."

"It's my secret party drink. Grape soda mixed with a small amount of alcohol so you feel a buzz but not so much that we're puking before dark."

He chuckles softly and passes the drink back to me. Our fingers brush during the handoff, and we hold eye contact a beat longer.

"So…Austin," Lacey starts like she's about to ask him the most serious of questions. "Blond or brunette?"

His smile remains as he considers the question. "That's too limiting. There is a rainbow of colors, and I like them all."

"Okay. Boobs or ass?"

"What is happening right now?" He looks to me for help.

"I have no idea."

Rachel tosses her hair over one shoulder. "We're trying to get an idea of your preferences. You've been at Frost Lake for a while now, and people are wondering when you're going to ask someone out. You played the new, mysterious guy for long enough."

"I didn't realize I was on the clock." He steals another quick glance at me. "It's more about personality for me and having that chemistry."

"Chemistry...interesting." Rachel taps a finger against her chin. "So you're saying it's someone in your science class."

Rowan plops down next to him. He has two beers stacked in one hand. He offers one to Austin, and I'm surprised when he takes it.

"What are you guys talking about?" Rowan asks.

"We're interrogating Austin," Lacey says.

"Oh yeah." Rowan's grin widens, and then his eyes light up. "Ooh, we should play never have I ever!"

Everyone agrees, and we move into a small circle.

It starts out with some easy ones. Never have I ever traveled out of the country. Never have I ever snuck out of the house. Never have I ever gotten a tattoo.

I don't have to drink at all. I considered it on the sneaking out one, but technically, I've only ever snuck people in.

"You have a tattoo?" Lacey asks Rowan when he drinks on the last one.

"Yeah." He pulls at the hem of his shorts, revealing the tattoo on his thigh. It's some sort of origami bird. It looks cool.

"How have I never noticed?" She leans forward to get a better look at it.

Everyone giggles as she basically puts her face in his crotch. Rowan gets an almost embarrassed look on his face, and then Lacey realizes what she's done and sits back on her heels.

"Okay, Austin's turn," she says.

He takes a drink while he thinks, then a slow smile spreads across his face. "Never have I ever tried out for the chess team."

My mouth falls open. I didn't think he was going to

come at me of all people. I drink, and everyone laughs and asks for an explanation, to which I just shrug and say, "I was trying some new things to see if it clicked. It didn't."

"Your turn, Claire," Rowan prompts me to go next when the laughter has died down.

"Never have I ever read the Jude Collins biography," I say, tossing one right back at Austin.

Austin narrows his gaze on me before putting the cup to his lips. Rowan drinks too.

"You're the other person who checked it out of the library?" Austin asks Rowan. Then, we all burst into giggles.

More people are gathering around. The soccer game has finally stopped, and people are ready to sit and chill. Eddie and Vaughn build a bonfire, and we move so we're sitting around it. Austin and I get farther apart as the circle expands, but he's across from me, and we sneak glances.

The guys use the game to air out one another's secrets. Like Barrett got caught in a compromising position with his therapist's daughter, and one of the guys on the football team waxed his butt for fifty bucks.

I'm enjoying the night and being out of Frost Lake and hanging out and even learning things about Austin that we haven't chatted about yet. He's not a virgin, but I hadn't assumed he was.

Vaughn and I came close, but we never went all the way.

Lacey's party drink has taken the edge off my worries, and I've forgotten the purpose of the game and what it feels like to be in the hot seat until Barrett takes his turn. He grins right at Austin and then me. "Never have I ever kissed anyone for a dare."

Austin flips him off as we both take a drink. But so do

several other guys around the circle, which leads to people wanting to know who and when.

I find Vaughn in the circle. He looks relaxed, beer in his hand, resting on one knee. He isn't shooting me or Austin daggers at the reminder we kissed, which makes me feel like maybe it's all going to be okay.

When it gets to his turn, I can tell he's more than a few beers in. One side of his mouth lifts as he says, "Pass. I can't think of anything."

"I got one," Eli says. "Never have I ever felt up anyone sitting in this circle."

I have a little rush of panic, because I know when Austin drinks, people are going to be very interested to know who he felt up, but then Lacey drinks, and everyone's gaze goes to her instead.

"Lacey, babe." Barrett's brows rise. "Tell me everything."

"I feel myself up all the time," she says, then cups herself over her shirt. "That counts, right?"

Some of the guys boo, and I pull her hands away from her breasts. "No, Lace...just no."

She grins at me, and I realize this wasn't Lacey having a ditzy moment. It was Best Friend of the Year in action.

"I knew it!" Hunter points to Austin. "Disco, you stud. Was it..." He trails off, then tips his head not so subtly toward Jenn sitting next to him.

Jenn shoves at his shoulder. "It's none of your business who feels me up."

"It's literally the game," Hunter says.

Austin just laughs it off, totally at ease except for the slight tightening of his jaw when he thinks everyone has stopped paying attention to him.

Eventually, we run out of questions, and people get

bored of playing. Most everyone has headed inside to warm up or to the hot tub on the deck.

It's cold, even with the heat from the bonfire, but I'm not quite ready to go in yet, and the hot tub is crammed full of couples making out.

I pull the sleeves of my sweatshirt down over my hands and hug my knees. Lacey is doing cheers with Jenn and some of the other cheerleaders from both squads. I'm watching and applauding after each one.

"Here." Austin drops a blanket down onto the ground in front of me and then takes a seat next to me.

"Thanks." I drape it over my legs and then hold up the side to offer it to him.

He moves closer until our legs and shoulders touch. We don't say anything as we stare out toward the lake. The cheerleaders are attempting a pyramid. As Lacey tries to climb up to the top, Jenn shifts, and they all tumble to the ground.

"Did you have a good day?" Austin asks, leaning into me.

"I did, yeah. You?"

"Yeah, this was pretty cool." His breath is visible in the cold night air. Mine too. "Wish we could have hung out more though."

"Yeah, me too." I don't want to just hang out though. I want him to kiss me again.

He gives me a wicked grin like he can read my thoughts. "Uh-oh. Whatcha thinking there? You're blushing."

"Nothing." I play it off, but he absolutely knows what I'm thinking.

I wonder if I should suggest that we just kiss right here and right now, let people realize we're hooking up. What would happen if we just stopped hiding? Would Vaughn really be that upset? I wish I knew the answers.

"Yo, Disco!" It's Rowan's voice that's yelling from the deck.

The two of us turn.

"Get your asses into this hot tub before you catch a cold. Tell 'em, Cap. He'll get pneumonia out there."

I don't see or hear Vaughn's response, but Austin pulls away. "I think I better go keep an eye on him." He gets up and dusts off the sand from his shorts, then looks down at me. "Meet me later?"

"Meet you where?"

"There's a small deck off one of the rooms. If you walk around the side of the house, you'll see it. I'll be waiting there as soon as everyone goes to sleep."

"Okay." My stomach somersaults as he winks, then backs away. He finally turns after he's put a few feet of distance between us and jogs up to the house.

When Lacey is done attempting cheerleading stunts, we walk up together.

"I'm gonna go change," I tell her. She already has her bikini on underneath her clothes.

I change into my suit, grab a towel, and am heading out to the hot tub when I spot Vaughn in the living room. I hesitate for only a second before I pull the towel around me and go to him. It feels like my chance to get a gauge on things between us.

He's alone, head back on the couch, beer in hand. He never used to drink that often, but when he does, he's the kind of guy who gets quieter and more reserved instead of turning into a party animal like Rowan.

"Everything okay?" I ask as I take a seat next to him.

His head slowly turns, his dark blue eyes locking on me. His lips curve up. "Hey, Claire. Yeah, I'm fine. Just taking a moment. It's so loud outside."

I doubt it's the noise alone that has him in here. He's used to the chaos of the soccer team.

"You don't seem fine. What's up?"

He doesn't act like he's going to answer, but then he heaves out a sigh. "I just found out I'm failing Algebra II."

"Oh." There's a part of me that expected it to be about me, and it both relieves me and makes me feel like the most self-centered person for even thinking it. I angle my legs toward him. "I'm so sorry. Does your dad know?"

He huffs a strange, strangled noise—a mixture of a laugh and a groan. "No, not yet, but he's going to be pissed."

"Algebra II is no joke. Is there someone in your class who can help?" I'd usually suggest Lacey, but one, she hates tutoring people, and two, I'm not so sure she doesn't still hate Vaughn.

"Yeah. Probably. I don't know. I'll figure it out." Some of the fog lifts from his eyes. "How are you doing? How's your foot? School? Your mom? I feel like we haven't talked in ages."

"We haven't."

"I'm sorry," he says, dropping his gaze from mine. "I didn't know how to be around you and not be us. But being apart has been good. It's given me perspective."

Sober Vaughn would never have admitted any of this, but I'm glad he is now. It makes me feel good about moving on. And it's not like I blame him for not talking to me. I made it pretty clear that I wasn't interested in getting back together. We both needed some space.

"Yeah, me too." I take his hand and squeeze lightly.

He glances at our fingers and then squeezes back.

I stand. "Are you coming back outside?"

"Nah." He shifts so he's looking back at the ceiling. "Think I'm gonna chill here for a while."

I leave him to brood alone and head back out. My smile feels freer as I aim it at Austin. I feel like everything is going to be okay. He's playing cornhole with Rowan and some other people, but he finds me the second I step outside. Lacey and some of the girls are in the hot tub, and I join them.

For the next couple of hours, Austin and I orbit around each other but don't interact. Each minute feeds into the anticipation of seeing him later.

When people start heading to bed, my heart rate spikes. I go inside with Lacey, change out of my suit into pj's, and then wait until she falls asleep.

Getting up, I pad through the house quietly. I have the fleeting thought that I can't imagine how anyone can sleep right now but then realize it's only because my heart is racing, and adrenaline spreads through my limbs, making me feel shaky and lightheaded like I've had too much caffeine.

Outside, the music is still playing, but there's no one in sight as I walk around the side of the house and locate the deck. Austin stands on the bottom step.

The wind blows his dark hair, and moonlight dances across his face. He holds out a hand, and I slip mine into it. The stairway leads to a small deck. There is an outdoor couch with black cushions and a glass coffee table in front of it. Lit candles are scattered across the top of it, and there's a blanket draped over the arm of the couch.

I look at him wide-eyed and jaw dropped. "Did you do this?"

"The candles were already here. I found a lighter in the kitchen." He looks more bashful than I've ever seen him.

My gaze flicks to the bedroom beyond the sliding door of the deck. "Who are you rooming with?"

"Rowan, but he's down on the dock with Sophie's friend Amanda, stargazing and finishing off a bottle of whisky. He'll be occupied for at least another hour."

"I think you will be too." I step to him and wrap my arms around his neck.

He guides me over to the couch. He sits and then pulls me onto his lap.

My already tingling body heats further as our bodies lock into place. My knees rest on either side of his hips, and our stomachs press together.

"Wanna stargaze?" He tips his head back just enough to ask the question.

"No." I press my lips to his. In this moment, the stars feel insignificant. I'm vibrating with so many emotions and feelings. My heart is galloping in my chest and warmth spreads through me. Every part of me wants to fuse our bodies closer, to capture him and this moment and hold on to it forever. Kissing Austin is exciting and thrilling in a way I didn't know it could be.

He groans into my mouth, pulling me tighter against him. The only sound is the quiet rustling of the wind blowing through the trees and the faint sound of the music. His fingers climb up my rib cage and slip under my T-shirt.

My breaths are ragged when he pulls back again. His green eyes have taken on a darker hue. "We don't have to do anything you don't want to do. I could literally kiss you all night long."

"But you want to do more?" I ask.

He gives me a look that could easily be interpreted as "Are you serious right now?"

"I haven't had sex before," I admit. "Vaughn and I..." I

stop myself and give him an apologetic smile for bringing up my ex. "We didn't."

His hands settle on the curve of my waist under my shirt, and his gaze locks on my lips. "I didn't sleep around in Arizona or anything, but I had a girlfriend for a little while."

White-hot jealousy sweeps through me. I know he didn't even know me then, but I still hate the idea of him kissing or touching anyone else.

"I've never felt this way about anyone," he says.

I believe him. I haven't either. I'm falling for him. *Have* fallen for him.

"I want more too." I pull my shirt over my head and drop it to the deck floor, then reach behind me to unhook my bra. Austin's stare drops to my chest as I pull the material from my body and let it fall on top of my shirt.

"So perfect," he murmurs. His palms are warm against my cool skin as they return to my waist, and heat curls in my lower stomach.

The compliment makes another dizzying rush spiral through me. He kisses me, and we move so we're lying side by side on the couch, breaking apart only to pull off my shorts and his shirt. Austin pulls a blanket over our heads so we're hidden in this little fort.

His fingers trail over my stomach and hips. His mouth licks and nibbles down my neck and lower while I explore the hard ridges of his chest and abs. He's still wearing his jeans, but when I hook a finger into the band, he takes them off for me.

He flings them out of our cozy spot and then shucks off his boxers too. My heart hammers in my chest as I wriggle out of my last piece of clothing.

"I meant what I said earlier." His fingertips whisper down my stomach and up in lazy strokes. "We don't have to do anything. Being with you like this is everything I wanted."

"Everything?"

His mouth quirks up on one side. "It's enough. Any time I get to spend with you is enough."

Pressing my lips to his, I climb on top of him. Heat flashes in his eyes.

I don't know if Austin is falling for me the same way I am him, but I know that I want to be with him in every way.

"Are you sure? I don't want you to have any regrets or feel like we're taking things too fast. I'm not going anywhere. We have lots of time."

The only promise I need from him is that he feels the same way that I do right now. Things change in an instant. I know I'll regret it more if I hold back than if I don't. That's how I feel about skating. I don't regret one second I spent practicing or competing, only that I didn't approach each time like it might be my last.

I nod. "I want everything."

He rolls me off him and goes into the attached bedroom for a moment before returning with a condom. Nerves mixed with excitement pulse over me as he puts it on.

"You and me," he says, stare so intense that it makes butterflies soar in my stomach. His mouth swipes over mine, and then he drops his forehead against mine. "No regrets."

CHAPTER TWENTY-NINE

I KICK CLAIRE'S FOOT UNDER THE TABLE, THEN TRAP IT WITH both of mine. She looks up from her art project. We're working at the dining room table because Wyatt wanted to hang with us. Then he ditched us for video games after about twenty minutes.

We've managed to hang out every night since we got back from the cabin, and I can't get enough.

"Are you done?" she asks me.

I've barely done a thing. I'm too distracted by her. Claire gives me a knowing look and then returns her attention to her painting. We've finished all our pieces and are working on flyers for the show. Well, she is. I'm working on memorizing her face.

"Austin." My mom comes into the kitchen with her phone in hand. She looks up from the screen. "What kind of cake do you want for your birthday?"

"Oh, uh…I don't care. Chocolate on chocolate, I guess."

Mom wrinkles up her nose playfully. She prefers vanilla. "Are you sure?"

"Positive."

She holds her disgusted face for a beat longer before smiling. When I glance back across the table, Claire's eyes are wide and locked on me.

"When is your birthday?" she asks.

"Friday," I say.

"How have you not mentioned this?"

I shrug it off. "I don't know."

Except I do know. I haven't mentioned it to anyone after I found out that Dad wasn't going to be able to make it back for the day. Usually, Mom makes our favorite meal, and we have cake and ice cream and then play board games. Then we'd do stuff with friends another day if we want. It's yet another tradition that won't happen this year. I swallow down the disappointment. I'm turning seventeen, not seven, so I know it's dumb to want my dad here. It's just that I thought it was one thing for sure he wouldn't miss.

"We should get everyone together and do something," Claire says.

"We have a game the next day."

"Not a party, just a little get-together with your closest friends. It's your first birthday in Frost Lake. It should be celebrated."

"Is that in the Frost Lake community handbook?" I tease.

"If it isn't, it should be." She continues smiling at me. "Seriously. It'd be fun."

I glance at Mom. "Is it all right if some of my friends come over Friday night?"

Her smile tells me instantly that she's more than happy about the idea. "I don't see why not. And it'll give me a good excuse to order chocolate *and* vanilla. I'm sure some of your friends have better taste than you do." Mom goes into full party-planning mode. "How many people?" she asks.

"Maybe some of the guys on the team and a few others. Fifteen?" I look to Claire.

With her thumb raised, she raises it, indicating I should go higher.

"Thirty?" I ask.

She grins sheepishly.

Leaning over, I quickly swipe my lips over hers.

"Thirty what?" Torrance asks as she walks into the kitchen.

"People," I say, pulling away from Claire. "For my birthday."

Torrance glares at Mom and then me. "You're throwing him a birthday party with all his friends, and you won't even let me go visit one of mine?" If looks could kill, my sister would have murdered me a hundred times over the past two months.

"Torrance..." Mom starts.

"No. Forget it. I don't want to hear it." She turns on her heel and runs for the stairs. As usual, a moment later, her door slams and music starts.

Mom sighs. "I should probably go talk to her."

"And I need to get home," Claire says.

After she packs up, we walk outside.

"You still seemed bummed." She bumps her shoulder against mine. "What's up?"

"It's nothing."

"It's obviously something. Do you not want to celebrate your birthday? I'm sorry if I overstepped. I love birthdays. Lacey always goes over the top and makes the whole day special."

I notice she doesn't mention her parents, and that makes me upset for her and then disappointed all over again that my dad isn't coming home.

She sits on the bottom step of the porch like she's prepared to wait until I'm ready to talk about it.

So I sit next to her and exhale a long breath before I say, "I'm just bummed that my dad isn't coming. He's missed all my games and now my birthday. And the worst part is, I can't even be mad, because it's my fault."

"Who says you can't be mad?" Claire asks, brows pinching together as she angles her body toward mine. Our knees lock, and I absently drop one palm to her calf.

"If we'd stayed in Arizona, he wouldn't have to miss everything. And he's not just missing my stuff. He's only seen a couple of Wyatt's games, he and Mom used to have date nights every Friday, and Dad and Torrance made pancakes on Sunday mornings and then watched cartoons. He's missing all of it because of me."

"You have a right to your feelings, and pretending like it's fine won't help anyway."

"Neither will complaining about it."

Her smile softens. "You have the best family, Austin, but even the best families aren't perfect. Your family picked up and moved across the country because they love you and they believe in you. And in doing that, things got more complicated. You can be frustrated or mad or sad or whatever. Just know that it will work out. This is just a rough patch. You all will find new traditions and ways to show up for each other, because that's who you are. You're so lucky. Your family loves you unconditionally. Not everyone has what you have."

Her words cut through me. By not everyone, I think

she means her. Guilt slowly seeps in. Here I am complaining, and she has had it far worse. "You're right. I'm sorry. I know it's dumb."

"No, don't be sorry. It sucks that your dad won't be here and that he's missed all your games. But it's not because he doesn't want to be."

I wrap my arms around her middle and rest my head on her shoulder. "Thank you."

"For what? I'm just stating all the obvious things."

My phone buzzes in the front pocket of my hoodie. I pull it out and read the text from Rowan. "I see the news has somehow already gotten out."

She laughs. "I put Lacey in charge."

"Dear god, help us." Or my mom anyway. Did I tell her thirty people? Not with Lacey planning it. I chuckle as I put my phone away and then keep on hugging Claire.

Somehow, she's become my lifeline. I don't know what I'd do without her anymore. And that is a terrifying and exhilarating thought.

CHAPTER THIRTY

Austin's hands slide down the front of my shorts. His fingertips graze along the lace of my panties. I hold my breath as the ache between my legs intensifies. He removes his hand before going any farther and then rolls on top of me. His weight blankets my body, and the pressure makes every part of me vibrate.

We haven't had sex again since the cabin, but I want to. And I can feel that he wants to too.

The electric hum of the garage door, followed by the sound of a door slamming shut makes us both freeze. My heart jumps in my throat.

"My mom's home." I disentangle myself from Austin, adjusting my bra and finding my T-shirt on the floor.

He sits up on my bed, looking frustrated, rumpled, and so sexy. I toss him his shirt with a smile.

"Sorry, birthday boy. I planned on letting you get to at least third base."

"Kissing you is all the birthday present I need." He hooks his shirt on over his head and then grabs me around the waist, kissing me and pulling me back onto the bed. I wish we could keep going, keep kissing and touching all night.

"If my mom finds you in here again, she might lock me in the house forever."

With a groan, he frees me. He looks so disappointed it makes me steal one more kiss.

"I'll be by at eight with Lacey," I tell him as I run my fingers through my tangled hair. Austin likes to run his fingers through it while we're kissing.

"If you want to come early, I wouldn't hate it. We could sneak up to my room and..." His mouth captures mine again, and one of his hands cups the back of my head, then fingers slide through the strands, making me laugh and sigh all at once.

"You have to go." I step back and push at him playfully. "If you don't go now, she'll see you."

I open my bedroom door and peer out, then we hurry down the stairs.

I pull him back to kiss him again. He laughs, then groans, lingering a second longer. "You're going to be the death of me."

I just get him out the front door and close it behind me when Mom appears in the kitchen. Ruby is behind her. Her cheeks are red from exertion. She was sick earlier this week and still looks like she's recovering.

"What are you doing?" Mom asks, eyeing me critically. "Was someone here?"

"Austin and I were studying in the living room."

Her gaze goes to the dark room that has no signs of anyone being in it.

I head for the stairs without meeting her gaze. "I gotta get ready."

I pick up Lacey on my way to Austin's house. She comes out of her house carrying a massive bundle of balloons that look like they could carry her away in a breeze. She opens the back door and then tries to wrangle them into the back seat.

"What is that?" I ask when she finally manages to force them in the car and gets up front with me. "I can't even see out the back window."

"I couldn't decide what to get him. I wanted to get condoms, but you said his family was going to be there, so I thought that might be awkward."

"And it wouldn't be awkward for me?"

"I was doing it for you." She beams.

"We've got it covered. And since when are you in favor of sleeping with high school guys?"

"I'm still not, but if you're going to keep having sex with him, I need to make sure you're being safe. Do you need to borrow my book on the female body?"

A laugh escapes from my lips, but my stomach does a funny flip, thinking about that night with Austin.

When we get to the birthday boy's house, the guys are out back. Some are playing cornhole, others Ping-Pong, and everyone else is sitting around the firepit to keep warm.

When Austin spots me, he tosses his last remaining bag and then heads for me. He hesitates like he was going to hug me, then does, letting go too quickly. He hugs Lacey too.

"You guys made it." His smile stretches across his face.

"Happy birthday," Lacey says. "I left your present inside."

"You didn't have to do that," he says.

"I know, but I'm just that kind of girl, Disco."

"Here." I hold up the little gift bag with the present I got him.

With a grin, he digs into the bag around the tissue paper and pulls out the disco ball key chain. He palms it, smile widening. "I love it. Thank you."

"Austin!" his dad yells, beckoning him back to the game.

"Your dad's here," I say as his presence finally clicks. Austin said he wasn't going to make it.

"Yeah." Austin looks happier than I've seen him look in a while. "He surprised me. Staying through the weekend."

"That's great."

His dad and the other guys playing cornhole call for him again. "I'll catch up with you guys later. There's pizza and cake inside, stuff for s'mores over on the table, and drinks in the cooler."

After he runs off, Lacey looks at me. "They really do have a whole Disney family vibe going on here, don't they? Are you sure they aren't all secretly serial killers?"

I feel a hint of defensiveness creep in. "They're just one of those rare families who all get along."

"Weird," she says. Her voice drops. "I wonder what that's like."

"I think it's nice." I turn and walk over to the cooler. I grab a sparkling water for myself and Lacey. Torrance and a girl I don't recognize are sitting around the firepit roasting marshmallows.

I start toward them.

"Is that his sister?" Lacey whispers the question.

Torrance has on way more makeup than normal, and both she and her friend are in tight dresses and heels like they're going to a dance or something instead of sitting outside at a family-friendly birthday party. And the girl with her…as we get closer, I finally recognize her. It's Sophie, dressed up like I've never seen her before.

"Hey, Torrance," I say as I take a seat across from her. I smile at the girl next to her. "Hi, Sophie."

Lacey lifts a hand in a wave.

I wait a beat to see if Torrance will introduce herself, but she doesn't, so I add, "Lacey, this is Austin's sister, Torrance."

Sophie's phone rings. She rolls her eyes, "Oh my gosh. It's my mom again. I'll be right back."

She takes off with her phone to her ear, strutting through the party in her heels. All the guys watch her go. I can't even blame them. Her skirt is so short, *I'm* having a hard time looking away.

Torrance has never once spoken directly to me, but she leans forward like we're the best of friends. "Oh my gosh, wouldn't they be so cute together?"

"Who?" Lacey asks.

"Austin and Sophie. She's so pretty, right?"

Lacey scoffs next to me. Torrance might be acting like a bitch, but I don't want her to know she's getting to me.

"Yeah, she is." I swallow around the tightening in my throat. "Excuse me. I think I want some pizza."

Lacey comes with me but doesn't say a word until we're inside.

"Okay, so not Disney."

"She's just pissed at her brother for uprooting her life."

"More wicked queen than princess." Lacey's reassuring half smile makes me feel worse. "Since when did they become friends?"

"I don't know."

Lacey shoots a glare in their direction. "Do you want to go?"

"No way. It's his birthday. Who cares if Sophie is here looking gorgeous and Torrance is playing matchmaker?"

"*You're* gorgeous."

A small laugh eases the tension in my chest. "Thanks."

We avoid Torrance and Sophie, but I don't get to see a lot of Austin as the night continues either.

Around ten, the guys lose interest in the games and all start to take seats around the patio. They have a game tomorrow, and curfew is eleven.

"We should play truth or dare," Sophie says. I haven't seen her or Austin interact much tonight, but she smiles at him now.

My stomach is a ball of nerves. What if someone dares me to kiss Austin? What if he gets dared to kiss someone else, like Sophie? The thought makes me want to throw up.

"Hell yeah!" Barrett says.

Most of the guys jump in as well. I catch Austin's eye across the room. He shrugs. Maybe I'm making too big a deal out of it.

"What about you, birthday boy?" Rowan asks, slapping him on the shoulder.

"Yeah, all right."

We get in a circle for the game. Sophie goes first and dares Barrett to take off his shirt. It's cold outside, but he whips it off and tosses it at her.

"His nipples could cut glass," Lacey says next to me.

We giggle, and the game continues. Barrett dares Brandon to kiss Torrance.

"No way," he says. "I'm not making out with anyone but my girlfriend."

"Fine, fine." Barrett changes it to them kissing, and they go at it so long that we all cheer and catcall them.

Lacey gets dared to sit in Eli's lap, and Andie has to tell whether she and Brandon have had sex—they still have not, but I know their anniversary is coming up soon. Torrance gets dared to prove she can shove her entire fist in her mouth. I've been happily left out of it so far, but I'm nervous because there are only a few of us left. I don't want to kiss anyone, but all the truth questions have been really invasive. There is no good option.

I'm relieved when the next person called is Sophie. Torrance thinks for a moment and then says, "I dare you to kiss my brother."

"No," Austin says immediately.

Relief sweeps through me, but my pulse still races, and my entire body flushes.

"Why not?" Barrett asks. "You're not dating anyone."

There's a moment where I think he's going to say, "Actually, I've been seeing Claire, and I'm in love with her," and I'm scared but excited. We've been living in this happy bubble where no one really knows, and it's been great, but how much better will it be when I can kiss him and be with him all the time instead of little moments when no one is watching?

Torrance laughs. "Oh my gosh. I'm such a dummy. I forgot. My bad."

The circle all looks from Torrance to Austin.

"Forgot what?" Eli asks.

Austin's sister smirks as she meets my gaze. My pulse skitters to a stop as I inhale sharply. Blood pounds in my ears.

"He's hooking up with Claire." She points at me like they don't know who Claire is.

Everyone goes silent.

"Was that supposed to be a secret?" She smiles, all fake innocence. "I thought—"

"Shut up, Torrance." Austin's jaw is tight as he glances to me.

The world around me slows as everyone in the room looks from Austin to me and finally to Vaughn. The silence is heavy and thick. Vaughn's face flushes and hardens. His usual mask has slipped and the hurt and betrayal in his expression makes my stomach twist with guilt.

He stands, glaring across the circle at Austin. "You're hooking up with Claire?"

Austin gets to his feet and puts his hands out as he crosses toward him. "I'm sorry. I was going to tell you."

My throat is thick with emotion and panic makes my pulse race. The moment stretches out and fills with tension. I can't seem to do or say anything except hold my breath as they stare each other down.

Vaughn's nostrils flair and the tension snaps as he lunges, punching Austin and sending him stutter-stepping backward. Austin looks shocked at first, then his rage seems to match Vaughn's.

"What the fuck?" Austin goes after him and pushes his chest.

The movement throws Vaughn off-balance, but he recovers quickly and stalks toward Austin. "You know how I feel about her. How could you do that?"

The rest of the team is on their feet, quick to break it up. Rowan grabs Vaughn around the waist, and the other guys stand in front of Austin.

The back door opens, and his mom stands there wide-eyed, taking in the scene.

The fight is over, but I know the fallout has just begun. I barely notice my surroundings as I stand and walk away from the chaos. Unshed tears blur my vision and I'm hit with a wave of nausea.

When I get to the driveway, I let the tears fall. This is all my fault. I wanted to wait until the end of the season, not Austin. If we had just told Vaughn, maybe this wouldn't have happened.

I hear footsteps behind me as I walk to my car, and I don't even have to look back to know it's Lacey.

"Are you okay?" She hugs me, and I bury my face in her shoulder as I cry. I am so humiliated and ashamed. I have told myself a million times that there was no reason to hide. I like Austin. He likes me. We weren't hurting anyone. But if that was true and there really was no reason to hide, then why were we, and why do I feel so awful?

A second later, I hear Austin calling for me from the front door. I wipe my eyes and look up. Lacey blocks him from getting to me.

"I'm not going to hurt her, Lace," Austin says.

"Do you want me to tell him to get lost?" my best friend asks without turning around.

"No. It's okay."

She glances over her shoulder at me, giving me a sad smile. "I'll be right inside if you need me. We'll go as soon as you want." She rubs at her arms and then hurries back into the house.

"I'm sorry," Austin starts as soon as she's gone. "I'm so mad at Torrance. I had no idea she would do something like that."

It's hard to blame her. We did this. Not her.

Sophie is the next to come out. Her steps are hesitant as she approaches. "Austin, can we talk?"

"It isn't really a good time," he says, sounding exasperated.

"I didn't know about you and Claire. Torrance invited me. She said..." She stops herself and then winces, looking embarrassed. "I thought you were into me."

"I'm sorry she dragged you into this," he says to her. "I think you're a cool girl, but..."

"I get it," she says quickly before he can finish his sentence. Her stare moves to me. "Sorry, Claire."

I try to smile, but another cramp in my side distracts me.

Austin moves closer to me, concern marring his handsome features. His hand comes up to the side of my face, and his thumb strokes my hot cheek. "Come inside. We'll figure this out."

"I think I should go. I don't feel well." The pain in my stomach is almost unbearable.

More voices filter outside, but I double over in pain, unable to process who it is or what they're saying.

Suddenly Vaughn is squatting down in front of me. Lines of worry crease his face. "Are you okay?"

"Fine." I force myself to stand straight. Something is wrong.

Austin and Vaughn continue to hover. Plus their twins. There are double of them.

"You guys can go back inside. I'm gonna go home."

"Please don't go," Austin says, taking me by the elbow. "I'm so sorry she did that."

Vaughn pushes Austin aside to get between us.

"Haven't you done enough?" he asks Austin. "Let her go if she wants."

"I didn't do anything," Austin grits out.

They get in each other's faces again.

"Stop it!" I yell, and another stab of pain takes my breath away. I'm hot, nearly sweating, and everything is spinning around me. I reach out to steady myself on my car, but when I lean, I miss it.

"Claire!" Austin yells. Or maybe it's Vaughn.

CHAPTER THIRTY-ONE

Claire crumples into me as I step forward. "Something's wrong. I think she's sick or something."

"No kidding." Vaughn's jaw hardens. "Let's get her back inside."

We flank her on either side and walk Claire back into the house. The guys on the team are all preparing to leave, as are the rest of the party. They're giving me and Vaughn worried looks. My eye throbs where he punched me.

Rowan and Lacey move toward us.

"What's going on?" Rowan asks.

"I don't feel so well," Claire says. "I think I'm gonna be sick."

She breaks free from us and rushes toward the downstairs bathroom.

"I've got her," Lacey says, hurrying behind her.

"I was going to head out, but do you need me to stay?" Rowan asks.

"No, I'll make sure she gets home." She went from seemingly fine to really sick fast. I'm kind of freaked out.

I must look as worried as I feel, because Rowan places a hand on my shoulder. His gaze bounces between me and Vaughn. "She'll be okay, but are *you two* going to be okay?"

"I'm gonna go check on Claire." Vaughn's response is confirmation enough.

"He's pissed," I say.

"Yeah, I got that."

"Fuck." I run a hand over my head. How did tonight get so messed up? "I should go check on her too."

"Yeah, do what you gotta do."

"Thanks for coming tonight, man," I say as I walk backward away from the front door.

Rowan nods. "Any time. Call me if you need anything."

The bathroom door is open, and Claire is sitting on the ledge of the bathtub while Lacey squats down in front of her and Vaughn hovers nearby.

"Are you all right?" I ask, not moving into the small space even though I want to.

"I think I have the flu. Ruby had it earlier this week. I felt fine earlier. It just hit me."

"I'll take you home," Vaughn says.

Fuck that. "I can take her."

We glare at each other.

"*I'm* going to take her," Lacey says, forcing herself between us and shooting each of us a glare.

"I'm coming with you," I say. "I can help or not, but I'm not leaving her."

"Me either." Vaughn stands tall and crosses his arms over his chest.

Lacey stands and jabs a pointy finger at Vaughn and then me. "This is not the time to act like cavemen. You're not going anywhere with us if you can't put your shit aside for the rest of the night. Got it?"

"Yes," I say quickly.

Lacey arches a brow at Vaughn.

"Yes." His tone is dry and bitter.

I give my mom a brief explanation. She's pissed about the fighting, but I promise to come right back home after I make sure Claire gets home.

Lacey drives, and Vaughn and I pile into the back seat with Claire between us.

"I feel like I'm driving my children around in a minivan." She adjusts the rearview mirror. "And I am not afraid to stop this vehicle, so don't test me."

Claire rests her head against my shoulder. She's burning up but has her arms wrapped around her middle like she's cold, and her teeth chatter.

"We're almost there," I promise her.

It's after midnight by the time Lacey pulls into the driveway. The lights inside aren't on, but Claire says her mom and sister are home. The three of us manage to get Claire inside and in her room without waking anyone.

"Claire Bear." Lacey sits on the edge of the bed next to her best friend. "What do you need?"

"Sleep."

"Do you want to change first?"

In reply, Claire pulls one edge of the comforter around her, wrapping herself up like a burrito.

"Okay then." Lacey stands and eyes the hovering boys in front of her. "Everybody out."

"I'm gonna stay," I tell her. "Just for a little bit to make sure she doesn't get sick again."

"And then what? Hold her hair back?" Lacey asks.

"If she wants."

"I'm not leaving either. You know how Claire is when she gets the flu, Lace," Vaughn says. "She's got a long night in front of her."

"You're right," she says, still looking angry at us and sad for her friend. "My dad is out of town, so I have to go home and let the dog out, but I can come back."

"You don't need to. I can handle it," Vaughn says. He kicks off his shoes and gets into the bed next to Claire. I want to push him off onto the floor, but then Claire moves closer to him, and I can tell his presence comforts her.

Lacey looks to me like she's making sure this isn't going to be a problem.

"Whatever she needs," I say.

She hesitates, and I can tell she doesn't really want to leave us with her best friend, but eventually Lacey does go.

Not long after, Claire gets sick again. For the next hour, she's up and down. I feel awful for her. She's emptied her stomach, and tears stream down her face as she dry heaves.

"Maybe we should wake up your mom," I say, smoothing her hair back.

"No," Claire and Vaughn say at the same time.

Vaughn lowers his voice. "She'll be pissed we're here, and she's shit at comforting Claire when she isn't feeling well."

So basically, she sucks like normal. I think about what my mom does when I'm sick and have to swallow down my guilt and disappointment that Claire doesn't have that.

"I want Tank Tank," Claire says, eyes closed as she gets back into bed. We managed to get her shoes off and all the covers pulled down so she's a little more comfortable.

"What's a Tank Tank? Like a tank top? A shirt?"

"No," Vaughn says in a tone that suggests I'm an idiot. He motions with his head toward the closet. "Look on the top shelf. There's a purple box. Grab that."

I'm too anxious to get whatever she needs to question him. I find the purple box and bring it out of the closet. Setting it on the bed, I pull the lid free. At first, I'm not sure exactly what I'm seeing, and then it comes through with a clarity that's yet another gut punch to the night. Letters, dried flowers, photos...her and Vaughn at a party, her and Vaughn dressed up for some sort of event, and so many more. Not all of them include him but enough that I get this is some sort of memento box.

"It's a little pink rhinoceros," Vaughn says. "Her dad gave it to her when she was little."

It doesn't take a lot of searching to find it. It looks old and like it's been well-loved. I hand it over, and Claire clutches it to her chest.

A small, petty part of me is glad it's not something Vaughn gave her, but the history between them is still fresh in my mind.

She falls asleep quickly. Vaughn and I sit on the floor on either side of the room, not speaking or looking at each other.

I can feel my eye swelling, and it's tender to the touch.

"I can't believe you punched me," I say. I'm going to have a hell of a black eye tomorrow.

"I can't believe you've been hooking up with Claire behind my back," he throws back. "You know how I feel about her. I trusted you. I welcomed you onto the team and helped you. I thought you were my friend."

"I am your friend," I bark back in a hushed voice. "You don't own Claire or my feelings. I tried not to fall for her, but I did. I'm sorry. I should have told you, but it just happened."

"Yeah, I'll bet." He makes a deep, throaty sound of disbelief. Another quiet moment passes with our anger hanging between us before he asks, "How long?"

The question catches me off guard.

"How long have you been hooking up with her?" he repeats.

"Awhile," I admit. "But—"

"No, forget it." His icy, blue eyes cut through me. "I don't have anything else to say to you. We're done."

CHAPTER THIRTY-TWO

Claire

When I wake up, I lie there for a moment, wondering if I'm going to be sick again. My stomach hurts but not in the same way it did last night. My head feels fuzzy, and my skin is gritty from sweat. I'm clutching my favorite childhood stuffed animal to my chest. It smells like dust and the perfume I was obsessed with when I was twelve.

I roll away from the light streaming in from the window. Austin is sleeping in the bed next to me. He's on top of the covers, about as far away from me on the mattress as he can get, but he has one arm stretched out toward me. I smile at his messy dark hair and his rumpled shirt.

My bedroom door opens, and I freeze, then relax when Vaughn steps quietly into my room. He's holding a glass of water and saltine crackers.

Sitting up, I feel the aches and pains of last night return. My body feels like I got beaten up.

"Hey," I say, voice rough and throat sore.

Vaughn closes the door behind him and walks over to my side of the bed.

"Is anyone else up?" I ask as he hands over the water and then sets the crackers down on the bed in front of me.

"Your mom is showing a house," he says. "She left a note on the counter. Ruby is watching TV."

"I bet she was happy to see you," I say.

"I was happy to see her too. I told her she was a shit for getting you sick." He smiles happily, but it falls off quickly, and he glances over to where Austin is sleeping. "He stayed up all night watching you like a worried mother hen."

"Sounds like you did too."

"I pretended to sleep mostly."

I guess that means they didn't work things out. Though I'm not really surprised.

"Why did you stay then?"

"Come on, Claire. You know why."

But the thing is I don't.

"It was supposed to be me and you against the world forever."

I open my mouth to remind him that he's the one who broke up with me, but he beats me to it.

"I know. I fucked up, but I never stopped loving you. I just didn't know how to be everything for you and the team, my dad, myself. I thought..." The blue of his eyes is so intense. Just like him. "You were so mad at me, and I get it. I should have been there for you when you got hurt. I just didn't know how to be. I felt like an ass being able to go do the things I love when you couldn't. The thought of calling you while I was gone at camp having the time of my life felt like I was kicking you when you were down. So I didn't. And I'm sorry." He blows out a breath. "I thought that we'd find a way back to each other when things were easier. And now I don't know... Maybe it doesn't get easier."

There's an awkwardness between us, and I don't know what to say to make things better. My brain is still foggy, and after last night, I don't know what's what anymore. I loved Vaughn. I know I did, but I know that loving someone doesn't mean that being with them is easy.

Take my mom. I don't understand her, and most of the time, I'm sure that she's wildly disappointed in me, and I still love her. She doesn't make my life easier. You can't choose your parents or family, but you get to choose who else you let in. Why wouldn't you choose people who make living easier instead of harder?

But I understand where he's coming from.

"You said that the time apart had been good for you. I hoped that meant you were moving on."

"It was good because it made me realize what a jerk I was," he says. "Not because I moved on."

"Oh." I consider everything he said. How he thought we'd find our way back. How he didn't know how to be what I needed. I'm sure I didn't make it easy on him. I was a mess after I found out that I wouldn't be able to skate competitively anymore.

"It would have been hard for me to hear about your awesome summer playing soccer," I tell him honestly, "but I would have, because I care about you. My dream ended, but that didn't mean I didn't want you to still have yours."

He nods, lips folding into a thin line.

Vaughn and I didn't make things better for each other when we were a couple, but maybe eventually we can do that as friends.

"You remembered." I lift the crackers and take out two.

"Saltine crackers and Sprite Zero," he says, some of the tension in the room leaving. "I didn't see any soda downstairs."

It's my favorite combination when I'm sick. When I was really little, my mom would pile a big stack on a plate and sit with me while I watched a movie on the couch. I can't remember the last time she did that.

"Thank you," I say. "I'm glad you stayed."

We fall into a more comfortable silence. Vaughn takes a seat on the floor underneath the window. I eat slowly in case it doesn't sit well in my stomach. I haven't had the flu in so long. I forgot how hard it hits me. I don't get sick often, but when I do, it's always awful. Ugh.

I lean back against the headboard and sneak another glance at Austin. I don't remember a lot from last night after I got sick in the bathroom at his house, but I have this faint memory of him kissing my forehead and pulling my hair back into a ponytail when I said it was too hot.

"You could have told me," Vaughn says eventually. "I think that's what hurt the most. We used to be able to tell each other everything." The hurt in his words makes me feel bad for not being honest.

"Would you have been okay with it?" I take another drink of water to wash the crackers down.

Instead of answering, he shakes his head. "I should go home. My dad is going to be pissed that I bailed on practice this morning."

"You missed practice?" I ask. "I thought you had a game today." Unless I'm still delirious from being sick.

"We do. Dad scheduled an early practice so we could walk through a few things this morning, work out the nerves before the bus ride."

"And you missed it? Why?"

He gives me a look like "isn't it obvious?" But in all the time we dated, Vaughn never missed practice. Not when I was sick, not when I got hurt, never. To have him suddenly putting me before soccer doesn't make any sense.

"My actions haven't always backed up my feelings. I figured if I was ever going to prove to you how I felt, it was now."

My heart feels heavy. Here he is, giving me exactly what I wanted months ago, but my feelings have changed.

He must read the emotions on my face, because he clears his throat as he gets to his feet. "I'm glad you're feeling better."

"Wait, Vaughn." I feel like there's so much more I need to say. I swing my feet over the side of the bed. Swaying, I take a moment to steady myself. He pauses at the door and looks back at me. "I'm sorry you found out the way you did. We've barely talked in months, so no, I didn't feel like I owed anything to you, but I did knowingly keep it from you. The way we ended things sucked. I was hurt, but that doesn't mean I don't understand where you were coming from. I hope we can at least be friends eventually."

A muscle in his jaw flexes as he continues to stare at me but doesn't speak.

"As for Austin…you didn't give him a lot of options. He knew telling you would impact your friendship and his role on the team. Look at what you put him through at the beginning of the year over some stupid dare. Can you really blame him for not wanting to go through that again? All that he wants is to play soccer and not let his family down. You of all people should know what that's like."

Movement on the bed catches my attention. Austin stretches and then opens his eyes, blinking a few times. His right eye is purple and puffy. My stomach clenches again, but this time, it's not because I have the flu. When his gaze locks on me, he studies me carefully, then glances to Vaughn.

"Hey." He sits up and runs a hand through his messy hair. He looks like he's gauging the situation carefully before he asks me, "How are you feeling?"

"Better," I say.

"What time is it?" he asks.

"We're late," Vaughn says, opening my bedroom door, but instead of stepping out, he comes to a halt and mutters a curse under his breath that has both me and Austin craning our necks to figure out what's going on.

The door swings open, and Coach Collins steps in, surveying the room with a scowl. He looks like he was the one who was up all night. His hair is sticking up, and his five-o'clock shadow is more pronounced.

My mom stands behind him. *Oh no.*

"Son," he says to Vaughn in a hard, clipped tone. "Keller. You both missed practice."

Austin's eyes widen.

"Oh shit," he says under his breath.

"Yeah, oh shit," Coach says dryly. "The bus leaves in an hour, and if either of you aren't on it, you're cut from my team. Do you understand?"

"Yes, sir," Austin says.

"Dad, I—"

"Not now." His dad closes his eyes briefly and shakes his head. "Do you understand?"

They both nod their agreement.

"I got the flu," I tell him, feeling like I'm the one in trouble. Coach C is scary when he's mad.

"I hope you feel better, Claire," he says, then looks at Vaughn. "You can find your own way home. I'm sorry for the interruption this morning, Ms. Crawford," Coach says. "We're all just leaving."

"Claire, what were you thinking?" my mom hisses. She looks so disappointed in me, but it's become such a common reaction that it's hard to continue to be upset about it.

"I wasn't," I admit. "I got sick."

"We'll talk about this later." She huffs, then smiles at Coach. "Let me walk you out."

I can hear her apologizing and assuring him that she has no idea what I was thinking having boys in my room all night. I fall back into bed, too tired to care.

CHAPTER THIRTY-THREE

THE BUS RIDE IS QUIET. I'M TIRED, AND MY HEAD IS NOT ON soccer, but I'm on my feet ready to go as soon as we pull up to the curb outside the school. Vaughn and I rush the door at the same time. The hard set of his jaw is as good an indication as any that the few words we exchanged last night didn't fix the situation.

I let him go first and fall into step behind him. We change and prepare to take the field for warm-ups. Coach hasn't spoken to anyone. He doesn't even come into the locker room for our pregame pep talk. I'm glad. I don't know if I can handle the disappointed look in his eye that he gave me this morning.

I shouldn't have missed practice, but I'd do it all over again to be there for Claire when she needed me. Besides, it was just a walk-through to go over a few last-minute reminders for today's game. Rowan gave me the rundown, and it doesn't sound like I missed much.

I don't know if the rest of the team who weren't at my house last night know what's going on with me and

Vaughn, but everyone gives me space as I try to push out everything else and focus.

When the whistle blows indicating the end of warm-ups, we jog over to the sideline for final words from Coach. I'm ready to play. The field is the one place I've always been able to block it all out, and I want that today more than ever.

I'm not sorry about Claire, not about falling for her and not about taking care of her last night, but now it's time to get to work. This opportunity is everything, and if that means putting my differences with Vaughn aside, that's what I'm going to do. When I glance over and catch his eye, I think he feels the same. I know what soccer means to him too. We may not have a lot of common ground right now, but we both want to win today.

"All right, Knights," Coach says, ducking his head down so we can hear him over the crowd for the game. We're playing Ralley today. They have a good turnout of fans to cheer them on, and lots of Frost Lake families made the trip as well. "Ralley is looking sharp. They'll come out strong and try to control the pace. Keep your heads. Make them play at our tempo." He looks around the circle, and we all nod along, letting his words soak in and fill us with hope and determination. "Eli and Eddie, you're taking Vaughn and Austin's spots today."

Wait, what? My head snaps up, and an icy dread trickles down my spine.

"You can't do this," Vaughn says. "You need us."

"I need team players, not children who can't control their tempers or remember their priorities." His dad has the same stubborn set of his jaw. "You fought, you missed curfew and practice. You knew the rules." He flicks his head to the side. "Take a seat, boys."

I avoid the stares of my family as I take a seat on the empty bench. Vaughn sits all the way on the other side, and anger radiates between us. We don't speak as we watch the game.

Ralley is good. Maybe even better than I expected. Their eyes light up when they realize we're down two players. Not any two players either. Vaughn is an opponent no player wants to go up against, and I've been making a big impact that hasn't gone unnoticed. Their glee seems to give them a burst of confidence and energy.

I feel hopeless as I watch Rowan try to keep the team working together. He fills Vaughn's shoes, leading them on the field. They do their best, and they're able to stop them for a while, but after the first breach in defense that leads to a goal, our team starts to look tired.

Vaughn goes up to his dad halfway through the first half, and they exchange a few words. A flicker of hope blooms in my chest, but when he turns back around looking angrier than before, I know his dad hasn't changed his mind. Vaughn tosses a water bottle along the sidelines, muscles clenching as he balls his hands into fists.

I feel sick to my stomach. The first game my dad comes to watch me play all season and I'm stuck on the bench.

By halftime, I'm convinced I caught whatever flu Claire had. My stomach hurts, and my head aches. I'm so fucking disappointed and frustrated. I should be out there. I *need* to be out there.

The team heads out of the locker room, and I hang back. I let my head fall back against the locker, close my eyes, and let out a long breath.

The squeak of shoes on the floor alerts me that I'm not alone. I open my eyes. Vaughn is still here too. His head is between his knees, and his shoulders are tense. As if he can sense me staring at him, he looks up.

"This is all your fault." He sits straight and then stands.

"How is this my fault? You didn't have to stay at Claire's all night. You made that choice. Same as me."

"Not that." His face scrunches up. "You heard him out there. He's pissed that I hit you and that you put our shit before the team."

"*I* put our shit before the team?" I want to laugh at the absurdity. "Every decision I've made has been about the team."

"You knew how I felt about her. Then you lied to my face and pretended to be my friend. And for what? So that I'd help you with soccer? Who does that?"

"I wasn't pretending. This team is just as important to me as it is to you. My family moved across the country for me. Now they're watching me sit on the sidelines." I run a hand through my hair. "I should have told you about me and Claire. I'm sorry about that but not the rest. I like her. I like her a lot, and I'm going to keep seeing her whether you try to take another swing at me or not. If you can't handle that, then too damn bad."

CHAPTER THIRTY-FOUR

I SPEND THE DAY IN BED. RUBY BRINGS ME SPRITE ZERO AND Jell-O, and we watch TV together. Mom stopped in only long enough to tell Ruby not to get too close because she has a big dance competition next weekend. She did also ask if I needed anything, but she meant medicine, not the thing I really want, which is for her to dote on me like she used to when I was little.

I don't know what happened. It's like once I started winning trophies, I stopped being her daughter and became her employee.

At some point, I fall asleep, and when I wake up, Ruby is gone from my room and the house is quiet.

Lacey stops by after I text to check in and let her know I'm alive. When I answer the door, she hands me a new box of saltine crackers and a two-liter bottle of Sprite. She smiles sadly. "You look like crap."

"I actually feel better."

She comes in and goes to the living room, sitting in the big armchair adjacent to the couch. "Well, you might not after I tell you about the game today."

The ache in my stomach intensifies. "I don't know if I can handle more bad news."

"Coach Collins benched Vaughn and Austin today. They lost to Ralley. Four to zip."

I groan and walk over to the couch, slumping into it and cradling the crackers to my chest. "This is all my fault."

"And that's why I wanted to be here when you found out. This is not your fault."

I open my mouth to protest, but she shakes her head.

"Nope. Uh-uh. Repeat after me. Boys are dumb, and they did this to themselves."

I don't repeat it, but it does pull a small laugh from me.

"I know that I didn't owe it to Vaughn, but I should have talked to him anyway. He and I have so much history."

"And you and Austin?"

"I don't know. It all feels so complicated now."

"High school is complicated."

"Is it, or do we just make it that way?" I shake my head. "The last few months have been some of the worst and best, and I can't help but wonder if the good only felt that way because the lows were so low."

"Yeah, I can see where you might feel that way. You've been dealing with a lot."

"Or not dealing," I say quietly. "It hit me this morning. The semester is half-over, and I have no better idea what I'm going to do about college next year than I did two months ago."

She smiles. "You're doing amazing if you ask me. Honestly, some days I don't know how you're still standing. Skating was your whole world. You had your entire life planned around it. So if you want to keep avoiding the future, I say that's A-OK. You'll figure it out in time. College isn't everything."

I snort. That is basically the opposite of the pep talk my mom has been giving me since I hurt my foot.

"Don't let your mom get you panicked. Your grades are fine, and plenty of schools don't care about having dozens of extracurriculars and awards."

"I know you're right."

She smiles smugly.

"But it's not just her. I want to find other things to do. You have cheer and student council. Andie has theater. Everyone has found their place, and I'm just floating aimlessly."

She comes over to the couch and takes the spot next to me. Lacey folds her legs underneath her so she can sit facing me.

"What if I don't ever find something I love as much as I did skating?" My throat tightens. I'd give anything to just perform one last time to soak up the feeling and bottle it in my heart forever.

"You will," she insists. "Do you remember when we went to that adventure summer camp the summer before fifth grade?"

"Vaguely," I say, thinking back on it. We slept in cabins and did outdoor things each day like hiking and kayaking, archery and other things. I only went because Lacey's mom signed her up, and she convinced me it'd be fun if we did it together. I was not a fan of the outdoors—I'm still not—but Lacey was very persuasive. Also still true.

"Remember how miserable we were on day one?"

"Sort of."

"But by the end of the week, we didn't want to leave. And you got really good at reading a compass."

"I think I blocked it. All I remember is staying up all night talking in our bunk beds." I smile. That part was fun. It was like a weeklong sleepover.

"My point is love isn't always automatic. Maybe whatever you fall in love with next is going to take a little bit of patience and practice."

"A lot of practice." I sigh. "I spent so much time figure skating, I'm basically terrible at everything else."

"Not true. You're a great friend."

"So are you. I don't think I would have made it these past few months without you."

I abandoned my phone earlier on the coffee table, and it buzzes now with a text.

Lacey looks over at the screen and then smiles. "Your boyfriend is checking up on you. The new one, not the old one."

I push at her shoulder lightly. "Not funny."

Her voice softens. "These last few months, I've seen you smile a lot, and most of it has been because of him. I don't think that's because you were feeling low. He really likes you, and I think you really like him."

"I do," I agree. I'm just not sure if it's enough.

"You're going to be okay. I promise." She takes my hand and squeezes it. "I've always got your back. Whatever you need."

She stays for a little while longer and catches me up on all the other drama I've missed overnight. Apparently, Ashley and Eddie broke up, one of the girls on the cheer-leading team had to get her stomach pumped after drinking too much, and there's a new rumor that the high school volleyball coach is hooking up with his assistant coach. I'm pretty sure she's just trying to make me feel better about my own drama, but it works.

After she leaves, I finally check my texts from Austin.

Austin: How are you feeling? Sorry I had to bail so fast this morning.

I'm typing out a reply when my phone rings in my hand. Austin.

"Hello," I answer tentatively.

"Are you home?" he asks. "I'm outside."

I walk over to the front door and pull it open. Seeing him makes me feel better than I have all day. He smiles, but he has a tiredness about him that reminds me of the game. And then of course, his purple-and-black eye. It looks like it hurts.

"Hi." I step back to let him inside.

"Are you okay?" he asks. "Can I hug you?"

"I feel better, but I might still be contagious."

Before I've finished the statement, he has his arms wrapped around me. He holds me like he's been waiting to do it all day long.

"You scared me last night," he says against the top of my head. He continues to keep me tight against him. I rest my cheek against his chest and breathe him in. He smells like laundry detergent and his body wash.

"I'm fine. Really. How are you?"

"Better now." He eases his grip and looks down at me.

"Do you want to sit?" I ask. My legs still feel a little shaky.

"I can't stay," he says, and it's not the words but the

tightness in his expression that tells me something else is wrong. "I'm grounded, but I had to stop by on my way home to see you."

"You're grounded because of last night?"

"I think it was a combination of the fight, not coming home, missing practice, getting benched for the game, and then yelling at Torrance." He tries to smile, but it doesn't light up his face like normal.

"I heard about the game. I'm so sorry."

"It'll be okay."

Will it though?

"Why did you yell at Torrance?" I ask.

He gives me a look like it should be obvious.

"What she did was *awful*, but we were the ones hiding it."

"She knew exactly what would happen if she told everyone. She wanted to hurt me, and that's fine, but not you. You've done nothing to her."

I can see how mad he is at her, but I don't know. I don't blame her. She's hurting, and she saw an opportunity to hurt someone else. An opportunity we gave to her by keeping things a secret when we should have been honest.

"Anyway. I better get going. If you're feeling up for it, do you want to come over tomorrow to work on our art project?"

"I thought you were grounded."

"They have to let me do school stuff."

I chuckle lightly, but the knot in my chest tightens. "I don't know. Maybe we should wait until things die down a bit."

He gives me a weird look.

"I just don't want you to get in more trouble because of me. Vaughn, Coach, your sister..."

"That's not on you. None of it. I take full responsibility, and I'd do it again."

I know he would, which is scary. I don't want him to screw up his opportunity with the team and make a mess of his family.

"Look, it's okay. I need to figure some things out for me anyway. I've been spending so much time with you and putting off dealing with everything else. I don't want to keep doing that. It's time to pick myself up and move on."

He looks so hurt that I have to hold my ground instead of hugging him. I need him to hear me first.

"You don't want to keep seeing each other because Vaughn is pissed? He's always pissed."

"No, that's not it." I take a breath. "You need to fix things with the team and your sister. I need to fix myself. Maybe it's better if we each focus on ourselves, just for now. I would never forgive myself if being with me cost you opportunities with soccer or created a rift between you and your sister. Maybe you can't see it right now, but us being together is causing problems for you. Even without the tension between you and Vaughn. You missed practice this morning. You never would have done that."

"You're right. There is a small circle of people who mean enough to me that I'd risk it, but you're one of them. I don't regret it."

"And that means so much to me. I can't even begin to tell you." I think of all the times Vaughn put me second. All I wanted was someone to put me first, but now that it's happened, I don't think I can stand by and watch him do it. Not at this cost.

"Does it?"

"You are so talented, and you deserve to have everything

you want. I know how much soccer and your family mean to you. I would give anything to still be able to chase my dreams. I can't stand by and watch you risk losing yours." My chest feels like it's going to crack down the middle as I say each word, but if I can save him from the heartbreak I felt after losing skating, then I will. I never want anyone else to feel that. Especially him.

"I can't believe this," he says. "It doesn't have to be a choice. I can chase my dreams and be with you. You're not a risk. And if you are, then fine, I choose that risk. I choose you."

"You don't know what you're saying." My voice is a whisper. He thinks he understands what it feels like to lose the very core of who you are, but he doesn't.

"I like you. I really, *really* fucking like you. I like you so much it's hard to breathe sometimes. I thought..." He trails off. "You know what? It doesn't matter. I thought you felt the same way, but I guess not."

I want to tell him that he's wrong. I do feel that way about him, but if I do, I'm afraid he'll stay.

"I guess I'll see you around." He pauses at the door like he's waiting for me to tell him not to go.

I don't. And then he's gone.

CHAPTER THIRTY-FIVE

TODAY SUCKED.

I spent Saturday night and Sunday feeling sorry for myself, but when I woke up this morning, I thought, *Maybe today won't be so bad. Maybe it was all one big nightmare.* Wishful thinking.

I toss my bag on the floor in the kitchen and grab a water glass from the cabinet. Torrance comes in as I'm gulping it down. Coach made us run for most of practice, and when we weren't running, we were doing push-ups.

Dad had to leave again for work, so at least I don't have him frowning at me. I've never been glad for him to be gone before, but when he left last night, I felt relief that there was one less person in the state of Michigan who was disappointed in me.

"Can we talk?" my sister asks, lingering in the space between the living room and kitchen.

Instead of answering, I arch a brow and set my empty glass in the sink. I have a feeling this day is about to get worse—something I didn't think was possible two seconds ago.

"I know you're pissed at me, but I wanted to say I'm sorry. It was a crappy thing to do, outing you in front of your friends and teammates." It sounds like an apology that Mom wrote for her.

"You're sorry," I repeat flatly. "Now that my life is turned completely upside down, you've found a crumb of empathy. How nice for me."

My sarcasm gets exactly the reaction I expected from her. She rolls her eyes.

"Oh please. You fall this far from perfection, and you act like you're some kind of sad case." She holds her thumb and pointer finger an inch apart. "You're Austin Keller, golden child, adored and beloved by all. Mom can't even look you in the eye because she feels so bad she grounded you."

Now it's my turn to roll my eyes. I've gotten in trouble from Mom plenty of times. Not as many as Torrance, but I'm much better at not getting caught than her.

"We moved halfway across the country so you could follow your dreams, but what about the rest of us? I gave up my friends, my swim team, the sun! It's not even November yet, and it's freezing outside!" She yells like I personally ordered winter weather to ruin her life. "And it's not just me. Wyatt has reverted back to sleeping in Mom's bed at night, Dad's never around, and it's all your fault." Her eyes are filled with tears when she's done.

I do feel bad that they all had to give up things to move here. I don't take that lightly. But what she did was still shitty.

Her voice softens, and a fat tear rolls down her cheek. "You have no idea what it's been like for me here. I'm a *nobody*. No, worse than that. I'm Austin Keller's little sister. In Arizona, people knew me before you became this big soccer star, but here the only thing people know about me is that I'm related to you. I was so excited when Sophie started talking to me, acting like she wanted to be my friend. But it was only because she likes you."

"I'm sorry. That was shitty of her." It's hard for me to wrap my head around someone being that cruel for such a dumb reason.

"And this guy in my homeroom invited me to a hockey game, and then when I got there, he kept bugging me to introduce him to you, and when I wouldn't, he called me a bitch and left."

"I didn't know it was that bad for you," I admit. And just like that, I have someone I hate more than her. "Who is he?"

"I'm not telling you."

The hurt in her eyes is so raw that I can barely look at her.

"Look, Tor, that guy is an asshole. Being my sister is the least cool thing about you. Especially right now."

She laughs a little between sobs.

"People just need time to get to know you."

"How?" A little of that whine continues in her voice. "I've had the same friends since elementary school. I'm not a soccer god or dating the most popular girl in school." She sniffles. My anger dissipates slowly as I watch her break down.

"Yeah, well, neither am I anymore."

Judging by the surprise on her face, I'm guessing it hasn't spread around school yet. "You broke up with Claire Crawford?" My sister looks at me like I'm the biggest idiot on the planet.

Maybe I am, but not for the reason she's thinking.

"No. She broke up with me."

"Oh." Again, she seems taken aback by that. "I'm sorry."

"I'll bet." I understand her frustrations and hurt, but I'm still upset about what she did. Maybe it all would have gone down the same way regardless of when and how we told people, but she took that option away for the sole purpose of being cruel.

"I am." She looks pained to admit it. "I'm really sorry. I was just so mad. We moved here, and everything is different. My friends back home are all moving on and forgetting about me, and everyone here already has their group or clique. It sucks."

We're both quiet. I'm still hurt by what went down, but I get it too. I'm not quite ready to tell her it's all fine, because nothing feels fine.

When Mom comes out of her office and finds us in the kitchen, she looks between us, concern turning to interest.

"How do you guys feel about ordering pizza tonight?" she asks finally.

"Fine," Torrance says.

I nod. "Sounds good."

Mom gives us another assessing glance and then walks back out. Torrance seems like maybe there's more she wants to say, but the moment is gone.

I look in on Wyatt as I pass his room. He's shooting Nerf darts at a target on the wall, chattering happily to himself.

Once I'm in my bedroom, I grab my soccer ball and lie on top of my bed, staring up at the ceiling with the ball resting on my chest. A week ago, I was happier than I can ever remember being, and now everything is so messed up. I know it's not what she intended by confiding in me, but now I've got Torrance's problems weighing on me with all the rest of it. Try as I might, I can't wish we'd never come here. That'd mean never meeting Claire or Rowan or Lacey, even Vaughn, and never working with Jude Collins.

I don't know how long I lie there playing the last few months over and over in my head, but when Mom yells up the stairs, I have to shake myself out of my thoughts. I'm half-convinced I dreamed it, but then she yells again. "Austin, you have company."

I sit up, still clutching the ball. My heart is in my throat as I rush to my feet and jog down to the first floor. I come up short when I spot Rowan.

"Hey." My feet slowly close the distance between us.

Mom's smile is tight as she glances at me. "Fifteen minutes."

I nod my agreement, and she leaves us alone in the entryway. I lead him into the living room where Wyatt is playing video games.

"Hey, W-dude." Rowan offers him a fist bump and then takes a seat.

I slump into the chair next to him.

"I'm guessing by the disappointed look on your face when you saw me that you were hoping I was someone else."

I did but admitting it feels too pathetic.

"What's up? Why are you here?" I ask, trying to sound friendly and not like I want to crawl back upstairs and mope some more, which is exactly what I want to do.

"What do you mean, why am I here?" He chuckles. "I'm checking in on you. That's what friends do."

"I wasn't sure I had any of those left," I admit. I wouldn't even blame him. Maybe I didn't do it to him, but my actions cost him all the same.

"You do, but I don't think that's why you're sitting at home feeling sorry for yourself."

"I'm grounded," I say.

"Uh-huh." He dismisses my reasoning like he knows it's not why I'm so doom and gloom. "Have you talked to Claire?"

Ah, and there it is. The knife twists in my chest.

"No." I avoided everyone at lunch, and during art class, she barely looked at me. "It's over. No point in trying to change her mind."

"Come on, you don't believe that. Everyone can see how into you she is. If they were surprised you two were hooking up, then that's on them. I knew you were gone for each other weeks ago."

I sidestep that, not totally surprised he knew, to ask a more pressing question. "If that were true, then why would she end it?"

"In case you've forgotten, you did sort of blow up your life in the last week. And Claire has been avoiding her issues with her mom and skating for a long time. It was bound to come to a head eventually. You just got mixed up in all of it."

"I don't think so. I all but told her I was in love with her, and she just shrugged it off."

"Yeah, well, when you don't grow up with people saying it very often, it can be hard to hear and even harder to accept."

I wonder about Rowan and his family situation. He never says much about the fact that his parents never come to his games, but that has to be hard. My dad had never missed one before this year. My family has always showed up for me when they could.

"What am I supposed to do?"

"You can start by fixing things with Vaughn."

I grind my back teeth.

"He's not a bad guy."

"I know." He's a lot of things, but a bad guy isn't one of them.

"You two are so much alike, you know?"

"Because we're both stubborn and hardheaded and only care about soccer?" I joke.

He meets my gaze with a serious expression. "I've never known anyone who loved soccer as much as you two, but you're also both incredibly smart and genuine dudes."

"You love it just as much," I say. I know he does. You have to at this level. Coach rides us, the pressure is intense, and it eats up a lot of time we could be playing video games or partying.

"Sure, but not in the same way. For me, it's about the team. You guys are family. My parents are never around, and I'm an only child who'd rather not sit at home bored." He grins, but again, I wonder if there's more to it than that. "You should have talked to him," Rowan says. "He would have been pissed, and he probably would have made your life hell at practice for a while, but then you wouldn't be sitting around feeling like shit. He's your friend, and you lied. You gotta own that part. The rest is on him to get over or not."

He's right. I feel awful about not telling Vaughn. I can tell myself time and time again that I didn't owe it to him, but that's not why I didn't tell him. I kept it from him because it was easier than dealing with the fallout. Because I cared more about my spot on the team than I did my friend. Because he is my friend. We started as teammates, became rivals, and then somehow friends.

My actions have a prick of guilt spreading through me. One more shitty emotion to pile on what a jerk I've been. Maybe Claire was smart to get away from me.

I put my head in my hands. "I really messed things up."

Rowan pats me on the back, laughing lightly. "Don't be so hard on yourself. There are mistakes that you can't come back from, and there's this. You'll be alright."

I hope he's right.

After Rowan's gone, I climb the stairs back up to my room. I pull out my phone to text Claire, thumbs hovering over the keyboard as I try to figure out what to say. I miss her. I'm sorry. I miss her. Fuck, do I miss her.

I lock my phone and set it back on the nightstand. I don't want to add more complications to her life, and right now, my life feels like one big complication.

CHAPTER THIRTY-SIX

FOR THE PAST FIVE MINUTES, I'VE BEEN PACING OUTSIDE THE local skating rink. Young girls walk by me with their skate bags over their shoulders, boys with hockey sticks, and parents carrying more gear. They're all just going about their everyday routine. That used to be me.

A little girl follows behind her mom. She looks back at me, grin showing off two missing front teeth, and holds the door open in invitation.

"Thanks." I hesitate, but then my feet are moving. Forcing a smile back at her, I finally step into the rink.

The smell halts me. I close my eyes and breathe in the ice, feel the coolness in the air against my skin. Emotions swirl in my stomach. Not for the first time since I pulled into the parking lot, I wonder if this is a good idea.

Pulling my bag higher on my shoulder, I move forward. The guy at the front desk nods his head to me and smiles.

"Hi, Warren," I say. He's worked here for as long as I can remember, and seeing him is like nothing has changed. Except everything has. "Is the ice open?"

"For you? Always." He motions with his head to the left. "A couple of skaters are just finishing up. I'll have them clear the ice for you when they're done."

"Thanks."

The closer I get, the faster my pulse races. The sound of skates gliding over the ice is drowned out by the music, but each time a skater lands a jump, I can hear it. My chest tightens. My brain screams at me to leave, but my heart pushes me on.

I stop at the last row of chairs and change out of my shoes. As I'm lacing my skates, Zoey is coming off the ice. A huge smile spreads across her face. "Claire!"

"Hey." My voice is quiet.

"Is this your first time back, or have I been missing you?" She puts on her skate guards and takes a seat next to me.

"First time," I admit.

"Wow."

"Yeah." A lump has worked its way into my throat.

We stare out at the ice together. She doesn't push me to say anything. I think she must realize how hard this is.

"I'm sorry I never texted back," I say when I can't stand the silence. "It was too hard."

"I can't imagine what you were going through," she says. "I probably could have made more of an effort too. I didn't know what to say or do. I still don't."

"You don't need to say anything."

"Okay." We continue to sit in silence until my body is cold and I feel numb all over.

"I better go." Zoey stands. "If you ever want to hang out, we don't have to skate. We could grab dinner or whatever…"

"I'd like that."

She smiles. "It's really good to see you back. The rink wasn't the same without you."

"Thanks."

I sit there a while longer and watch the other skaters. Lauren falls on a jump, and the frustration on her face makes tears fill my eyes. I remember that feeling. Skating is not a forgiving sport. The smallest mistakes can put you on your ass so fast.

She lifts her chin defiantly and gets back on her feet to do it again.

That's the other thing about skating. You have to get back up.

So I do.

When everyone else is finished and the Zamboni has cleared the ice, I pull myself up and step out onto the ice again.

Home. It feels like home.

It's my favorite spot in the whole world. This rink made me into the person I am. I swear I can breathe easier with skates on my feet and my mind is clearer than it's been in months.

I move slowly at first, gliding from one foot to the other. Muscle memory takes over quick, which is good because my legs shake, and I can barely see through the tears that have started to fall down my cheeks.

A million memories play through my head. My first skate lesson. Landing my first lutz. Winning. Losing. Planning for the future. All my hopes and dreams were created right here.

I stop at center ice. Inhaling deeply, my chest fills with the cool air. As I exhale, I let all those dreams go to make room for new ones.

CHAPTER THIRTY-SEVEN

"I NEED YOUR HELP." I SET MY BACKPACK DOWN ON THE TABLE in front of Lacey.

My best friend quirks one brow and then says, "It better not be algebra. I can't look at another math problem today."

"It's not homework." I sit down and move my bag off the table onto the floor and take a deep breath. "I think I want to join the hockey cheer team."

A slow smile creeps onto her face. "Since when?"

"I went to the rink yesterday."

"You went to the rink..." Her mouth hangs open.

"Yeah. It was...great. I mean, a little sad at first, but great. I missed it. I thought it would be hard to be there and not be able to do all the things I used to be able to, but it wasn't like that. I still love it even though I can't do it the same way."

"Of course you do." She covers my hand with hers. "I'm so proud of you for going. That had to have been difficult."

I nod. It was, but I feel a sense of relief. Like it was the last step in grieving my old dreams. "So I was thinking, maybe I don't have to give it up completely. The hockey cheer team would allow me to skate, but it shouldn't aggravate my old injuries if I don't go back to practicing like before. What do you think?"

"It's a great idea. I wish I had given you this same speech weeks ago."

Even if she had, I'm not sure I would have listened. I needed to remember how good it felt to be on the ice without the pressure of preparing for a competition.

"One problem. The season has already started."

"Barely," she says. "They've only had two home games so far."

"But I missed tryouts. Do they let people join this late? You don't."

"Hundreds of people try out for cheerleading every year, babe. The hockey cheer squad gets far less interest."

That's true. Despite our hockey team having a good record each year, the hockey cheerleading squad is small.

"Is it even worth asking Jenn?" The thought makes me slightly nauseous. Austin said they were just friends, but she could be into him. And even if all she feels for him is friendship, she might not be my biggest fan right now or want to do me any favors.

"Yes, definitely. New members are at the team's discretion, and you are a goddess on skates." Her smile dims ever so slightly. "Are you sure you want to do this? You've thought it through and everything? You're not usually one to rush into something this quick."

"I am." I nod. "I can't explain it, but I really think it'll be good for me. I have missed skating so much, and I know it won't be the same, but maybe it'll allow me to hold on to a small piece of the person I was before, while pushing me to do something new."

"The outfits are cute," she says.

"They are." I laugh lightly. "So you don't think it's dumb?"

"No, I absolutely do not. Is that what your mom said?" She narrows her gaze.

"I haven't told her yet." I know she's going to freak if I manage to make it on to the team. I'll deal with that when and if it happens. "Okay, well, will you help me figure out what to say? I see Jenn right after lunch on my way to the east building."

"Yeah, of course." Lacey leans forward on her elbows, and we spend the rest of lunch coming up with a script.

I'm dizzy with excitement at the idea of it. I think it could be really fun.

"Wish me luck," I say when the bell rings. I won't see Lacey again until after school.

"You don't need it. If she doesn't want you, she's an idiot."

"Says the girl who won't let me on her squad," I call, walking backward, smiling. It's the lightest I've felt in days.

And the feeling completely evaporates when I spot Austin. He's standing with Jenn at her locker. They're only talking, but it feels like someone ripped my heart out. There's no way I can approach her now.

I find my escape by ducking into the library. I wait a few seconds, then peek out to see if he's still there. The past two days have been torture. I miss all his cute texts and glances between class, and the way he'd so casually hand me his sketchbook and I'd open it up to see he drew something for me.

Yesterday, I only saw him in art, and he had this sad, broody look on his face that nearly broke me.

But now he looks…better. He's smiling as he and Jenn talk. It's not like I think he's suddenly hooking up with her two days after we ended things, but eventually he will. He's a good guy, and he deserves to be happy.

"Who are you hiding from?" The deep voice catches me by surprise and makes me jump. I turn and spot Vaughn sitting at a table in the library. His laptop and books are spread out in front of him.

Forgetting Austin and Jenn, I walk over to my ex.

"What are you doing in here?" I ask, even though it's obvious. But Vaughn being in the library studying is more surprising than me deciding to try out for the hockey cheerleading squad.

"Trying not to fail Algebra II."

I wince. "Still not going great, huh?"

"That would be an understatement." He closes his laptop and puts it and his books in his backpack. "I spent all day Sunday studying and somehow did worse on yesterday's test than any of the others. I think I actually made myself dumber. So," he says when he's done and I haven't moved. "Still hiding from Austin?"

"How'd you know?"

"He's been wearing a permanent frown, and I haven't seen you two together all week."

I bite the corner of my lip. Confiding in my ex about my heartbreak feels strange.

"I ended things," I confirm. "He has a lot on the line with soccer, and I'm still figuring out what I want."

"He said that?" Vaughn asks. "Sounds more like something *I* said."

"He didn't need to. I know what it means to him."

He nods thoughtfully, staring at me in a way that makes my skin feel too tight. I know I hurt Austin by ending things. It hurt me too. But Austin deserves to have everything that he's worked so hard for.

"You know that night you were sick, he stayed up all night long watching over you like he was afraid you'd stop breathing. He was even googling your symptoms and what to do. I think he was on the verge of taking you to the emergency room. Never seen a guy so spun up over the flu."

"Why are you telling me this?"

"Because you look as sad as he does. And because as much as I hate seeing you move on, I do want you to be happy. Don't let my fuckup ruin things for you. He's not me." The corners of his mouth turn down.

Vaughn's words spark something inside of me. Hope, maybe. I don't know what to do with it yet, but it's there.

"Thank you." I step forward and hug him.

It's awkward at first. Vaughn is not really the cuddly type—even when we were dating, he wasn't—but when he finally wraps his arms around me, I feel a sense of closure with him that has been missing.

Stepping back, I glance up at him. "Does your dad know about algebra?"

"Ha!" He doesn't actually laugh as he says it. Instead, his blue eyes darken. "I can just hear the lectures now."

"Better than him finding out when he sees your report card."

He groans. He actually groans.

"Do you think..." He trails off, looking conflicted as he considers his words. "Do you think Lacey might be able to help me?"

My first thought is *Hell no*, but he's already so upset, I don't want to pile on.

"I'm not sure. She's pretty busy." Which is true. Lacey's schedule is packed full.

"Yeah, I get it," he says.

"You should ask her anyway. It's better than failing," I find myself saying. She's going to glare so hard at me.

When we get back to the hallway, I glance over at Jenn's locker. Neither she nor Austin are there.

"Coast is clear," Vaughn says.

"Yeah." I ignore the disappointment of not talking to Jenn. I'll just have to find her another time. Or maybe it's a sign that this was a bad idea.

Vaughn and I go our separate ways. I just barely make it to art as the tardy bell is ringing. Mrs. Randolph gives me a disapproving look as I take my seat. We're painting today, and everyone has already started grabbing supplies.

Austin has gotten two of everything for our table.

"Hey," I say as I take my seat. His head snaps up, surprise clear in his expression. We didn't speak at all yesterday, and it was awkward and weird, and I don't want it to be like that between us. I don't hate him, and I hope he doesn't hate me. "Thanks for getting my supplies."

"It was no problem." There's a flatness to his tone that makes me miss his laugh. He hesitates a beat, then looks back down at his work.

"Also..." I wait until his green eyes find mine again. "I had an idea for our project."

Austin's brow furrows and then smooths out quickly. "Okay." He sets his paintbrush down and gives me his attention.

"What if for the centerpiece, we do a blank canvas?

We decorate the edges, almost like a frame, and then have markers and pencils that people can use to leave their own mark, so to speak."

"That's a good idea." He leans back in his chair. "It's a really good idea. And I think we found the title of our show."

"Make Your Mark." I hadn't thought of that, but I like it too.

We smile at each other, then he seems to catch himself and looks away. "How'd you come up with it?"

"I don't know." Except I kind of do. I've had several days with nothing to do but think, and since obsessing about Austin wasn't accomplishing anything, I switched gears to figuring out all the other things in my life. This project was the simplest one on the list.

"I like it. I can sketch a design for the frame tonight."

"Okay."

After another awkward beat passes between us, Austin picks up his abandoned paintbrush and gets back to work.

We don't talk again until we're cleaning up.

"Hey," he says, pausing as everyone else heads out the door. "Are you free Friday night?"

My heart skips several beats. "Yeah, I think so. Do you want to work on the project together?"

I can tell immediately by his expression that I've guessed wrong.

"It's Rowan's birthday. We were planning on taking him to dinner."

"Yeah, I think Lacey mentioned something about that earlier." My face heats with embarrassment.

Of course he doesn't want to hang out with me and fall back into our old patterns. I told him we should take time apart, and he is respecting that while still trying to make things as normal as possible for our friends. It's better than giving each other the silent treatment. Though that was easier on my heart. Talking to him and being around him make the reality of our breakup that much harder.

He's still waiting for a response, so I snap out of it and force a smile. "I'll be there."

He nods. "Great."

Except by his tone, I can't tell if he means it or not.

CHAPTER THIRTY-EIGHT

I GET TO THE RESTAURANT FOR ROWAN'S BIRTHDAY DINNER A few minutes early to see if we can get a table for a large party. Vaughn is already waiting out front.

"Hey," I say, steps slowing as I reach him.

Hands in his pockets and face tipped down into the collar of his jacket, he tips his head slightly and gives me a muffled, "Hey."

"Did you already check in with the host?"

"They said about ten minutes while they pull some tables together."

I fall in next to him, shoving my hands down into my pockets as well. It's cold out. I can see my breath in the night air. It feels good to be out of the house though. I'm still technically grounded, but Mom likes Rowan, and she has a real soft spot for birthdays. Begrudgingly, she let me come but told me if I wasn't home by ten, I'd be grounded for another two weeks and she'd take away my phone.

Neither of us says anything. We've talked a little in practice, but things are definitely still strained. The air between us feels as thick as the big puffy coat I'm wearing. I wonder if I'll ever get used to winters in Michigan.

I know Vaughn could stand here in silence forever, but every second feels like an eternity.

"I've been meaning to talk to you," I start. I've thought about how to apologize a million times, and there never seems to be a good time or place. Standing in the cold while I freeze my nuts off seems like as good a time as any.

He says nothing, but his gaze locks on me and doesn't waver.

"I'm sorry that I wasn't honest about how I felt about Claire. You are my friend, and I should have talked to you before I let anything happen. I owed you that much at least." I apologized before, but it feels like it didn't count since I basically yelled it at him.

I can't tell anything about his emotions from the reaction on his face or body language. Vaughn is a stone wall when he wants to be.

"Anyway. I don't expect you to forgive me, but I am sorry for keeping it from you and for how you found out. I don't blame you for getting pissed and decking me."

"I wasn't pissed at you." His jaw tightens. "I mean, I was, but really I was just mad at myself."

There's a long silence where I think that's all he's going to say about it, but then miraculously, he keeps going.

"I lost Claire a long time ago, and I've been holding on to who we were or who I thought we could be. She was the coolest girl in fifth grade, and she's still the coolest girl I know." A hint of a smile tips up the corner of his lips. "But we aren't those same kids anymore."

I think of the mementos Claire has tucked away in that purple box. It's a lot of history to have with one person.

Fuck, I've only known her for a few months, and I don't want to let her go.

He clears his throat. "Anyway. It's not really my place anymore to act like a possessive boyfriend. She's moved on. I'm gonna try to do the same. I know how much you care about her," he says the last part like it pains him.

"I do." Not that it really matters anymore, but I'll always care about Claire.

"And I know if you hurt her, Lacey will destroy you without me having to lift a finger." He smiles for real, an honest-to-god smile at the thought of my demise.

"She would for sure, but, uh, we aren't together anymore."

"I know," he says. "But it's still reassuring to know." With a side-eye, his smile turns teasing. "Parents still pissed about the fight?"

"No, not really. Your dad?"

He shakes his head. "He's too worried about the game next weekend." Conference championships. We'll more than likely face Ralley again.

Blake walks up, and we stop talking to greet him. After that, everyone starts to slowly arrive. We head inside and are seated at three tables pushed together lengthwise on one side of the restaurant.

I glance up at the doors as Claire walks in with Lacey. My breath gets caught in my chest. She's smiling at her best friend, sharing some private conversation. Her cheeks are red from outside, and her blond hair is covered by a black beanie that matches her coat and gloves. It hurts to look at her. She's so damn beautiful and no longer mine.

She waves around the table as she and Lacey take a seat at the opposite end. Would it be too desperate to move closer? Probably. I consider it anyway. I just want to be near her.

Dinner is nice. Rowan eats up the attention as half the restaurant sings "Happy Birthday" to him, and I'm next to Hunter, who wants to talk about practice and the upcoming game. Any other time, I'd be thrilled to talk soccer, but tonight I'm too busy sneaking glances down the table.

After we finish eating, people start to slowly trickle off. We have early practice tomorrow, so nobody is going out tonight.

Rowan and I move down to where Vaughn, Lacey, and Claire are still sitting.

"I feel like I didn't get to talk to you two all night," Rowan says to the girls as he takes a seat next to Lacey. "What'd I miss?"

Lacey glances at Claire, smiling big. Claire looks a little embarrassed as she smiles back. It's obvious something happened.

"What?" Rowan asks.

She still looks bashful, but she twists her lips together and then says, "I joined the hockey cheer squad."

Her gaze briefly drifts to me. Lacey squeezes Claire so hard, I watch the latter visibly wince as the air is knocked out of her.

"No way!" Rowan says, face lighting up as he holds up a hand, looking for a high five. "I'm happy for you."

Claire fits her smaller palm against his. "Thank you."

For the next several minutes, Rowan asks her a bunch of questions about it, and Claire answers, Lacey jumping in with all her excitement and hugging her best friend every few minutes.

A weird sensation spreads through me. Pride. Excitement. And this lingering sadness that I wasn't there to cheer her on while she did it.

When we all eventually get up and head for the front door, I fall into step beside her.

"Congratulations. That's really awesome news."

She puts her arms through her jacket sleeves, then smiles. "I have you to thank."

"Me?"

"Yeah, you helped me realize how much I missed being a part of something, having a purpose." She laughs lightly. "Even if that purpose is just to skate around and yell some cheers. I don't need to win medals or be the best at something. I just want to enjoy myself, and I missed skating."

Her words make my chest tighten. I'm glad for her, but seeing her all lit up and excited just makes me miss her all the more.

"It's only a start. I applied for a job too."

"You did?" I don't know why, but it makes me smile. Maybe it's seeing her come alive with all the possibilities that have been waiting for her.

"Yeah. The rink is looking for weekend help running the front counter." She sort of shrugs it off.

"You went to the rink?"

She nods. "Yeah. You were right. It was time."

"You've had a big week."

"I had a lot of time on my hands," she says, and I wonder if she's felt like every day has lasted an eternity not talking or hanging out like I have. "My parents don't know about the cheer team, so I probably shouldn't go around telling everyone."

It's none of my business, but I want to have a stern talk with her mother in advance to make sure she doesn't kill Claire's happiness like she seems to be so good at doing.

"I'm really excited for you. About all of it."

"Thanks."

Lacey calls her name from the door. I keep staring at her as Claire turns her head. Lacey motions that she's leaving.

"I gotta go," Claire says. "I'll see you later."

"Yeah."

I watch her go, wishing things were different. Maybe she was right to end things like she did. The time apart seems to have been good for her. But it doesn't make me miss her any less.

Rowan throws an arm around my shoulders, and Vaughn steps up to my other side.

"Now what?" Rowan asks.

"What do you mean, now what?" Vaughn's voice has a teasing edge to it. "We have practice in the morning."

"And I'm still grounded." I angle my body to face him.

"So we'll go to your house," Rowan says. "Your mom loves me."

"I've gotta get home and study," Vaughn says.

"Nope. Uh-uh. It's Friday night, and it's my birthday, which means tonight I'm the captain. And with my first order, I demand that you come with us. Sleepover at the Kellers' house." His eyes light up. "Do you think your mom will make me pancakes in the morning?"

I actually do think she will, but I just shake my head at him.

"Ooh...pancakes." Vaughn suddenly sounds a little more interested. "I could go for some pancakes."

"If you two get me in more trouble, I'm kicking both your asses," I say, starting for my car.

"As if he could," I hear Rowan mutter behind me, followed by an agreeing scoff from Vaughn.

"I heard that," I call over my shoulder.

CHAPTER THIRTY-NINE

Claire

Over the next week, I fall into a new normal. Immediately after school, I have cheer practice. We meet at the school rink, and while the hockey teams are using the ice, we work in the lobby area, rehearsing cheers and coming up with ideas for new ones. As soon as the boys' team is done and heads to the training room, we go out on the ice. It's my favorite part.

The team has been so nice and welcoming. I wasn't sure what to expect, especially of Jenn, but if she's harboring any bad feelings toward me, I can't tell.

And it's fun doing things on skates as a team. Aside from practices and just goofing around, I skated alone most of the time before my injury. I thought it helped my focus, and maybe it did, but I'm enjoying this aspect of it the most and getting to know my new teammates. Some of them have figure skating or hockey backgrounds, but they've found a place on this squad that lets them just have fun. I feel really grateful.

Most nights, I go straight from the school rink to the

club rink and skate for a little while longer. If I still don't feel like going home, I sit at the little café and watch the other skaters practice difficult jumps and combinations while I do homework.

Sometimes when I see that look of pure ecstasy on someone's face after landing a new skill, it still feels like someone ripped my dreams out from under me, but it's getting easier. I don't want to run from it anymore. I want to heal and figure out how to move forward. I think it's working, or I'm busy enough that those moments don't consume me like they did before.

What does consume me is Austin. Everything reminds me of him. Something he said or did, something I want to share with him. We're on talking terms, but it's not the same. We talk about our art project, or I ask about soccer and he asks about the cheer practices, but everything in between—all the important stuff—has become off-limits.

I saw him and Vaughn talking in the halls today. They were laughing and joking around, two things Vaughn reserves only for people he's really close with. They've become real friends, and I'm not sure that would have happened if we were still together.

When I get home, Mom is in the kitchen throwing away takeout containers and putting dinner plates in the dishwasher.

"You missed dinner," she says, then eyes the skate bag in my hand. "Were you at the rink?"

"Yes," I say, dropping it to the ground.

"You're skating again?" She stops what she's doing to stare at me in surprise.

"Sort of. I joined the hockey cheer squad."

I brace myself for her reply. I've avoided her for the past week because I knew this was coming.

"Why?" Her eyes widen, and her voice rises in shrillness and volume.

"Because I was bored of sitting around and watching all my friends have things they do and love and because I still love to skate."

"I understand wanting to skate again in your free time, but you should be focusing on school. You have an A-minus in Chemistry and a B-plus in Algebra II. Those grades will not cut it."

"I'm not even sure I want to go to college yet. And if I do, I want to go somewhere with a good art program."

She holds up a hand like she physically cannot stand to hear me say more. "Don't make decisions now that will impact your entire future."

"Fine, but I'm not going to quit the cheer team."

"There has to be some other activity. Anything would be better." She paces, hands going to her temples. "Ten years of figure skating with the best coaches in the state and now you're skating with a group of girls who probably can't land a single axel."

I have no idea if any of them can, and I don't care. We're not trying to win a figure skating trophy.

I will never win one again. And that's okay. It has to be. Sitting around and wishing it were different won't do any good. I want laughter and excitement and to live my life instead of mourning the past or worrying about the future. Things change in an instant. The plans I made two years ago were shattered, but I can make new ones.

"Maybe we can word your admission letters to sell the hockey cheer team as an act of school spirit and generosity."

She sighs, then mutters under her breath, "It certainly feels like charity."

"Absolutely not. I want to be a part of the team. I'm having fun. More fun than I had the last few years competing." Which is true. I loved skating, but the schedule was tough. There wasn't a lot of time for fun.

She stares at me, lines of exasperation written on her face. Her phone rings on the counter behind us. She glances over at it but doesn't move before saying, "We're not done here, but I have to take this."

"It's fine. There's nothing else to say." I pick up my bag. "I'm doing it. I already committed to the team."

"We'll talk about this later," she says, already bringing the phone up to her ear.

⁓

I don't sleep well. Mom didn't try to talk to me again last night. She was on the phone on and off with clients. She has a three-million-dollar listing that she's been obsessing about, and for once, I was happy to be invisible. But her response, though expected, still left me in a funk.

In art class, we have the entire hour to work on our show.

Everything is done, and we're deciding how we want to display them. Eventually, we head out in the hallways to hang up our flyers. The show is next Tuesday night. The whole class will set up in the gym, and parents and students can walk around and view all our art. I've caught glimpses of the other groups artwork and everything looks amazing.

Austin is taping a flyer on the door going out to the breezeway.

"More tape?" he asks, eyeing me carefully with a look on his face I can't quite decipher.

I tear off another strip and hand it to him. "What?"

"I don't know. You look…off or something. Is everything okay?" He grins. "A cheerleading emergency?"

Despite the weird mood I've been in all day, I laugh. "No. Cheerleading is great."

He finishes taping the flyer and smiles at me, then we slowly walk through the hall to find another good spot to hang up our last show announcement.

"How's everything with you?" I ask him. "Ready for the big game tomorrow?"

He blows out a breath and plays it off with his smile still intact, but I can see the flash of worry that crosses his face. "It's gonna be tough, but the whole team is looking for redemption."

Redemption because he had to sit out the last time they met. I know that wasn't my fault, but I still feel bad about it. He wants to win so badly.

"Are you coming?" he asks, and I think there's a hint of hopefulness in the question.

"Of course. Me, Lacey, Andie, both cheer squads."

"Are you bringing your pom-poms?" That glint of amusement is back in his eyes.

"No," I say, trying not to laugh.

"Too bad."

We head back to class shortly after, then the bell rings, and we go our separate ways again. That feeling of missing him so much it hurts creeps back in. I forgot how good it feels to have Austin's support. Even when he's teasing me, I can feel how much he cares about me.

I'm still thinking about it when I open my locker after

my last class. Austin's sketchbook catches my eye, and for a moment, I think maybe he left it in here weeks ago or I accidentally picked it up in class, but for some reason, I flip to the last page just out of habit.

And there I am. Well, not me, but a sketch of me in skates with pom-poms. I'm smiling in the sketch, and I look happy and carefree. My heart flutters, and my smile is bigger than it's been in days.

I like the way he sees me. The way he draws me. The way he always seems to know exactly what I need.

I glance around for him, but he must have dropped this in my locker before he went to practice.

I grab a pencil and quickly add to the sketch. My pulse is racing by the time I'm done. Blake is walking down the hall, and I hurry to him.

"Hey," I say, falling into step beside him. I hold out the sketch pad. "Can you give this to Austin?"

He glances at it, then shrugs. "Sure."

I hope it's not too late to be exactly what he needs too.

CHAPTER FORTY

MY STOMACH IS IN KNOTS THE SECOND MY FEET HIT THE floor. It's game day. We play at home, so I hurry to get ready and head downstairs. I come up short when I spot Dad at the kitchen table.

"Morning," he says as he brings a cup of coffee to his lips. He's in sweats and a T-shirt like he slept here last night, but he was not here when I went to bed.

"Morning." My steps slow as I head to the pantry for cereal. "When did you get in?"

"Late last night, early this morning." His voice is deep like he just woke up.

I'm shocked to see him and hesitant to be excited. "I didn't know you were coming."

"I wasn't sure I could get here in time, and I didn't want to disappoint you again if I couldn't."

There's a tiredness in his voice that makes me realize that maybe this has been as hard for him as it has been for me. I hadn't considered that before. All I can manage to say is, "Oh."

"What's the plan for this morning?" he asks. "Are you heading to the field early to get out the game-day nerves."

I smile as I grab a bowl out of the cabinet. I set both that and the cereal on the table and get the milk out before taking a seat across from him.

"No. Coach doesn't like for us to show up too early. I usually kick the ball around out back until it's time to head to the field."

"It's going to be cold out there." He laughs softly. "Not like playing in the cold in Arizona either. I saw that the high today is thirty-eight degrees."

"No kidding. I'll be freezing out there for sure, and the ground is hard when it's this cold. The ball feels different. I'm wearing so many layers, it's not even funny." I chuckle softly as I think about playing in shorts and a T-shirt this time of year in Arizona. "It's taken some getting used to for sure."

"I can throw on my tennis shoes and a jacket after breakfast and kick it around with you if you want."

My stomach drops. That sounds perfect. I've missed doing that with him. "A couple of the guys are coming over in twenty. Our backyard has become the unofficial game-day practice spot."

"Ah." He nods. "That's why your mother went to the store to stock up on groceries before dawn."

It hits me then. My mom has gone to great lengths to make my friends feel welcome at our house. The same way she used to do that for Claire. I've taken that for granted. I've taken a lot of things for granted.

"You know what?" I say. "Come out anyway. The guys won't mind."

One corner of his mouth lifts. "Sounds good, as long

as you take it easy on your old man." He pats his stomach. "All this travel and eating in airports and hotels is catching up with me."

"No promises," I tell him.

An hour later, a handful of the guys have made it over, and we're outside in the backyard. Vaughn and I are passing the ball back and forth, and Rowan is playing one-on-one with Dad. Dad looks like he is feeling the burn, but he's smiling too. Everyone else is standing around doing more stretching and talking than playing. We all have our own routines to work out the pregame nerves. Barrett's version of that is running his mouth. Hey, whatever works. Come game time, he's quiet and focused.

When it's time to head to the school, Dad pats me on the shoulder and wheezes. "Good luck today."

"Are you going to make it over to watch the game?" I ask, fighting a laugh.

"Oh, yeah. Quick shower and I'll be good as new." He winces as he takes another step. I did warn him we weren't going to take it easy on him.

"I'm glad you're here. We've missed you." I bob my head to the side. "I've missed you. Game days don't feel the same without you."

"Yeah, me too. I'm sorry things have been hard since the move. I'm proud of you."

My throat works around a lump as I swallow. "Thank you.

"Your friends seem great," he says.

"They are." I scan the yard filled with my teammates. "Most of the time."

With one final squeeze of my shoulder and a smile, he hobbles off. I can't explain the peace it gives me, knowing he'll be there today, but it ignites a new hunger in me.

Rowan walks up behind me as Dad disappears into the house. "Your dad is cool."

"He is," I agree, then turn to him. "Are your parents coming today?"

He hesitates, then shrugs. "I'm not sure. I think it depends on their work schedules."

I nod my understanding. Families are complicated, and he never seems that upset that they don't come to his games. Maybe I've just been projecting my own disappointment onto him.

"Are you ready to do this thing today?" he asks.

"Yeah," I say, a steely resolve spreading through my body. I am definitely ready.

In the locker room, I get dressed in my uniform while the guys do the same around me. A low chatter fills the room. I can't wait to get out there. Sitting out the last game was torture, but I'm ready to bring it today.

Blake steps up next to me and opens his locker. He glances over and gives me a chin lift. I respond the same way, but as I glance away, something catches my eye. A black notebook and not just any notebook: my sketchbook. The torn cover and splotches of paint make me certain it's mine.

"Where'd you get that?" I ask him, pointing to it. Confusion and unease prick my skin.

"Oh shit," he says, reaching for it. "I completely forgot. Claire asked me to give this to you yesterday, but when I got into the locker room, you were already out on the field. Sorry."

I hold it in my hands for a moment, a weird sensation

spreading through me as I flip to the last page. She added to the drawing I did yesterday. She put a thought bubble over her head and in it wrote, "Go, Austin!" Then she scribbled out a little note next to it:

> *Good luck tomorrow. I'll be cheering for you. I'm always cheering for you.*
>
> *x, Claire*

"Everything cool?" Blake asks, giving me a weird look. Then I realize I probably have a strange look on my face too.

She wrote back. Not just that, but she wanted to make sure I knew she would be cheering me on.

Suddenly, all I want to do is go see her. This thing between us can't be over. It just can't. I know that she's figuring things out, and I am too. We can figure it all out together. Life is so much easier when people show up for you. We can be that for each other.

"Everything is great." I close the sketchbook and put it in my locker. We have about thirty minutes until the game. Maybe she's already here. I turn to go find her, but Coach Collins steps into the room, halting me.

"Keller," he says.

"Hey, Coach."

"Are you ready for today?" His hands go to his hips as he assesses me.

"Yes, sir. I could barely sleep last night."

"I remember that feeling." One side of his mouth quirks up a fraction. "You're the most talented young player I've seen in a long time, and you're hungry for it. That's good. Use that grit today, huh? We're going to need it."

I nod, a little dumbstruck. Jude Collins, my hero, just said I was the most talented young player he's seen. I leave off the "in a long time" as I repeat it in my head. I'm the most talented young player he's seen. Period.

Coach pushes past me. Everyone quiets down, and he moves into the center before he starts talking. "Ralley is here."

The mood in the locker room shifts immediately.

"They think they've already won," he says. "They're betting that we're going to walk out there scared, thinking about our last meeting and so in our heads that we can't pull it together. But we aren't going to do that."

There's a low murmur of agreement.

"You are the better team. I believe that with every fiber of my being. But it's going to take each of you playing your best to beat them today. They're not going to make it easy. They are hungry for it. They want to be the team that cost Frost Lake a conference title for the first time in four years. We have to be hungrier. Play our game. Work together. We don't win or lose alone. We are a team. Don't let them rush you or force easy mistakes." He stops talking and lets his gaze scan the room. "All right. Let's walk out there with our heads held high. Show no fear."

He tips his head to Vaughn.

"All right, boys," Vaughn says, placing his hand up in the air.

I feel the collective shift in the mood. We all step closer, joining the circle with our hands raised next to his.

Vaughn's voice has that ring of authority laced with inspiration. He's a good captain. "Knights on three. One, two..."

"Knights," we all say in unison, dropping our hands.

CHAPTER FORTY-ONE

It feels like the entire town is here to watch the game. Lacey and I are standing because the bleachers were full by the time we got here. Parking was insane. Frost Lake High has gone to state the last two years, and during that time, the community support has grown, latching on to the success like it's their own.

It might be slightly delusional, but the truth is, people like to be a part of something great. And the Frost Lake High soccer team has been phenomenal since Coach Collins became head coach.

I bounce on my toes as the teams take the field. Austin scans the crowd briefly, tipping his head to his family. The entire Keller family is in the front row, wearing Frost Lake colors. Even Torrance is clapping as her brother gets ready to play. Austin continues glancing around the stadium like he's looking for someone else. I stare at him, willing him to spot me standing in a crowd of hundreds.

I thought he might call last night after the back-and-forth in the sketchbook. It's dumb, I know. I should have just gone over to his house or texted him. The truth is that I was scared to put myself out there after everything that happened.

It's my fault we aren't together. I pushed him away because I didn't want to ruin things for him. I should have at least told him how much he means to me. I don't know how I would have survived the past few months without him. He showed me that there was so much to look forward to still. And I don't want to survive the next month or year just being friends.

"Let's go, Knights!" I yell loudly as Vaughn prepares for kickoff.

Lacey smiles, bumping my shoulder. "You sound like a cheerleader. Good volume and clarity." Her smile turns down at the corners in an impressed expression.

"I learned from the best." I bump her back.

The intensity of the game from the start is like nothing I've witnessed. It reminds me of some of my biggest skating competitions. The air crackles with tension. Even the weather seems to be taking its cues from the field. The temperature has dropped, and the wind is brutal.

Neither team lets up as the minutes tick by. It's back and forth from one side of the field to the other. Ralley is fast, and their defense is mean. The crowd yells at the ref as one player throws an elbow that gets Vaughn in the lip. To his credit, Vaughn doesn't react except to send a glare so icy that I swear the temperature drops another few degrees.

The response by Frost Lake is to dig deeper. I can see it in their expressions and the renewed energy as they race down the field. They are a different team with Austin and Vaughn out there working together.

They set up for the play. Rowan has the ball, and he

dribbles, weaving through players and then passing to Vaughn. Vaughn immediately sends the ball to Austin, who takes it toward the goal, passing it back to Vaughn at the last second when the goalie is focused only on him. The ball soars into the goal, just beyond the goalie's fingertips as he tries to leap back into position to stop it.

"Goal! One-zero Frost Lake."

Screaming, Lacey and I jump up and down, grabbing on to each other and smiling. It's only one goal, but it feels so monumental in the shift of energy in the team. Austin and Vaughn celebrate on the field, hugging and yelling things we can't hear from here.

The rest of the first half is all Frost Lake. They don't score again, but the momentum at halftime is in our favor.

Lacey and I get hot chocolate and crowd around a heater to warm up. A light rain has started to fall, but no one has left.

"You seem more nervous than the players," Lacey notes as I toss my empty cup in the trash, then rub my gloved hands together. She smiles.

"I'm not," I argue. "I have the same level of nerves as everyone else."

She chuckles lightly. Having a best friend who knows you better than you know yourself is annoying sometimes.

"I want him to win. His entire family is here and..." I trail off. "I guess in some twisted way, it'll feel like the breakup was worth it."

She lets her head fall to one side and sticks out her bottom lip. "You miss him."

"Of course I do."

"You haven't said. You've been all woman on a mission. New job, joining the hockey cheer team, studying like you've never studied before. I thought maybe you were moving back into your single girl era with me."

"Keeping busy was easier than sitting around sulking. I've done enough of that for a lifetime. Besides, I needed the time to figure things out. That part wasn't a lie. I want to be good for..." I start to say Austin, but it wasn't just about him. "...whoever I'm with next."

"You are the best friend I've ever had, and you are so talented in so many different ways. I'm glad you took time for yourself, but, babe, you don't need to be perfect to be ready for love. You just have to be willing to let people see *you*. You let Austin in, which is incredible all on its own, because you were in a bad place. And guess what? He liked you exactly as you are. He saw all the incredible things you are, not the amazing things you think you need to do with your life to please your parents or anyone else."

"I know," I say, because I do know, even if it's hard to wrap my brain around it.

"Tell him how you feel."

My throat tightens, and I swallow thickly.

Applause close to the field draws our attention. The team must be back on the field.

"I will," I say. "But right now, let's go watch them beat Ralley."

She nods, tosses her cup, then slips her arm through mine. We walk back huddled together closely.

This time, when I take my spot along the sideline where the team is back on the field preparing for the start of the second half, Austin looks up, and we make eye contact. I will all my feelings to him telepathically. And when he doesn't seem to understand that, I smile and lift a hand in a wave. He grins back. The rain makes his dark hair stick to his forehead. My breath catches in my throat.

He has no idea how I feel, and it's physically painful stopping myself from running out onto the field and telling him right now. I want him to know that I want to be one of the people in his life who always shows up. He has this great family and friends that he can count on, so he doesn't need me to have his own personal fan club, but I want to be a member of it anyway. Even if it's too late to be more than friends.

The second half starts with the same intensity as the first. Ralley has a renewed energy and determination. Not two minutes in, they score.

"Goal. One-one, Ralley," the announcer says.

The crowd groans as the red jerseys on the field celebrate.

The minutes that follow are painful to watch. The other team looks stronger and more rested as our guys make silly mistakes and turnovers that have Coach Collins looking angrier by the second.

Both teams are unable to score, as it's back and forth with close calls several times. Barrett and the Ralley goalie are ready and working hard to defend their goals.

With two minutes left to play, a Ralley player trips Eli behind the play. Rowan, always ready to stand up for his teammates, gets in the guy's face. Unfortunately, the ref sees only Rowan's actions and not what led to them. The ref pulls a yellow card and the crowd gets to their feet to show their support for Rowan. All day, Ralley has been pushing us around, so it's hard to blame Rowan for losing his cool.

Hunter is subbed in for him. Austin's jaw is clenched as he walks with Rowan toward the sideline. The two exchange words, and then Austin holds out his hand in a fist bump. Whatever he said, I know he's trying to reassure Rowan that he didn't make a massive mistake.

There's a hum of excitement as we watch the guys pull themselves together and see a new determination take hold of them. Losing Rowan is a huge loss, but it's fired them up. They want this so badly.

Lacey and I hold hands, squeezing each other's fingers tight as the seconds tick down. The score is still tied, and the rain is coming harder. Extra time in these conditions isn't a guarantee, and there's a chance they'll reschedule if they think it's too risky.

Hunter kicks the ball into play from the corner. Austin dribbles by players, scanning for his teammates. Less than a minute to go now.

Ralley has two guys flanking Vaughn. I can see the irritation all over his face. But even two defenders aren't enough to keep him from breaking free. In a pass that seems impossible, Austin kicks it up into the air to Vaughn. Ralley immediately shifts toward our best player. Everyone is expecting him to take the shot, so when he jumps up and headbutts the ball, sending it back to Austin, who's moved to the wing, the other team isn't ready for it.

I hold my breath as Austin kicks the ball toward the goal. Silence falls over the crowd, the only sound is the steady patter of rain. Time ticks by slowly as the ball soars through the air, cutting through the downpour, before finally slamming into the back of the net seconds before the buzzer sounds.

My heart lurches in my chest and then chaos erupts like I've never seen. People are hugging and yelling and jumping around. The team is one big huddle on the ground. Even the players from the bench have joined in.

My pulse races with the excitement of it all. They did it! They won!

I bounce up and down with the rest of the Frost Lake fans. The celebration on the field is broken up only long enough for the two teams to shake hands. As soon as the Ralley players leave the field, the bleachers empty and the crowd walks out to congratulate the boys.

"Come on. Let's go." Lacey pulls me, but I'm just as giddy and eager to get to Austin. It's not easy. He has quite the fan club.

Lacey and I hug Rowan and the others while Austin's family showers him with love. Torrance looks proudly toward her brother and Wyatt beams with excitement. When Austin and his dad hug, I can almost feel his happiness. His dad finally got to see him play.

Rain falls like endless confetti. Water seeps into my shoes as I stand there waiting for him. I lose Lacey as she gets swept up in the crowd. A group of girls from the soccer team runs past me toward Austin. Their excitement is palpable.

I stand on my toes and lean to either side for any small glimpse of him, but they crowd around him in droves. I want to push all of them out of the way and go to him, but there's a part of me that feels like I've lost some of that right.

I ended things so he could have this, and showing up now to tell him that I miss him and I don't want to go another day without being with him suddenly feels selfish.

I back away and then turn to leave. My steps are slow as I wonder if I've made the right decision. Waiting one more day won't kill me, although it feels that way with every step I put between us.

"Claire!"

I turn at Austin's voice. He's running toward me. The rain is coming down so hard it's difficult to make out his facial expressions. The crowd parts for him, and a few people reach forward and pat him on the shoulder or back as he goes by. I stop and turn as he comes to a halt in front of me.

There are so many things I want to say to him, but the only thing that comes out is "Congratulations!"

"Where are you going?" he shouts back over the rain. His smile is so big, like a guy who has just secured a conference title.

"You were celebrating with your family and the guys and everyone. I was going to text you later. You were unbelievable. I'm so proud of you."

"That's because my favorite cheerleader was here." Drops of water cling to his dark lashes.

My stomach dips. I have spent a lot of time over the past several months trying to decide what I want. I don't have all of it figured out, but I know I want Austin.

Surprising us both, I throw myself into his arms. He catches me, cocky smile sliding into place as his hands grip my waist and mine settle around his neck.

"You're my favorite everything," I tell him.

His lips crash down onto mine in a kiss that feels as good as stepping onto fresh ice. No, better.

Happiness spreads through me until I feel like I could float away.

He pulls back far enough that he can see my face. "I didn't see your note in my sketchbook until today."

"But I gave it to Blake yesterday right after school."

"He didn't see me, and then he put it in his locker and forgot..." He trails off with a shake of his head. "Thank you for cheering me on."

"Always."

"I wasn't sure if you still felt the same. I'm still not, but I'm hoping." He looks almost bashful as he grins down at me.

My heart flutters in my chest as his hands reach for mine. He links our pinkie fingers. Even through my gloves, the contact sends an electric current up my arm.

"I know that we're both still figuring things out, and I don't want to hold you back from discovering all these new things about yourself, but I don't want to miss it either," he says. "I am in love with you. I've been in love with you."

All the air in my lungs leaves with a whoosh that makes me feel lightheaded.

"You are?" My lips curve, and I can't seem to do anything but just smile up at him.

"Completely."

His hands come up to my face. Cold fingers rest along my cheekbones, and his light green eyes stare back at me with all the love and adoration I've felt in every action and word of the past three months. He has shown up for me time and time again. It's his day, and he's still showing up for me.

"I love you too. I'm sorry I pushed you away. I should have fought harder to show you how much you mean to me. I just didn't want to risk everything you've worked for. You've worked so hard, and you're so talented. You deserve to have everything you want."

"Even if what I want is you?"

"Even then. I'm done running away from you and my feelings. You are one thing I am absolutely certain about. I love you too."

"Thank fuck."

His lips cover mine again. I drape my arms around his shoulders, and his circle my waist and then pick me up. While he spins in a circle, my lips pull into a smile. I'm grinning so big it's hard to kiss him, but neither of us moves away as we laugh and smile with our lips pressed together.

When he sets my feet back on the ground, I'm dizzy with happiness. We stare at each other, the rain still coming down in sheets between us.

"Should we get out of here?" he asks.

My head is still swimming with excitement and anticipation, but I glance toward the field. I can make out the Frost Lake team and fans still celebrating.

"Not just yet." I take his hand and pull him back toward his teammates so he can celebrate with all the people who love him.

Including me.

CHAPTER FORTY-TWO

Austin and I arrive together at Doyle's cabin to celebrate the win today. The rain has stopped, but the temperature has continued to drop. Austin hurries from the car to the front door like another second out in the cold weather might kill him. He is not at all prepared for winter in Michigan.

"Brrr." He stops inside the cabin and rubs his hands together. He's wearing a sweatshirt and beanie pulled down over his ears, but he left his jacket and gloves at home.

"It's time to pull out your below-zero winter gear."

"I have a coat at the house, but after the game, I was still too hot, and I didn't think I'd need it." When he shivers, his entire body shakes.

"It's Michigan. You always need a coat. And a real winter coat, not the one you've been wearing." I reach up and tug on his thin beanie. "And a hat that will keep your head warm."

He takes my hand, lacing his cold fingers through mine. "Or I could just steal your body heat."

"You made it!" Rowan greets us as we walk into the kitchen area. He has a bottle of Jack Daniel's in one hand, and he looks like he started partying the minute the game was over. "And you came together." He puts one hand over his heart and speaks in a dreamy voice. "Young love is so sweet. Our Disco is all grown up, winning games and getting the girl."

Laughing, Austin shoves his shoulder playfully. "Shut the fuck up."

"You want something to drink?" Rowan asks, walking over to the counter where a variety of liquor and mixers is set up next to a stack of cups. "Beer and hard seltzers are in the fridge."

"The only thing I want right now is some hot chocolate or coffee. I'm never going to be warm again." Austin's shoulders hunch as he folds into himself.

"Take a few drinks of that, and you'll warm right up." Rowan holds out the bottle of Jack.

Vaughn walks in through the back door. He eyes the bottle and huffs a laugh. "Yeah, it'll keep you warm all right, until you're resting your head against the side of the toilet later tonight."

Briefly, Vaughn's gaze drifts to where Austin and I are still holding hands. My body tenses. I know I shouldn't feel bad, but I don't want to hurt him either. But Vaughn doesn't look mad or even surprised.

"Ah, lighten up, Captain. We won." Rowan's grin doesn't falter. I've actually never seen him sick or hungover. His tolerance is either high or he manages to cut himself off before he reaches that point.

A small smile creeps onto Vaughn's face, and he takes the Jack from Rowan and tips it back as everyone else in the small kitchen area cheers and hoots while Vaughn drinks straight from the bottle. He only gives a small grimace as he passes it back.

"Yes!" Rowan exclaims, grinning ear to ear. "Now it's a fucking party."

As more people arrive, the cabin gets crowded. There's a bonfire outside, but Austin refuses to go outside into the cold. It's going to be a very long winter for him.

I'm standing between his legs with my back to him. He leans forward and rests his chin on my shoulder, then slides his hands under the hem of my shirt.

I jolt at the contact and inhale sharply. "Your fingers are so cold!"

"I'm never going to be warm again," he whines quietly, sliding his palms along my rib cage.

My stomach flutters, and I melt under his touch. It feels so good to be with him, not hiding, hanging out with our friends, celebrating the game and this time in our life. I want to reach out and capture this feeling, this moment, and lock it away, so in five or ten years, I can remember every detail.

Rowan's laugh and ability to put everyone at ease, Lacey's smile and bubbly personality that never fails to make me feel better, the way Andie and Brandon are always teasing and flirting like they've been dating a week instead of a year, and the feel of Austin's body brushing against mine, his laughter vibrating through him to me. These are the things I want to remember instead of the classes and grades, the awards, and the failures.

Eli is sharing footage from the game, including Austin's game-winning goal.

"It was a great pass," Austin says, dodging the compliment and tipping his head to Vaughn.

"Who said I was passing?" He smirks. "I was aiming for the goal, and it just happened to get deflected to you."

Everyone laughs, and then Eli has to play it back again to determine if Vaughn is lying, even though we all know he is. It was most definitely a pass.

"It was a great end to a great game." Barrett holds up his beer in a silent cheers. He finishes it off and tosses the bottle in the recycling. "In fact, I think we should reenact it outside. Ten bucks says you two can't pull that off twice."

Austin's body shakes against me as he chuckles. "Oh no, I'm not going out there. Not even for soccer."

"Wow, you really do hate the winter." I swivel around to look at him.

His green eyes are lit up with amusement. "I'm sure I'll feel differently tomorrow, but tonight, I just want to be warm."

He pulls me against his chest and wraps his arms around me. I'm okay with being used for warmth like this. I dreamed about what this would be like, but the reality is even better.

"Ten bucks?" Vaughn scoffs, and the corners of his mouth pull down in a frown. "At least make it worth our while."

"Okay." Barrett is more than happy to up the ante. "Let's make it fifty."

Vaughn and Austin share a look like they're considering it.

"I don't have fifty bucks," Austin says.

"All right. Twenty-five from Vaughn, and for you, Disco, I'll make it easy. You lose, you take the dare of my choosing."

Laughter fills the kitchen again. Everyone here knows that's the exact bet he took that resulted in our first kiss.

"Same dare?" Austin's gaze flicks to my mouth, and my stomach flips in response.

"Ah, what the hell," Barrett says. "You lose, you have to kiss blondie here."

"Done." Austin jumps down off the counter next to me.

"But if I lose, then I get to kiss blondie." Barrett tosses me a wink. We've known each other since elementary school, so I'm aware he knows my name and is trying to get a rise out of Austin. Which he does.

"No fucking deal." His arms circle around me again, tightening protectively.

"Just kidding, New Guy." Barrett heads for the back door. "I'll let you pick the lucky girl. It worked for you, so maybe it'll work for me."

"Doubtful," Lacey says to me quietly. "He's about as smooth as sandpaper."

"Be right back." Austin brushes his lips over mine and then pulls his beanie down farther before following Vaughn and the rest of the team outside.

Lacey and I are slower to follow, letting them get out there and set up before we step outside.

"It really is cold." I pull my sleeves down over my hands, wishing I had brought my gloves. "Don't tell Austin I was complaining about it. I keep making fun of him for being such a baby."

Laughing, she slips her arm through mine. The guys are getting it all set up, and Austin and Vaughn are in position in front of an old goal.

"New Guy and Vaughn seem to have worked things out," she says.

"Yeah. I think they're going to be okay." The relief of

that is a weight off my shoulders. "Hey, by the way, did Vaughn talk to you?" I ask her.

"To me?" Her brows pull together in question as she shakes her head. "No. Why would Vaughn talk to me?"

"He's having some trouble with Algebra II." I wait for the words and the obvious follow-up question to sink in.

Her brown eyes widen, and she tries to pull away from me, but I hug her arm against my side.

"Oh no," she says, shaking her head and making her brown hair fall around her shoulders. "No. No. No."

"Just think about it," I plead. "You know what kind of pressure he's under, and his dad will freak if his grade makes him ineligible to play."

Her gaze narrows. "Why would you want me to help him? He treated you awful."

"A long time ago, before Vaughn and I were ever a couple, we were friends. I think we can be that again, and he needs help."

"Then why didn't he ask me?"

"You know why." Lacey has made no attempt to hide her dislike of him.

I pull one of her moves and stick out my bottom lip.

"Fine."

I squeal and bounce around.

"I will *consider* it," she says. "I make no promises." Then she mutters under her breath something about being more likely to strangle him than help him pass his class.

They're finally situated to redo the play. Barrett gives them five tries, but it only takes two before they get the timing right and the ball soars to the goal just like it did earlier today.

The guys on the team celebrate just like they did then.

Lacey and I watch, smiling and laughing. I catch Austin's eye across the yard, and he grins at me. He extricates himself from the celebration and jogs over to me. Lacey excuses herself, waggling her fingers as she leaves us.

"You didn't lose. I guess I can't kiss you."

"New dare." His hands find mine, and he closes the distance between us. "We kiss whenever we want."

And then he kisses me.

"Kissing you with everyone watching used to be exactly what I wanted."

"And now?" He cocks a dark brow like he's unsure where I'm going with that statement.

"Now I kinda wish we were alone."

CHAPTER FORTY-THREE

THE ART SHOW IS HELD IN THE BASKETBALL GYM. EACH GROUP is set up around the perimeter. Our collections are displayed on the wall against a white brick backdrop. It's not exactly museum-style lighting and presentation, but it looks pretty good.

Speaking of looking good…

Claire's smile is nervous as people start to filter in, but she looks gorgeous. Black long-sleeved dress and boots that come up over her knees. She is stunning. I know because every time I look at her, I feel stunned.

I'm a little anxious too. This collection is a big percentage of our grade, and putting my art up for people to see is not something I ever really wanted. I draw for me and sometimes Claire. Okay, most days, I draw for Claire.

We've kept exchanging my sketchbook. It's almost time to buy a new one, and I'll be sad to move on. This one is filled with pages of us getting to know each other and falling in love.

But since I don't plan to stop falling any time soon, I

imagine there will be plenty of used sketchbooks in our future.

Mrs. Randolph is the first to swing by.

I step up to her, blocking her from entering our little square. She could see behind me if she moved a foot either direction, but she plays along.

"Password?" I ask quietly.

"Knights Territory."

I step to the side to let her by. Claire stands next to our pieces, hands clasped in front of her. Underneath our centerpiece is a small table with colored pencils and markers. Mrs. Randolph takes it all in, smiling as she does.

"This looks great, you two." She glances between us and then back to our art. "I love the title. It's a great name for a show, and this is clever." She steps forward and points to the empty paper. "I assume this is for everyone here tonight to add their own art?"

"Yes." Claire nods. "Or just add their names or a quote, whatever you want. We all leave our mark on the people we meet and the places we go differently."

"That we do." Mrs. Randolph continues to soak in each piece before she goes over and grabs a red pencil from the cupholder, then she writes *A+* in the right-hand corner and circles it. "Well done."

"Is that for real?" I ask.

"Yes. This collection is fantastic. You two really worked well together, and you're both so talented. Congratulations. Enjoy tonight."

When she's gone, Claire and I hug and beam at each other with excitement.

"We did it," she says.

"Was there any doubt? Your paintings stole the show."

She looks like she's about to disagree or talk me up, but I kiss her so she can't. When we break apart, her face is flushed, and I successfully distracted her long enough that she seems to have forgotten what she was going to say.

"Break it up. It's a family-friendly event," Rowan jokes as he walks toward us with Lacey, Andie, and Brandon.

"You guys came." Claire rushes forward to hug her best friends.

"Password." My lips twitch with a smile as Rowan rolls his eyes.

"You were serious about that?"

"Completely."

"I can see over your head." He glances above me but then sighs. "Austin Keller is a..." He mumbles so low I can't hear the last two words.

"I'm sorry, what was that?" I cup my ear and lean forward.

He repeats himself, a tiny bit louder.

"I'm so sorry, but I still can't seem to hear you."

"Austin Keller is a soccer god!"

"Oh wow, that's so nice of you to say. Love you too, buddy."

With an exaggerated eye roll, Rowan brushes by me. The others tag along behind him to look at our art show collection.

"What was that?" Claire asks, coming to stand next to me.

I wrap my arm around her. I can't get enough of being able to touch her any time I want (which is always).

"I gave him a different password." I lift one shoulder and let it drop casually. "I wanted to hear him say my name one time."

"Austin Keller."

A shiver rolls down my spine. "I definitely like it better when you say it."

"Austin Keller is a soccer god," she says sweetly in a tone that's all flirt.

"Are you trying to kill me?" I bury my head in her neck and breathe her in. Now all I want to do is drag her out of here and make out in my car. I mean, to be fair, that's always on my mind, but I was doing a decent job of focusing on our art show until now.

Luckily or unluckily for me, there's a steady stream of people stopping by after that. Some of my teammates show up as well as a few girls from her cheer squad. My entire family blows in like the chaos that they are. Wyatt runs circles around the gym after signing his name in big blue letters across the middle of our centerpiece. Mom and Dad are excited and complimentary, almost to the point where Claire is uncomfortable with it. Torrance hangs back a little shyly. Things have been better between us since we talked. I've forgiven her. I just hope she can find a way to forgive me for everything else. Hopefully in time, she'll see that Frost Lake isn't so bad. When everyone is gone, I glance over at Claire. Something seems off with her.

"Hey, what's wrong?" I ask. "Is it my parents? They're a lot. I know. I'll talk to them."

"No, they were so sweet. I love that they showed up for you and wanted to hear all about each piece. And look! Your mom even wrote how proud she was of you on the paper." She points to the short note Mom wrote.

"Like I said. They're a lot." But they're mine, and I wouldn't change them for anything.

"It's not them."

"Okay." I wait for her to elaborate.

"I thought maybe my family might come. I sent both my mom and my dad all the information last week and reminded them yesterday."

Fuck. I hadn't even thought about them not showing up, which maybe says more about her family than my brain, but I should have realized that it would hurt. Especially when my family is here parading around like I created a masterpiece.

"I'm so sorry."

"No, it's fine." Her lips curve into a smile that if I didn't know her better, I'd believe is real. "I'm sure my mom had to work late, and Dad never remembers anything without being prompted ten minutes beforehand. And it's just a silly high school art show. Are you ready to go?"

Again, she flashes that gorgeous but totally fake smile. I really hate her parents sometimes, but saying so feels like dogpiling when all she obviously wants is to ignore it.

Snow is falling softly outside as we hurry from the door of the school to my car. We get in, shivering, and I start up the engine and get the heat going. It isn't the first time I've seen snow fall, but watching it accumulate on the side of the road as I drive is a novelty.

I drop off Claire, spend entirely too much time kissing her before letting her go, and then have to drive home going slow so I don't slide off into a ditch.

Wyatt and Torrance are in the living room staring out the front window, watching the accumulation cover the yard. I kick off my snowy shoes and strip out of my coat and hat.

"Shouldn't you be asleep?" I ruffle Wyatt's hair as I take a seat next to them on the couch.

"Mom said I could stay up since it's snowing." He barely takes his eyes off the window to glance at me. "Do you think we'll be able to build a snowman tomorrow or have a snowball fight or make snow angels?"

Every idea makes his face light up more.

"I hope so." Once, we drove up into the mountains to play in the snow all day. Wyatt was just three or four, so I doubt he remembers it. "Come on, little man. Let's get some sleep. It'll still be there in the morning." I stand and then scoop him up into my arms. He rarely lets me carry him around anymore. I won't be able to for that much longer. "You too." I nudge Torrance's leg with my socked foot.

"I just want to watch it fall for a little bit longer." She rests her head on her elbow and keeps staring out at the snowflakes glistening under the moonlight.

—

The next day, there is more snow than any of us could have imagined, at least eight inches, and it's so cold that it squeaks under our shoes. I spend all morning with Wyatt outside, building an entire snowman family and having an epic snowball fight. Torrance sits at the window, watching more than playing, but she helped Wyatt pack his snowballs good and tight so they hurt worse when he managed to hit me.

By afternoon, we're all too cold and tired to stay out, and we watch movies together and have the snow day we always imagined. The rest of Frost Lake is going about their normal routines. The roads are clear, and this isn't that much snow for them, but for the day, we just enjoy it.

"Do you want to come with me to the hockey game?" I ask Torrance as I'm about to head out.

"No." She looks up from the book she's reading. We haven't talked more about how she's fitting in here, but I've noticed she's home more often. Bobby Boone had another party last weekend, and I fully expected her to go and sneak in late, but she was home the entire time. I know I can't take on the guilt of that, but I hope she'll find friends here like I have.

Before I drive to the arena, I make a stop. The large brick house is quiet, but lights stream out the downstairs windows. I hit the doorbell, and then shove my hands in my pockets.

It takes a solid two minutes of me standing outside in the cold before Ms. Crawford answers the door.

"Austin." She says my name with a hint of surprise and a lot of dislike. I have not managed to win her over since Claire and I started seeing each other again. "What are you doing here? Claire isn't home."

"I know," I say. "That's why I'm here. I'm hoping I can convince you to come to the hockey game to watch her cheer."

"She sent you here to ask me to go to the game?" She crosses her arms over her chest.

I can tell she wants to shut the door and tell me to get lost, but if I don't say what I came here to say, it'll weigh on me for not doing everything I could to make Claire happy. I know what it's like to have the love and support of my family. It's better than any trophy or victory.

"No, of course not. She wouldn't. Claire knows how you feel about her joining the cheerleading squad, so I doubt she'll ever ask you to come, but I know it would mean so much to her. She just wants you to be proud of her and to know you're going to love and support her no matter what she does."

The annoyed stare Claire's mother aims at me doesn't waver, but she doesn't say anything.

"Your daughter is so talented. I never got to watch her compete, but she puts her all into everything she does. I know you probably worry about what she'll do or who she'll become without figure skating, but you don't need to. She's already the most incredible person I've ever met. She's good and kind, and I know she had to have gotten some of that from you. Anyway, I just thought you should know how much you showing up for her would mean. She wants to make you proud, even if she won't say it."

Claire's mom doesn't look any more convinced than when she opened the door, but at least I've said what I wanted. With a smile and a nod, I back off her steps and then hurry to the game.

Rowan and Vaughn are sitting in their usual seats, Lacey and Andie in front of them. The girls have signs made with a lot of glitter. Lacey hands me one, and I grin at the *Go, Claire!* written in big, bubble letters.

"We're cheering for the cheerleaders?" Vaughn quirks a brow but smiles.

"We're cheering for our friend." Lacey glares at him. I can't tell when she's teasing and when she's serious, but I would not want to be on the receiving end of one of those looks.

I don't spot Claire until a time-out. The cheer squad skates out onto the ice in their blue-and-white pleated skirts with matching blue sweaters. Claire's cheeks are pink from the cold, and her whole face is lit up as she cheers along with the others.

The way she glides across the ice is beautiful. Her movements have an ease to them that speaks to the many hours she's practiced.

We wait until they're done with the cheer, and then the five of us stand, screaming and yelling for Claire. The embarrassment splashed across her face is dimmed with a pleased smile.

The game becomes the sideshow, and I perk up every time Claire steps onto the ice. She's amazing. And the look on her face is pure joy.

When it's over, I wait for her by the locker rooms. She comes out still in her uniform but with a big coat over it, sneakers instead of skates, a bag on one shoulder and her pom-poms in one hand.

I hold up the sign Lacey gave me earlier over my head.

Laughing, she approaches me. "We lost."

"Didn't notice," I say. "I was too busy staring at you instead of the game."

I let the sign drop to my side and circle my free arm around her waist.

"You looked great out there. I've never seen anyone skate like you."

"Thanks. Maybe I can teach you sometime."

I scrunch up my face. "I don't think I'd do well on ice."

"Oh no, you're doing it. I played chess for you."

Laughing, I drop my mouth to hers. I never knew kissing could feel like this. The press of her lips to mine is like a jolt to my central nervous system every single time.

Someone clears their throat behind me, and I pull back reluctantly. Claire's smile falls. "Mom?"

I swivel around.

"Dad?" Claire adds.

Sure enough, both of her parents are standing three feet away. Ruby too. The latter comes forward and hugs Claire. "You looked so pretty out there. I missed watching you skate."

"Thanks." Claire hugs her back, still looking stunned.

Ms. Crawford meets my gaze briefly and gives me the smallest nod. I wouldn't say it's appreciation, but she's here.

"You still got it, Claire Bear." Her dad comes in for a squeeze next.

"I don't understand." Claire looks between them.

"You looked beautiful out there. Like you were meant to be there." Her mom speaks slowly, like she's realizing it only as she says the words. "Watching you skate still takes my breath away. I forgot..." Her voice breaks, then she steps forward and hugs her daughter.

The surprise on Claire's face makes her eyes widen and brows raise. Then something else crosses her face, understanding maybe. She wraps her arms around her mother without taking her eyes off me, then mouths, "Thank you."

"I love you," I mouth back.

CHAPTER FORTY-FOUR

WHEN WE GET HOME FROM THE HOCKEY GAME, I HEAD UP TO my room. Tonight was better than I imagined. Being out there skating with the other cheerleaders felt good. There is less pressure to be perfect and more room to just enjoy it all.

When I'm ready for bed and pulling back the covers, Mom knocks on the cracked door and then peers into my room.

"Can I come in?" she asks.

Nodding, I sit on the edge of the mattress.

She comes in and takes a seat next to me. My defenses are slightly lowered, but I don't think she's going to suddenly go easy on me just because she came to watch me cheer.

"You really looked beautiful out there. You are easily the best skater on the team."

I can hear the hint of condescension in her tone, and my annoyance level creeps right back up to high.

"Mooom." I'm so tired of fighting with her. Why can't she just accept that this makes me happy?

"Okay. I will lay off. I can tell how much this means to you."

Surprise shoots through me, and my voice is tentative as I ask, "Really?"

Just like that? I thought for sure she'd still try to talk me into quitting. Maybe not tonight but eventually.

"Yes. Believe it or not, I do want you to be happy."

That is hard to believe. The past few months have felt like she's cared less about what I want and more about what she thinks I need.

"I still think you should consider adding some AP classes and focus on bringing up your GPA."

I groan.

"You have such a big, beautiful future ahead of you." She reaches forward and tucks my hair behind one ear. "I know that I have been hard on you, but it's because I believe with enough hard work, you can have all the success you want. Look at how far you got with skating."

"And for what?" I ask, letting myself feel that familiar burn of disappointment that something I worked so hard for was taken away.

"For what?" She laughs quietly. "Is that really what you think? It's over so it was worth nothing? Honey." She reaches over and rests a hand on my knee. "If nothing else, it should have taught you how capable you are. You can do anything if you're willing to put in the effort."

I know it wasn't for nothing, but sometimes the sting of it still catches me off guard. She's right though. It did teach me a lot.

"I will think about adding in some AP classes next semester."

Her smile is immediate. She gets up like she wants to flee before I change my mind. Maybe we won't ever agree on everything, but I can compromise if she can.

"I want to visit some colleges with great art programs," I say as she reaches the door.

"Does this have anything to do with Austin?" Her gaze drifts to the wall next to where she stands. The first sketch Austin ever drew for me hangs there. The one where I'm skating.

"No." It doesn't. Besides joining the cheer squad, it's the only thing that I've found that feels right. Maybe I won't end up majoring in art and it will be something I just do for fun, but I at least want to explore it.

"It took a lot of nerve for him to show up here tonight." Her stare doesn't leave the sketch.

My stomach dips. I don't know exactly what happened or what he said, but it's obvious that whatever he did had an impact on her. I still can't believe they all showed up to watch me cheer. Even if they never come again, I'll remember tonight for a very long time.

"I'm glad he did." She finally looks back at me, and her usual no-nonsense mask slips back into place. "He's still not allowed in here with the door closed."

Fighting a smile, I nod my agreement. And without saying more, Mom steps into the hallway.

I pull out my phone to say good night to Austin before I go to sleep. A text from him is already waiting.

Austin: Night cheer girl. See you in my dreams.

EPILOGUE

Three months later

AUSTIN CAREFULLY STEPS ONTO THE ICE. THE LOOK OF TREPIDATION on his face is adorable.

"Are you sure I'm not going to fall through and get trapped under the ice?"

"The lake is frozen," I say for what has to be the third time since we parked the car and walked out here.

"Uh-huh." He doesn't seem convinced.

Stepping next to him, I take his gloved hand in mine. He's like a baby deer standing for the first time, legs at odd angles and hunched over.

"I can't believe you've never been ice-skating."

"There isn't a lot of ice in Arizona." He stands tall and then freezes. "Now what?"

"Okay, now push off and glide."

"I don't even know what that means," he says, but he does a pretty good job of it.

I let him set the pace as he feels out the ice. A very slow

pace. I show him a few basics and then skate ahead of him. By the time I've gone around the lake and am lapping him, he's figuring it out.

"All right. All right. I got it." He holds his hands out to his sides and wobbles backward, then corrects himself.

"Lean forward," I remind him.

He grunts his acknowledgment. I wish he could see himself. That stubborn set of his jaw and brow creased in concentration. I love that I get to be here to watch him do this for the first time. It's not chess, but I guess we can finally be even.

I breathe in the cool air and tip my head up to the sky. Today is a good day. Actually, most days have been lately.

I've made new friends with the girls on the hockey cheer squad and found the more time I spend with them skating and having fun, the less it hurts to think about my dreams of figure skating. I still don't know what I'm going to do after high school, but I'm not sweating it. My mother does enough of that for me. Speaking of, after our talk, she's eased up a little. She's now spending her time with the other hockey cheer moms trying to raise money and make the squad "a reputable and elite group." She told me I can be anything, and right now, all I know for sure is I want to be happy. And I am. Deliriously happy and in love.

She's making compromises, and so am I. And I'm happy to report Austin has nearly won her over. I think it helps that he was named to the all-state first team and finished the first semester with straight As (I'm fairly certain he did it just to get on her good side). There's a lot to love about him, but most of all, I love how he sees me and pushes me to keep dreaming.

I circle around him, watching him get more comfortable.

"You're making me dizzy," he says without looking at me. I think he's afraid to take his eyes off the ice, like that's what's keeping him upright.

I skate next to him, and he eventually picks up speed.

"You're getting it," I say.

"Was there any doubt?" He lifts his brows and aims a cocky smirk at me. His movements aren't smooth, but he looks like he's been doing it longer than five minutes.

I move in front of him, skating backward and showing off. I like it when he chases me.

He speeds forward and grabs me around the waist. He tips forward, and I'm helpless to keep us from falling. Laughing, Austin spins us so I land on top of him. Oops. I forgot to show him how to stop. His laughter stops abruptly, and he squeezes his eye shut.

"Did I hurt you?" As I try to move off him, his grip around me tightens.

"No. I was just waiting for us to bust through the ice."

My giggles start low, and then he joins in until we're both unable to talk because we're laughing so hard. When we finally stop, he leans forward and presses his lips to mine.

"I love you," he says. "But I think I should stick to cleats."

"You wouldn't be able to get around on the ice very well," I tease.

His hands move to my waist, and he tickles me until I squirm and beg for mercy. Then he slides his fingers under my coat and sweatshirt. "How many layers do you have on?"

"Enough to keep warm," I say as his cold, icy gloves move under my T-shirt and find my bare skin.

I retaliate by doing the same, except he has on far fewer layers.

"I give, I give," he says, wincing. His hands lift from my waist but remain under the layers. "Maybe we should head back to your place and cuddle in front of the fireplace. Drink some hot cocoa."

What he really means is *go make out somewhere warm*.

"Five more minutes," I say, untangling myself from him and getting to my feet. With some effort, I help him up, and our arms wrap around each other again. "You and skating, skating with you… I feel like my heart might burst. I love you so much."

"Are you talking to me or to the ice?" His green eyes spark with mischief.

"Both." I grin back.

"Hey," he says quietly, mouth hovering an inch from mine. "I dare you to kiss me."

WANT TO DISCOVER MORE BLOOM YA BOOKS?

READ ON FOR A SNEAK PEEK

AT MERCEDES RON'S

PROLOGUE

"LEAVE ME ALONE!" SHE SAID, TRYING TO GET AROUND ME and through the door. I grabbed her by the arms and forced her to look at me.

"You want to tell me what the hell's going on with you?" I asked, furious.

She looked back, and I could see her eyes were hiding something dark, yet she smiled at me joylessly.

"This is your world, Nicholas," she replied calmly. "I'm living your life, hanging out with your friends, and feeling like I don't have a care in the world. That's how you are, and that's how I'm supposed to be, too," she said and stepped back, pulling away from me.

I couldn't believe what I was hearing.

"You're out of control," I hissed at her. I didn't like who the girl I was in love with was turning into. But when I thought about it, what she was doing and *how* she was doing it were the same things I had done before I met her. I was the one who got her into all this. It was my fault. It was my fault she was destroying herself.

In a way, we'd switched roles. She had shown up and dragged me out of the black hole I'd fallen into, but in doing so, she'd wound up taking my place.

1

Noah

While I rolled the window of my mother's car up and down, I couldn't stop thinking what the next hellish year had in store for me. I couldn't stop asking myself how we'd ended up like this, leaving our home to cross the country on our way to California. Three months had passed since I'd gotten the terrible news that would change my life forever, the same news that would make me want to cry at night, that would make me rant and rave like I was eleven instead of seventeen.

But what could I do? I wasn't an adult. I had eleven months, three weeks, and two days to go before I turned eighteen and could go away to college, far away from a mother who only thought about herself, far from these strangers I'd end up living with, because from now on I would have to share my life with two people I knew nothing about—two men, to make matters worse.

"Can you stop doing that? You're getting on my nerves," my mother said as she put the keys in the ignition and started the car.

"Lots of things you do get on my nerves, and I have to put up and shut up," I hissed back. The loud sigh I heard in reply was so routine, it didn't even surprise me.

How could she make me do this? Didn't she even care about my feelings? *Of course I do*, she'd told me as we were leaving my beloved hometown. Six years had passed since my parents split—and nothing about their divorce had been conventional, let alone amicable. It had been incredibly traumatic, but in the end, I'd gotten over it...or, at least, I was trying to.

It was hard for me to adapt to change; I was terrified of strangers. I'm not timid, but I'm reserved about my private life, and having to share twenty-four hours of every day with two people I barely knew made me so anxious, I wanted to get out of the car and throw up.

"I still can't understand why you won't let me stay," I said, trying to convince her one last time. "I'm not a little girl. I know how to take care of myself. Plus, I'll be in college next year, and I'll be living on my own in another country then. It's basically the same thing," I argued, trying to get her to see the light and knowing that everything I was saying was true.

"I'm not going to miss out on your last year in high school. I want to enjoy my daughter before she goes away to study. I told you a thousand times, Noah—you're my child, I want you to be part of this new family. For God's sake! You really think I'm going to let you go that far away from me without a single adult?" she answered, keeping her eyes on the road and gesturing with her right hand.

My mother didn't understand how hard this was for me. She was starting a new life with a new husband she supposedly loved. But what about me?

"You don't get it, Mom. Did you never stop to think that this is my last year of high school? That all my friends are here, my boyfriend, my job, my team? My whole life!" I shouted, trying to hold back tears. The situation was getting the best of me, that much was clear. I never, and I mean *never,* cried in front of anyone. Crying was for weaklings, people who can't control their feelings. I was someone who'd cried so much in the course of my life that I'd decided never to shed another tear.

Those thoughts reminded me of when all the madness began. I still regretted not going with my mother on that damn cruise to Fiji. Because it was there, on a boat in the middle of the South Pacific, that she'd met the incredible, enigmatic William Leister.

If I could go back in time, I wouldn't hesitate a second to tell my mother yes when she showed up in the middle of April with two tickets so we could go on vacation together. They'd been a present from her best friend, Alicia. The poor thing had broken her right leg, an arm, and two ribs in a car accident. Obviously, she and her husband couldn't go off to the islands, so she gave the trip to my mom. But come on now—mid-April? I was in the middle of exams, and the volleyball team had back-to-back games. My team had just climbed from second place to first, and that hadn't happened as long as I could remember. It was one of the greatest joys of my life. Now, though, seeing the consequences of staying home, I'd happily give back my trophy, leave the team, and fail English Lit and Spanish just to keep that wedding from ever happening.

Getting married on a ship? My mother was out of her mind! And going and doing it without telling me a single word! I found out when she got back, and she said it all blithely, like marrying a millionaire in the middle of the ocean was the most normal thing in the world. The whole situation was surreal, and now she wanted to move to a mansion in California, in the United States. It wasn't even my country! I had been born in Canada, even if my mom was from Texas and my dad from Colorado. I didn't want to leave. It was everything I knew.

"Now, you have to realize I want what's best for you," my mother said, bringing me back to reality. "You know what I've been through, what *we've* been through. And I've finally found a good man who loves and respects me. I haven't felt this happy in a long time. I need him, and I know you'll come to love him. And he can offer you a future we could never have dreamed of before. You can go to any college you like, Noah."

"But I don't want to go to some fancy college, Mom, and I don't want a stranger paying for it," I replied, feeling a shiver as I thought how, at the end of the month, I'd be starting at a new fancy high school full of little rich kids.

"He's not a stranger, he's my husband, and you better get used to the idea," she added cuttingly.

"I'm never going to get used to the idea," I said, looking away from her face to the road.

My mother sighed again, and I wished the conversation would just end—I didn't want to go on talking.

"I get that you're going to miss Dan and all your friends, Noah, but look on the bright side—you're going to have a brother!" she exclaimed.

I turned to her with a weary look.

"Please don't try to sell this like something it's not."

"You're going to love him, though. Nick is a sweetheart," she told me, smiling as she gazed down the highway. "He's mature, responsible, and he's probably dying to introduce you to all his pals. Every time I've been there and he's around, he's stayed in his room studying or reading a book. You might even have the same tastes."

"Yeah, right. I'm sure he's crazy about Jane Austen." I rolled my eyes. "How old is he again?" I knew, of course; all my mother had talked about for months was him and Will. It was ironic that for some reason Nick had never managed to find a hole in his schedule to introduce himself to me. Moving in with a new family before I'd even met all the members of it just kind of summed up how crazy this all was.

"He's a little older than you, but you're more mature than most girls your age. You'll get along great."

Now she was kissing up to me. *Mature.* I still wasn't sure whether that word defined me, and I doubted a guy who was nearly twenty-two would really feel like showing me the city or letting me meet his friends. If I even wanted to, which was a whole different question.

READING GROUP GUIDE

1. Claire has suffered a career-ending figure skating injury. How do you think this injury affects her mindset? How does it weigh on her?

2. Do you think Austin feels pressure to perform well at Frost Lake High since his family moved there for him? How do you think this affects the way he thinks and behaves?

3. Does Vaughn have a right to be mad at Austin for kissing Claire? Why do you think Vaughn wants Claire back once he sees her with someone else? Why do you think he broke up with her to begin with?

4. Claire struggles discovering something new to do as a hobby once she can't figure skate anymore. How do you think she feels when she can't do the thing she loves? How does her mom make her feel about it?

5. Austin and Claire enter into a secret relationship. Do you think this was a good idea? Why do you think they wanted to hide their relationship from Vaughn for so long?

6. Austin tries to help Claire find something new to occupy her time that she could learn to love as much as figure skating. Why do you think this means so much to Claire?

7. Lacey is always there for Claire. What does it mean to have a best friend that will always stand beside you? How do you think Lacey does that for Claire?

8. Rowan is a good friend to Austin when Vaughn and the rest of the team box him out. Why do you think Rowan does this? Do you think Rowan's friendship helps Austin stay true to himself and his goals when the rest of the team seems to dislike him?

9. Austin's sister, Torrance, struggles in Michigan and wishes she was back in Arizona. She does something really mean to Austin and Claire. Do you think Torrance had the right to get back at Austin or do you think she was out of line?

10. Claire tries to break up with Austin to protect him from ruining his soccer career. Do you think this stemmed from the ending of her figure skating career? Do you think she was right to do this? Why do they both eventually realize they should be together?

ACKNOWLEDGMENTS

Thank you so much to everyone who picked up this book. I hope you enjoyed it. I love this new world with my whole heart and cannot wait to write more! Go Knights!

The team at Bloom Books, thank you for taking a chance on me and for all your guidance and support. I feel so lucky to work with you all.

To my team: Devyn, Jamie, JR, and Tori, I quite literally could not have finished this book without your help. I can't say thank you enough. I'm so fortunate that I get to work with each of you.

Sarah Jane, thanks again for the stunning character art. I love seeing my characters through your eyes!

Jamie and Katie, this book is so much stronger for your suggestions and notes. Thank you for always treating my words with such care while still pushing me to be a better writer.

My agent and publicist, Nina, this book and series is all thanks to you!

Amy, Catherine, and Laura, you each held my hand in

different ways while I wrote this book. From talking plot to cheering me on and so much more. Authoring is more fun with friends like you.

To my daughter, you are so brave and kind and smart. You inspire me every day. Thank you for being my first beta reader.

To my son, your curiosity and adventurous spirit make life endlessly entertaining.

Mom, Dad, Natalie, you're present in every story I tell, maybe this one most of all.

And lastly, to my husband. The reasons are too many to list. I love you.

ABOUT THE AUTHOR

Rebecca Jenshak is a *USA Today* bestselling author of sports romance for teens and adults. When she isn't writing, you can find her cheering on local sports teams, hanging out with friends and family, or curled up with a good book.